LADY REAPER
SERVING MAGIC
BOOK FIVE

TONI CABELL

CHAPTER 1

"Come sit wif me, lass, right 'ere." The paunchy bricklayer patted the empty barstool next to him. He hiccupped, his breath reeking of stale ale and cheap tobacco.

Mara wrinkled her nose. She shouldn't have poured another round for Mr. Redfield, despite his entreaties. The man never ordered more than two tankards, and now she knew why. "I am working, sir. And I'm meeting my boyfriend tonight." At least, Mara hoped so. Arnesto said he'd stop by later, but she wasn't sure whether he meant later in the evening or later in the week. Arnesto traveled so frequently between the fay and human realms his sense of timing was entirely out of whack.

Mara stepped back from the polished mahogany and brass bar and peered over Mr. Redfield's greasy cap, taking in the Cracked Cauldron's scarred, wide plank floors and dark wood booths lining its walls, each booth filled with customers stopping in for a pint and a bite after work. To one side of the bar was the requisite dartboard, where a group of young men guffawed as they relieved each other of their day's wages. Idyllic prints of pre-war Valerra dotted the pub's dark green walls, mostly scenes from the rolling farmland, valleys, and villages to the west of the city.

Mr. Redfield hiccupped. "Yer boyfriend's not around much these days, lassie. How about ye try out a real man and not some popinjay who talks weird and can't hold down a steady job?"

Mara chose to ignore him, usually the best course of action around drunken patrons. She served a pitcher of ale to three blacksmiths sitting at the mahogany counter before stepping from behind the bar to wipe down a vacated booth. She'd forgotten about Mr. Redfield, until he wrapped a beefy arm around her waist and spun her around. Mara stomped on his foot with the heel of her tall leather boot. The man howled and tried another grab for her. Mara pulled her fist back, ready to land a punch, when everyone froze around her—Mr. Redfield, the blacksmiths, the middle-aged couple at the rear booth, even her friend Gemala, owner of the Cracked Cauldron, who'd just stepped through the kitchen door with a platter of sandwiches.

Mara spun around. "Arnesto, is that you?" She tried but failed to keep the hopeful tone out of her voice. She hastily tugged off her hair tie, finger-combing her wheat-blonde hair before pulling it back into a long ponytail. She smoothed down her sea-green sweater, which fit snugly over her chest. Arnesto used to ogle her tall hourglass figure when he didn't think she'd notice. But that was *before*— before the dark fays kidnapped him, before his brother died during the rescue mission.

"Nay, lass. He is visiting a seer from the Suporra-Draca clan, said to be the wisest living dragon." Yelenarra dropped onto the vacant barstool next to Mr. Redfield, who looked ready to topple out of his seat, his arms outstretched toward Mara, his face twisted in a leer. Mara stepped well out of his reach.

Arnesto's aunt wore a shocking pink cape with a darker pink lining, a burnt orange evening dress with a beaded bodice, and a lime green pillbox hat on her flyaway hair. Mara noted the elderly fay tried to disguise her hair color with a glamour, but the magic seemed to be sliding in and out of focus. Yelenarra's curls switched from silver to ginger to their normal bright blue, and then the magical circuit repeated itself.

A thin line formed on Mara's brow. Yelenarra was a highly skilled fay mage who ordinarily had no problem maintaining a glamour. Something, or someone, had upset her equilibrium. "What's the matter? Has anything happened to Arnesto?"

"Nothing has happened to my nephew, other than what you already know," said Yelenarra. "He was injured by a speeding locomobile, imprisoned by the dark fays, and lost his dear brother. The only bright spot for him these days is you."

Mara debated whether to say anything to Yelenarra, but she trusted the fay woman, and she had no one else to confide in about Arnesto. "I've begun to wonder whether that's still the case."

Yelenarra canted her head to the side. "Of course it is... unless you have changed toward him?"

Mara twisted the damp dishtowel in her hands. "Arnesto has been so distant when we're together. I think he's the one who's changed toward me."

Yelenarra chuckled in her tinkling way, soothing Mara's jangly nerves. "A fay cannot pledge his friendship unless he is certain." The implication was obvious; on the other hand, human hearts were all too fickle.

Friendship among the fays meant something quite different than in the human realm. When Mara had promised to be Arnesto's *friend*, unbeknownst to her, she'd also become his *betrothed*. While Mara's feelings for her fay boyfriend ran deep, she was in no hurry to be married. They had agreed to take things slowly, but she'd only seen him twice during the past three weeks—even the hapless Mr. Redfield had noticed—and each time, Arnesto had been in a hurry to leave.

Mara told Yelenarra about Arnesto's short, infrequent visits, adding, "He seems distracted whenever he's with me, as if he's listening for something or someone. When I ask him what's wrong, he shakes his head and tells me not to worry. That makes me worry even more."

Yelenarra waved her hand, dropping her glamour entirely. Instead of the bright pink and orange hues she wore to visit the human realm, Yelenarra's cape and empire-waist dress were sparkly silver, and her hair vivid blue. "I thought perhaps you and he had quarreled, which would explain his behavior. Now I do not know what to think."

"I'm sure he is grieving for Efram. They were very close, and Arnesto looked up to him so."

"Aye, he misses his dear brother, as do I. But grief drives loved ones together, not apart. Nay, something else is bothering Arnestarious. He wanders about the estate, muttering to himself, lost in another world entirely. He works tirelessly, reading old scrolls and meeting with every seer he can find. When he is not studying or conferring with seers, he is practicing with his weapons, his sword, dagger, bow, and now the lasso."

Mara brought a hand to her throat. "Not the lasso." Reapers used ensorcelled rope to lasso and return undead creatures to the realms of the dead. Although Mara was neither a reaper nor a fay, she knew how to lasso the undead. Arnesto did not.

"Aye, he is determined to master the lasso."

"You don't think he'd attempt a reaping by himself, do you?"

Yelenarra nodded. "If Arnestarious believes doing so would keep you safe, I fear he might enter the realms of the dead alone. And we both know that never ends well."

"But why? We defeated Bazra and sealed him inside the lowest of the realms. He's no threat to us now."

"I would not be so certain. The dark fay king always poses a threat, wherever he resides."

Mara pulled out a leather-topped barstool and sat opposite Yelenarra, as far away as she could from the leering bricklayer, still frozen in place by the elderly fay's spell. "What should we do?"

Yelenarra patted Mara's arm. "This is something only you can solve. It is time for you to remind Arnestarious how much he has to live for."

"Huh?"

"I never interfere in the coupling activities of young people. However I must say, the two of you operate at a slug's pace." Yelenarra sighed. "If you move any slower, you shall be in retrograde. Live it up a little. Nay, live it up a lot!"

"Live it up?"

"My dear lass, you and Arnestarious need to have some fun. You have both been under extreme stress for an extended period. It is not healthy for you or your relationship. I believe a holiday is in order." Yelenarra rose from the stool, her hands fluttering excitedly. Mara thought the octogenarian might be recalling some holidays she'd taken as a young fay. "Tell my nephew you wish to visit all seven seasons of Havynweal. Ask him to take you to the Unicorn Sanctuary next to Toomsenbarra Parkway. It is quite lovely, and I hear they have several foals in the nursery. Oh, and you must call on Katrinareus and observe a fay council meeting, although not for very long because they are quite awful. You shall not forget to visit your old friend Grihm Farleigh. I had my doubts whether a wolf-man crossbreed could get along with a clan of feline hybrids, but I hear he is doing quite well. And then—"

Mara interrupted before Yelenarra could make any more suggestions about places to visit inside the fay lands. "What about a chaperone? I realize fays are more accepting of a single young woman traveling alone with a man, but that's not the case here in Valerra."

"But you and Arnesto are *friends*." Yelenarra emphasized "friends," as if that explained everything. Probably in Havynweal it did.

"Precisely. Human girls do not travel about the country-side with close male friends without some sort of chaper-one." *Although I'd love to spend uninterrupted time alone with Arnesto,* thought Mara. *And I haven't been on a holiday since before the war, when Father took us to the hot springs.*

Yelenarra glanced down at the pub's scarred wooden floorboards. She tapped her foot and murmured to herself. Half a minute passed before her head snapped up and she smiled, clearly pleased with her solution. "Gloria will do very nicely."

Mara's jaw dropped. She closed her mouth and cleared her throat. "You want my pet griffin to serve as a chaperone in Havynweal?"

"Certainly. In fact, Gloria would make an ideal chaper-one. She raised six griffins of her own, and she is well schooled in etiquette, both human and fay. And in Havynweal, Gloria will be able to speak her mind. Here, she must make do with clicking her beak and flapping her wings when she is displeased."

"And pecking my leg." It was true her miniature griffin could speak quite eloquently inside Havynweal. Fay magic enabled all animals to speak, if they wished. In fact, Gloria offered her opinions a bit too freely when in Havynweal. Yelenarra made a good point; Gloria would be an effective, if altogether unconventional, chaperone. Mara was beginning to warm to the idea. "I'll speak with Arnesto about it."

"You must speak with him very soon, lass. Do not delay. I fear he will do something rash otherwise."

Mara compressed her lips and considered. Yelenarra had raised Arnesto and knew him better than anyone. If she thought he might be in danger of getting himself injured or worse, then there was no time to lose. Mara nodded. "I'll contact Arnesto after the ribbon-cutting ceremony tomorrow."

"Thank you, lass, that is all I can ask." Yelenarra waved goodbye as her fay traveling vapors swirled about her silver ankle boots and snaked up to her waist. "I shall hasten to prepare the Amber Room for you and..." The rest of Yelenarra's sentence was lost as she vanished on her mists.

Yelenarra's spell lapsed, unfreezing all action and noise in the pub. Gemala hurried over to the bar with her platter of sandwiches as the blacksmiths laughed at a joke. The middle-aged couple called out for another round, while a toddler wailed behind Mara, her mother hushing the child. Mr. Redfield, his arms still outstretched, lost his balance and pitched headfirst onto the floor. Under other circumstances, Mara would have rushed over to assist the man. Instead, she stepped around him and retrieved fresh drinks for the couple in the booth.

Mara felt as if she'd run a relay by the end of the evening. The front door to the Cracked Cauldron seemed to be in almost constant motion, with customers coming and going, and she wound up working past her shift. By the time Gemala told Mara to go home, it was close to midnight.

Mara pulled her navy cloak off one of the hooks near the rear entrance to the pub. She slipped into her cloak, retrieved her reticule from Gemala's tiny office behind the kitchen, and called out goodnight. Then Mara remembered she might not be able to work for a few shifts and paused at the pub's front door. "I'm hoping to convince Arnesto to take a short holiday. If he agrees, I'll be gone about a week. I'm sorry, I know you're short-handed."

Gemala, her dark hair pulled back in a loose bun, looked up from wiping down tables. Her brown eyes twinkled with amusement. "Have you forgotten you rescued thirty people last month from the dark fays—including me? And then there's your boyfriend, who gave me a bag of gold to pay for a single meal. As far as I'm concerned, you can come and go as you please for the rest of your days, and I'll be nothing but grateful. Now go take that holiday and have some fun. You've earned it."

BRIGHT SUNSHINE FILTERED through the arched windows of Mara's small, one-room flat. She yawned and tried stretching, but something heavy pinned down her legs. Mara had a brief moment of panic until she saw her miniature griffin sprawled across the foot of her bed, clicking her beak as she slept. "Gloria, it's time to wake up."

Gloria squawked and hopped off the bed. Her reddish-brown mane, streaked through with white, stuck out in tufts around her eagle-like face. She had the body of a compact lion, with four paws and a long tail, and a pair of wings strong enough to propel her wherever she wanted to fly.

Mara swung her feet to the floor and slid them into her woolen slippers. "What do you think I should wear to the ceremony today?"

Martel "Vas" Revas, the provisional president of Valerra, had invited Mara to cut the ribbon for the new Bellaryss Children's Hospital. The president wanted to publicly acknowledge Mara's role in rescuing him and many others from the dark fays. Vas believed telling people about the dark fays and the danger they posed would help tamp down the anti-magic sentiment swirling about the capital. Mara didn't think it would make any difference. People would believe what they wanted, regardless of the evidence.

Gloria padded over to Mara's wardrobe and used her beak to pull open the latch. With her front paw, she pointed out a maroon split skirt and ivory blouse with a row of gold buttons down the front. As an afterthought, Gloria tapped an aubergine cape. Springtime in Valerra was generally blustery and often damp.

Mara folded her arms. "I was thinking of my new cobalt day dress with the matching spencer jacket. Madame Zostra assured me it's the latest fashion, and she said the color would accentuate my blue eyes." The stylish Madame Zostra was commonly acknowledged as the best dressmaker in Valerra, or at least in Bellaryss, the capital.

Gloria butted her head against Mara's leg, which meant no.

"But I wear split skirts when I know I'll need to run or ride or fight. They're not for fancy ceremonies."

Gloria squawked and flapped her wings. Mara narrowed her eyes. "You're expecting trouble, aren't you?" Gloria dipped her head. "Well, I hope you're wrong, but I'll take your wardrobe advice just in case."

Mara crossed the dark oak floorboards of her studio to the kitchenette on the opposite wall. Filling her teakettle with the hand pump above her sink, she placed it on top of the cast iron stove, scooped a scuttle of coal inside, and struck a match to light the coal.

Mara felt something sharp jabbing her in the knee and jumped. "Ouch. Stop that." Gloria tilted her head to the side and clicked her beak.

"What's the point of casting a fire-starter spell to light the coal when I have matches right at hand? I'm merely conserving my energy."

Gloria flapped her wings in a huff. Mara knew she owed her griffin an explanation, which she'd been putting off for weeks, claiming fatigue. Mara had been seriously injured while rescuing Arnesto and everybody else from the dark fays. The healer had reminded Mara she was only human and needed to rebuild her strength, but even Mara knew she wasn't healing properly.

"The truth is, I've not felt the same since I expended so much magical energy during Arnesto's rescue. I'm afraid I depleted my magic. At least, that's how I feel, kind of emptied out. It's hard to explain."

Her griffin slumped to the floor, dropping her head on her front paws. Mara knelt beside Gloria and ran her fingers through her mane. "I've been meaning to speak to Arnesto about it. I figure if anyone knows what's happened to my magic, it's a twelfth-level fay wizard. But he's so preoccupied whenever I do see him, I keep putting it off."

Gloria gave a low, throaty growl. "That's not fair. Arnesto is obviously worried about something." Mara stood up. "Let me open the window so you can find your breakfast."

After Gloria flew off, Mara dressed in the split-skirt ensemble and pulled on her tall brown leather boots. She fastened the dozen buttons on each leg, still pondering the problem of her magic, which made no sense. After all, she was a Serving mage who had conjured defensive wards during the war without thinking twice. Now, she couldn't magically light a candle without breaking a sweat. Mara sighed as she slipped her thin, narrow blades into the holsters stitched inside the shanks of her boots. She vowed to consult Arnesto about her magic.

She carried her breakfast of tea and overdone toast to the table and opened an old spell book Gemala had leant her. Mara had lost everything—her home, her belongings, and her family—during the war with Glenbarra. She shook her head, pushing aside the pain she felt whenever her mind wandered to the past. Starting over at eighteen hadn't been easy, but she was managing pretty well, except for her faltering magic and missing fay boyfriend. She closed the book, donned her aubergine cape, and locked up the flat, dropping her keyring into the matching reticule attached to her belt.

An hour later, Mara stood with a small crowd of Valerrans in front of the Bellaryss Children's Hospital, a three-story, yellow brick building with white shutters and trim. The wind whipped up Mara's cape as she waited for Vas to call her forward. Although he preferred baggy sweaters and rumpled corduroys over formal attire, Vas had dressed appropriately for the occasion, in a gray jacket and black slacks.

Bright blue highlights ran through Vas's brown hair and beard—the blue streaks inherited from his Faymon parents—and Mara noted he still cropped his hair far too short to be considered fashionable. His nose bent where it had been broken, and his face and hands bore the scars of someone accustomed to hard fighting. Vas's dark brown eyes narrowed as he surveyed the crowd. Mara figured he was probably making mental notes of who chose to attend, and more importantly, who had skipped the ceremony.

The provisional president had been a Royal Marine colonel before the war, a resistance leader during the occupation, and a reluctant politician afterward. Vas's speeches were short, lively, and to the point, which was the main reason Mara agreed to attend the ceremony and cut the ribbon. She ranked most politicians lower than street urchins in their trustworthiness, and far less likable.

"As you know, the recent fires in our capital were caused by arsonists linked to an anti-magic movement, which had its roots in a plot to overthrow our government. The chief leader of the movement, Harlan Lewyn, was later discovered to have been colluding with the dark fays." Vas waved his hands as he recapped the battle between the "forces for good, those who practice Serving magic," and the dark fay king, Bazra, and his minions. Vas praised the many Serving mages, human, fay, and other species, who'd lost their lives, and then he recognized Mara for rescuing him and many others from Bazra's dilapidated tower in the lower realms.

The audience applauded politely in all the right places and gasped a few times at Vas's colorful descriptions of events. Mara spotted her ex-boyfriend, Remy, in the crowd, along with Gemala, Vas's entire staff, several constables, and everyone else she'd rescued—everyone, except for Arnesto.

Vas handed Mara a pair of fabric shears. She felt the ground shudder slightly beneath her feet and thought a large carriage was rumbling down the cobblestone road behind them. As she slipped the shears' sharpened edges around the blue grosgrain ribbon, Mara felt another tremble underfoot. *That's an unusually large carriage. Or perhaps it's some sort of procession.* She noticed a few people glancing at each other, probably wondering about the tremors. Mara paused uncertainly but noticed Vas squinting at her, so she took a deep breath and cut the ribbon.

As the two ends of the ribbon fluttered in the breeze, three things happened: the street split wide open, sending Valerrans tumbling onto the cobblestones; fay traveling mists wound up Mara's legs and swirled about her waist; and Arnesto grabbed Mara's hand, tugging her into the black chasm in the ground.

CHAPTER 2

THE CRACK IN THE ROAD OPENED INTO A DEEP, DARK TUNNEL filled with mournful whispers, low murmurs, and occasional weeping that gave Mara goosebumps. Glancing down at her boots, she saw nothing but a vast, black void below her and gripped Arnesto's hand more firmly. Arnesto's fay magic was the only thing keeping them from plunging to their deaths.

"Arnesto! What are you doing? We need to go back and help Vas deal with this...situation, or threat, or whatever is going on. What *is* going on?" Mara's voice sounded too loud, echoing across the chasm and bouncing back at her. The air became warm and cloying. Fine beads of perspiration broke out on Mara's brow as she and Arnesto fell deeper. She glanced at Arnesto's profile, his wavy, vivid blue hair fluttering slightly around his broad shoulders. "Did you create this giant fissure?"

Arnesto squeezed her hand and leaned toward her, his breath tickling her ear as he whispered, "Nay, I arrived just in time to see you cut the ribbon when the ground split open. I merely used the opening to translocate us. Unfortunately, matters in the underworld have reached an impasse —quite literally. Wrongs must be righted and errors corrected, as it were." Arnesto's speech patterns reflected the influence of his Auntie Yelenarra. He became even more formal and stilted when he was nervous.

A knot formed in the pit of Mara's stomach. She preferred to spend as little time as possible in the realms of the dead. Although her nightmares had lessened, her harsh memories of the place had not softened with time. "What impasse?"

"You shall see for yourself shortly. Be brave, as always." Arnesto brought her hand to his lips and kissed her palm. Mara's heartbeat raced at his touch. She wanted to ask why he was showing her affection now, when he'd been avoiding her for weeks.

Arnesto's traveling vapors started to thin out, becoming silver wisps barely able to hold them afloat, before winking out entirely, which told Mara what she'd *suspected* but didn't want to *confirm*: they were entering the realms of the dead, where Serving magic no longer functioned.

They landed with a hard thud, taking several steps to steady themselves on the spongy ground. Mara was certain they'd fallen far enough and long enough to reach the bottommost realm of the dead, the final destination for departed spirits. Dark, scraggly trees surrounded them, silent sentries in the constant gloom, their leafless limbs stretching to the leaden sky above. Boulders of various shapes and sizes populated the area. Beyond the trees and boulders, deeper in the gauzy gloom where Mara had no intention of roaming, towered large sand dunes covered with tall, dull grasses. Black and gray defined the under-world; no other color, nothing vibrant or vivid, no reminders of life, could possibly hold sway in this place reserved for the lifeless.

Mara squinted through the gloom, trying to get her bearings. She heard churning water nearby and the same sad murmuring she'd heard as she tumbled through the chasm. The sound was louder and even more depressing, halfway between a chant and a low moan. *Eerie* was the only word she could use to describe it—and something she'd not encountered during her previous visits to the lower realms.

Mara peered at Arnesto and inhaled in surprise. Her gorgeous fay boyfriend looked almost...haunted. His large gray eyes, always so luminous, were clouded with worry, and the frown lines on his brow marred his smooth brown complexion. The angles of his face appeared sharper, as if he'd forgotten to eat his past few meals, his cheekbones more pronounced. He wore standard fay garb, a stretchy, silvery cape, trousers, and tunic, which normally strained in the most flattering way across his broad shoulders, but his clothes hung a bit loosely on his tall, muscular frame. "Arnesto, what's wrong? Are you unwell?"

Arnesto rubbed the stubble on his chiseled chin and didn't meet Mara's eyes. "I am sorry for dragging you here. I know how much you hate this place, with good reason. I have tried to fix this on my own, but to no avail. It seems I must ask for help. To be specific, I must ask for *your* help."

Mara placed her hands on either side of his face, care-worn with troubles she didn't understand, but still as ridiculously handsome as ever. "Tell me why we are here and how I can help. After all, I'm still your field coach. I'm supposed to be teaching you how to operate undercover inside Valerra, which you've barely visited this past month.

Or have you forgotten all about your training?" *And me, have you forgotten all about me?*

Arnesto's mouth twitched upward at the corners. *That's better. At least he hasn't lost his sense of humor.* He took her hands and tugged her toward him, his bow-shaped lips parting. She inhaled his tangy scent, loamy earth mixed with citrus, so unusual and so Arnesto-like. Mara knew kissing her fay boyfriend shouldn't be her highest priority in the realms of the dead, but she was affection-starved and not about to miss her chance.

A loud thump followed by an indignant squawk startled them both. They sprang apart, Arnesto's hand on the hilt of his sword, Mara crouching down to withdraw her twin daggers from inside her boots.

"'Tis only me, milady."

"Gloria! What are you doing here?" Mara straightened.

Her miniature griffin puffed out her chest. "I am your Griffin Companion. I promised to follow you everywhere, even into the lower realms." Gloria flicked her long tail. "I see Laird Arnestarious has finally made an appearance. What brings you to milady's side now, when you have been ignoring her for weeks? Hmm?" Apparently Gloria could speak as well in the realms of the dead as she could in Havynweal.

Mara blushed at her griffin's frankness. Perhaps Arnesto wouldn't notice her red face amidst the constant grayness of the underworld. "This is neither the time nor the place to have that conversation," she hissed. Gloria harrumphed.

"I have not been ignoring you." Arnesto ran a hand through his shoulder-length, wavy blue hair. "When you pledged your friendship to me in error, which was entirely my fault, since I had not explained about fay friendship customs, we agreed to take things slowly. I have been doing precisely that. I thought this is what you wanted."

Mara narrowed her eyes. "Your interpretation of 'taking things slowly' is to avoid me?"

"Not to avoid you, per se, but to create space so you do not feel any pressure to...move faster."

"Huh?"

"Maragold." Arnesto's voice grew husky. "What I am trying to say, in my very clumsy way, is—"

"What my nonsensical younger brother is trying to say is it's difficult for him to take things slowly when he is with you. His affections for you run very deep. So his solution has been to avoid you."

Mara yelped and jumped back. She knew the owner of that voice quite well. She'd held his hand and wept bitterly when he died. "*Efram?* I thought you would have crossed long ago—it's been nearly two months since your funeral rites."

Efram's ghostly form glided, rather than walked, toward them. He looked very much the same, a slightly shorter, translucent version of Arnesto, his curly hair cropped shorter. But unlike other spirits Mara had encountered in the realms of the dead, Efram flickered in and out, as if he couldn't maintain his ghostly form. Something was very wrong.

"Aye. I should've crossed over to the far shore, along with many hundreds of other spirits. We're all stuck here, on the wrong side of the river. Even worse, those of us who have been here the longest, like me, are starting to fade away entirely. I'm afraid we have botched things rather badly."

"This is not your fault, Efram. The error is all mine." Arnesto's shoulders slumped.

Efram shook his head, which detached from his neck, shimmering and floating in front of them as he spoke. "I should never have left you with the red sword, alone and unguarded, in your apartment in Valerra. It was far too easy for Bazra's creatures to capture you and the sword."

Despite the warmth in the lower realms, Mara shivered as she watched Efram's head settle back onto his neck. She didn't think she'd ever get used to seeing disembodied ghostly body parts fluttering about. Maybe if he spoke without shaking his head, it wouldn't happen. She wondered whether this was an example of how Efram and the other spirits were fading away. Bits of themselves flew off in various directions.

Arnesto drew his sandy eyebrows together. "But I am a twelfth-level fay wizard. The undead creatures should not have been able to overcome me."

"True, but I still should have—"

Mara raised her hands before the blue-haired brothers started bickering. "We know what happened, how Bazra got the red sword. Let's not forget I was the one to seal him and the sword into this realm. But what I don't understand is why the spirits are unable to cross over or why they are beginning to fade. What has that to do with the red sword?"

"Everything," said both brothers.

Efram clarified, "Since the red sword is one of the Swords of Five, forged by melding Serving magic with elemental magic, Bazra is able to use the sword to upset the magical balance in this realm."

According to fay legends, the Swords of Five were made by a giant and sprinkled with magic dust from the ancient forests by a powerful fay girl. Mara owned another of the Swords of Five, the blue sword. Mara and her schoolmates had discovered the five fay-spelled swords while hiding out in the Valerran Museum during the war. Her friends kept the other three swords safely locked away, under a web of spells and wards, deep in the forests of Faynwood.

During Arnesto's rescue mission, Mara learned she could use her blue sword to cast spells inside the lower realms, where the weapon's elemental magic still functioned. Her Serving magic spells, and even the dark fays' Fallow sorcery, went dormant inside the realms of the dead.

Arnesto added, "And since you sealed Bazra and the red sword into the lowest realm, it seems that only you can help us retrieve the sword now."

"To clarify, we need *both* you and your blue sword. You'll need to channel your sword's magic, as you did before." Efram waved one filmy hand, which bobbed in front of Mara's face before reattaching to his wrist. Mara swallowed and tried not to become distracted by Efram's floating body parts. "Your sword magic is the only thing confining Bazra to the lowest realm, and restraining the red sword as well."

Mara knew she had no choice but to come clean about her missing magic. "I'm afraid that's going to be a problem."

"Why is that?" Efram raised his hands, palms outward. Apparently he could still do that without misplacing them; something to be grateful for.

"Something happened to my magic the last time I visited the realms of the dead." Mara blew out a puff of air. She'd hoped to have this conversation in private with Arnesto.

"When you rescued me?" said Arnesto.

"When Bazra's guards killed me?" said Efram.

Mara looked around for a place to sit down. She spotted

a boulder covered in black lichen and wandered over to sit on it. Efram waved his hand frantically, the hand detaching and bobbling toward her. "Don't sit on that!"

"Why ever not?" Mara was crouched over the boulder but paused as Efram's hand continued bobbling.

"It's a hibernating undead creature. Best to let it sleep."

Mara swallowed down a squeal. She had no idea anything hibernated inside the realms of the dead and sprang away from the lichen-covered rock-thing. She pushed Efram's floating hand back toward him, where it reunited with his wrist.

Arnesto turned his large, gray, puppy-dog eyes on Mara. "Why am I only hearing about this now? If you are having difficulties with your magic, or anything else, I want to know about it right away."

Mara waved her hand and quickly checked to make sure it was still attached to the end of her arm. She would be having nightmares again about the realms of the dead, without a doubt. "I wanted to tell you but I kept hoping my magic would right itself. I just figured I needed more rest."

"And this transpired following my rescue?"

Mara bit her bottom lip. She didn't want Arnesto to think it was his fault or believe he had to solve this for her. She nodded. "But keep in mind I'd never used my sword's elemental magic that way before—and I'd never commandeered a dragon—or sent undead creatures back to the lowest realm." Mara gulped and said in a low voice, "I sent them back here...where are they?"

"The monsters you sealed in here are not the problem," said Efram. "You showed them mercy, and they are content to ignore Bazra because of it. Of course, there are new arrivals all the time, some of them quite nasty, whom he is influencing."

"But you expended all your magical energy saving me." Arnesto pinched the bridge of his nose. "I should have known this would happen."

"What do you mean, you should have known?" Mara folded her arms.

"A human girl cannot possibly save a twelfth-level fay wizard without incurring lasting damage to her magic. In fact, there is no recorded instance of a human ever saving a fay wizard by magical means." Arnesto flattened his lips.

"Well I did, and now we need to figure out how to restore my magic," said Mara crossly.

"It is not that simple. In fact, it may not be possible at all. Ouch!" Arnesto yelped and rubbed his knee. He stared down at Gloria. "Why did you peck my leg?"

Gloria flapped her wings. "Because you are not helping my mistress. You are simply stating the obvious and feeling sorry for yourself. Now get to work figuring this out." The griffin stomped her front paw for emphasis.

I adore having a pet griffin, thought Mara. *She's more than a companion for me—she's my champion too.*

Efram flickered in front of them, fading in and out. "Whatever you do, Arnesto, do it fast. I need to go rest now. I'll find you later."

Arnesto addressed Gloria, although it was clear to Mara his message was intended for her. "I did not mean to give offense, Griffin Gloria. Mara's magic saved many others and me that day. I shall never forget the vision of her calling down that magnificent dragon with her blue sword—" Arnesto paused mid-sentence and started murmuring to himself. He did this whenever he was recalling a passage from one of the books or scrolls in his aunt's library. He muttered under his breath, "It cannot hurt, anyway."

"What is it? Have you thought of something that will

help my mistress and restore balance here in the lowest realm? Do speak up." Gloria pecked Arnesto's boot for attention. He scooted backward to avoid any more pecking.

"It is simply this: I wish to re-read the primary sources on the forging of the Swords of Five, in case I have missed anything. It will require a trip to Havynweal, of course." He turned to Mara. "But first, there is someone here you must meet."

Arnesto took Mara's hand and guided her past the scraggly black trees toward the river. Gloria padded along on her other side, a steady, calming influence on Mara's already frayed nerves. The only people Mara could imagine wanting to see were those who had already crossed over to the far shore, such as her mother. "Who is it?"

Arnesto didn't respond directly but asked a question of his own. "Have you noticed anything different since your last visit to the lowest realm?"

"Other than seeing your brother's ghost, not really. It's as gray, gloomy, and uninviting as ever. No wonder the spirits want to cross to the other side of the river as quickly as possible."

"Nothing else?" Arnesto raised one eyebrow and lowered the other, which he did when he was trying to make a point.

Mara frowned, thinking about her last visit. Everything was the same, except for that eerie murmuring sound. Then it came to her. She snapped her fingers and immediately regretted making the small popping noise in the otherwise nearly silent realm. "There's no chanting from the spirits across the river. They aren't beckoning to those who led good lives. Is that why Efram can't cross to the other side?"

"Aye, it appears that without the singing spirits and their hymns, none are able to traverse the river."

"What happens when they try?"

Another voice spoke up from behind them. "None try, because we are unable to welcome them with our hymn. And because we are unable to raise our voices in song, we cannot conjure the boats and smooth out the river for the good spirits to cross over."

Mara jumped, her heart pounding. "Mage Mother Pawllah? What are *you* doing here? Surely you would have made the trip across the river many months ago." Pawllah had literally saved Mara and her friends after they escaped from Valerra during the war. They'd made it to Sanrellyss Island, where Pawllah had sheltered them, nurturing their wounds —both physical and emotional—and ensuring they studied their Serving magic spells. The elderly fay mage no longer looked ancient, but ageless.

Pawllah's dark brown skin glistened with dew, and her hair flowed in translucent blue wisps all around her head, as if blown by some invisible wind. She wore a silver gown that cinched at the waist and billowed around her legs. "I am no longer Mage Mother of Sanrellyss Island. I now serve the newly departed, ensuring a seamless transition for those who led commendable lives. I am the Choirmaster."

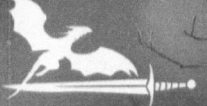

CHAPTER 3

PAWLLAH SHOOK HER HEAD, HER BLUE HAIR FLOATING BEHIND HER. "But the dark fay king has silenced my choir. Before long, we will begin to lose good souls such as Efram to the ether. Once they are gone, they are lost for all time."

Despite the warmth of the lower realms, a chill prickled Mara's scalp and rippled down her spine. *What a horrible fate.* "I don't understand how a person's soul could be lost forever."

Pawllah turned toward the river. Mara and Arnesto walked alongside the ghostly mage. "Those who are worthy must cross the river to the far shore, where they are reunited with others who have passed on before them. They join their forever family, kindred spirits who affirm and sustain one another."

"What happens to the spirits deemed unfit to cross the river?" Mara had a good idea, but she wanted Pawllah to confirm it.

The Choirmaster waved her hand, which Mara was relieved to see remained firmly attached to her wrist. "I believe you have seen some of what occurs here. The unworthy ghosts fight each other for any means to cross over, piling into boats that flounder in the rough waters. Most are swept along into the lake of fire downriver. A few manage to break free of the coursing river and crawl back to the beach. Over time, their twisted, unhappy spirits shrivel up, losing all semblance of what they once were. Some become the monsters you have encountered. They roam about, seeking a means of escape. Others curl up and hibernate for so long they become part of the landscape." She swept her arm to indicate lumpy rock formations, covered in gray dune grass and black lichen, scattered along the shoreline.

Mara peered more closely at the boulders and quickly covered her mouth with her hand to stifle a cry. She could just barely make out a pair of eyes on top of the nearest mound, staring up at the gauzy gray sky, and what looked like a yawning mouth etched into the stone surface of another. *If anything could convince someone to lead a decent life, it was a visit to the realms of the dead.*

Pawllah paused at the river's edge. Across the water, on the far shore, the otherworldly choir sat huddled together, murmuring in low, eerie tones, as if trying to harmonize once again. The Choirmaster nodded at her unhappy singers. "So long as Bazra possesses the red sword, discordancy and chaos shall reign in this realm—and spread to yours. Look at my choir; without their harmonizing voices, the entire realm is off-kilter."

She pointed at the beach behind them, where ghosts were fighting over a few rickety boats beached in the sand. Other spirits had retreated from the water's edge and watched the scuffling from a safe distance. Mara noticed many of the peaceful ghosts flickered in and out, like Efram.

"Please help me restore balance inside this realm,

before it is too late to save Efram and the others. Otherwise, both our worlds will be forfeited. That single crack in front of the children's hospital was Bazra's opening volley. There will be more incursions into your realm as well."

"I want to help, Mage Mother, I mean Choirmaster, but how?" asked Mara.

Pawllah held one hand over the water's surface. A flat stepping-stone emerged from the riverbed. She stepped onto the stone and turned back around to address Mara. "By all magical means necessary. You must help Arnestarious retrieve the red sword. It must not remain in this realm. Act with all due speed, Maragold, and be not afraid."

"But—"

Pawllah's voice faded as the stepping-stone carried her across the water. The choppy river became smooth as glass around the stone transporting the Choirmaster. "May your magic serve in peace and lead through service. This is the true path."

"Aye, this is the true path," echoed Mara glumly, repeating the last part of the Serving mage's pledge. She felt as if she'd been handed an impossible assignment, one that she was ill equipped to take on since she'd depleted her magical reserves the last time she'd visited the realms of the dead.

Gloria glanced up at her. "How are you supposed to defeat the dark fay king when you are unable to cast a fire-starter spell?"

Arnesto put his hands on his hips. "Is this true? You are unable to cast even a simple child's spell?"

"Perhaps fays consider a fire-starter spell appropriate for children, but that's not the case in Valerra." Mara knew she was deflecting from the real issue, but she didn't need a lecture from Arnesto about how easy a fire-starter spell should be for her. No one needed to tell her what she already knew, especially not her missing-in-action fay boyfriend.

"Fine," Arnesto huffed, "it is an adolescent's spell, appropriate for a mage apprentice. Even so, you have been casting that spell for years. We must get to the bottom of your magical malaise, and we must do so quickly, before my brother wanes any further."

"Agreed. I think the first thing to do is reunite me with my blue sword. Perhaps being separated by such a great distance has slowed my magic's healing process." After Mara's near-death experience rescuing Arnesto and battling Bazra, his necromancers, and the undead creatures they'd raised, she'd turned her sword over to Yelenarra for safekeeping. She reasoned it would be far more difficult for Bazra to steal her ensorcelled sword from a fay stronghold in Havynweal, than from a human girl's apartment in Valerra. Arnesto had agreed with her.

"I do not believe that alone is the answer, but it is an interesting theory, and as good a place as any to start," said Arnesto. "Follow me to the portal." He began walking briskly away from the river through the copse of scraggly trees toward a row of sand dunes covered in spiky, gray grass.

Mara lengthened her strides to keep up with Arnesto. "You discovered a portal between the fay lands and the realms of the dead?"

"Not precisely." Arnesto wouldn't make eye contact with her, which meant he was avoiding telling her the truth about something she probably wouldn't like hearing.

"Oh?" Mara stopped walking. She wasn't about to let Arnesto off the hook. As a fay, he couldn't tell an outright lie, but he was masterful at skirting the truth. When

Arnesto saw she wasn't keeping pace with him, he turned around with a sigh and stared down at her boots. Definitely not a good sign. Gloria padded over to Arnesto and pecked his leg.

"Ouch! Please desist from further pecking, Griffin Gloria."

"Stop dithering and tell milady what you have done." Gloria angled her head and gave Arnesto a withering glare.

Arnesto threw his hands in the air. "Fine. I confess that I conjured the portal. But I can assure you it is perfectly safe."

Mara stared at Arnesto. Since Serving magic did not operate inside the lower realms, even a powerful fay wizard such as Arnesto was unable to cast the simplest Serving magic spell. However, Arnesto's advanced wizardry skills enabled him to draw upon elemental magic for short periods of time, which Mara suspected he'd been doing. It was the only explanation she could come up with for why her fay boyfriend looked so drained and exhausted, and how he'd managed to conjure the portal.

"You *intentionally* connected Havynweal to this realm? What if something undead escapes, like happened last time?" Mara shook her head. Bazra had sent stinking, bristly monsters from the lower realms into Havynweal twice before. The creatures had terrorized the fays and destroyed everything in their path. She was shocked he would take such a risk.

Arnesto squared his jaw. He had a stubborn streak as wide and long as the crack in front of the children's hospital. "I have set up the appropriate defensive wards. No undead creatures shall be able to climb up past the second lowest level."

"And what about the dark fay king himself? He's a bit wilier than the creatures he controls."

"Your sword magic has confined Bazra to this realm for the time being. Rest assured, the portal is quite secure."

Arnesto led Mara and Gloria behind the sand dune directly in their path. He walked up to a large boulder that stood twice as tall as Mara and ran his hand over a fissure along its surface. Mara gulped, worried he would awaken a hibernating creature. But instead of the roar of an angry beast, the fissure opened with a creaking hiss. Pebbles, sand, and scores of brown spiders the size of Mara's fist poured out of the widening gap.

"Eek." Mara leapt back. "I'm not going in there. You know I *hate* spiders."

Arnesto's lips twitched but he restrained himself. A good thing, because Mara was in no mood to be teased. "This is our only means of traversing between realms."

"Are you certain this is the only way back to Havynweal?"

"Aye. This is how I have been able to visit Efram and meet the Choirmaster."

Despite the warmth in the lower realms, Mara had kept her cape with her and pulled up the hood. She carefully tucked her hair inside and grumbled, "Alright. Show me the way."

Arnesto said, "It is best if we lock arms."

"What about me?" asked Gloria, who looked as if she might peck Arnesto's leg again.

Arnesto crouched down beside the miniature griffin. "I would be honored if you would permit me to hold you whilst we enter the portal. I have only ever traversed between the realms by myself. I do not wish us to become separated."

Gloria squawked. "This is most irregular. Griffins are not accustomed to being carried. But under these special circumstances, I grant you permission." The griffin folded her wings tightly against her compact body as Arnesto scooped her into his arms.

Arnesto nodded at Mara. "Ready?"

She took a deep breath and looped her arm securely through his. "Aye."

Mara and Arnesto, clutching Gloria, leaned into the wind as they stepped inside the portal. Fierce gusts tossed leaves, twigs, and bugs—lots of them—in great swirling spirals all around them. Mara clamped her mouth shut to make sure she didn't accidentally swallow any of the creepy-crawly things twirling past them. The portal smelled loamy, a bit like Arnesto, but without the pleasing citrus notes, and vibrated as they drew closer the end, or what Mara assumed was the end, a small, narrow finger of light that grew wider as they approached.

The wind whipping around them stilled suddenly. The portal shuddered, expelling them with a loud, belching wheeze. Arnesto's traveling mists encircled them even before their feet touched the ground, so they didn't stumble and scrape any knees or elbows as they landed on a bright, lime green lawn.

Mara flung off her cape and yelped as two brown spiders scurried away. She shook her head, worried spiders might have crawled into her hood, and breathed a sigh of relief when nothing else fell from her hair to the ground. "Your portal is an amazing achievement, but the bugs are awful," she huffed, "no offense."

"None taken," said Arnesto as he carefully deposited Gloria on the grass.

The griffin shook herself vigorously and arched her back, extending her claws as if testing the solidness of the ground. She sat back on her haunches and smoothed her mane with her front paw. "Thank you, Laird Arnestarious, for a most unusual experience, one I am not anxious to repeat but will do so for milady's sake. I must take my leave for now, as two of my sons live nearby. I shall see you back at the manor." Her long, tufted tail flitting with purpose, Gloria bounded away.

Arnesto gazed thoughtfully after the griffin, but clearly, his mind was still working out the intricacies of his latest invention. "I have not yet figured out why insects are drawn to the portal."

"Perhaps the wind draws them in." Mara shrugged and glanced around. Given the giant purple and teal butterflies zooming in and out of the hot pink honeysuckle, they'd arrived in one of Havynweal's summer seasons. "I don't see Yelenarra's manor anywhere. Where are we going?"

Arnesto rubbed the stubble on his chin. "The wind's suction power is a possibility I had not considered. If I could reverse the polarities at the portal's midway point, then I may be able to blow the insects away, and—"

"Arnesto, please answer my question." Mara had no interest in polarities or portals. She wanted a simple, direct answer from her wizard boyfriend.

"To confer with your healer," said Arnesto. Mara stifled a groan. Zornamayne was both highly skilled and quite terrifying. And Mara knew she was in for a scolding from the feline-fay healer.

A large cat roared somewhere off to Mara's left, followed by the howling of a wolf. While wolf howls normally sent shivers down Mara's spine, this one sounded familiar. A huge wolf-man crossbreed burst through the neon orange sunflowers and wrinkled his muzzle in a canine grin. "Mara, friend! You visit me?"

Mara smiled at the panting grihm. "Aye, Farleigh, we only just arrived. It's good to see you again."

Though many grihms lost the power of speech during crossbreeding, Farleigh and his friend, Jerdahn, had retained some speaking abilities. Mara had no trouble understanding their garbled words, although she was convinced Arnesto cast a translation spell whenever he conversed with the two grihms.

"I happy here. Jerdahn too."

Mara smiled. "That's good news. You deserve to be happy after everything you've been through." Most grihms were about the size of an average man, but Farleigh had been a six-and-a-half foot-tall Royal Marine before the Glenbarrans had captured and forcibly crossbred him with an oversized wolf.

Grihms had a bushy tail and four wolfish legs, with a pair of furry human hands for paws up front. While their forehead and eyes looked like a man's, their snout and muzzle were completely wolfish. Farleigh and Jerdahn had escaped from their Glenbarran captors and assisted Mara during the war. She had returned the favor, by helping to find a fitting sanctuary for her ferocious-looking friends.

Mara heard a throaty purr and spun around to find a lovely feline-fay hybrid, one of Zornamayne's clan, watching her. The hybrid bowed low. "Welcome, Lady Maragold. Master Healer wishes to see you immediately. Please come with me." Unlike the misshapen forms that grihms had been forced into during crossbreeding, Zorna-mayne's clan were natural hybrids—part large feline, part fay—and stunning. This young hybrid had sleek black fur and a small, pert nose.

Farleigh yipped, "Bye, Mara. See later."

Arnesto started to accompany them, but the young

hybrid bowed a second time. "With all due respect, Master Healer expressly asked to see Lady Maragold alone. When she is finished, I will escort her to wherever she wishes to go."

Arnesto sputtered, "But Maragold does not know her way around Havynweal."

The hybrid tilted her head to one side and glanced up at him through glittering gold eyes, the whiskers above her pink rosebud lips twitching. "Nay, sir, but I do."

Mara put a hand on Arnesto's arm. "It's fine. I will meet you back at the manor."

He placed his hand protectively over Mara's and glared at the young feline-fay. "If Lady Maragold has not arrived at the manor by sunset, I shall return and retrieve her myself."

"As you wish, Laird Arnestarious."

Arnesto's traveling mists coiled up his legs and waist. Before he winked out, he gave Mara a quick, chaste kiss on the cheek. Her pulse quickened, and she almost followed him into the mists. They still had a great deal to discuss about their relationship, and she needed a better grounding in fay friendship customs if her heart was going to survive Arnesto's conflicting signals.

CHAPTER 4

"Master Healer, it is very good to see you again." Mara bowed, lower than perhaps necessary. She respected the talented feline-fay who had saved Arnesto's life and her own. The young hybrid had deposited Mara inside the kitchen of Zornamayne's snug stone cottage. Dried herbs, tied up with string, hung overhead, filling the room with a piquant scent. Brightly colored bottles lined the shelves above the sink, which Mara noticed had no hand pump. She assumed that like Arnesto and Yelenarra, Zornamayne merely snapped her fingers and conjured running water. Inside her own home, the hybrid dispensed with the layers of veils she typically wore. Instead, she was draped in a gossamer gown, and Mara was struck again by the healer's beauty, simultaneously catlike and feminine.

Zornamayne's champagne-colored fur looked freshly groomed, the touches of black on the tips of her ears, paws, and tail gleaming. Mara noticed the healer's tail flicking briskly and refrained from taking two steps backward. "Maragold." The hybrid's piercing green eyes flashed. "Is it true you are not in control of your magic?"

"Unfortunately, that is correct." Mara needed to have a chat with her officious but well-meaning griffin. "I suppose Gloria has just left?"

Zornamayne grunted. "Why must I learn of this from your griffin? I asked you to get in touch after eight moon-rises if your magic still remained elusive. This is not uncommon, given the amount of magical energy you wielded. When I heard nothing, I assumed you were recovered." Zornamayne had provided Mara with her full fay name so she could contact the healer from anywhere, including Valerra. It was an unusual act of trust, especially between a feline-fay hybrid and a human girl, which Mara had earned by rescuing several hybrids from Zornamayne's clan during the battle with Bazra.

Mara lowered her head. She should have consulted with Zornamayne as soon as she realized she wasn't improving. "I'm sorry for not contacting you sooner, but I kept hoping—"

"Foolish girl! While you were hoping, I could have been seeking answers for your cure. We have lost precious time."

Mara's head snapped up. "Is there a cure for my condition?"

Zornamayne waved her front paws impatiently. "Of course there is a cure."

"Arnesto believes otherwise."

"I expect Arnestarious told you no human has ever been able to command a dragon or rescue a twelfth-level fay wizard. So therefore, your magic must be fully depleted."

"How did you know?"

Zornamayne snorted. "Arnestarious is a powerful fay wizard who was careless enough to be captured by the dark fays and then needed rescuing by his human girlfriend. His perspective is limited by his ego."

"But I know Arnesto wants to help me."

"Aye, I am sure he does. He will go to great lengths to aid your recovery, but he is *not* a healer."

"There is something else you should know, something I just discovered." Mara told Zornamayne about meeting the Choirmaster and what was happening—or more precisely, *not* happening—inside the realms of the dead.

Zornamayne yowled. "This is unprecedented. We have no time to waste. Where is your blue sword?"

"With Yelenarra for safekeeping."

The hybrid tapped her chin with one claw. "A wise choice on your part. I shall retrieve it myself." Zornamayne pointed toward the front of her cottage. "Please make yourself comfortable and help yourself to refreshments. I shall return shortly, and we will get to work." The healer disappeared on a puff of traveling mist.

Mara wandered down the hallway, her boots clacking on the bare wooden floors. She turned to her right and entered a cozy pink, green, and yellow sitting room. A riot of florals covered every available surface—tables, windows, and sofas. Fresh hibiscus, roses, and snapdragons filled vases scattered about the room, and floriated chintz hung at the windows and adorned twin sofas by the fireplace. The plush carpet was a swirl of flowers in what Mara thought of as fay land colors, hot pink, lime green, neon yellow, and bright orange. A low table between the two front windows was set with tea service for two. The tray of chocolate-covered biscuits looked especially inviting.

Mara sank down onto one of the pink floral floor cushions. She picked up Zornamayne's porcelain teapot, admiring its delicate green vine pattern, and poured the jasmine-scented black tea into a matching teacup. The cup had an extra-large handle to make it easier for someone with paws to grip it. Mara took a sip of tea and nibbled on a biscuit, wondering whether Zornamayne really could find a cure for her missing magic. The hybrid seemed confident she could help Mara, and yet Arnesto was just as convinced her magical reserves had been permanently depleted during the rescue operation.

Mara was on her second biscuit when Zornamayne emerged from the mists, carrying a long, flat navy trunk by the handle. "I informed Yelenarra and Arnestarious that you would be here for the day, and I would personally deliver you to the manor when we are finished. I wish to observe you with your sword, to see whether your natural magic will assert itself again when in contact with an ensorcelled object that has imprinted on you."

"My sword has imprinted on me?"

"Aye, and the reverse is also true. You have imprinted on your sword. Please open the case and withdraw it. Let us see how your blade responds to your touch."

Mara pulled the trunk toward her and set it on the carpet of Zornamayne's sitting room. She reached into the aubergine reticule attached to her belt, and withdrew a ring containing three keys: the large brass key opened the front door of the Cracked Cauldron, the dingy tin key fit the door to her flat, and the small, ornate silver key matched the silver lock on her trunk. Mara's hands trembled as she unlocked the trunk and flipped back the lid. She hadn't seen her sword since placing it in Yelenarra's care six weeks earlier. *Could simply touching my sword reawaken my magic now?*

Mara removed the dark blue leather scabbard from the trunk's velvet lining. Dozens of blue gemstones were embedded into the handle protruding from the scabbard, with the largest sapphire Mara had ever seen covering the base of the hilt. Mara took a deep breath and rose to her feet. She gripped the hilt with her right hand and withdrew the sword, raising it above her head. The ancient fay hieroglyphs on the blade, which normally blazed bright blue at Mara's touch, winked on and off a few times, and then fizzled out.

Mara bit her bottom lip, blinking back the tears stinging her eyes. Re-sheathing her sword, Mara chanced a glance at Zornamayne, whose whiskers were twitching furiously. "That has never happened to me before. My sword always shines brightly when I grip it. Perhaps Arnesto is right after all, and my magic has truly expired."

"Nonsense." Zornamayne shook her head, her tail lashing the floor. "Something else is at play here." The healer glanced at the tea tray. "I must think, and I think best with tea in one paw, and chocolate in the other." She sat on a mint green floor cushion and poured herself a cup of tea.

Mara returned her sword to the trunk but didn't lock it. Zornamayne might want her to try again later, although Mara couldn't see any point. Clearly, she'd used up all her magic when she'd rescued Arnesto and the others. It was a hefty price to pay, but she would do it again if given the choice. Mara sat at the table and sighed at her tepid tea. Zornamayne touched the side of Mara's cup with one claw and reheated the tea, something Mara used to be able to do for herself by casting a basic kitchen spell. She sighed a second time and took a sip of the now-hot tea.

"Arnestarious is partially correct," said Zornamayne in between nibbles of a shell-shaped biscuit drizzled with chocolate. "It is true there is no recorded instance of a human commanding a dragon or rescuing a fay wizard."

Mara's shoulders slumped, and Zornamayne hastened

to add, "However, I have drawn a different conclusion from your pessimistic friend. I do not believe your magical reserves are depleted. Why should they be? If someone is able to accomplish the near impossible once, then why conclude she will not be able to do so again? That is not logical, and feline-fays are known for our logic, especially in all things magical and mysterious."

Mara frowned. She had never heard of the logic of magic. If anything, magic seemed quite illogical and altogether impossible. However, Zornamayne seemed so certain she would find a cure Mara felt a twinge of optimism. Zornamayne sipped from her teacup and placed it carefully in its saucer. "Further, your sword did respond to you. The imprinting between you and your sword is as active as ever."

Mara waved her hand at the navy trunk sitting in the middle of the parlor. "And yet the hieroglyphs barely lit up for me."

Zornamayne nodded. "Aye, but the blade did react at your touch, although not with its usual power." She reached for another chocolate-drizzled biscuit, this one shaped like a bell. "When I went to retrieve the sword from Yelenarra and explained why, she asked if she could try an experiment. She used the duplicate key you had given her to unlock the trunk. Both she and Arnestarious attempted to hold your sword. When Yelenarra tried, nothing happened. The blade remained a dull gray. When Arnestarious tried, the sword shocked his palm, and he immediately dropped it."

Zornamayne rose from the cushion, crossed to the center of the parlor, and crouched by the navy trunk. Flipping back the lid, the healer glanced at Mara. "May I try?"

Mara said, "Of course. But do be careful. As Arnesto learned, the sword can be temperamental."

Zornamayne's whiskers twitched. She lifted the scabbard from the trunk and turned toward Mara. The healer gripped the scabbard in her left paw, and grasping the hilt with her right, slowly withdrew the blade. Nothing happened, not a single spark lit the hieroglyphs along the blade.

Zornamayne nodded. "You do see what I mean now, do you not?"

Mara scratched her head. "Not really."

The healer grunted. Mara thought she might be frustrating the feline-fay with her obtuseness. Zornamayne closed the trunk with a decisive snap. "Your blade's runes lit up for you; however, your sword did not fully awaken. The magical connection between you and your sword is still active, but something is blocking the flow of energy."

Zornamayne returned to her mint green cushion, reheated her tea with a touch of one claw, and took several sips. Mara stared at the half-eaten chocolate wafer in her hand and returned it to her plate. She didn't know what to think. Although Zornamayne was giving her reason to hope, she couldn't imagine how to free her magic when she had no idea what had blocked it in the first place. Then an idea struck her. "Could Bazra or one of the other dark fays have cast a spell to block my magical energy?"

Zornamayne shook her head. "You defeated the one and showed mercy to the rest. While it would be easy to blame Bazra, I do not sense any dark magic." Zornamayne stroked her whiskers. "Perhaps there is a clue somewhere in the past. Tell me about your heritage."

"My *heritage*? What do you need to know, other than I'm a human girl from Valerra?"

Zornamayne waved her paw, a six-sided chocolate star clutched between her claws. "It is common for fay healers to know their patient's parents, siblings, and even extended family. We are often able to see connections and reach a proper diagnosis faster when we consider the patient's generational and situational context."

Mara didn't think her family history would be much help but she shrugged. "Alright. What would you like to know?"

"Tell me about your parents. Were they mages? If so, describe their abilities to me."

Mara shifted on her floor cushion, wondering how much to tell. She hated delving into her father's failed military career and never discussed her mother, except to say she had passed on. Her memories of her mother were fragmented, mere impressions. She'd been barely four years old when her mother died.

Zornamayne must have detected Mara's hesitation. Her green eyes softened. "There is another way for me to acquire your family history, if you are willing."

Mara sat up straighter. "And what is that?"

"A memory spell, which would enable me to peer into your past, without you needing to actually tell me about it. I may ask a few questions afterward, but I assure you, it is painless and quite efficient."

Mara nodded slowly. "Very well. If you think there might be a clue in my past or in my family tree, then let's try your memory spell."

CHAPTER 5

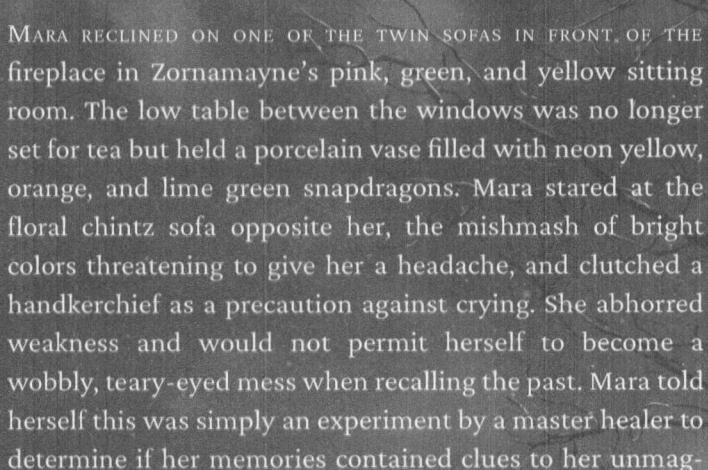

Mara reclined on one of the twin sofas in front of the fireplace in Zornamayne's pink, green, and yellow sitting room. The low table between the windows was no longer set for tea but held a porcelain vase filled with neon yellow, orange, and lime green snapdragons. Mara stared at the floral chintz sofa opposite her, the mishmash of bright colors threatening to give her a headache, and clutched a handkerchief as a precaution against crying. She abhorred weakness and would not permit herself to become a wobbly, teary-eyed mess when recalling the past. Mara told herself this was simply an experiment by a master healer to determine if her memories contained clues to her unmagical condition.

Zornamayne sat down on the sofa opposite Mara, hissing and buzzing the words to a spell Mara couldn't possibly translate, other than a few of the fay words, such as "past," "memory," and "lost." Prompted by the feline-fay's singsong voice, Mara grew sleepy and yawned. Perhaps reclining on the comfy chintz sofa had not been such a good idea.

Mara blinked and found herself standing at the edge of the pretty, leafy park across from the old parliament building in Bellaryss. She must have been in a pre-war memory, since the old parliament building, along with half the other buildings in the city's downtown, were now ruin and rubble. Mara watched as a tall man with wheat-colored hair, heavily salted with gray, and a well-trimmed beard to match, purchased toffee from a pushcart vendor. He bent down to hand the treat to a little girl, about four years old, with large blue eyes and two wheat-colored braids. Zorna-mayne stood next to Mara and asked, "Am I correct in assuming that little girl is you?"

"Aye." Mara felt a tingling sensation in the back of her throat and swallowed down a large lump forming there. "And that's my father." When her mother's illness had progressed to the point she was entirely bedridden, Mara and her father would go for long walks together. Her mother insisted they both needed the fresh air and sunshine, although often as not, they walked in gray driz-zle. Mara suspected Mother wanted to give them a respite from the constant sadness shrouding their home, from the knowledge her health was not improving despite Father's insistence otherwise.

Little Mara polished off her toffee and smiled up at her father. He took the small girl by the hand, and Mara wondered when she had last felt so loved and safe. The child and gentleman walked beneath a canopy of trees, the pale green leaves signaling the arrival of spring.

Mara took several steps in their direction and then stopped, wrinkling her brow. A middle-aged man with a large handlebar mustache and silver-topped walking stick stalked over to the pair. Mara glanced down at her boots, avoiding eye contact with Zornamayne.

"What you're about to witness happened often to my father, but he remained undeterred. He might have gripped my hand a bit more firmly when some stranger berated him, but otherwise, Father carried on. He learned to live with the mistake that cost him his officer commission. He still served in the Royal Marines, but as a corporal, not a captain."

The mustached man walked up to them and spat on the ground, some of the spittle landing on her father's polished leather boots. "Chicken-livered coward! How many men and women did we lose because you turned and fled? You should be ashamed to show your face in public!"

Little Mara started to cry, and her father bent down to soothe her. Mara curled her hands into fists, took several steps toward the mustached man, and shouted, "Be gone from here, you bully!" Neither the mustached man nor her father reacted.

Zornamayne placed a paw gently on her arm. "We are observers only, mere shadows in the realm of your memories."

Mara grumbled, "Have you seen enough?" She heard the bitterness in her voice and took a steadying breath. "I know you're trying to help me, but this just hurts."

"Unfortunately, painful bits of memory often reveal the most relevant clues." Zornamayne waved her paw, and the scene faded away, to be replaced by another.

Mara shook her head. "Not here, please. There can be nothing to learn from watching her final moments."

Zornamayne murmured, "Turn away if you must, but this is where your memories have directed us."

Mara brought her hand to her chest and held it there, as if to ward off what came next. Her mother's slender form huddled under a swath of blankets reaching to her chin. Her white-blonde hair, so pale as to be almost translucent, fanned out on the pillow and framed her oval face. She appeared to be sleeping, her breathing shallow and raspy.

The healer, a matronly woman who'd taken up residence in one of the guest rooms to nurse her mother, whispered, "She'll not be with us much longer, sir."

Mara's father wailed, "No, no, it's much too soon. I can't say goodbye to my Gracelyn. I refuse." He stumbled from the room.

Tears trickled down little Mara's cheeks, but she stood by the bed. Her mother's breathing became erratic, and the healer leaned over to dab her forehead periodically with a lavender-scented cloth. "Look!" cried little Mara, pointing at her mother's violet eyes, which had flickered open.

Mara frowned. *Mother's eyes were blue, not violet. And her hair had been several shades darker, not the platinum blonde on the pillow. Why am I seeing her differently now?*

"I'll go find your father, Miss Maragold," whispered the healer. "He should be here."

Little Mara leaned over and kissed her mother's cheek. "Don't leave, Mama. Stay here in this realm, with me."

Mara turned away with a dull ache in her chest, unable to watch any more. Her memories of her mother's death were fuzzy, and she preferred it that way. She saw no reason to relive it now. "Please, let's go."

Zornamayne extended her paw toward the bed. "Just a bit longer." Mara scowled but turned back around.

The little girl leaned over to whisper in her mother's ear. "I may get lost visiting the other realms without you." Mara drew closer to the pair. What was this about visiting other realms? Mara hadn't realized she'd been such an imaginative little girl. She remembered being quite solemn, defensive even, especially when it came to protecting her father's reputation.

Her mother moved her lips. "Promises."

"What promises?" asked the child.

Mara had no recollection of her mother saying anything in her final moments. She didn't even recall she'd been left alone in the room with her dying mother. Mara gripped the bed's footboard, hanging on every word.

"Must keep our promise."

"Is it a secret promise?" whispered little Mara.

"Aye." Her mother had a coughing spell. The child grasped her mother's hand until she settled onto the pillows again. "You are different, dearest."

"Is that the secret, Mama?"

Mother nodded and seemed to fall asleep, but her eyes fluttered open. "Master your blades...and magic...and lasso. Master your craft."

Mara's knuckles turned white as she tightened her grip on the footboard. *Master my craft? What is my craft? My blades are useful, lifesaving even, and magic is essential for any mage. But only reapers need to master the lasso. I'm a girl from Valerra with wobbly magic and a malfunctioning sword. I'm definitely not a reaper—and I don't want to be!*

One final, shaky breath escaped from Mother's lips and she fell silent. Young Mara collapsed onto the carpet and sobbed. Her father dashed back into the room with the healer, spotted Mara sobbing on the floor, and lifted her to his shoulder.

The healer pulled back the bedcovers, checked for a pulse, and shook her head. "I am sorry, sir."

Father stared at the bed, his daughter in his arms, and stammered, "How can I raise her without Gracelyn? I know nothing of the other realms. My poor child!" Father kissed the top of little Mara's head as tears streaked down his cheeks. "Our promise is an old one," he mumbled under his breath, "let us hope he forgets."

"Look! Mama is shimmering," said young Mara, reaching a hand toward her mother's still form, where a rainbow of sparks hovered near the bed.

Her father knelt by the bed and placed Mara on the carpet next to him. "That's your mother's magical energy, departing this realm along with her spirit. She wants you to indwell some of her sparks—that way, a bit of her magic will be with you always."

"I'm here, Mama!" shouted the little girl, twirling around as the tiny flashes of magical energy landed on her hair, face, and arms.

Mara's head swirled, and she feared she might vomit at any moment. She leaned over the footboard, closed her eyes, and wept. Zornamayne murmured something, probably the counterspell, and Mara found herself back in the hybrid's snug cottage, leaning forward on the colorful floral sofa. She wiped her eyes with her crumpled handkerchief and slowly swung her feet to the floor. She didn't trust herself to stand just yet. Feeling weak as a kitten, her body shaking and her stomach roiling, Mara dropped her head between her knees and gulped some air.

Zornamayne placed a comforting paw on her shoulder. "Stay put whilst I mix a draught for you. Memory spells are powerful, and you have had quite the shock, I daresay."

Mara gritted her teeth to keep the bile down and nodded. Her mother's final words ran through her head, and she could make no sense of them. Neither could she comprehend the meaning behind her father's response. He seemed to confirm Mother not only visited other realms, but took Mara along with her—which she could not remember—and what was all that talk about a promise to keep?

Father had never mentioned anything about a promise to her. He eventually remarried a plump, pleasant, unmagical woman and had two more daughters. Mara had lost contact with her family during the siege of Bellaryss, when they joined other evacuees headed for the colonies. She didn't know whether they'd survived the arduous journey.

"Here, sip this slowly." Zornamayne handed Mara a cut-crystal goblet.

Mara took a few sips of the amber liquid, which tasted both sweet and bitter, and burned slightly as she swallowed. "What is this stuff? It tastes like orange peel and a spot of brandy."

Zornamayne's whiskers twitched. "Something like that, with a few herbs as well."

Mara felt herself growing warmer with each sip. Her insides eventually stopped quaking. "It's quite nice, actually."

Zornamayne smiled but said nothing. Mara figured the healer was waiting for her to break the silence. Mara continued sipping the delicious drink. She'd finished more than half before placing the heavy crystal glass on a small side table. "I don't know what to think. What other realms did I visit with my mother as a child? What promise must be kept—and why? Who demanded the promise in the first place? It's all so strange."

"Did your father say anything when you were older, give you any clues?"

"No, quite the opposite in fact. Father seemed to shut down after Mother died. He grew quieter, more introspective. Sometimes he would glance at me, his brow furrowed and his lips pursed, as if he weren't quite sure what to do with me." She shrugged. "I figured he was missing Mother, same as me. My father certainly ensured I never wanted for anything—I had a lovely governess and many tutors through the years, from the old mage who taught me basic spells, to a dashing young fencing instructor I was sure I'd marry one day. He broke my heart at the age of ten, when he eloped with a 'spinster' twice my age."

Mara chuckled and then glanced down at the crystal goblet in her hand. She hadn't realized she'd been sipping from it again. Shaking her head, she placed the empty glass on the side table. "I haven't thought about my governess or fencing instructor in years. What's wrong with me?"

"It's the aftereffects of the memory spell, combined with the draught."

"It seems you've managed to shake loose both my memories and my tongue. But I'm not sure whether we've learned anything useful."

Zornamayne purred. "We have learned a great deal, and some of it is quite useful for diagnosing your condition."

"Oh?" Mara waited. Her head was fuzzy from the amber liqueur, and she felt drained from what she'd witnessed during her mother's final moments. She didn't want to guess; she wanted Zornamayne to tell her what she knew.

Zornamayne uncurled herself from the other sofa and stood before the unlit fireplace. She clicked off her points on each claw of her left paw. "One, your mother was exposing you to other realms from an early age. Why would she do that? Probably to provide you with some sort of training. Two, your father chose not to reveal aspects of your heritage, for reasons unknown. Three, whatever promise your parents made regarding you seems to have its source in a different realm—and involves mastering the tools of a reaper. Four, you have inherited your mother's extraordinary eye color—a clue for all the world to see—and which I did not notice until now. I believe an old protection charm may have been involved."

"What does my eye color have to do with anything? And why would anyone bother with a protection charm?"

"Have you met anyone else in Valerra with violet eyes? They are quite distinctive."

Mara stammered, "I have blue eyes, not violet."

"Your eyes are most definitely violet, and your hair color is lighter than I've previously noticed too. The memory spell must have unwound the old protection charm someone—presumably your father—had placed to hide your ancestry."

Mara wondered whether Zornamayne might have been affected by the memory spell. She found it difficult to believe her hair and eye color were suddenly different. "Do you have a looking glass? I want to see this for myself."

"Of course." Zornamayne waved a paw and produced a gilt-framed oval mirror with a long handle, which she handed to Mara.

Mara held up the mirror, took one look, and gasped. "Queen's Crown!" A pair of violet eyes peered back at her. Mara touched her shoulder-length hair. The color was halfway between platinum and wheat; she'd gone from dark blonde to light blonde during the span of the spell. "I don't understand what's happening—and what we've learned about my mother—and me."

Zornamayne said, "We have learned your mother was a reaper, and she hailed from Alfweard."

Since her mother had mentioned visiting other realms and the importance of mastering the lasso, Mara had guessed the part about her being a reaper. "I've never heard of Alfweard. Where is it?"

Zornamayne's tail swept the rug as if to clear away Mara's mental cobwebs. "No one knows the precise location of Alfweard, although most believe it is true north, beyond the mists of Havynweal's seven seasons. The kingdom is difficult to reach—practically inaccessible."

"But what does it mean? Who was my mother?" Mara tapped her foot impatiently. Zornamayne seemed to be enjoying drawing this out.

"My dear Maragold, it means a very great deal. All the signs are there. Your mother was elven."

CHAPTER 6

"Wait—what?" Mara started to rise from the chintz sofa but thought better of it; she was still lightheaded. She rubbed her temples, which had started to throb, either from the memory spell or Zornamayne's special draught, or both. The jumble of fay land colors and floral patterns in the healer's sitting room weren't helping matters. "Are you trying to tell me my mother was an *elf?*"

"I am not trying to tell you. I *am* telling you."

"But I thought elves were just made-up fables. My father used to read me stories about elves when I was a child. They seemed very fantastical and not at all real."

"Oh I can assure you, elves are quite real."

"But in the stories they were extremely secretive, always kept to themselves; even the fays rarely saw them, and they never spent time in the human world. They carried coils of silver rope wherever the went and," Mara grabbed the mirror from her lap and brought it up to her face. She pulled back her light blonde hair—something else to get used to—examined both her ears and blew out a sigh of relief. "And the elves had very pointy ears, which as you can see, I don't have."

Zornamayne's whiskers twitched. "What is wrong with pointy ears?"

Mara glanced up at the hybrid's cute, fur-covered pointy ears. "Your ears are quite lovely and suit you perfectly. I just can't imagine them on me."

Zornamayne nodded gravely. "You are quite right. Not everyone can pull off pointy ears. But to be accurate, elves do not have pointy ears, so much as ears that tip up slightly at the top. Hardly noticeable, and not nearly as attractive as cat's ears, but then again, not everyone can be feline."

Mara brought the mirror back up and inspected the tops of her ears, which seemed as rounded as always. She arched an eyebrow at Zornamayne. "Or perhaps the story-books got it wrong. For example, I've never come across any tales about feline-fay hybrids."

Zornamayne drew back her lips in a catty grin that revealed sharp, white teeth and four large, jagged incisors. "We are as reclusive as elves and eschew human contact more than they. You are the rare exception, the only human I have ever invited into my home. And now, of course, it makes much more sense."

"How so?"

Zornamayne shrugged. "You are only half-human, and the elven half will always be dominant."

"And we know that how?"

"History, my dear lass. Your parents are not the only elven-human couple to produce offspring, although it has been more than a century since the last incident."

Mara sighed. Did she really want to know? "What was the last incident?"

"It had something to do with a waterway and a tremor in your realm."

Mara sucked in her breath. "You mean the Great River Quake?" When Zornamayne nodded, Mara added, "That earthquake changed the course of the Windrun River, creating all sorts of border issues between Valerra and Glenbarra. I find it hard to believe something like that could have been caused by someone like me."

Zornamayne said, "Elves, like fays, are magical beings. However, elven magic is more volatile, unpredictable even, and no one knows why."

"But I suspect you have an idea."

Zornamayne's tail flicked. "I have more of a hypothesis in need of testing."

"Go on."

"According to the old fables humans like to read—most of which are accounts of actual events, disguised as fantasies so as not to scare human children—elves guard the portals between the living and the dead." Zornamayne canted her head to the side. "What magical system operates in the lower realms?"

"Elemental magic, of course," replied Mara. "Neither Serving mages nor Fallow sorcerers are able to cast spells inside the realms of the dead. Only a wizard such as Arnesto, who has learned how to wield elemental magic, can conjure inside the lower realms." Mara thought about the implications. "So if elves guard the portals between the living and the dead, then they must be able to control elemental magic to a very great degree. And I expect elves would also be masters of Serving magic."

Zornamayne agreed. "Those are logical conclusions."

"And since elves can wield both Serving magic and

elemental magic simultaneously, are you suggesting their spells are sometimes more volatile?"

"Not precisely." Zornamayne waved her paw at the fireplace, and a low blaze sprang to life, which Mara found comforting despite the fact it was summer outside the cottage. A tray laden with fruit-filled pastries and a fresh pot of tea materialized on a pink cart between the floral chintz sofas. "We were speaking of their children—particularly, any offspring of elven-human couples."

Mara leaned over, selected a lemony puff pastry, and took a bite. She chewed her pastry slowly as she considered Zornamayne's hypothesis. "You believe half-elven children must learn to master both Serving magic and elemental magic, which seems a tall order to me. And if they don't master both magical systems adequately, they could cause another incident like the Great River Quake?"

"I believe that is very likely the case." Zornamayne sipped from a delicate pink teacup with a gold rim and an extra-large handle.

"But I have never had any sensibilities when it comes to the elements. It all seems rather farfetched to me."

"Your mother did not live long enough to train you in elven ways, and your father hid your ancestry from you."

Mara wiped her fingers on a linen napkin. If she spent too much time in Zornamayne's snug parlor, munching on her delicious sweets, she might not fit into her new cobalt day dress with the matching spencer jacket. "Frankly, I can't imagine I would ever be able to master elemental magic. If it's incredibly difficult for a fay wizard such as Arnesto, how much more challenging would it be for a human girl from Valerra?"

"A half-human girl, whose mother was elven."

Mara shrugged. "Even so, I don't see how it's possible, at least not without my mother to help me."

"And yet while rescuing Arnestarious, you commandeered a dragon from Havynweal, repelled scores of undead creatures, and sealed the dark fay king into the lowest realm of the dead," said Zornamayne.

"Well it wasn't really *my* magic. I channeled my sword's magic—which, as you know, was ensorcelled by a powerful fay girl—and embodies both ancient Serving magic and elemental magic."

Zornamayne chuckled, which sounded like a cross between a purr and a yowl. "No wonder Arnestarious believes you have depleted your magical reserves. What human girl could possibly channel the elemental magic of an ensorcelled object, accomplish all that, and rescue scores of people besides?"

Mara ran a hand through her hair, which had become a tangled mess. Somewhere between the ribbon-cutting ceremony in Valerra, the visit to the realms of the dead, and Zornamayne's powerful memory spell, she'd lost the ribbon tying back her ponytail. "But Yelenarra and Katrine encouraged me to use my sword's magic inside the lower realms. They thought the sword's elemental magic would function—and it did."

Katrine had been Mara's boss before an arsonist set fire to her Valerran toyshop. Katrine was also a distant cousin of Arnesto. Mara had learned many things from her old fay boss—how to reap in the lower realms, how to spy for the Valerran resistance, and how to fix a clockwork toy. Katrine now lived in Havynweal, serving as the interim Chief of the Fay Nation, subbing for her brother until he returned from his first-ever holiday. Given the obstreperous fay council meetings over which Katrine now had to preside, Mara suspected Katrine's brother might decide to extend his holiday indefinitely.

"I spoke with Yelenarra and Katrine in the early days of your recovery," said Zornamayne. "I needed to understand what happened in the lower realms, so I could determine how to best treat your injuries—not the physical ones, which I addressed immediately—but the magical ones.

"Katrine has long believed you were more than you seemed. She'd never met anyone, human or fay, who learned the fundamentals of reaping as quickly as you. Yelenarra suspected you had some trace elven blood; she has the ability to sense magical auras."

Mara wondered aloud, "What about Arnesto? Did he guess anything about my ancestry?"

The healer shook her head. "He held himself responsible for your injuries and was consumed with worry and guilt. I could get nothing useful from him. That young fay wizard is entirely besotted with you."

Mara blushed but said nothing. While her heart beat like a drumroll whenever Arnesto was near, she felt confused about his conflicting signals and wasn't entirely convinced he still loved her. They had a lot to discuss, and he seemed to be avoiding the inevitable sit-down, which only increased her doubts about their relationship. On the other hand, recent events in the underworld were understandably distracting him.

Zornamayne said, "Arnestarious did tell me about the peculiar circumstances surrounding your friendship pledge. He feels guilty about that as well. He is faulting himself for a very great deal at the moment, and he certainly bears some of the blame for rushing into a friendship pledge with you, for allowing himself to be captured by Bazra, for the loss of the red sword, and for his brother's death."

"Plus what's happening in the lower realms. He's feeling terribly guilty about that as well." Mara sighed. "I need to help Arnesto find a solution before Efram's spirit fades away entirely."

"And you must find a way to help Arnestarious forgive himself, as these are heavy burdens to bear alone. Which brings us back to your magical malaise and the clues we uncovered from your memories. You will not be able to restore balance in the underworld until we have found a way to restore your magic."

"And how are we supposed to do that? I have no idea where to begin," grumbled Mara.

The feline-fay gave her a stern look. "You are behaving in a distinctly human fashion. I forbid any grumbling. It is unproductive and lowers one's spirits."

Mara apologized and Zornamayne continued. "The answer is as obvious as the whiskers on my face. We must travel to Alfweard and seek an audience with the elven king."

CHAPTER 7

"I THOUGHT YOU SAID NO ONE KNOWS THE PRECISE LOCATION OF Alfweard," objected Mara. She'd hoped now that Zornamayne knew she was part elf, the healer could simply conjure another potion to drink or cast one of her powerful healing spells, and restore her magic. Mara feared an extended trip to Alfweard would take up precious time Efram and the other spirits didn't have.

"We know it is located in true north. If we ask around, I believe we will be able to piece together an itinerary that will get us close enough for the elven king to take notice."

"Do you know any elves who would agree to serve as our guides?" Mara figured that would be the most efficient way to get to Alfweard. Of course, first they would need to convince some antisocial elf of the worthiness of their mission.

Zornamayne shook her head. "Nay. As I said, elves are reclusive. They are either in Alfweard, or guarding the portals, or hiding themselves under powerful protection charms."

"What about an elf in disguise, such as my mother? Perhaps we might discover an elf that way."

"I know of no others such as your mother at present. Besides, if an elf has disguised herself, how are we to find her? Nay, we must seek information here in Havynweal, amongst those who have their own reasons for wanting an audience with the elven king."

"And who might that be?" asked Mara. "I can't imagine there are many fays with such an interest."

Zornamayne took a sip of tea. "I know of several clans with such an interest, including the Suporra-Draca clan."

"What could a dragon possibly want from the elven king?"

Zornamayne waved her paw. "A dragon would want the same thing as the rest of us—access to the Alfweard Archives, which house the world's oldest scrolls and manuscripts."

"Now the war is over," said Mara, "it's far easier to visit the Valerran Museum, which contains many ancient, priceless scrolls and artifacts from both the human and fay realms. That's where I first came across the blue sword."

"Aye, your museum is quite impressive. But the Alfweard Archives are even older and the only place where a scholar may study elven books on magic, history, and prophecy."

Mara groaned and then covered her mouth with her hand. "I'm sorry. It's just whenever I hear the word 'prophecy' I cringe. During the war, my friends and I discovered that seers and prophets don't see eye to eye on very much. They provided us with a great deal of conflicting advice."

"I see. Well, perhaps we shall leave the prophecies to those who want to study them. I am merely suggesting some clans would wish to access the Alfweard Archives and may be prepared to help us with our quest. Others, like us, will seek a meeting with the elven king."

"What can you tell me about the king? Is he the sort of man who would grant us an audience, or could this be a wasted trip?"

Zornamayne angled her head. She appeared to be listening to a noise outside her cottage, which Mara couldn't hear. "Please excuse me. Someone is at my door." Zornamayne's tail swished as she left her sitting room. A few moments later, Mara heard the healer exclaim, "Xenestra, what an unexpected and pleasant surprise. I was planning to pay you a visit."

Mara dashed to the front window. An enormous green dragon, with gold and teal flecks on her scales and wings, crouched on the front lawn, her belly grazing the grass. Mara assumed the dragon had lowered herself so Zornamayne could speak to her without the need for shouting. When Xenestra stood on her powerful hind legs, she could peer over the roof of any two-story building. Her spiked tail ran the length of the garden path leading to Zornamayne's door. Long, teal eyelashes fringed intelligent emerald-green eyes. The dragon waved one of her forearms and flared her nostrils slightly as she spoke. "Please ask Maragold to join us. I wish to speak with her."

Mara scratched her head, astonished the dragon knew she was in Havynweal, visiting Zornamayne. Now that she was here, Mara resolved to thank Xenestra properly for the important role she played in rescuing Arnesto and the others from Bazra's prison. Without an enormous dragon to transport the captives, many of whom were injured, Mara had no notion how they would have made the trip out of the lower realms.

"Of course," said Zornamayne. "Please make yourself comfortable in my little wilderness, and we shall be along in a moment."

Mara heard the door close and hurried into the foyer. "How does Xenestra know I'm here? I don't think Yelenarra or Arnesto would have traveled to her clan to inform her."

"Let us go and ask Xenestra directly. It is most unusual for her to make a social call. She generally sends one of the younger dragons to summon me if she requires my healing services." Zornamayne waved her paw. The teacart, laden with fresh pastries and biscuits, levitated several feet and preceded them through the door.

Zornamayne's "wilderness" consisted of a woodsy area behind her cottage, filled with silver maples, golden oaks, and blue pines. A wide path led through the woods to a clearing with several benches scattered about, a pond filled with neon-colored fish, and a large grassy area suitable for visiting dragons. Xenestra was nestled on the grass, her enormous spiked tail curled behind her.

Zornamayne poured tea into a porcelain bowl the size of a washing tub, decorated with white and yellow daisies around its base. She placed the tea bowl on the ground in front of the dragon, along with a large platter of puff pastries. The dragon lowered her head for a sip. "Delicious, as always," said Xenestra. Zornamayne nodded her appreciation.

Mara waited as Xenestra lapped up her tea and swallowed down the pastries in two bites. The dragon picked up a square piece of linen between two talons and dabbed her mouth. She sat back with a contented sigh, discharging two puffs of smoke from her nostrils, and nodded at Mara. "I am glad to see your physical injuries are healed."

"Thank you for your bravery during the rescue," said Mara. "You saved many lives that day, including mine."

"We had an agreement, signed in dragon's blood. A dragon never countermands a blood oath." Xenestra waved her forearms. "However, I have not come to receive your thanks, although I appreciate the sentiment."

"You rarely make house calls." Zornamayne tilted her head to peer up at the dragon. "And yet you knew Maragold was in Havynweal."

Xenestra snorted. Fortunately, Mara and Zornamayne were out of range of the two small fireballs that fell to the ground and fizzled out. "Come now, have you forgotten? Griffin Gloria's eldest son is my head steward. Whenever Gloria visits her son, she always pays her respects to me."

"And so you were informed of Maragold's presence?" asked Zornamayne.

"Aye, and the fact her magical reserves are running on empty."

Mara refrained from an eye roll, wondering how many more residents of Havynweal would be hearing of her problems before nightfall. She much preferred her griffin's moody silence in Valerra to her gossipy nattering in Havynweal. But perhaps she wasn't being entirely fair. Gloria was extremely loyal, and she was spreading the news among friends whom she believed might be able to offer assistance. But how could a two-story tall, fire-breathing dragon help restore her magic?

Xenestra drew back her lips to reveal sharp, jagged teeth. Mara thought the dragon might be grimacing at a spot of indigestion, but soon realized Xenestra was smiling —at her. "I have come to offer my services again, young Maragold."

Mara eyebrows peaked. *How do I respond to such a*

gracious offer when I have no idea what sort of aid I might need from a dragon? However, Mara's stepmother had always taught her girls to display good manners in every situation. She replied, "Thank you, Madame Xenestra of the Suporra-Draca clan. You are very kind to offer your services."

Zornamayne surprised Mara by clapping her paws together. "Splendid! I had planned to visit you and apply for assistance."

"Of course, I must first petition the Dragon Mage for permission to travel to Alfweard," said Xenestra. "She shall require several days of reflection before reaching her decision."

"Of course," agreed Zornamayne, "although I expect her natural curiosity will outweigh her caution in the end."

"I expect she will grant my request." The dragon nodded gravely. "And then she shall need to fast and meditate whilst she composes her message."

"Her message?" Mara worried about the amount of time all of this draconic reflection and meditation would require.

"Aye," Xenestra waved her forearm. "The Dragon Mage will write a letter of introduction to the elven king, with an offer of hospitality should he wish to send an emissary to the Suporra-Draca clan. We must follow all the diplomatic protocols."

"Agreed." Zornamayne stroked her whiskers thoughtfully. "You will need three days, perhaps four, to complete your visit to the Dragon Mage. Let us meet on the coast—the Dragon Mage will foresee our arrival and can direct you to our location."

"An excellent suggestion." Xenestra rose onto her hind legs, bid them goodbye, and trundled down the path toward Zornamayne's lawn. Mara and Zornamayne followed behind her. When Xenestra cleared the last of the trees, she ran forward on her powerful hind legs and spread her wings, which glimmered gold, teal, and green in the early afternoon light. The dragon circled once overhead, dipped to the side in a sort of salute, and winged away toward her stronghold.

Mara had never seen anything more beautiful and awe-inspiring than a dragon in flight. She noticed Zornamayne watching as well and commented on the sight. The healer agreed. "I do enjoy watching a dragon take wing." She brought her paws together in a soft clap. "I had half-expected Xenestra would need some persuasion to aid us, and instead, she has volunteered. She has taken a genuine interest in your wellbeing. And then there is the added inducement of gaining access to the Alfweard Archives. After all, Xenestra is our foremost scholar of creature lore in Havynweal."

"Creature lore?"

"Aye, she has written ten volumes on magical creatures, covering everything from dragons and unicorns to griffins and trolls. She even devotes three chapters to feline-fay hybrids."

"That's...interesting," agreed Mara. "But I still don't see how she will be able to help us."

Zornamayne looked at Mara as if she'd grown an extra limb. "Once we arrive at true north, Xenestra will be able to fly us to the elven king's stronghold, tucked somewhere in the mountains of Alfweard."

Mara had her doubts about traveling to Alfweard and appealing to the elven king for an audience, but if it was the only way to learn more about her heritage and what might be happening to her magic, she was prepared to see it through. "Can't we simply translocate ourselves there on fay traveling mists?"

Zornamayne shook her head. "Once we journey beyond the coasts of Havynweal, fay traveling mists become unreliable. We are apt to transfer ourselves to someplace quite inhospitable. Nay, we will need physical transport of some sort in Alfweard, and what better conveyance than a dragon?"

Mara wrinkled her brow, and Zornamayne hastened to ask. "Do you have any concerns about dragon-flying?"

"Oh, not at all. I think that's a brilliant solution to the transportation problem. You mentioned the coasts of Havynweal. Will there be some sort of seafaring transportation needed as well?" When the feline-fay nodded, Mara groaned.

Zornamayne waggled her whiskers. "The ships have a reputation for being quite safe. Felines are not especially fond of the sea, as a rule, but I have no qualms about trying an Alfweardian seafaring vessel."

"It's not that. I get seasick, terribly seasick. Perhaps Xenestra could fly us over the sea, and we could avoid the ships altogether?"

"I am afraid that will not work. The Unseasonable Sea —that is its elven name, translated—forms a barrier between the fay and elven realms. None may navigate that barrier, except by specially outfitted vessels, designed and magically spelled for the trip."

"So even a giant dragon such as Xenestra must cross the sea on one of these vessels?"

"Aye." Zornamayne nodded. "The ships are reputed to be quite large."

The teacart levitated once again, and Mara followed Zornamayne into her cottage. Inside the foyer, the feline-fay said, "We must inform Yelenarra and Arnestarious of what we learned from the memory spell, and where we are heading now. I have no doubt Arnestarious will find this a difficult pill to swallow."

"I'm not sure I'm following you." Mara felt a headache coming on—probably due to the amount of chocolate she'd consumed—and she didn't want to confront Arnesto about anything at the moment. She'd hoped they could take a short holiday together, as Yelenarra had suggested.

Instead, Mara just discovered her mother was an elven reaper, and her parents had made some vague promise concerning her before she was born. Meanwhile, she was no closer to solving the mystery of her magical problems, although Zornamayne seemed convinced the answers lay in Alfweard. Mara had to hope the master healer knew what she was doing, and Mara hated relying on hope alone.

"Mark my words. Arnestarious will argue you cannot possibly be half-elven, because as a twelfth-level fay wizard, he would have sensed it."

Mara shrugged. "So? Why should he care, so long as this new knowledge helps us solve the issues with my magic, which is the only way I'll be able to help his brother and the others in the lower realms."

Zornamayne murmured an incantation to sort out her tea things and clear away the cart. She picked up the carrying trunk containing Mara's blue sword and guided Mara back outside, explaining as they walked. "Fays and humans can pledge themselves to each other without receiving formal permission from a higher authority. Elves, however, cannot. All betrothal pledges—which in fay terms, is the friendship pledge between you and Arnestar-ious—must receive approval from the elven king to be binding."

Mara ran a hand through her hair, considering. "So in other words, if I am half-elven—"

"You most certainly are half-elven," interjected Zornamayne.

Mara conceded the point. "Since I am half-elven, I should not have pledged myself—accidentally or intentionally—to Arnesto, without first seeking permission from the elven king?"

"Aye, that is the case."

Mara rubbed her temples. "You're right. I'm afraid Arnesto isn't going to like this one little bit."

CHAPTER 8

"But this is preposterous! There is no conceivable way Maragold is anything other than a human girl. I simply refuse to believe it." Arnesto jumped up from his chair and folded his arms across his chest. At any other time, Mara could not help but notice the bulge of Arnesto's biceps beneath his form-fitting silvery tunic, but she was too irritated to observe anything other than the stubborn set of his perfectly chiseled jaw. Despite the dark circles under his eyes and worry lines on his brow, her fay boyfriend was as dashing as ever—and every bit as frustrating.

They sat in a small courtyard outside of Yelenarra's sprawling manor, perched on top of a mountain in the Havynweal season of auburn summer, which Mara knew was Arnesto's favorite. Six towers formed the perimeter of the imposing gray stone home, which soared four stories in the air and contained so many rooms Mara had given up trying to count them all. Visitors to the manor entered through a tall, arched doorway, covered in gold and silver runes that flared up as they passed beneath them.

Yelenarra had conjured four cushioned wicker chairs, a

glass-topped wicker table, and icy glasses of lemonade when they arrived. Zornamayne and Mara had taken turns describing the memory spell and what they'd learned, but Arnesto had stopped listening when Zornamayne revealed Mara's elven heritage.

Mara rose from her chair and skirted around the wicker table, drawing closer to Arnesto. "Fine. Don't believe what we just told you about the memory spell—memories are always tricky. But take a closer look at me."

Arnesto raised one eyebrow and lowered the other. "Whilst it is always pleasing to look upon your lovely face, I do not know what it is you wish me to see."

"Notice anything different?" Mara's voice had an edge to it, which Arnesto must have noticed.

He took a step closer and peered at her. His gray eyes widened in surprise. "Mara, your eyes...they are violet! And your hair, well, it is much blonder. But I do not understand how this can be. I saw you this morning, and your appearance was unaltered."

Zornamayne set her glass on the tabletop with a *clink*. "I believe a powerful protection charm had been placed on Maragold, which shielded her true nature until now. My memory spell appears to have rendered the old charm obsolete."

Arnesto reached a hand toward Mara, who closed the distance between them. He picked up a lock of her hair and stared at the bright blonde strands. He swallowed hard and seemed to be mulling over the evidence. Arnesto must have decided the facts were irrefutable, because he eventually nodded. "I shall of course accompany you to Alfweard. Let us hope the elven king can provide us with some answers regarding your magic and whatever this old promise might have entailed."

"And then there is the matter of your friendship pledge," Yelenarra said gently. "The elven king must approve."

Arnesto's chest heaved as he glanced at Mara. "Aye. When the time comes, we shall need to make a formal request of the king." He paused and then locked eyes with Mara. "This unexpected trip shall provide you with additional time to ponder the friendship pledge you made unawares—and reconsider, if needs must." He drew himself up to his full height. "My feelings must be secondary."

Mara opened her mouth to speak, but Arnesto placed a finger on her lips. "Do not say anything now. Wait until we are in Alfweard, and the king has granted us an audience. Until then, we shall be merely friends in the human sense, but no longer betrothed." As if to make his point, Arnesto took two steps back.

Mara alternately wanted to throttle him and rush headlong into his arms. At least he could have asked Mara what *she* wanted before releasing her, temporarily, from their fay friendship pledge. Instead, she took a deep breath and nodded. Arnesto was right about one thing; this was the ideal time for her to take stock and determine, once for all, whether she wished to be Arnesto's special friend, in every sense of the word.

Zornamayne cleared her throat. "Now that is settled, we must discuss our preparations for the journey."

As Mara and Arnesto returned to their seats, he said, "We must also determine who should accompany us. Many fays have an interest in visiting Alfweard. However, very few would prove to be an asset on the trip."

Mara glanced at Arnesto in surprise. He gave her a head nod. "I have learned much from you, my straight-speaking friend...ah, I mean mentor. I am not quite so naïve as when I first arrived in Valerra as your trainee."

Mara sipped from her glass of lemonade, which Yelenarra had magically refilled. It was true; when Efram had introduced her to Arnesto and told her he was her new trainee, Mara had despaired of ever being able to teach the gorgeous but incompetent fay anything useful. He'd managed to get himself arrested within the first few days. He'd antagonized Vas, the provincial president of Valerra, and he botched his initial assignments.

But Arnesto's sense of duty—of doing what was right, despite the dangers—had won her over. That, plus the way he would look at her, his eyes full of admiration. Arnesto hadn't stopped looking at her with admiration. He'd simply stopped spending time with her.

While she understood Arnesto's grief at losing Efram and his anxiety over what was happening in the lower realms, Mara couldn't help feeling hurt, first by his neglect and now by his declaration they were no longer "friends," at least for the duration of their trip to Alfweard. Arnesto was as challenging as ever, but she had to set the record straight about their work in Valerra. "It's true, I nearly sent you back to Havynweal, because I didn't see how I could help you become a fay scout like Efram. But now I think he had something else in mind all along."

Arnesto leaned forward in his chair. "And what was that?"

"Efram wanted you to spend time in Valerra with someone who could introduce you to the human realm, to our virtues and foibles, and to our magic. I believe he wanted you to see there is good and bad in each of us, human or fay."

Arnesto stared into his glass. "You may be right about

my brother's intentions. Regardless, you trained me in many things—how to work undercover, how to assist a customer, how to assess a situation with an unvarnished eye, and how to laugh at myself. I shall never forget our time together in Valerra."

Arnesto continued staring at his glass, and Mara's heart gave a painful lurch. He looked so forlorn and friendless, as if their future together—which they'd discussed in the early days of their accidental friendship pledge, while she'd been recovering from her injuries—was over before it began. *I may not be ready to pledge myself in marriage just yet, but I'm also not ready to break up with my boyfriend. We need to talk things through, without Yelenarra and Zornamayne listening to every word.*

Mara thought of the formal gardens in the rear of Yelenarra's manor, which would offer them ample privacy. "Arnesto, perhaps you and I could go for a short walk, before we begin our preparations for the trip to Alfweard?"

Arnesto's head snapped up, and he smiled tentatively. She smiled back, and he gave her one of his heart-stopping, bedazzling grins that always left her feeling overly warm and slightly breathless.

"Aye, that is an excellent suggestion." Yelenarra fluttered her hands. "Zornamayne and I will carry on here." Mara had no doubt Arnesto's aunt would do everything in her power to encourage their friendship. Yelenarra had always made her feel welcome; from their earliest acquaintance, the elderly fay behaved as if Mara were already a member of her extended, eccentric family.

As Mara and Arnesto started down the gravel-lined path leading toward the gardens, a swirling mist arose in front of them. Arnesto reached out his hand to stop her. "Wait." He glanced at his aunt and Zornamayne, who'd risen from their seats and joined them on the path. "Are we expecting anyone else?"

"Nay," said Yelenarra. "And I do not recognize those traveling mists."

Mara had no idea fays could recognize the traveling mists of other fays. She supposed it was akin to recognizing the magical signatures of other mages. Havynweal was full of surprises, and she wished, not for the first time, she could take a holiday inside the fay lands with Arnesto, rather than rushing from one peril to the next. Perhaps life with Arnesto would always be thus, dashing headlong from one mystery or disaster to another.

Mara could see two forms inside the mists, a woman and her male companion. As the vapors evaporated, she gasped in recognition. Vas stepped out of the traveling mists with his fay girlfriend, Chief Inspector Penray Talias. Something must have been seriously amiss inside Valerra for them to make an appearance. Vas and Talias weren't here for tea and scones.

Yelenarra hurried forward and bowed. "Well met, President Revas and Chief Inspector Talias. This is an unexpected pleasure. Please, join us for refreshments and tell us the news—for I am sure you have come with news to share."

"Aye," said Vas. "Much news and little time, but something to slake our thirst would be welcome."

Yelenarra snapped her fingers and the seating area around the glass-topped table expanded to accommodate two more wicker chairs. Mara stifled a sigh; her private chat with Arnesto would have to wait a bit longer.

Vas glanced at the rest of the group as he took his seat. "We have a serious issue inside Valerra, and I can't think of anywhere else to turn for assistance. I'm sure Mara has told you about the chasm that opened up along the road in front of the children's hospital."

When the group nodded, he continued. "Two more have opened up; one by the main gate into the city, and the other in front of the Valerran Museum. In addition, there have been fresh sightings of King Roi, although we've been unable to pin down his location. Our scouts think they see Roi, but when we investigate, he's gone, or it's a case of mistaken identity.

"Penray and I are concerned there's some connection between the former Glenbarran king and these chasms that appear to connect directly with the lower realms. But we know Roi can't be working alone. He may be a Fallow necromancer, but he lacks the power to be opening up pathways to the underworld. That takes dark fays and elemental magic—old Bazra's specialty."

Mara swallowed hard, her mind filled with images of creatures climbing out of the lower realms and swarming the streets of the Valerran capital. The two cruel kings—Glenbarra's Roi and the dark fays' Bazra—had collaborated once before and nearly succeeded. Mara, with a lot of help from both her human and fay friends, had been able to avert the disastrous consequences. She felt entirely helpless now, and without her magic, she would be nothing more than a hindrance. "Has anything undead emerged yet?" she asked.

Vas and Talias shook their heads in unison. Penray Talias was every inch the chief inspector, with her long brown mackintosh—it must have been raining in Valerra—gold-rimmed spectacles, and crisp air of authority. The only clue to her fay ancestry was her vivid blue hair color; well that, and her ability to conjure traveling mists. Talias kept her hair under strict regulation inside Valerra, employing a glamour to change its color from bright blue to glossy black.

"We have posted guards along all three cracks, which we're attempting to explain away with a combination of magical persuasion and misinformation," said Talias. "Our story is that the destruction wrought by the war with Glenbarra, and the recent fires set by anti-magic arsonists, have weakened the city's infrastructure. We're managing to tamp down the panic, temporarily at least, among the non-magical population.

"Mages and mage apprentices, of course, know something is seriously wrong. Some of them have complained about a sulfurous odor emanating from the cracks, while others claim to hear a peculiar murmuring that gives them goosebumps. Only those with magic in their bloodlines seem able to detect these disturbances. However, everyone is on tenterhooks, fearing an invasion from the lower realms."

Arnesto pulled his brows down in concentration. "If this is happening in Valerra, then I fear it may be happening elsewhere. Didn't the Choirmaster indicate as much?"

"Aye." Mara nodded. "She said the chasm in front of the children's hospital was Bazra's opening volley, and she predicted more 'incursions'—that was what she called them—in our realm."

Vas thrust out his lower lip and grunted, "Who is the Choirmaster? What does she know about this?"

Mara described her visit to the underworld with Arnesto, leaving out the part about him conjuring a portal, about which she suspected even Yelenarra knew nothing. She also explained about the issues with her magic and her blue sword, which she needed to restore balance. "Bazra is using—or rather misusing—the red sword to silence the choir that welcomes the spirits of those who led commendable lives. As a result, Efram and other worthy spirits are unable to cross the river to the far shore. The Choirmaster is powerless to intervene. She has told us we must act soon, before the good souls fade entirely into the ether."

Yelenarra cried out, "Oh, my poor nephew!" before disappearing in a swirl of fay mists.

Mara brought her hand to her mouth and glanced across the table at Arnesto. "I'm so sorry. I should have realized you were trying to resolve this without worrying Yelenarra."

Arnesto ran a hand through his shoulder-length blue hair. "I was trying to protect her, but the truth was bound to come out. Please excuse me whilst I attempt to comfort my aunt." He waved his hand and blinked out in a puff of vapor.

Zornamayne spoke with a low hiss, each *S* popping with urgency. "We must inform Katrinareus of these incursions in the human realm immediately, and we must plan for our trip to Alfweard. Chief Inspector Talias and President Vas, could you please visit Chief Katrinareus before you return to Valerra and bring her this news? I must help Maragold prepare for our visit to the elven king."

Talias stared at Mara, her eyes widening slightly. "I knew *something* was different about you, but I hadn't guessed the truth. This certainly adds another wrinkle."

"What truth? And what wrinkle?" asked Vas impatiently.

Mara stared at her hands in her lap. "It's a lot for me to take in, but a trip to Alfweard seems the best course of action at the moment. We need the elven king's advice on how to restore my magic."

"Why do we need to involve the elves?" grumbled Vas, glancing in confusion at Mara and Talias. Zornamayne leaned back in her wicker chair, her tail curled around her legs, an impassive look on her face. Mara suspected the feline-fay enjoyed stirring the cauldron occasionally. Her announcement about a visit to the elven king certainly caused a stir with Vas, who had no idea what elves looked like. Even if he did, he hadn't noticed the transformation in Mara.

Talias continued staring at Mara, seemingly lost in thought. She gave Mara a curt nod. "Let's hope the king agrees to an audience. Who is accompanying you on your journey? Whatever you do, you must make haste."

Vas threw his hands up in the air. "Would someone please explain to me why we're talking about elves? And what this has to do with Mara?"

Talias spoke in quiet tones that seemed to have a calming influence on Vas. His shoulders relaxed slightly as she explained, "You recall we have always been surprised—and ever so grateful—that Mara's remarkable sword magic worked in the lower realms? Without Mara's intervention, we would still be sitting in Bazra's tower."

"Aye," Vas grunted. "It was amazing magic. Now tell me about the elves."

"As it turns out, Mara has elven blood."

"She does?"

Talias nodded. "The evidence is before us, although some sort of a spell had obviously been employed to mask her elven bloodline until now." Talias pointed out Mara's violet eyes and pale blonde hair.

Vas squinted at Mara. "And now your magic is wonky, and you think a consultation with the king of the elves might be the answer?"

When Mara nodded, Vas let out a loud puff of air. "How long will this trip take?"

Zornamayne waved her paw. "We do not know for certain. No one has attempted to call on the elven king in recent memory, but my best guess is anywhere from five days to twenty."

"Twenty days!" Vas exploded. "How are we supposed to manage the situation on the ground in Valerra for that long, without some sort of fay assistance in the meantime?"

Zornamayne sipped from her glass and eyed Vas over the rim. "I recommend you take that up with your good friend, Katrinareus." The fay healer seemed to enjoy provoking the provisional president of Valerra. On the other hand, Zornamayne was right—Vas and Katrine had run the Valerran resistance during the war—and Mara had no doubt Katrine would want to help her Valerran friends again.

Talias rose from her chair. "Zornamayne is right. We need to inform Katrine and formally request magical assistance from the Fay Nation."

Vas stood up, his brow deeply furrowed. "I really thought we'd defeated the dark fay king when Mara sealed him into the realms of the dead. It seems Bazra can wreak havoc wherever he resides."

"That is true," Zornamayne agreed. "And it will continue to be the case until we can restore Mara's magic, and then travel to the underworld to confront Bazra and relieve him of the red sword. In the meantime, I would advise you to get that crazy human king under control. He is as unpredictable as he is dangerous."

The fact that Vas had been unable to capture King Roi and bring him to justice was a sore spot with the provisional president. As Vas's countenance darkened, Talias quickly interjected, "Aye, we are pursuing every lead and very soon, we trust, we will capture Roi."

Vas nodded at Talias before turning to Mara. He gave her a stern look, coupled with one of his fatherly lectures, which used to annoy her but no longer did. If anything, she appreciated Vas's concerns for her safety. "That's a tall order for anyone, Mara, even if you are part elf. As always, be careful, and let me know if I can help you in anyway."

"Aye, sir," said Mara. "When the time comes, I may need help from anyone who can twirl a lasso." Vas had helped her and Katrine in the past, during Mara's first visit to the realms of the dead. Although Vas wasn't a reaper, his father had trained horses for a living, and Vas himself was a fair hand with a rope.

"You let me know, and I'll be there. Not my favorite place, of course, but we have to stop Bazra—whatever it takes," said Vas.

As traveling mists encircled their ankles and coiled up their legs, Talias recited the Serving mage's pledge with a small bow. "May your magic serve in peace and lead through service. This is the true path."

Mara and Zornamayne, who had joined her on the gravel path, returned the bow. They watched as Vas and Talias faded away on the mists, repeating the final words of the pledge. "Aye, this is the true path."

CHAPTER 9

"How long do you think we'll have to wait before Katrine arrives?" Mara started down the gravel footpath; she felt the need to walk a bit and clear her head. She wondered how Yelenarra was doing and regretted giving the elderly fay such a shock.

Zornamayne ambled alongside her. "Not long. Katrinareus will no doubt want to join us on our trip to Alfweard."

"Really? But she is Chief of the Fay Nation—at least until her brother returns from his holiday. Can she really afford to take that much time away from the fay council meetings?"

"Katrinareus is not one for pompous speeches and empty posturing, nor is her brother, for that matter. She will be quite content to join us and allow the fay council to bumble along, not making decisions of any consequence."

"I suppose you're right." The path wound through the lime green lawn, with hot pink, yellow, and blue flowering shrubs lining the walkway. Mara wondered aloud who else should join them on their trip to Alfweard.

"There are the four of us, of course—Yelenarra, Arnestarious, you, and me—plus Gloria, Xenestra, and Katrinareus." Zornamayne canted her head to the side, her whiskers twitching. "We shall ask one of the grihms to join us, Farleigh, I think. The elven king would not have encountered a grihm before; the novelty will appeal to him. And what is the name of the human boy who once wielded the red sword? An old schoolmate of yours, I believe?"

"You mean Remy?" The last thing Mara needed was for her ex-boyfriend to join their traveling party. "But Arnesto cast an unremembered spell over Remy, so he would forget all about the red sword. Arnesto broke the bond between Remy and his ensorcelled blade."

"We will need Remy to join us." Mara jumped at the sound of Katrine's voice. The fay emerged from her traveling mists wearing her signature blue turban on top of her short, vivid blue curls. She was dressed like a proper fay, in a sparkly silver-and-blue tunic, cinched at the waist with a wide sash, and silver slacks.

A small woman halfway between Vas's fortysomething years and Yelenarra's eighty, Katrine's dark brown eyes were focused on Mara's pale blonde hair. Katrine waggled her eyebrows and gave Mara a brief nod. Mara had to restrain herself from reaching over and giving her old boss a quick hug. Katrine was not the demonstrative sort.

Zornamayne waved her paw. "Well met, and right on time too. You shall accompany us, of course?"

"Wouldn't miss it for all seven seasons." Katrine grinned. "We must get to the bottom of Mara's magical malaise—which I'm now convinced is linked to her elven heritage—and I'm intrigued by the opportunity to meet the elven king face-to-face. I told the fay council I would be traveling to Alfweard in an unofficial capacity, which naturally spawned a debate regarding trade relations with the elves. I appointed three of the most vociferous fays to form a committee and slipped away."

Katrine turned to Mara. "I know you're wondering why I want Remy to join us, when it had been my idea for Arnesto to cast the unremembered spell in the first place."

"Aye, I'm more than a little confused." Mara and Remy had been childhood friends, attending all the same schools. When King Roi decided to invade Valerra during their senior year, they'd fought side-by-side, losing family and friends during the war. Afterward, they dated briefly, Mara breaking it off when Remy started talking about their future together.

While Mara trusted Remy, her ex-boyfriend was as over-protective as her current boyfriend, and a teensy bit jealous besides. *Wait a minute...is Arnesto still my boyfriend? Or is he an ex-boyfriend too?* Mara bit her bottom lip as she considered what Arnesto had said about releasing her from their fay friendship pledge—for now. *I don't need the complication of two ex-boyfriends accompanying me on this trip to Alfweard, especially when I'm still trying to sort out my feelings for Arnesto.*

Katrine sighed. "I was wrong."

"Did I hear you correctly?" Mara canted her head to the side. "You're never wrong, or at least, never wrong about spells and magic."

"I shouldn't have encouraged Arnesto to try to break the bond between Remy and the red sword, which had imprinted on him in the same way the blue sword imprinted on you. Although Bazra is able to wield the red sword, I don't believe it's imprinted again—at least that's my theory—because some of what's going on seems out of character for the dark fay king."

"Such as?"

"Such as silencing the choir on the far shore. Why would he bother? It's to Bazra's benefit for the commendable spirits to pass swiftly across the river, so he can recruit the remaining unsavory souls to do his bidding."

"Are you saying the sword has a mind of its own, sort of?" Mara ran a hand through her hair, trying to understand how a sword—even an ancient, fay-spelled sword—could have a mind of its own.

"Aye, in a way. I believe the sword knows its rightful owner still lives, and until the sword and Remy are reunited, I'm afraid the havoc in the underworld will continue."

"Wow, if that's true, then..."

"Then I bungled things badly." Katrine put her hands on her hips. "And I want to help set things to rights."

"Have you told Arnestarious your theory about the red sword?" asked Zornamayne.

"I've tried," said Katrine, "but he wants to take all the blame on himself. He's so guilty over his brother's death, he can't see past it, I'm afraid."

The feline-fay nodded. "Aye. Unfortunately, Arnestarious has been working himself to a frazzle, so consumed is he with grief. We must help him see the bigger picture— many magical forces are at work here—and one single fay wizard, however powerful, is not responsible for all that is happening inside the realms of the dead."

Mara sat on one of the benches scattered about the garden, suddenly weary with all she'd learned and all she needed to do, including a trip to Alfweard to heal her magic —that is, if the elven king even agreed to help her. She asked, "Can an unremembered spell be reversed?"

Katrine raised her shoulders in a half-shrug. "I don't

know. I've been doing research but haven't come across any other, similar cases. But I want to try. I don't think we have much choice."

"What about the prophecies that someone—we assumed Arnestarious, since he is a twelfth-level fay wizard —needed the red sword to defeat Bazra? You don't think those prophecies were about young Remington, do you?" Zornamayne raised her front paws, palms up. "Does it make sense the owner of the red sword would be human and not fay?"

Katrine removed her turban and ran her a hand through her bright blue curls. "Mara and her blue sword defeated Bazra, sealing him into the lowest realm of the dead. The prophecies got it wrong—again."

Mara felt the need to remind them of one important fact. "You're forgetting Efram had asked me to smear his blood on my blade, one of the hardest things I've ever done. It was that combination of my sword's magic with Efram's blood magic that did the trick. So the prophecies were partially right about needing a red sword, blood red, to be specific."

Efram, Arnesto, and Yelenarra each had unique magic coursing through their veins. Yelenarra's blood could raise an undead army. Arnesto's blood could return the undead to their eternal resting place, either the far shore for the commendable spirits, or the lake of fire for the unworthy. Efram's blood could bring the undead under control, which was how Mara had been able to get Bazra's undead minions to listen to her.

She'd given them an ultimatum: ignore Bazra and never rise again, and she would show them mercy. Otherwise, they would be banished to the lake of fire. Every last crea-ture, except for the dark fay king himself, chose the path of mercy. Bazra snatched the red sword and escaped to the lowest realm before she could permanently dispatch him.

Katrine sighed wearily. "I think the lesson here is that prophecies are hazy at best, and inaccurate at worst, especially when they involve the Swords of Five. But I have no doubt we're going to need Remy's help retrieving the red sword."

"That means we'll be putting Remy in danger, when he has no idea what we're asking of him. The unremembered spell wiped all his memories involving the red sword." Mara kicked at a stone with her boot. "I don't like exposing him at the off chance you can reverse the spell."

"I agree with Mara." Arnesto walked out of his traveling mists and onto the lawn. "I tested Remy's memories after the spell, and he had no recall whatsoever of the red sword. It doesn't seem fair to place him in harm's way now."

"Hmm. Why don't you tell us what happened when *you* picked up the red sword?" Katrine lowered her brow, waiting for Arnesto to reply. Mara sucked in her breath, surprised at the sharpness in Katrine's tone. *If Arnesto had tried out the red sword, he would have mentioned it before now —wouldn't he?*

Arnesto stared at his boots, a sure sign he was avoiding something. "Everything happened so quickly. Suddenly I was under attack by three of Bazra's scaly, stinking, undead creatures."

"But you did pick up the sword's hilt and test it, did you not?" Katrine narrowed her eyes. The air seemed to crackle around them, probably caused by Arnesto's obvious discomfort. As an elemental mage, he could affect the weather patterns. Mara leaned forward, her stomach in fresh knots, waiting for Arnesto's answer.

Arnesto's shoulders sagged as he continued peering at

his boots. "Aye," he grumbled. "The sword didn't respond to my touch. Not so much as a sparkle. I tried everything."

Mara jumped off the bench and hurried toward him. "Why didn't you say anything sooner? You've let all of us believe you are the rightful owner of that sword. And now poor Remy has to be dragged back into this hot mess, when we thought we were giving him a normal life, free of dark fays, undead monsters, and battles with evil sorcerers."

"I do not believe this." Arnesto glared at Mara, his gray eyes flashing. "You are more worried about Remy than you are about Efram and the others. Humans are a fickle bunch, and you are the most fickle of all, Maragold Gracelyn—"

"Stop this instant." Yelenarra emerged from her mists before Arnesto could finish saying Mara's full name, which always had unexpected consequences, particularly when Arnesto was upset.

Yelenarra's eyes were red-rimmed, and there was a slight tremor in her voice, but otherwise the elderly fay was as feisty as ever. She stood next to Mara and shook her finger at Arnesto. "You shall not insult any humans in my presence, and you shall certainly address your friend—for Maragold is your friend—with respect. She risked her life and her magic to save you. Or have you forgotten?"

Arnesto's shoulders drooped lower, and he bowed deeply. "You are right, of course, Auntie." He straightened and locked eyes with Mara. "I seem to be apologizing quite a bit lately, with good reason. I have been overwrought and not thinking clearly since we lost Efram. I am sorry, Mara. I owe you a very great deal."

"You don't owe me anything, except the truth." Mara waved her hand. "It's not your fault the red sword didn't bind itself to you. Why have you kept it a secret?"

"I felt as if I let everyone down, Auntie Yelenarra,

Katrine, and especially you. After all, if you own one of the Swords of Five, and your other human friends own the rest, then..."

"Then why not you, an accomplished fay wizard? I see." Mara sighed. Arnesto's ego had gotten in the way of the truth. On the other hand, the ensorcelled swords *were* confounding. "I suppose it is one of the mysteries of the Swords of Five."

Katrine began pacing in a circle around them. "Perhaps something else is at play here. History tells us all previous owners have been fays. This time around, the swords selected human owners. Why?"

Mara stared at a cluster of deep purple asters, thinking. She preferred not to watch Katrine pace; it made her head spin. "But as it turned out, some of us are not entirely human. I'm half elven. Your niece, Linden, is part fay and now the Liege of Faynwood." Mara and Linden had been not-so-friendly rivals throughout their school years, until the war forced them to work together to survive. Mara had learned to respect Linden's leadership traits and magic skills. By the time the war with Glenbarra was over, she counted Linden as a close friend.

Katrine paused and turned toward Mara, picking up the thread. "Her husband owns another of the swords. Chief Corbahn is a Faymon, and we know Faymons are roughly ninety-eight percent human and two percent fay."

"But what about Jayna?" Mara thought about Linden's kindhearted best friend and confidante. Although Mara had been occasionally envious of their close relationship, she'd always admired Jayna, who was a remarkable healer. "She's entirely human."

Katrine crossed her arms. "Jayna was eighteen when

she became a master healer. Have you known any other human healers who achieved mastery at that young age?"

Mara shook her head. Most master healers she'd known were ancient or an entirely different species, such as Zornamayne. "So you think Jayna may be part fay as well?"

Katrine shrugged. "Jayna is so amiable and self-possessed, and she moves with an almost cat-like grace. Perhaps she has a trace of feline-fay in her ancestry. That might explain the lack of blue streaks in her hair and her remarkable healing skills."

Zornamayne's black-tipped tail flicked back and forth. "How fascinating. I hope to meet this young woman one day. I should like to compare healing methods."

Arnesto rubbed the stubble on his chin. "Even if Jayna has a hybrid ancestor, what about Remy? He seems one hundred and ten percent human."

Mara smiled. Arnesto was right about Remy. With his love of food, amazing cooking skills, and goofy sense of humor, he was just an ordinary boy who'd been forced to fight Glenbarrans, sorcerers, and undead creatures with his red sword. Yet even after devastating losses, including the death of his best friend, Remy still retained his boyish charm. "I have to agree with Arnesto. Remy is happiest when he's baking and eating, preferably full puff pastries."

Katrine nearly shouted. "That's it! It's been at the back of my mind ever since I first met Remy. It's so obvious I could smack myself, but I'll restrain the impulse."

"What are you going on about, Katrinareus? Please tell us your hypothesis." Zornamayne seemed exasperated, pronouncing each *S* with extra emphasis.

"Alright. I'll curb my enthusiasm." Katrine gave them a small, sly smile. "How do you calm a troll?" Mara stared at her old fay boss, wondering what trolls had to do with anything they'd been discussing.

Yelenarra shrugged. "Everyone knows all you need to do is offer them food, preferably full puff pastry."

Mara shook her head, finally catching on to Katrine's theory. "Oh no. You've got to be joking. Remy is not some short, hairy little creature with a bulbous nose and horsy teeth."

Arnesto laughed out loud. "Have you ever met a troll?"

"Well, no, but in every illustration I've ever seen, that's how they're pictured."

Arnesto, still chuckling, said, "Trolls are quite respectable looking, about my height, with a burly build and droll sense of humor. They are wonderful bakers and chefs. And once you have gained their trust, they are loyal until their dying day. I am very fond of trolls."

"You just described Remy to a *T*." Mara's ex-boyfriend and oldest chum was probably part *troll*? "I'm feeling a bit lightheaded. I think I'd better sit back down."

CHAPTER 10

Mara returned to the bench in Yelenarra's garden. She'd had far too many surprises in a single day and needed something solid beneath her. Arnesto sat down next to her and took her hand gingerly, as if afraid she would snatch it back. "I promise we will sort this out. And when we have visited the elven king, healed your magic, retrieved Remy's memories, defeated Bazra entirely, and restored balance in the underworld, we will take a holiday together."

Mara appreciated that Arnesto was trying to make her feel better, but she was hurt he hadn't trusted her enough with the truth about the red sword. She glanced down at her hand in his, and her traitorous heart skipped a beat. Their complicated relationship would have to wait a bit longer to sort out. Mara gave Arnesto a weak smile. "That's a tall order, even for a twelfth-level fay wizard."

"Aye," said Zornamayne, her whiskers twitching as she stood in front of them. "But we must begin by placing one paw in front of the other. It is past time we gathered the rest of our group and prepared to leave in the morning. I shall speak with Farleigh and bring him back with me.

Mara, I believe you and Arnestarious must go to Valerra and convince Remington to join us."

Mara nodded. "It will be difficult to explain about his memories, but I'm sure he will want to help."

"I am afraid Remy is going to hate me when I explain what I did." Arnesto's mouth bent downward. "I had good intentions, which I hope he realizes."

"You did *what* to me?" Remy, Arnesto, and Mara stood behind the Triple B Bakery in a narrow, gravel-covered alley strewn with discarded food wrappers, empty boxes, rusted cans, and a couple of old barrels. Mara heard the clip-clop of horse hooves striking the cobbled road in front of the bakery, and an occasional steam-powered locomobile chugging alongside the horse-drawn buggies. The traffic in downtown Bellaryss still hadn't returned to pre-war levels, but more people were out on the streets, which Mara took as a good sign for Valerra's beleaguered capital.

As Arnesto tried explaining again about the unremembered spell, Mara hung back, remaining in the shadows cast by the bakery's building. Remy hadn't noticed the changes to her appearance yet, but he'd see the alterations soon enough. She felt as if she'd betrayed her ex, even though protecting Remy from Bazra had been her goal all along. She'd been wrong—they'd all been wrong. Remy had been captured, along with Arnesto, by the dark fay king's undead creatures and taken to the lower realms.

Remy had a dusting of flour across the bridge of his nose, and his white apron was covered with dabs of dried dough, smears of jam, and streaks of chocolate. His hazel eyes clouded over as Arnesto repeated his explanation of the unremembered spell, the red sword, and why he'd cast the spell in the first place. "What gave you the right to mess around inside my head, mate?"

Arnesto compressed his lips and shook his head. "I did not have the right, and I am deeply sorry. The prophecies indicated—"

"Whoa! Not 'the prophecies.'" Remy raised his hands in front of his chest. "I never want to hear another word about prophecies, or dark fays, or Fallow necromancers. I just want to live a normal life. Is that too much to ask?"

Mara stepped closer to Remy. "Of course not. That's why Arnesto cast the spell in the first place. Katrine thought she was protecting you. She thought if you no longer possessed the red sword, then Bazra would leave you alone."

Remy snorted. "Instead I wound up in Bazra's dilapidated tower, wondering whether I'd live long enough to see sunshine again. I still get nightmares about that gloomy place." He shuddered. "And now with those cracks showing up in our roads, and the creepy feeling I get when I'm near one of them, I just know nothing's going to be normal for a while yet."

Mara sighed. "Things are even worse in the lower realms—that's why the cracks are showing up. We're going to need your help one more time."

Remy glanced at her, and his face softened. Mara knew he still had feelings for her, and she cared for him, but not in the "happily ever after" storybook way. Remy was her oldest friend. They'd been through a lot together, both good times and really, really bad. "Tell me what's happening and how I can help."

Arnesto explained how the underworld's choir had stopped singing and how Efram and many other spirits were beginning to fade away. "There's more, but it's Mara's story to tell, not mine."

Mara sat down on an overturned barrel and patted the scarred wooden side. Remy sat next to her. "Whatever it is, you know you can tell me."

Mara took a deep breath and plunged in. "My magic's gone dormant ever since the rescue, my sword fizzles out whenever I pick it up, and well, I just found out my mother was an elf."

Remy's mouth hung open. "No way!" Then he leaned closer, as if seeing her for the first time. "Your hair—it's much blonder—and your eyes are different too, kind of purple. Wow!"

"*Violet.* Elves have violet eyes," said Mara, "and before you ask whether I have pointy ears, the answer is no." She explained about the trip to Alfweard, and her hope the elven king would provide some answers about her heritage and her missing magic. "We need my blue sword to start working again—and to retrieve your red sword—if we're going to defeat Bazra for good." She glanced at Arnesto. "Maybe you should explain to Remy about the next part."

Arnesto ran his hand through his wavy blue hair and blurted out, "I believe you are part troll." Mara rolled her eyes. For such a brilliant wizard, Arnesto could be so clumsy at times.

Remy hopped off the barrel and stalked toward Arnesto, his hands curled at his sides. "First you take my girlfriend, then you mess with my memories, and now you insult me." Remy hauled back his fist and threw a punch at Arnesto's nose. Arnesto moved so quickly Mara felt a slight tremor in the air. Remy swung wildly, missed, and stumbled forward.

He spun around, ready to charge again, but Mara jumped off the barrel and stepped in front of him. Remy dropped his hands to his sides and shook his head wearily. "So you think I'm a troll too?"

Mara tucked a chunk of hair behind her ear. "I think it's likely you had a troll ancestor. Arnesto wasn't trying to insult you. He likes trolls, quite a lot, and it turns out they seem to have a lot in common with you and your mum." Mara told him what she'd learned about trolls from Arnesto.

"You're kidding. Trolls love full puff pastry? And they're about my height, and about my build, and are great bakers and chefs?" The corners of Remy's mouth turned up. "I've got to tell Chef Desna about this. His grandmother was a fay, you know."

"That's a good idea, and you may as well ask the chef for time off so you can help us deal with the dark fays. We'll wait out here." Mara watched as Remy dashed through the rear door of the bakery. "That went better than I expected."

Arnesto shook his head. "I certainly did not expect him to throw a punch. He nearly caught me too."

"Well, you weren't exactly delicate about his troll heritage. It's not something you can just spring on someone without a bit of an explanation."

"We do not have the time for explications and revelations. We need to bring Remy back to Havynweal and plan our trip."

"And we need to talk—you and me."

Arnesto turned his puppy-dog gray eyes toward her. "I am prepared to listen, even if what you are about to say is not what I want to hear. But please know that regardless of your feelings for me, mine are unchanged toward you. When I pledged myself as your friend, I knew what I was doing. I have no regrets—well, other than the fact I was too injured to tell you what the friendship pledge meant."

Mara wanted to tell Arnesto he was jumping to the wrong conclusions again, and she did have feelings for him —the kind that made her stomach tighten and her heart flipflop whenever he drew near—but she also needed him to understand he must never mislead her again. Before she could say anything, the bakery's rear door swung open, and Remy emerged with a striking bald-headed man dressed in chef's whites. The man's stern face relaxed into a grin. "Miss Pensk, Mr. Luca, it is good to see you both again."

Mara and Arnesto bowed from their shoulders. The chef had employed them briefly when they were working under-cover as baker's apprentices, and he'd been another of Bazra's prisoners whom Mara had rescued. Mara said, "It is good to see you again, Chef."

The chef lowered his voice. "Remy tells me he must leave for an assignment in the lower realms."

Mara said, "Aye, Chef. We need Remy's help."

The chef narrowed his ice-blue eyes. "Problems with the dark fay king?"

Mara and Arnesto both nodded. Chef Desna thrust out his lower lip. "Well then, be on your way. And do take care. I'd like to have my best baker's apprentice returned in one piece."

"Thank you, Chef." Remy's chest puffed with pride.

Desna opened the door to his bakery and paused. "Let me know if I can help in any way."

"Aye, sir," replied Mara, as Arnesto's traveling mists snaked up their legs. They emerged in Yelenarra's library, where the elderly fay and Katrine leaned over a walnut table, peering at a heavy old book with an inscribed wooden cover.

Katrine looked at Remy and nodded. "Well met, Remy. It is good to see you again. Please accept my deepest apology. It was my idea for Arnesto to try the unremembered spell. I'd hoped to save you from a showdown with Bazra."

Yelenarra added, "And I am the one who composed the spell. I owe you an apology as well."

Remy glanced down at the jewel-toned carpet underfoot and cleared his throat. "I realize you were doing what you thought was best. However, I'd prefer to fight my own battles, rather than have my memories scrambled by magic. For the record."

"Understood," said Katrine. "Thank you for agreeing to help us now."

Arnesto wandered over to the table. "Rezebella's journal?" He sounded surprised, almost dismissive, as if they were wasting precious time.

"Aye," replied Katrine. She tapped the open page, yellowed and brittle with age. "We are planning our route to true north."

"But how can that old diary help us?"

"Your great-grandmother was the most accomplished fay reaper in her day," Yelenarra reminded Arnesto. "Rezebella handled the most difficult cases; nothing undead ever escaped her lasso and sword. Her reputation spread throughout Havynweal and beyond. Eventually, the elves recruited Rezebella to guard a particularly leaky portal. Every other year, an elf would show up to relieve Rezebella, and she would disappear for thirty days."

"And you think she visited Alfweard while she was gone?" Mara stood next to Arnesto and peered at the book bound in wood. She wondered what it would be like to guard a portal and prevent the undead from seeping out.

Yelenarra patted the tabletop. "I remember Rezebella sitting right here, writing in her journal. I was a young woman at the time, and she was very old. It occurred to me she might have recorded her expeditions. According to her journal, Rezebella traveled to true north seven times!"

"Did she record her itineraries?" asked Mara.

"Aye." Katrine folded her arms. "Unfortunately, Rezebella took a different route north each time—different landmarks, different stops along the way."

"Can't we just use a compass to guide us north?" Remy scratched his head.

"Hmm. What happens to mechanicals around too much magic?" Katrine waited for Remy to respond.

"They malfunction, of course, which is why Royal Marines carry both pistols *and* swords. But that doesn't apply to a compass, since its magnet always points true north," said Remy.

"That is true in Valerra, but not here in Havynweal, where even the magnetic field is disrupted, or overridden, by magic," explained Arnesto.

"So we have seven potential pathways to Alfweard. Can we determine which is the fastest?" Mara wanted to get past the maps and itineraries and figure out what to pack for her trip. Yelenarra always kept the Amber Room—Mara's sumptuous bedroom suite inside the manor—well stocked with everything she could possibly need, from whimsical day gowns to practical tunics and leggings. Mara had no idea what would be appropriate attire for an audience with the elven king, but between Yelenarra's magic and Gloria's advice, she'd be ready.

Yelenarra waved at the book. "We have eliminated four itineraries already, since Rezebella indicates those routes lengthened her trip by several days. Another path contained too many twists and turns along the way. So that leaves us with two potential pathways to Alfweard that have been tested by Rezebella."

"But she made that trip many decades ago," pointed out Mara. "How do we know the landmarks haven't changed, or there isn't some other impediment?"

"We don't know"—Katrine pursed her lips—"but the first leg of the trip is the same regardless, so we'll leave in the morning as planned. We can decide on our course after the second day of travel."

"How many jumps will we be making tomorrow?" Arnesto carefully turned the old parchment pages of Rezebella's journal, tracing the pencil-drawn routes with his finger. He was referring to the number of times they would travel by fay mists and then touch down to gain their bearings. Fays translocated from point to point, and they needed to understand their geographical boundaries when they made their jumps. Mara leaned forward for a closer look.

Yelenarra counted off on her right hand. "About thirty jumps, more or less, five of which will require a meal break. We shall need first breakfast, second breakfast, midday lunch, afternoon tea—Zornamayne must have her tea and chocolate—and then dinner, once we make camp."

Mara stifled a sigh. Traveling with an octogenarian fay and a tea-loving hybrid would prove challenging, given the number of meal stops they'd be required to make along the way.

"We shall not have time to prepare five daily meals whilst we are traveling," Arnesto gently informed his aunt. "Let us plan on three meals at most—second breakfast, afternoon tea, and dinner—and rely on snacks in between."

"Very well." Yelenarra's earlier her enthusiasm waned somewhat.

"Speaking of dinner...could you please point me to your kitchen wing? I'm happy to rustle up something for us to eat." Remy cocked his head hopefully at Yelenarra, reminding Mara of a large, friendly sheep dog. She was grateful Remy didn't hold grudges, or the trip would be uncomfortable for all of them. On the other hand, she'd forgotten how frequently Remy liked to eat; he'd require just as many meal stops as Yelenarra could conjure.

"Come with me, Remington. You shall assist me in the kitchen." Yelenarra placed her hand on Remy's arm. "Dinner shall be served between sunset and moonrise this evening. Let us make this a formal affair. After all, it will be our last real meal together in the manor."

Arnesto looked up from the book, his brow furrowed. With a flutter of her hands, she amended, "Until we return, of course."

Arnesto nodded. "Aye, Auntie, let us make this a night to remember."

CHAPTER 11

Arnesto offered to translocate Mara to the Amber Room, located at the top of one of the manor's six towers. Since the alternative was climbing a twisty four-story staircase, Mara gratefully accepted the lift. She exited Arnesto's traveling mists on the landing in front of the door and turned to invite him inside.

"We shall assemble in the parlor at sunset and then head into the dining room together." Arnesto gave her a brief bow, the mists swirling about his legs. This might be their only opportunity for a private moment for some time, but he seemed in a hurry to leave.

Mara couldn't tell whether he was avoiding conversation or simply distracted. "Why are we so formal tonight?"

"My aunt wants to commemorate this special occasion."

Mara enjoyed a good dress-up party as much as any other girl. "I'm not complaining. Just curious, I guess."

"It is not every evening we prepare to depart for Alfweard." Arnesto gave her a small wave as he vanished on his traveling mists.

Mara sighed, wondering again at Arnesto's haste...and avoidance. She pushed open the thick wooden door and stepped inside. Like the rest of the mansion, the room's floors, doors, and trim were dark wood, and its walls whitewashed. Decorated in warm shades of coral and peach, the Amber Room could swallow up two of Mara's tiny flats back in Valerra.

A large bed occupied one side of the room, with a small sofa and low table on the opposite wall. Eight narrow windows, evenly spaced around the chamber, provided a breathtaking view of Yelenarra's mountain and the valley below. Mara's favorite feature was the tall wardrobe standing between two of the windows, which contained fresh outfits every time she peeked inside, all magically supplied by Yelenarra.

Mara pulled off her tall boots, wriggling her toes on the plush orange and yellow carpet. She surveyed the room; other than fresh flowers on the low table in front of the sofa and on her bedside table, everything looked the same. Mara crossed the room and pressed her hand against a seam, barely visible, in the wall opposite her bed.

Part of the wall shifted, and she stepped into a white-tiled bathroom with a brass tub, shell-shaped sink set in a marble shelf, and water closet. As Mara had discovered during her previous visit, everything filled, drained, or flushed magically—a good thing, since the usual faucets, pulls, or levers were nonexistent.

After her bath, Mara slipped into a fluffy white robe hanging on a large hook behind the tub and slid her feet into matching slippers. She yawned and thought longingly of the canopied bed as she re-entered the bedroom. Perhaps she might squeeze in a short nap before dinner.

A loud squawk and flap of wings dislodged that notion.

Yelenarra always left one window open in the Amber Room whenever Mara was visiting, so her griffin could come and go as she pleased. Gloria clicked her beak, her wings extended as she glided into the suite. She dashed headlong for Mara, who knelt on the thick carpet and wrapped her arms around the trembling miniature griffin. "How is your family? Is everyone well?"

Gloria burrowed beneath Mara's arm. She nestled there for a few moments before lifting her head to reply. "My children and grandchildren are quite well, milady, thank you for asking. But I have felt rumbles in my belly and prickles down my back since we arrived in Havynweal."

Mara frowned; Gloria never got sick. Could the griffin have eaten something that caused her to feel poorly? "Do you need to see a healer?"

Gloria unwound herself from Mara's arms and leapt onto the sofa. "Nay milady. If I could be cured by a healer's potion, I would be most grateful. Unfortunately, I recognize my symptoms, and invariably they portend change—an unwelcome, unwieldy upheaval—heading our way."

Mara sat on the sofa next to Gloria and ran her hand through her griffin's soft reddish mane. Mara could think of many adjectives to describe Gloria—gossipy, opinionated, and bossy came to mind—but she wasn't one for gloomy, prophetic pronouncements. Something had set her off. "I suppose this is connected to Bazra in some way. After all, he has disrupted the natural order of things in the realms of the dead. That's going to have consequences."

Gloria clicked her beak. "While you are correct about the dark fay king disrupting the natural order of things, I am speaking of change that is much closer to home, much more personal in nature."

Mara rested her hand on Gloria's back and considered. "Then this is about me...and, and Arnesto?"

"Aye. You, Laird Arnestarious, and the rest of us, but mostly about you." Gloria canted her head and peered up at Mara as if seeing her for the first time. "I can see some things have already changed. Your eyes...your hair. You have news for me, do you not?"

Mara took a deep breath and told Gloria about Zorna-mayne's memory spell unlocking an old protection charm, which revealed Mara's elven heritage. Gloria hopped off the couch and flapped her wings excitedly. "Such a remarkable revelation! And to think I am the Griffin Companion to a Lady Elf. Perhaps the king shall grant us admittance to his court. Now that would be something to behold."

Mara folded her arms and shook her head at her silly griffin. "What are you going on about? At most I'm half-elven. I have no connection to the elven king's court, or to anyone else in Alfweard, other than to my mother, who is long gone."

Gloria squawked. "Why else would there have been an old promise, a powerful protection charm, and so many secrets, if there is not some connection to the king himself?"

"I could think of a dozen other reasons." Mara paused, weighing Gloria's words. "You sound as if you know some-thing of the elven king."

"Oh, you know, we griffins hear many things."

Gloria proceeded to preen her wing feathers, until Mara threw her hands in the air. "Gloria! Tell me what you've heard from the other griffins—please."

Gloria purred, "Of course, milady." She padded over to a pillowy armchair adjacent to the sofa, hopped on top, and kneaded the cushion until it suited her fancy. She finally settled and turned her bright eyes toward Mara. "Many years and seasons ago, my mother's cousin, Abigail, became Griffin Companion to Rezebella, Arnesto's great-grand-mother, who was a renowned—"

"Fay reaper, recruited by the elves to protect a portal in the lower realms," said Mara. "Aye, I've just learned all about her. She used to travel to Alfweard every other year, and she recorded each of her itineraries."

"Oh, well, since you know all about Rezebella and her visits to the elven court, I suppose I have nothing more to add."

"Wait a minute, are you saying Rezebella used to call on the king and his court?" When Gloria gave a quick head nod, Mara said, "That would have been fifty or sixty years ago. I wonder how much has changed since then?"

"I do not know what has changed, only what Abigail told my mother, who in turn told me." Gloria paused dramatically.

"Please do continue." Mara nodded, hoping her griffin got to the point soon.

"Aye, milady." Gloria extended her neck for another rub, purring when Mara complied. "Abigail said true north is very chilly, sort of like the elves themselves. She also was surprised to discover elves are very blonde—she did not see a blue hair amongst them—and contrary to popular belief, their ears are not pointed. They merely tip up a bit. She also mentioned their eyes are violet."

"Can you recall anything else?"

"Let's see..." Gloria cocked her head. "Oh, Abigail did mention the king and queen had two young children. A son, who must be the elven king by now, and a daughter, who pouted and frowned and pulled Abigail's tail more than once."

"That's an interesting bit of background." Mara stifled a yawn. She would have gotten more benefit from a good nap than from listening to Gloria's meager, second-hand intelligence, but she would never say so to her griffin. "I do hope the elven king grants us an audience."

"I suppose we shall have to rely on elven hospitality and hope for the best." Gloria jumped off the chair and padded over to the wardrobe. "Should we select something for you to wear to dinner?"

Mara glanced down at her robe and slippers. "Aye. Let's see what Yelenarra has designed since I was here last." Gloria pulled open the doors and drawers, oohing and aahing over three new ball gowns, all in colors far too bright for Mara's taste: magenta, cobalt, and tangerine. The décolletage was cut low and revealed more of Mara's unmentionables than she liked. Mara shook her head. Since she had no magic of her own, she wouldn't be able to make any alterations. "I'm not sure what Yelenarra was thinking when she conjured these, but they are simply too bold for me."

Gloria said, "I think perhaps Yelenarra has designed these gowns to show off your figure to full advantage so Arnestarious would notice"—Mara groaned aloud—"and to compliment your new pale blonde hair color."

Mara pursed her lips, realizing her griffin was probably correct. "Fine. What about the magenta? I'd never wear anything like it back home."

Gloria nodded. "An excellent choice, milady. And while you are changing, I shall accessorize for you."

"I'm still wearing my leather boots with my blades. No fancy little slippers for me, thank you very much," called Mara over her shoulder as she headed toward the private bathroom, where she exchanged her fluffy robe for the magenta gown, which had a fitted bodice and a skirt that flared from the waist. Mara appreciated that she didn't have to wear either a corset or hoops beneath the dress, thanks to Yelenarra's fashion-magic.

Mara and Gloria descended the winding stone stairway, Gloria alternately chatting about her sons and then about the trip they would be taking in the morning. Mara listened with half an ear, still grappling with her newfound elven ancestry.

They were the first to arrive in the parlor, a large, elegant room on the main floor of the manor. Three tall, arched windows dominated the right side of the room, with three pairs of canary-yellow, wingback chairs angled in front of the windows, and glossy black side tables tucked between each set of chairs. In the middle of the room, four cherry-red, camelback sofas were arranged at right angles on a plush red, yellow, and black rug. A heavy, black marble coffee table sat on the rug, in the enclosed square created by the four sofas. Mara didn't think the table could possibly be moved, except by magic.

On the left side of the room stood a long, mahogany sideboard with delicately carved doors, and a row of matching mahogany chairs with red-and-black striped bottoms that could be pulled out to provide extra seating. The largest gilded mirror that Mara had ever seen hung above the sideboard. Tall, potted plants occupied the corners of the room, and vases filled with fresh-cut flowers sat on the tables and sideboard. Glass bric-a-bracs were scattered about the room, on the coffee table and the curio shelves lining either side of the entrance to the parlor.

Hanging on the long wall opposite the entrance was the most eye-catching point of interest in the parlor, a triptych about Mara's height, which she'd studied carefully during her previous visits to the home. She was drawn to the painting again, which depicted the legend of the Swords of Five, how they were forged by a giant and sprinkled with magic dust by a powerful young fay girl. Mara liked to see her blue sword, sparkling with power, captured with such precision by the unknown artist.

Mara narrowed her eyes as she examined the painting; something was off. Then she gasped and gripped the back of the red sofa facing the triptych. Elves peeked out from the flowers and from behind the forge, and on the hill, half hidden from view, one of the elves gripped a sword—a fiery, orange sword that Mara had never seen before—a *sixth sword*.

Had elves been there all along, captured in paint and wood by some long-ago artist—and only now made visible?

CHAPTER 12

"Do you need to sit down, milady? You are suddenly quite pale." Gloria leaned against Mara's leg, her warm, furry presence soothing Mara's nerves.

Mara found her voice. "I've never noticed them—I'd swear they weren't there before."

"What should I be noticing?" Gloria followed Mara's line of sight. "I do not see anything new."

Rather than stepping closer to the triptych, Mara moved back to the threshold and gasped a second time. "It requires a change in perspective to see them, and perhaps in my case, a powerful memory spell as well."

Gloria padded to the entrance of the parlor, which was large enough to host a fencing match or dance assembly, and turned to face the painting on the opposite wall. She tilted her head to the left and then to the right, and then sat on her rump with a squawk and flap of her wings. "Elves! Why, they are sprinkled throughout the painting, hidden in plain view."

"Elves? Where?" asked Yelenarra as she came alongside

them. She'd changed into a teal caftan with a bright yellow turban topping her blue flyaway hair. She'd clipped a sparkly brooch, a ruby-studded dragon, to the center of her turban, and a long, pink feather sprouted from the top, making her seem nearly as tall as Mara.

Mara sidestepped and gently positioned Yelenarra in the precise center of the threshold. She rested one hand on the elderly fay's shoulder and pointed with the other to each section of the triptych. "See? There, and there, and tucked down there, peeking out of that cluster of asters, and another one, kneeling in the grass, and again, at the top of that hill."

"Oh my stars!" Yelenarra brought a hand to her mouth. "I have peered at this painting for eighty years, but I believe this is the first time I am truly seeing it." She ambled slowly into the room and drew closer to each section of the triptych, examining the painted wood. She eventually turned to face Mara. "This is the confirmation I have been seeking."

Mara drew her eyebrows together. "Confirmation? Of what?"

"Of why you are here, or rather, why you have entered our lives at the precise moment you did. Do you recall our first meeting, in Katrine's cramped office behind her old clockwork toyshop in Bellaryss?"

"Aye," Mara smiled wistfully. She'd loved her job at Katrine's Klockworks—both of her jobs, actually—her daytime job of running the shop, and her nighttime job of spying for Vas, who headed the provisional government. She'd even gained admittance to the president's inner circle of trusted friends and operatives. Nothing had been the same since anti-magic arsonists had burned down portions of the capital, including Katrine's shop. "Arnesto had just started working with me, and you wanted to check me out, make sure I was qualified to train your nephew in Valerran culture and undercover work."

Yelenarra wandered to the pair of yellow chairs angled in front of the middle window. Mara sat next to her, a glossy black table wedged between them. "I had no doubt you would be a fine coach, given the high praise you received from Katrinareus. I gave you a hint, at the time, of my true purpose."

Mara smoothed the folds of her magenta gown. "Which was not the same as Katrine's or Arnesto's, as I later learned. Arnesto's primary mission was to prevent the ensorcelled swords from falling into Bazra's hands. Meanwhile, I was focused on protecting Arnesto from himself. He struggled somewhat to blend into our culture." That was an understatement. Arnesto had been a downright handful to train. "You must have guessed why Katrine wanted Arnesto to train with me in Valerra."

"I was aware of the need to protect the swords—and their owners, you and Remy—from the dark fays." Yelenarra compressed her lips and seemed to be choosing her next words with care. "Fays, like humans, often have multiple, complex motives for what we do. The difference is that fays cannot tell an outright lie. Oh, we are quite adept at obfuscation and misdirection, but when asked a targeted question, we must provide an honest response. Do you understand my meaning?"

Mara nodded slowly. "I think so...you want me to realize we are more alike than not, and the main difference is humans can lie and fays cannot. When I put it like that, it makes me think we humans are just not worth all the fuss and bother."

"Never think that, my dear. Human beings are the

bravest creatures of all, braver than fays or elves or dragons. Men and women are the first to charge headlong into danger, risking death or permanent injury for a cause they believe in. Fays debate endlessly, elves retreat to the icy north in Alfweard, and dragons head to the mountains. It is humans, the most fragile and least magical of creatures, who stand in the valleys, in the trenches, in the depths of their own despair, and fight back against evil. I can think of no worthier allies than you and your human friends."

"I'm glad you feel that way. I know many fays would disagree. But why are you telling me this now?"

"Because you seem to be forgetting what I said to you during our first meeting."

Mara recalled thinking Arnesto's aunt was quirky, flighty, and perhaps not all together there. While the quirkiness part proved true, the rest did not. Yelenarra was completely at ease with herself, a rare quality in anyone, whether human or fay. "When we first met, you spoke of a partner for Arnesto, and I misunderstood your meaning at first."

Yelenarra laughed in her tinkling way. "Actually, you were closer to the mark than I let on. I wanted to see for myself what sort of young woman you were: did you have your priorities straight; did you understand the importance of protecting Serving magic; and most importantly, would you be able to gain my nephew's trust? I was trying to determine whether you would be a good partner for my nephew—in every sense of the word."

"Oh." Mara mulled over Yelenarra's words. Arnesto's aunt had always been supportive of her, and perhaps even doting. "You did seem very pleased later, when Arnesto announced our friendship."

"Aye, I was thrilled, until I realized he had not explained

about the fay meaning behind a declaration of friendship. I wanted to throttle my nephew, but he had been injured at the time, and so I did not scold him, until tonight."

"Why tonight?" Mara turned in her seat toward Yelenarra.

"Because I have observed his behavior around you, and I am deeply disappointed. When you told me Arnestarious was avoiding you and cutting his visits short, I had hoped you were exaggerating. If anything, it is worse than you indicated."

"I don't see how scolding him will make a difference." Mara shrugged, suddenly sad, as sad as she'd felt while under the effects of the memory spell, watching her painful past unfold before her.

"Perhaps not, but he is stuck fast. I am attempting to unstick him." Yelenarra reached beneath her turban with one finger to scratch above her left ear. Mara waited for the older woman to readjust her headgear and explain. "My nephew clearly wants you to feel the same way about him as he feels about you, but he does not want to force the issue."

"Which I respect and appreciate."

"Aye, except he is going about it all wrong. Meanwhile, we have a major threat in the lower realms, which is affecting his dear brother's spirit and many others, and is creating rifts the human realm as well. Arnestarious must stop being a silly, besotted boy and thrust out his manhood."

"Thrust out his manhood?" A warm flush spread across Mara's face and neck. "I think perhaps we ought not to speak about this..." She tugged at her bodice, wishing her gown had a higher neckline. While Yelenarra often twisted her words in much the same way Arnesto did, this conversation was beyond awkward.

Yelenarra giggled. "Oh dear, a mere slip of the tongue. I told my nephew to grow up and tackle the issues we are facing head on, with you at his side. If you work together again, as partners, then perhaps everything else shall fall into place."

Mara nodded. "That's good advice. But what do elves hidden in the painting have to do with us partnering together?"

Yelenarra waved her hand at the triptych. "Half a dozen elves suddenly appear in a painting about the forging of the Swords of Five. And even stranger, there appears to be a sixth sword, wielded by an elf, standing in the background. Elves must have some connection to the legend, which has gone unremarked until now. This new piece of the puzzle was first revealed to you—a girl who has just learned she is half eleven—and owns one of the swords of legend. I do not believe in coincidences, Maragold, especially where magic is involved. You are here, at this time and place, to help Arnestarious defeat the dark fay king and restore order in the lower realms."

"Which I won't be able to do until we fix my magic."

"True enough, lass." Yelenarra pushed herself up from her chair. "Let us go to the dining room. The others must be gathered there by now."

"Oh, I thought everyone was meeting here in the parlor first and then heading into dinner together." Mara rose from her seat.

Yelenarra gave her a mischievous grin. "A small misdirection on my part, I am afraid. I asked Arnesto to tell you to meet us in the parlor, whilst I told him and everyone else to go straight to the dining room. I wanted to have this chat, just us two girls."

"I see." Mara should have been irritated with Yelenarra for the small subterfuge, but she found it amusing.

"I hope you can forgive an old woman her fay ways."

Mara chuckled. "Aye, no harm done."

Gloria, who'd managed to keep silent during the entire exchange, clicked her beak several times. "I shall go on ahead to the dining room and let the others know you are coming."

Mara watched as the miniature griffin trotted from the room, her tail held high. "Her real motive, of course, is to inspect the first course and snag a good spot at the table." Mara offered her arm to the elderly fay, who seemed inclined to stroll toward the dining room, rather than translocate them both in an instant on her mists.

Yelenarra looped her arm through Mara's. "It is good to have a griffin in the house again. Arnestarious and I have rattled around this manor by ourselves for far too long."

"He never got another pet after the attack?" Arnesto's mother and pet griffin had been killed by a hideous, bristly, underworld creature sent by the dark fays. Arnesto had been barely five years old at the time and had witnessed the attack.

"Nay, we both feared the same thing would happen again, and so we kept to ourselves. It was quite lonely for Arnestarious, especially after his father sent Eframallium away. Arnestarious was too young to be sent to boarding school with his brother, and well, you know why we kept him secluded here on this mountain. I wonder sometimes whether we made a mistake."

Mara recalled the first time Arnesto had told her about his blood magic. Arnesto's family believed if given the chance, the dark fays would misuse Arnesto's blood magic, threatening the undead creatures under their command with an eternity in the underworld's fiery lake. They kept young Arnesto isolated on Yelenarra's mountain retreat for the duration of his childhood.

"Why do you say that?" While Mara thought their decision had been flawed, they had just lost Arnesto's mother—Yelenarra's younger sister—to the dark fays, and they'd been understandably fearful.

Yelenarra and Mara turned down a long corridor, the whitewashed walls cocooning them on either side. Their footsteps produced no sound as they trod on the plush carpets lining the hallways. The rugs' swirly patterns added bright, cheerful splashes of color as they walked. "It does not take a wizard to see my youngest nephew is different—and I do not mean his magical talents or boyish charm—but his struggles to fit in, whether here in Havynweal or in the human world. He often alienates people, including even-tempered Remington, who gave me an earful when I asked him how well he knew Arnestarious."

This was the first time Yelenarra had confided in Mara about her nephew. Mara wanted to reassure the older woman, but she couldn't exactly prove Yelenarra wrong. Arnesto had struggled with his undercover assignments because he was different—he stood out, rather than blended in—on the other hand, Remy was not the most reliable witness. When Mara explained Remy was her ex-boyfriend, Yelenarra nodded. "I thought that might be the case. Still, much of what Remington told me did have the ring of truth."

As they turned down the hallway that led to the dining room, they heard a happy yip, followed by Gloria exclaiming, "Farleigh, watch your tail. You almost knocked over that planter."

Farleigh mumbled an apology, and then he woofed, "Remy, friend. Miss you."

"I've missed you too, mate," said Remy. "Life in Havyn-weal must be agreeing with you—I think you've grown a few inches."

"Of course life is better here for Farleigh," hissed Zorna-mayne, her voice drifting down the hall. "No one is trying to capture him or experiment on him or pretend he does not exist simply because he is a crossbreed."

Katrine said, "Aye, we're all grateful to you for providing a home for our grihm friends."

"It has been a mutually satisfactory arrangement. We are pleased Farleigh and Jerdahn have joined our clan."

"Like it here," agreed Farleigh.

Yelenarra smiled at Mara. "As I recall, it was your inspired idea to ask Zornamayne to provide sanctuary for your two grihm friends." They were standing by the room's entrance. The door, slightly ajar, was inlaid with colored panes of glass, reminding Mara of the kaleidoscopes she used to sell in Katrine's toyshop. Arnesto had enjoyed twirling the scope as he peered inside.

"Farleigh and Jerdahn helped us during the war," said Mara as she pulled open the door. "I was glad to return the favor. They'd needed a new home, and Zornamayne had needed help securing her clan's boundaries."

A long, low teakwood table occupied the center of the dining room. Chandeliers hung from the ceiling, casting soft candlelight across the room, which could easily accommodate Mara's entire flat within its four white walls. Mirrors of various shapes and sizes covered the wall to the right of the doorway, and tall windows lined the other two walls. The cheerful silk rug covering the dark wood floor muffled her footsteps.

Since she was the last to arrive, everyone else was seated on gold-tasseled floor cushions, each cushion a different color of the rainbow. Mara knew this was Yelenarra's "small" dining room; she had another huge space she used to accommodate larger groups, with upholstered, straight-backed chairs and an even larger table.

Farleigh woofed a greeting, Remy complimented her "fancy hot pink dress," and Arnesto glared at Remy staring at her neckline. *I don't think this evening is going to go well at all. Throwing an ex-boyfriend and a maybe-boyfriend together is asking for trouble.*

Yelenarra thanked everyone for coming as they sat down to the first course, a chilled peach soup, which Mara enjoyed despite the knots forming in her stomach. Gloria and Katrine sat on the tasseled cushions on either side of Mara, as if to provide her with moral support. Remy and Zornamayne sat across from her, and Arnesto and his aunt anchored opposite ends of the oval table. Arnesto wore a navy sateen cape over his sparkly, silver tunic. The only guest not seated was Farleigh, happily gnawing an enormous bone on the floor next to his water bowl.

Zornamayne asked about their itinerary, and Katrine and Yelenarra described Rezebella's journal and the course they would take for the first two days, the feline-fay nodding as she listened. Remy helped himself—twice—to the next course, roast pheasant, broiled whitefish, and an assortment of seasoned root vegetables. Mara picked at her food while Arnesto ate in stony silence, his eyes darting occasionally between her and Remy.

The silence lengthened until Mara couldn't take it anymore. She asked Katrine whether she had ever heard of chasms opening up in the human realm before. The fay chief shook her head. "None with a supernatural cause—at least none that I've come across in my studies."

Arnesto agreed. "I have not encountered any previous mention of fissures opening up as a result of disruptions in the lower realms."

Remy took a bite of his potato and chewed slowly before asking, "Isn't this the first time the choir's stopped singing in the underworld?" When Katrine nodded, he added, "Seems to me that's pretty unprecedented too."

"What are you implying?" Arnesto narrowed his eyes.

Remy shrugged. "I'm not implying anything. I'm merely pointing out that whatever Bazra is doing with the red sword—*my* red sword—seems to be creating chaos in multiple realms."

"The meaning behind your words is quite clear. You are blaming me for the red sword winding up in Bazra's hands, for the imbalance in the underworld, and for the rifts in the human realm," growled Arnesto, which made poor Farleigh whine.

Remy raised his hands. "Look, I'm here to help Mara. As to the rest, if the boot fits—then wear it."

Arnesto drew his brows together, obviously trying to interpret Remy's last remark, an old Valerran expression. Arnesto's face clouded as he deduced the meaning, but before he could reply, Yelenarra waved her hands, replacing their dinner plates and mugs of wine with dessert and coffee.

As she pecked at a biscuit on her plate, Gloria said, "I wonder what the elves have to do with the Swords of Five? And why do you think they have popped up in Yelenarra's painting?" Mara suppressed a sigh. She'd hoped to get through the meal without any further discussion of swords, or for that matter, elves.

Arnesto laid his fork on his plate, his chocolate cream pie forgotten. He glanced at Mara. "You have seen *elves* in the triptych?"

Mara nodded reluctantly; she would have liked to postpone this particular conversation indefinitely. Arnesto threw down his napkin and waved his hand, disappearing in a puff of mist.

CHAPTER 13

REMY SAID, "WHILE THAT SOUNDS INTERESTING, I'LL FINISH MY dessert first and then go take a look. This pie is amazing, as good as any piece of artwork, in my opinion."

'Thank you, Remington," said Yelenarra, who took a tiny bite of her pie and then set down her fork. While Yelenarra had maintained polite conversation during dinner, Mara had noticed her casting worried glances at Arnesto throughout the meal.

Katrine wiped her mouth with her napkin. "If you'll excuse me, my curiosity has gotten the better of me. I must see this for myself."

Zornamayne smoothed her whiskers with one paw. "I shall accompany you."

"Me too!" Farleigh yipped.

Mara climbed to her feet, her appetite gone. She wasn't sure why, but she didn't think Arnesto would like the new additions to the painting. Before Bazra had captured him, Arnesto had been much more self-assured and optimistic. He'd been convinced he was the rightful owner of the red sword and confident he would be the one to rout the dark fay king. He'd also been more openly affectionate with Mara, and more patient with her need to explore her feelings following their accidental—at least for Mara—friendship pledge.

Yelenarra remained seated. "Please go on ahead. I shall stay behind with Remington whilst we finish our dessert. We will be along shortly."

Gloria clicked her beak several times. "Please, may we travel by mist? It is a long walk back to the parlor."

Katrine and Zornamayne nodded in unison, their traveling vapors twining around everyone, except Remy and Yelenarra, still seated at the teakwood table. The group touched down gently, the thick carpet of the parlor muffling the sound of their arrival. Mara's eyes searched the room and spotted Arnesto standing before the triptych, his arms folded across his chest, his shoulders hunched forward, as if in defeat.

He's stopped believing in himself and in the singularity of his magic. He's realized he is not some hero of legend, but a fay boy who still needs the help of others—possibly even the elves—to defeat Bazra and fix the mess in the lower realms. Mara wanted to wrap her arms around him, but Farleigh broke the silence by knocking over one of the planters with his tail.

"Sorry." Farleigh dropped to all fours, his head down.

Katrine righted the planter and twirled her finger to redeposit the spilled soil. She patted Farleigh's shoulder. "No harm done."

Arnesto spun around, his navy cape whirling behind him. His eyes locked on Mara's. "You continue to confound me," he said, his mouth bent downward. "I thought I knew you, but clearly I was wrong. Your ensorcelled sword, your elven heritage, and now this"—he pointed over his shoulder at the painting—"are all so perplexing. I cannot wrap my head around your untamed magic. Who is the *real* Maragold Gracelyn Raeburn Pensk?" Arnesto uttered Mara's name with such force all the glass bric-a-brac and planters rattled.

The floor beneath Mara's feet heaved, and she braced herself. The last time Arnesto was upset and spoke her full name, she wound up outside, in the dark, frightened and lost until Efram had shown up and guided her back to the manor. She closed her eyes and reached inside, probing for any sparks of magic, anything to counterbalance Arnesto's tantrum. Mara took in a ragged breath. She felt nothing, not a spark of her old magic, nothing she could draw upon to anchor herself. She could feel herself being pulled into a vortex of doubt and anxiety and fear. Was this a window into Arnesto's tumultuous emotions? Or her own?

The gilded mirror crashed to the ground, shattering. The potted plants, crystal vases, and curio cabinets fell over, sending dirt, water, flowers, leaves, and shards of glass flying in all directions. Katrine and Zornamayne cast spell after spell to reverse the damage, as poor Farleigh ran howling from the room, his tail drooping behind him.

Gloria flapped her wings, squawking, "Chaos! Calamity! Catastrophe!"

No one, however, seemed to be dealing with Arnesto, or if they were, it wasn't working.

Mara fell to her knees as the floor beneath her gave another heave. Gripping the back of one of the cherry red sofas and pulling herself up, Mara knew she had to get Arnesto's attention. But without magic to help her, she did the only thing that came to mind—she shouted, "Arnestarious Aziel Windstorm Lucato the Fourteenth!" She'd only spoken his full fay name aloud once before, under very different circumstances. Then, she'd needed to gain his attention so she could kiss him. This time, she just wanted him to stop and listen.

A lightning bolt shot out of the ceiling and struck the middle panel of the triptych, the one that showed the forging of the swords, and burned a hole through a section of wood. Flames licked at the image of the swords. Katrine cast a spell to put out the flames and restore the painting, but a long, slim scorch mark remained.

Arnesto shook himself, as if stunned, his wavy blue hair a wild halo around his head. He looked from the damaged panel to Mara, his face hardening. "I believe I have my answer. You obviously have powerful elven magic but are unable to control it. You are a force to be reckoned with, Maragold—but I do not know whether that is a good thing or bad." He snapped his fingers and disappeared in a swirl of mist.

Mara's legs shook, and she half-collapsed onto one of the sofas. Gloria padded over and leaned against her shins, whether to provide comfort or be comforted, Mara wasn't sure. She ran a hand through her griffin's fur as her eyes welled up. For the first time she could recall, Mara didn't attempt to hide her tears but let them flow freely down her cheeks. Somewhere behind her she heard Yelenarra and Remy arriving, and Farleigh grunting, "Scary magic. Don't like."

Yelenarra whispered, "Oh dear, did Arnestarious do that?"

Katrine replied, "Indirectly. Arnesto caused a disturbance, and Mara stopped him. Zornamayne and I were able to undo all the damage, except for that blackened section in the triptych."

Remy must have noticed Mara slumped on the sofa. He

didn't say a word, didn't reach out to pat her shoulder or take her hand, but he simply sat down quietly next to her. Mara appreciated his solid, uncomplicated presence. He reached into his pocket, withdrew a handkerchief, and handed it to her.

Mara accepted the square piece of linen gratefully. She mopped her face and blew her nose. "Thanks."

"Anytime."

"Come along, lass. I'll give you and Gloria a lift," said Katrine. Mara nodded mutely and stood as Katrine's mists spiraled up her legs and waist. She was surprised when they landed on soft grass, slightly damp with dew, rather than the carpeted landing outside the Amber Room.

The air was cool, and Katrine handed her a light wrap she'd conjured from somewhere—probably from the wardrobe inside the Amber Room. A bright, white moon hung above them, and stars dotted the sky all around. Katrine walked over to a stone bench, sat down, and patted the empty spot next to her. Mara sniffled and took a seat. She could tell her old fay boss was working up to a lecture she was in no mood to hear.

"This thing between you and Arnesto—it's gotten way out of hand."

"This thing? You mean our friendship pledge? It may be meaningless after tonight. You saw how Arnesto looked at me, as if I was some monster from the realms of the dead. He pledged himself to a human girl, not some half-breed with wild magic who makes elves appear in paintings and shoots lightning bolts from the ceiling." Mara's broiled whitefish sat like a boulder at the bottom of her stomach. She wished she'd skipped dinner entirely.

"While you did shoot that lightning bolt and scorched the painting, I don't think you can take credit for embedding those elves in a very old triptych," Katrine pointed out. "It's obvious they'd been there all along—painted by the original artist, since the style and brushstrokes are the same—but we've not *observed* them until now."

Mara shrugged glumly. "I may not have sketched the elves, but my presence—and my elven ancestry, which is now quite obvious—caused them to be revealed."

"Aye, that is the likeliest explanation." Katrine crossed her legs and sighed. She seemed reluctant to speak her mind, which was unusual for Katrine. She toed the grass with one of her boots and sighed again. "Look, it seems to me you and Arnesto might work together better if you dissolve your friendship pledge now, before we depart for Alfweard in the morning. We have a great deal of ground to cover and none of us—you most of all—can afford this constant upheaval."

"But what about the penalty for breaking off our pledge? Wouldn't we both be permanently banished from Havynweal?"

"Who told you there was a penalty?"

"Well, Arnesto strongly implied it."

Gloria added, "We all know it is against fay ways and laws to break an oath. And banishment is the typical penalty for oath-breakers."

"Aye," agreed Mara.

"That's true in general, except for friendship pledges, which are an entirely different matter. It's also true friendship pledges are rarely dissolved, because fays understand what they are promising. On the other hand, you had no clue. Furthermore, the only penalty for going your separate ways would be hurt feelings, or possibly a bruised heart, both of which eventually mend."

Mara rubbed her forehead. "It's been such a long, eventful day. I don't know what to think."

"What do you feel?"

"Confused, hurt, and sad. I really like Arnesto, or at least, the Arnesto I thought I knew. I feel numb, I guess."

Katrine compressed her lips. Finally, she slapped her thighs and rose from the bench. "I can't tell you what to do, but I can tell you what I would do in your boots."

"Which is?"

"I'd release myself—and Arnesto—from this emotional carousel. Focus on traveling to Alfweard, fixing your magic, and defeating Bazra. That's more than enough for a pair of eighteen-year-olds who may or may not be in love. Time will tell; until then, heads down, lassos coiled, and swords drawn. We have much to do and not much time."

Katrine was right. Those heady days immediately after Arnesto's rescue, when they'd both been smitten and grateful for every moment they had together, were gone. Later, after Mara recovered from her physical injuries and returned to Valerra, the plans they'd made seemed to evaporate on Arnesto's traveling mists.

Yelenarra saw things quite differently, however, and Mara told Katrine about their pre-dinner conversation, after discovering the elven images hidden in the triptych. Katrine listened carefully, her arms folded. "Yelenarra appears to be indulging in wishful thinking. However, she didn't see what transpired in the parlor. Arnesto blew a gasket when he saw the elves in the painting."

"I still don't understand why that bothered him so much."

"He's not a fan of the elves, ever since his mother was killed by an undead creature."

"What's that got to do with Arnesto's dislike of elves?"

"He blames them for not properly securing the portals to the lower realms. If the elves had been doing their job, he reasons, then his mother would still be alive."

"Oh." Mara dropped her head in her hands and mumbled, "And he's just discovered his girlfriend is half-elven, with out-of-control magic and a malfunctioning sword."

"Aye."

Mara raised her head, her mind made up. "Fine. I'll speak to Arnesto, but I'm not sure how to find him at this late hour."

"I know where he is," said Katrine. "I'll translocate you there, and I'll take Gloria back to the manor with me."

Mara blinked rapidly a few times and rose from the bench. She was still gripping Remy's handkerchief. She balled it up and stuffed it in her reticule, squared her shoulders, and gave her old fay boss a firm head nod. "I'm ready."

As Katrine's mists enveloped her, Gloria raised her paw. "Do not be sad, milady. This is for the best, I daresay." Which, of course, made Mara feel even worse.

She found herself in a vast, empty room, which Mara immediately recognized as the old ballroom, rarely used anymore. Her boot heels rapped against the wooden floorboards. Arnesto stood by the windows facing the moonlit garden. Mara knew beyond the lawn was a sheer drop of seven thousand feet. She thought again of the isolation on that mountain and Arnesto's lonely childhood. He did not turn around but spoke to their reflection in the darkened windows. "You have come to make it official, then?"

"Make what official?" asked Mara, although she suspected Arnesto knew the reason for her visit.

"Please do not toy with my affections."

Mara's temper flared, and she quickened her pace

across the floor. "*Your* affections? What about mine? I'm the one you've ignored for weeks on end."

Arnesto spun around. He waved his hand and lit a candelabra at each end of the cavernous room, which cast just enough light for Mara to see his chiseled cheekbones and strong chin, covered in a week's worth of stubble. "My brother explained—in his accurate yet inelegant way—the reason I was avoiding you."

Mara stopped ten feet in front of her former fay trainee, who was as infuriating and impossibly handsome as ever. "Because you liked me so much you found it easier to avoid me. You wanted to give me the space to explore my feelings." She shrugged. "I suspect you had other reasons as well."

"Such as?"

"You wanted to prove to yourself you could take on the dark fay king without me—you wanted to go it alone—and you knew I would uncover your plans if you spent too much time with me."

Arnesto dropped his gaze and ran a hand through his hair. "Whatever my reasons, I daresay they no longer matter."

Mara wasn't sure that was true, but she decided not to press the point. "Your words tonight hurt me deeply. You obviously hate my elven heritage, which, like my magic, is not something I can control."

Arnesto took a step toward Mara and then another. Her heart pounded in her chest, but she resisted the urge to close the distance between them. "I could never hate you, Mara."

Mara waited, but Arnesto said nothing more. She bit her bottom lip, which quivered slightly. She would not cry in front of him. "I don't think we can go on like this—I know I can't."

Arnesto bowed his head. "I shall accede to your wishes, of course."

Mara's stomach twisted into a hard fist. "So you agree with me?"

He raised his head but didn't meet her eyes. Instead, he stared at a point above her left shoulder. "I shall not debate with you, Maragold. I must bow to your conviction that you know best."

Infuriating man. Why does he leave it up to me to break off our friendship pledge, after all that happened in the parlor, after everything he's said—and left unsaid? Mara threw her hands in the air. "Alright then, I'll say it. We're done, it's over—I release you from our friendship pledge. You are free to do whatever you wish."

Arnesto gave her a wistful head nod. "So be it. I am sorry—"

Mara put her right palm up. "No! Don't you say dare you're sorry now. I've shed enough tears over you. I have to go." She spun around and walked the length of the ballroom, her boots click-clacking on the floorboards.

She was almost to the door when Arnesto shouted, "Wait!"

Mara took a deep breath and turned around. "What is it?"

"Did you truly shed tears over me?"

"Aye." She turned toward the door half-hoping Arnesto would call her back and apologize again. If he did, she'd listen this time. But he remained silent.

No matter, she thought. *I have to focus on tomorrow, on the future—a future without fay boyfriends, friendship pledges, whirlwind tantrums, or lightning bolts.*

CHAPTER 14

After Mara left Arnesto in the empty ballroom, she wandered the silent corridors until she wound up in the parlor, where she sat in the dark. A thin beam of moonlight streamed through the windows, striking the middle panel of the triptych. Mara stared at the scorch mark she'd made, unsure how she'd been able to fire off the lightning bolt. Eventually a cloud scuttled across the moon, and Mara stumbled off to her chamber, where Gloria snored quietly at the foot of the bed.

The first bands of orange streaked across the indigo sky as Mara slipped out of the mansion. Yawning, she rubbed her eyes, bleary from lack of sleep. Mara had no luggage, just the clothes on her back—a lightweight blue cape, layered over a dark yellow blouse and split skirt, perfect for riding anything from a horse to an aero cycle—and polished brown leather boots, her blades holstered inside. Gloria and Katrine had packed for her while she'd been speaking with Arnesto, and then Katrine had transferred Mara's saddlebags outside with the other bags and supplies.

Although a cool breeze fluttered through the trees as Mara approached the manor's archway, she knew the day would grow warm once the sun had risen fully. She glanced at the runes as she passed beneath the arch, warded by Arnesto and every one of his ancestors, including Yelenarra. Mara jumped as the arch emitted an obnoxious screech, like a strangled foghorn, and the runes remained dark. Usually, the arch's gold and silver runes twinkled brightly—and silently—whenever she crossed its threshold. She shook her head, her ears ringing.

A skinny, wraith-like man wearing thick goggles, brown leather jacket, and a green top hat scampered over to Mara, startling her. The odd man bowed deeply. "Milady Maragold the Merciful."

Mara returned the bow, realizing this was one of the Bazeerka, whose ancestors had been banished from Havynweal to the lower realms and then forced to serve whichever dark fay king was in power at the time. Bazra, like his predecessors, gained power by dint of his wickedness. He'd shown not a trace of decency toward his underfed, overworked subjects. When Mara had rescued Arnesto, Vas, and the others from Bazra's prison tower, the pathetic Bazeerka had begged her to allow them to return to Havynweal.

Mara hadn't seen anything wrong with showing them mercy; after all, they'd committed no crimes themselves. Yelenarra had agreed with her and constructed a small settlement partway down the mountain to accommodate the formerly dark fays, who were still considered banished by most of the fays of Havynweal. Katrine had proposed legislation to lift their banishment, but so far the fay council had vetoed it.

"Please follow me, milady. Yer horse is saddled and bags stowed." The skinny man pointed to a long caravan of

TONI CABELL

horses lined up on Yelenarra's side lawn. Mara's brow furrowed. She hadn't realized they would be traveling by horse as well as fay mist. Yelenarra must have been busy half the night with the preparations.

Mara felt a twinge of guilt. She should have been helping Arnesto's aunt, rather than sitting in a darkened parlor staring at a scorched painting and feeling sorry for herself. "Oh, I had no idea. How many horses are we taking?"

"There's two dozen of 'em, milady, and half as many of me countrymen to assist on yer expedition."

Mara thought that seemed excessive, but then she realized they would be hard-pressed to carry their own supplies for a five-plus-day journey otherwise. She fell into step behind the skinny Bazeerka, his tall green hat bobbing as he jogged to the lead horse. He picked up the reins and waited for her to mount. Gloria was sitting on the ground in front of the horse, clicking her beak softly. The horse neighed, raising his head up and down as if in agreement.

Mara pursed her lips and frowned. "I don't understand why I'm the lead rider. I don't know the route nearly as well as Yelenarra or Katrine." Or Arnesto, but she wasn't going to say his name aloud any more than necessary, because every time she even thought his name, she felt a tiny stab of pain in her chest. Mara had never felt that way after her breakup with Remy, or any of her other boyfriends, for that matter. Perhaps ending a fay friendship had weightier consequences.

"Lady Yelenarra the Generous says you are not to worry, because she and Lady Katrinareus the Wise will guide the jumps."

Mara sighed and stepped up to the huge bay stallion, which was at least sixteen hands tall. She gripped the saddle, placed her right foot in the stirrup, and swung herself onto the horse's back. "What's his name?"

"Seaworthy."

"Seaworthy? That's a peculiar name for a horse." She leaned over and patted his neck. The horse turned to look at her and batted his long eyelashes. Mara could have sworn he actually *winked* at her. *Do horses in Havynweal have some sort of equine magic?*

The skinny fay shrugged. "I dunno, maybe he likes swimmin' er somefin'."

Mara nodded. "Well, thank you for joining us on this trip, Mister, er...what is your name?"

He swept his top hat off his head. "Me name is Helfyre Harley, but most folks just call me Har. And yer most welcome, milady."

A thin woman in an ankle-length red-and-green plaid duster approached Mara and Har. Like the rest of the rescued Bazeerka, she wore thick goggles to protect her eyes from daylight; after living all of their lives in the lower realms, the formerly dark fays had highly sensitive eyes. She bowed low from the waist, her long blue braid flopping over her head. "All are present an' accounted fer. Lady Yele-narra the Generous sez we can leave anytime."

Gloria flapped her wings and landed gently behind Mara's saddle, settling in for the first jump. She was far too small to fly alongside Mara for five days straight. Mara glanced around to confirm everyone was present. Katrine, sitting directly behind her on a palomino, gave her a wave. "Ready when you are, Mara!"

Yelenarra, Remy, Arnesto, and Zornamayne sat on their horses behind Katrine; only Farleigh was not riding. As a wolf-man crossbreed, he'd be running alongside the horses on all fours.

Mara noticed Arnesto studiously avoiding eye contact with her, which bothered her more than she cared to admit. She didn't have time to dwell on that, however.

"Then I suppose we are ready to leave." Mara addressed Har and the woman in the plaid duster. "Please mount your horses and prepare for the first jump." The two gave her a quick bow and scurried to the back of the line. Mara felt more than a little overwhelmed. She had no business leading twenty-four horses, a dozen Bazeerka, and the rest of their group to Alfweard. She was the only person present who had no active magic—or at least, none she could control.

Mara recalled a conversation she'd had with Linden, shortly after her friend had been crowned Liege of Faynwood. Mara had been teasing Linden about suddenly being thrust into the limelight—everyone bowing to her and accommodating all her wishes—but also expecting Linden to judge every magic contest, sit at the front of every procession, and basically be visible whenever and wherever her advisors suggested. Linden had smiled sadly and said, "I really do miss being just Linden. You know I never asked for this...but I'll do what I must."

Not for the first time, Mara wished she could turn back the timepiece and tell Linden she understood her so much better now. Even after they had gotten over their awkward phase in high school and become friends, Mara had been a little jealous of all the attention Liege Linden received—but not any longer. Mara fully sympathized and wished she could be just Mara again, working in Katrine's Klockworks and training her ridiculously handsome fay employee, Arnesto. Becoming a leader was definitely overrated, in Mara's opinion.

Large puffs of traveling mist entwined themselves

around Seaworthy's legs and traveled up to Mara's shoulders. She felt the ground beneath them give way and they were airborne. A vaporous film, almost like incense, surrounded them, obscuring Mara's view. She felt adrift in a thick, dense cloud, without any sense of what was up or down.

Seaworthy's hooves touched down along a wide river in one of Havynweal's chillier seasons, perhaps frosty fall. He jogged along the shoreline, kicking up sand and a spray of cold water as he ran. Dry leaves, in shades of metallic gold, amber, blue, and silver, crunched underfoot, fallen from tall trees overhanging the riverbank. Mara heard Katrine and the others landing behind her. She glanced over her shoulder but it was impossible for her to confirm that twenty-four horses, with their assorted riders, had landed safely. "Do we need to regroup to ensure all are accounted for?" she shouted at Katrine over the pounding of the hooves.

Katrine called out, "No need. Yelenarra, Zornamayne, and I have connected our traveling mists to you, the pack-horses, and the Bazeerka in the back of the line. Arnesto is also connected to you, as well as Remy and Farleigh. We're waiting for a word from you, or better yet, a hand signal for the next jump."

"Let's keep going," hollered Mara. She faced the front, raised her right palm above her head, and waved her hand forward. The last Bazeerka in line blew through a horn of some sort—likely taken from a dead ram, since the formerly dark fays hadn't lost their instincts for scavenging among the dead—after all, that had been their only means of survival in the lower realms. The mists began twining around Seaworthy and Mara once more.

On their second jump, they landed in dead of winter.

Although Mara's blue cape immediately sprouted a thick wool lining, and warm knit gloves appeared on her hands, courtesy of Yelenarra's magic, Mara was still cold and saw no point in lingering. She waved the group forward for the next jump. After dead of winter followed chilly spring, where a storm was blowing through, and so Mara pressed on, despite the fact her stomach was grumbling. She'd discovered a packet of nuts and dried fruit in the pocket of her cape, which she'd consumed between frosty fall and dead of winter. She figured that was first breakfast, minus a hot mug of coffee.

When they touched down in pretty little valley surrounded by low green hills, Mara breathed a sigh of relief. Yellow, orange, blue, and white daffodils dotted the valley, and butterflies the size of her palm flitted about. She turned Seaworthy sideways, pointed to the ground, and yelled down the line, "Let's stop here!" The Bazeerka at the opposite end tooted twice through his horn, and people began to dismount.

Har ran over and took Seaworthy's reins, guiding her horse and Katrine's toward a stream. About half the Bazeerka took charge of the horses, while the rest aided Yelenarra with preparations for second breakfast. Saddlebags levitated from the backs of the packhorses and floated across the grass; colorful blankets, cushions, napkins, plates, mugs, and utensils flew out of the bags and landed in perfect precision on the ground. Yelenarra, the Bazeerka woman in the plaid duster, and another, younger woman wearing a burnt orange cloak with black stripes, clapped their hands in unison, conjuring poached eggs, cinnamon scones, crispy bacon, small crocks of currant jam, and pots of tea and coffee. Mara decided the Bazeerka's nickname for Arnesto's elderly aunt—Yelenarra the Generous—was an apt description.

Mara approached the inviting breakfast spread across the row of blankets and waited. Everyone seemed eager to sit down, and Farleigh gave a low whine, but no one moved. Yelenarra came alongside Mara and whispered, "The Bazeerka will not sit until you do, and everyone else is waiting as well, out of politeness."

Mara hastily waved her hands. "Please do be seated and enjoy this lovely food, courtesy of Lady Yelenarra." She sat down, waited until everyone else had found a cushion, and picked up a piece of bacon, figuring she'd better start eating in case they needed her to take the first bite too. That seemed to be the correct action, because at the sound of her crunching, everyone else picked up mugs or utensils and dug in. Mara expelled a puff of air. She had no idea her every movement would be scrutinized for the entire journey. How had she gotten to this weird place—her magic missing, her useless blue sword stowed among Zornamayne's belongings, and her eyes and hair color distinctly elven—and also, somehow, the leader of this peculiar pack?

Yelenarra sat on the cushion to her right. Mara had been standing at the end of the row of vivid blue, lime green, dark red, and neon orange striped blankets, so she had no one on her left, which was just as well. She was weary, sad, and quite hungry, but sitting next to Yelenarra felt soothing, despite the fact she'd just broken up with her nephew.

Yelenarra ate daintily and chatted with Remy to her right, until Mara had finished eating and was sipping from her second mug of strong coffee. Yelenarra leaned close and spoke softly. "I have heard about Arnestarious's temper tantrum in the parlor and how you stepped in to stop him. I gather, by the storm clouds in his eyes and the sadness in yours, that you have called an end to your friendship pledge."

Mara bit her bottom lip and nodded. "I hope you're not angry with me."

Yelenarra patted Mara's hand. "My dear lass, I consider you a member of my extended family. You shall always be welcome in my home. The Amber Room is yours, and none other shall use it."

Mara's eyes burned, and she blinked rapidly a few times. She refused to cry; if she started, she might not stop for quite some time, and she didn't want Arnesto to see her breaking down over him. Plus, her nose turned bright red whenever she had a good cry, and that simply wouldn't do. "Thank you. I am so fond of you, and I'd be even sadder if you pushed me away too."

Yelenarra brushed a stray wisp of her flyaway blue hair out of her eyes. "That shall not happen. I promise."

"I'm glad to hear it. It's just, well, Arnesto is your nephew, and I know you adore him, and rightfully so." Mara gave her a half-smile. "But then when I passed beneath the arch this morning, it made the most awful sound and didn't glow like it usually does for me, so I wondered."

Yelenarra's mouth twisted. A shadow flitted briefly across her face, and then she forced a smile. "Did it now? I thought I heard a peculiar foghorn sort of noise but was too busy to investigate. Think nothing of it, my dear. I must have those wards checked when we return home."

Mara had a feeling Arnesto's sour mood had disrupted the wards, but she said nothing to his aunt. Mara finished her coffee and peered down the row of blankets. Plates and mugs were empty, and it was time for the next jump. She glanced at Yelenarra, who said, "Are you ready, lass?"

"Aye."

"Then if you would stand, the others will hop to it, and we shall be able to leave shortly."

"Alright." As soon as Mara climbed to her feet, all the Bazeerka jumped up in unison. They magically cleared away the remains of the meal, cleaned plates, mugs, and utensils, and repacked the saddlebags in less than two minutes. No evidence remained of their meal, except the slight depressions in the grass where they'd been sitting. Yelenarra waved her hand, and the grass sprang back up. Apparently, when fays traveled, they did not leave any trace of themselves behind.

Mara led the group through six more touchdowns before she paused on a white sand beach, with not a cloud in the sky overhead, in the middle of sweet summer. While she didn't have the complete itinerary memorized, she knew they were making good progress toward their final destination for the first day of travel. Seaworthy pawed the sand while she quickly surveyed the area, which seemed ideal for afternoon tea. Mara turned Seaworthy sideways and pointed down at the sand to indicate a meal stop.

As before, Har took the reins and led Seaworthy to a segment of beach farther down the shoreline. He and a couple of Bazeerka linked hands and bowed in front of the horses, which Mara thought quite odd. When they straightened, she saw they'd conjured fresh water troughs on the beach, along with buckets of oats. Meanwhile, the remaining Bazeerka helped Yelenarra set up the blankets, cushions, mugs, and plates for tea.

Mara decided to sit in the middle of the row of blankets, closer to where Arnesto sat last time. She wanted to see the storm clouds in his eyes mentioned by Yelenarra. However, he was off to the side speaking with Katrine, both of them waving their arms about. *Are they having an argument?* Mara didn't have time to investigate. Everyone else was standing in front of the blankets, waiting for her to be seated and take the first sip of tea. Mara gritted her teeth and then reminded herself they were traveling to Alfweard to help her connect with her elven heritage and hopefully, find a means of repairing her magic.

When Remy sat next to her, his plate piled with cheese-and-meat finger sandwiches, squares of apple tart, and chocolate-drizzled cookies, Mara figured Yelenarra automatically gave him extra. After he'd cleaned his plate and had thirds of everything with chocolate, he glanced over at Mara. Katrine and Arnesto had found seats on opposite ends of the row of blankets. Remy hooked a thumb in Arnesto's direction. "So what's up with your twelfth-level fay wizard? For a guy who used to be obnoxiously cheerful, he's looking more like an undertaker these days."

"He's not *my* anything." Mara lowered her voice. "You missed all the action in the parlor last night. It was...very upsetting. Arnesto said some things that, well, I couldn't let slide."

Remy nodded knowingly. "I heard about it from Farleigh, but I thought he was exaggerating. Powerful magic frightens him, poor fella. So what exactly happened?"

"Arnesto threw a magical tantrum and right in the middle of it, he said my full name—and he was really upset."

"Queen's Crown! I'm surprised there wasn't more damage; just those scorch marks on the painting." The first time Arnesto had said her full name had been in front of Remy. Mara had fainted dead away, but Arnesto had caught her in his arms before her head hit the floorboards. She'd probably fallen half in love with the impossible fay right then and there.

Mara explained that Zornamayne and Katrine had cast spells to reverse the damage caused by Arnesto's meltdown. "But Arnesto kept going and wouldn't listen to anyone. Finally I shouted out *his* name to get his attention, and somehow I burned the painting with a lightning bolt in the process. I don't have a clue how I managed to do that, when I can't even light a candle with magic these days."

Remy patted her shoulder. "I'm sorry I stayed behind for the second piece of pie, although it was scrumptious. You and Arnesto dueling it out—that must have been quite a sight."

"It wasn't a duel," grumbled Mara. "I was just desperate for him to stop and listen to reason." *Did Arnesto see it that way, like it was some sort of magical duel? He did seem stunned at my power—but then again, so was I.*

"I think it's just as well you've broken it off. I used to like the chap, but I'm afraid he's earned his Bazeerka nickname."

"Oh?" Mara arched an eyebrow.

Remy gave her a mischievous grin. "They call him Laird Arnestarious the Turbulent."

"Oh no, he couldn't be happy with that title."

Remy chuckled. "Arnesto stormed away, and neither Har nor the others realized he was upset. They figured that's just the way he is."

Mara's mouth turned up at the corners. She didn't want to laugh at Arnesto's expense, but the nickname *was* fitting, given his recent outbursts. Unfortunately, Arnesto chose that exact moment to look at her for the first time all day. He couldn't miss the fact she was sitting with her exboyfriend, chatting and smiling. Squaring his jaw, he dropped his gaze, but not before Mara saw the hurt in his eyes. Her stomach clenched, and she put her unfinished apple tart back on her plate. "I suppose we'd better prepare for the next set of jumps."

Remy wiped his mouth with his napkin. "Aye, aye, Captain. Ready when you are."

Mara knew he was trying to help her feel better, but she shook her head. "I had no idea a trip to Alfweard would involve all this." She spread her hands wide. "All I want is to find a cure for my magic and help Efram and the others in the lowest realm."

"Plus defeat Bazra, and stop anymore Bellaryss streets from splitting wide open."

"Aye, that too." She smiled ruefully. "And let's not forget about crazy King Roi. I want him behind bars."

Remy paused and seemed to be choosing his words carefully. "These are not easy problems to deal with, and they're not problems you can take on alone. Don't be too proud to ask for help when you need it."

Mara tapped two fingers to the side of her forehead in a mock salute. "Message received, sir." She rose from the cushion and watched as the Bazeerka sprang into action. Before long, Mara climbed onto Seaworthy's broad back and gave the hand signal to move forward.

As the mists enveloped her, Mara's scalp prickled and a tingle ran down her spine. The ground gave way and they were airborne, but Mara recognized the sensation. Bazra was using his mage sense to probe for her whereabouts. She inhaled shakily; Mara wouldn't rest easy until she faced the dark fay king one last time.

CHAPTER 15

Mara gripped Seaworthy's reins and peered around cautiously before the next jump—they'd touched down in an ice-filled valley in dead of winter, which she immediately rejected with a hand signal—and the next jump, landing on a snow-topped mountainside, and the one after that, a brief stop on the banks of a frozen lake. Gradually the prickling and tingling lessened, and her shoulders relaxed. Perhaps she was simply overwrought, totally understandable under the circumstances.

When they touched down on the outskirts of a small village in harvest fall, Mara gave the hand signal to stop. The Bazeerka divvied up their duties and soon horses were munching their oats, while everyone else was gathered around Yelenarra's colorful blankets, sharing meat and potato stew, fresh bread, mugs of hard cider, and pear crisp.

After clearing away all remnants of dinner, the Bazeerka followed Yelenarra's instructions and erected pup tents for each traveler, the women in one row, and the men in another. Yelenarra positioned the two rows of tents so their flaps faced outward, in opposite directions, ensuring an extra measure of privacy. Mara noticed her tent was as far away as possible from Arnesto's tent; they'd wound up on the opposite ends of their respective rows. Mara wondered whether Yelenarra was trying to drive home the point she and Arnesto were no longer friends. The elderly fay did nothing by accident.

Mara decided to go for a solitary stroll and headed away from the village, where most of their group had gone after dinner. She followed a footpath through a copse of amber, gold, teal, and indigo trees, their leaves beginning to turn metallic, a sign they'd be falling to the ground before long. She wandered through the woods until she reached a wide clearing, where some thoughtful fay had conjured a ring of stone benches around a fire pit, the wood laid for lighting.

Mara took a seat and snapped her fingers, whispering, "Turn stick and log to flames so bright. Stop when burning true and right." As usual, nothing happened. She shook her head in disgust, drawing her cape more firmly around her shoulders.

Suddenly, a cheery fire burst forth, and Mara pulled back, glancing around suspiciously. She heard a twig snap. Bolting from the bench, she reached down to withdraw the twin daggers tucked inside her boots.

"There is no need for your blades, Maragold, at least, not yet," said Arnesto wryly.

"Oh." Mara sank back onto the hard stone seat, her heart rate refusing to return to normal. "It's you."

"As you can plainly see." Arnesto sat on a stone bench opposite her. "It is I." He folded his arms and frowned at her. The bright moon above the trees highlighted his wavy hair, which seemed wilder than usual, and bluer, if that were possible.

Arnesto was the last person she'd hoped to encounter

on her walk. Mara stared into the fire. "Did you follow me here?"

"Aye."

She glared at her ex-boyfriend and former trainee, the single most maddening person—fay or human—she'd ever known. "Why now? I've been trying for weeks on end to catch your attention long enough for a good heart-to-heart chat."

Arnesto waved one hand, which Mara noticed had fresh scars across the knuckles. "Is it not apparent?"

"No, it's not apparent," Mara grumped. *Whether we're socializing, working, or simply training together, Arnesto is just so frustrating.*

"Since you dissolved our friendship pledge, this seems like the ideal time for that talk you have been so eager to have."

"That makes no sense," huffed Mara, "and by the way, I 'dissolved' our friendship pledge because of your behavior toward me. It's clear you've lost whatever feelings you once had for me."

Arnesto grimaced, rubbing his chest with two fingers. Mara chalked it up to heartburn. She noticed he'd drunk an extra glass of wine with dinner. "My feelings are complicated, but that is not what I am here to discuss."

Mara rolled her eyes to hide her disappointment. She *wanted* to discuss Arnesto's feelings. Maybe then she could understand how everything could go so wrong so quickly, and all because she discovered she was part elven. "Go on, I'm listening."

"We must be able to work together to resolve the issues with your magic and restore balance in the underworld. My focus right now is on helping Efram and the others cross to the far shore—and also defeating Bazra."

Mara shrugged. "Our goals are aligned; of course we can work together. Although given how much you despise elves, isn't that going to be a problem for you?"

Arnesto sighed. "I do not despise elves, and I certainly do not despise you. I do hold Alfweard partially responsible for my mother's death. However, I also realize my mother was a fay reaper, and her work always involved a certain amount of risk."

He hesitated, and Mara probed further. "You hold someone else responsible, as well, don't you?"

Arnesto's bow-shaped mouth turned down in the corners. "You know me so well, Mara. Too well at times."

"You blame yourself for not being able to fight back when that creature attacked." When Arnesto nodded, Mara shook her head. "Oh, Arnesto, you were a five-year-old boy. What could you have done?"

Arnesto took his time before answering. "Something, I could have done something. I knew my basic defensive spells by then. Instead, I ran."

Mara resisted the urge to skirt around the fire pit, sit next to Arnesto, and grip his hand. Old Mara would have comforted him, but the new, half-elven Mara needed to make sure Arnesto was ready for the battle to come. She needed a strong twelfth-level fay wizard by her side, and not someone reliving the past, wishing for different outcomes. "I'm seeing a pattern here."

"What are you talking about? What pattern?"

"You blame yourself for your mother's death, for Efram's death, and for Bazra obtaining the red sword. You can't see past your own nose long enough to realize there's so much more going on here. Take Yelenarra, for instance."

"What about my aunt?"

"I'm worried about her...but I can't put a finger on why."

"You have concerns about Auntie Yelenarra, all the while your magic is missing, your hometown is splitting apart, you discovered your mother was an elf, and you just broke up with me. Is that an accurate assessment?"

Mara crossed her arms. "Thank you for pointing out the obvious. I'm convinced something's not quite right with Yelenarra, whether you realize it or not."

"Other than her worries about Efram, my aunt is perfectly fine. Besides, she is my concern, not yours. Particularly as the two of you are no longer connected by our friendship pledge."

Mara shook her head. "Nothing's changed between Yelenarra and me. I care deeply for her."

Arnesto's face softened. "I know you do." He leaned forward, toward the flames and Mara seated on the other side. "All I am trying to say is you have enough else to be concerned with at present. It is critical we arrive at Alfweard as soon as possible—that must be your sole focus for now. I am anxious about Efram fading away completely, if we run into any serious delays."

Mara stood up. Despite the fire, she felt suddenly chilled, and the hard stone bench wasn't helping. "I understand my responsibilities, Arnesto. I trust you understand yours, as well."

Arnesto stood and snapped his fingers, putting out the fire. Nothing but charred, blackened ash and bits of wood remained. "Have no qualms on that point. I know what I must do." His traveling mists swirled around him and he winked out, leaving Mara to wend her way back to the tents alone.

MARA KEPT TUGGING the blanket up around her chin, but it seemed to be snagging on something. Her eyes tightly shut, she pulled it up, but her blanket slipped back down toward her feet. Then she heard a familiar clicking sound. "It can't be time to rise. It's still fully dark outside."

Gloria hissed. "Your two ex-boyfriends are fighting, 'man to man,' as Remy calls it, without using magic. I tried to stop them, but they are ignoring me."

Mara flung off her blanket and shoved her feet into her boots. She glanced down; she was wearing a pale green nightgown. She shrugged, tossed her cape around her shoulders, grabbed her reticule, and crawled out of the pup tent. "Where are they?"

"Follow me." Gloria dashed toward the village square. Mara hiked up her nightgown and ran after her griffin, who led her to a darkened alley behind a tavern called Almost The Last Stop. Mara idly wondered where The Last Stop was located.

Half a dozen Bazeerka, in various states of inebriation, were calling out encouragements to Remy and Arnesto, both of whom had their fists up and were squared off against each other. Mara strongly suspected the Bazeerka had laid odds on the winner. *Gambling and drinking, just lovely,* she thought. Then she recalled they were formerly dark fays, and some habits might be more difficult to break than others.

Mara marched to the edge of the fight. Blood dripped from Arnesto's nose and his split bottom lip. Remy looked no better. His right eye was swollen nearly shut and blood dribbled from his mouth to his chin. He spit out something, which Mara thought might be a tooth. "Stop this instant!"

she hollered, but they didn't seem to hear her. She frowned; perhaps Arnesto and Remy had agreed to an enclosed fighting circle, which would magically prevent anyone from interfering.

Har cupped his hands together and shouted, "Go on, now, Laird Remington the Humble, yer doin' jest fine lad!"

Mara yelled in Har's ear, "We need to stop this fight before anyone gets seriously injured."

Har glanced over at Mara and hiccupped. His eyes were slightly out of focus. "Lady Marigold the Merciful," he barked. The other Bazeerka stopped cheering long enough to give Mara clumsy bows. One fay bowed so low he toppled onto the ground, where he began snoring.

At least she had their attention. "Use your magic to open up this fighting circle, please. I need to get inside there." Har and the others stared at her as if not comprehending. She shouted, "That's a direct order!"

"Aye, milady." Har gave her a second, tipsy bow. The Bazeerka raised their hands, mumbled something unintelligible, and clapped twice. A slight breeze ruffled Mara's hair, and the sounds of two men landing blows and grunting became suddenly louder.

Mara charged into the fray and grabbed Remy's fist, which he'd pulled back, ready to pack another punch. She bit down hard on his knuckles, and Remy howled. She ran between the two men and raised her arms, palms outward. "Stop hurting each other! Look at what you're doing!"

"Well he started it!" grumbled Arnesto, swiping his bloody nose with the back of his hand.

"Ye frew da fers' punsch!" lisped Remy.

Mara pointed at his mouth. "Um, you're missing your front teeth. It's not a good look for you, Remy."

Remy clapped his hand over his mouth and mumbled,

"'Nesto, hel' me find da teef! D'ya 'fink Z'namin can 'tuff 'em back in?"

"Did I really do that to you?" Arnesto dropped his fists, a look of alarm passing over his face.

Remy rolled his one good eye and winced. "Yer boxin's bett'r. Now 'thop gawpin' and hel' me find da teef!" He snapped his fingers, and a small fireball materialized in his palm. As a pyro, Remy could conjure fire without casting a spell, a magical gift that he and Mara had put to good use during the war. Of course, Remy being Remy, he'd also been expelled from school multiple times for inappropriately conjuring fire in class.

Arnesto, Har, and the rest of the fays spread out and began looking in the unlikeliest places—under rocks, behind the tavern's shutters, even down the road, in front of the haberdasher's.

Mara scanned the hard-packed dirt of the alley, occasionally leaning over for a closer inspection. "I found them!" She withdrew a handkerchief from her reticule and scooped up Remy's teeth. Twisting the top of the handkerchief, she tied a knot to prevent them from spilling out.

Mara extended the handkerchief to Remy, who stuffed the handkerchief inside his pants pocket. "Here, take them to Zornamayne's tent, and don't be surprised if she is very out of sorts with you"—she glanced at Arnesto, who'd joined them—"with both of you. She's not alone." Mara turned on her heels and headed back toward the tents, hoping to reclaim whatever small measure of sleep remained before dawn.

Remy called out, "Aw, Mawa, dun' be 'fat way. We 'er fightin' o'er yew."

Mara spun around, her violet eyes flashing. "No, you weren't. You both know me well enough to know I hate that sort of thing. You were fighting because you're tired and frustrated and maybe just a little bit scared, too, of the crazy stuff happening in the lower realms, and the chasms appearing in Bellaryss, and finding out I'm part elf, and I can't access my magic. I get it, because I feel the same way. But fighting with each other isn't going to make any of us feel better."

Remy sighed. "Yer right, a'course. Yer al'ays right. 'Fat's whut make 'thit 'tho har' ta..." His voice trailed off.

Mara glanced at Remy, then at Arnesto. "That's what makes it so hard to be in a relationship with me. Fine. But we're stuck together for now, so let's try not to kill each other. We have real enemies who would be happy to do that for us." Mara stomped across the village square, back toward the tents, Gloria keeping pace with her, a silent, comforting presence.

Gloria clicked her beak softly a few times before speaking. "Both boys are foolish in their own ways. Laird Remington finds humor in the most unusual circumstances and can behave inappropriately at times, and Laird Arnestarious believes he is destined for great things while continuing to stumble over his own two boots. But they both care about you."

"Do you think I was too hard on them just now?"

Gloria flapped her wings. "Nay. I am merely reminding you that while neither were model *boyfriends*, particularly Laird Arnestarious, both are very good *friends*, in the human sense of the word."

Mara crept into her tent, tossed aside her cape and reticule, and sat on her bedroll. Gloria padded in after her. "I don't want them fighting because of me. It makes me feel...I don't know...like some prize, an object to be won."

"Aye." Gloria used her front paws to knead a spot at the

foot of Mara's bedroll. "But boys can be stupid where girls are concerned. I raised a passel of them myself. They were quite a handful during their courting days."

Mara pulled off her boots and then slipped under her blanket. "I care about them too, you know. But my feelings are engaged in different ways."

"Laird Remington is like the brother you never had, but Laird Arnestarious, well—"

"Please, let's not talk about Arnesto just now. It's still too fresh." *And too painful.*

"Aye, milady." Gloria nestled against Mara's feet and began purring almost instantly. Mara lay awake a long time, Arnesto's words from the previous evening running through her head: *"You obviously have powerful elven magic but are unable to control it. You are a force to be reckoned with, Mara, but I do not know whether that is a good thing or bad."*

CHAPTER 16

THE SECOND DAY OF TRAVEL PROCEEDED MUCH AS THE FIRST, WITH Mara selecting the best locations and seasons to share a meal and water the horses, while the fays' traveling mists did the real work of advancing them through their itinerary. As before, she routinely dismissed any stopovers in dead of winter, despite the fact they seemed to land on snow-capped mountains and frosty valleys more frequently than the day before. And although fays could conjure anything they might need to stay warm, Mara preferred warmer, gentler seasons.

During the jumps, as the silvery mists swirled about her, obscuring everything except Seaworthy's mane and the tips of his ears, Mara pondered her elven heritage. Did she have any family living in Alfweard? The idea filled her with equal parts excitement and dread. If she discovered elven relatives, would they welcome her despite her human father, or despise her half-breed status? She didn't want to think about rejection from her mother's relations, not on the heels of Arnesto's rejection.

The tingling and prickling anxiety she'd felt the day

before was gone, but Mara knew enough about dark fays to remain vigilant at every stop. She was worried about her friends in Bellaryss, particularly with renewed sightings of King Roi in and about the capital. Roi's Fallow necromancy, combined with Bazra's control of the red sword, could spell even more trouble for her hometown. Mara's head swirled with images of undead monsters crawling up through the cracks in the pavement.

She gripped the reins more tightly and scolded herself; she had to focus on the problems at hand and not borrow trouble. The undead creatures hadn't started swarming Bellaryss *just yet*.

Seaworthy's hooves landed at the grassy edge of a wide meadow filled with sunflowers—the mustard-yellow variety Mara was familiar with, as well as rusty orange, deep purple, and bright crimson—their cheerful blooms waving in the summer breeze. She gave the hand signal to stop and slid off Seaworthy's back as Har sprinted up to take the reins. Although they weren't technically riding their horses, they still sat atop them all day. Mara's legs, thighs, and bottom ached, and the tension between her shoulder blades, which had begun as a small, tight band a few days earlier, had hardened into a painful knot.

She wished for a long soak in a tub but dismissed the idea immediately. The fays could conjure a little hot spring behind the juniper bushes lining one end of the meadow, or fill a large cauldron with warm water, but Mara would never feel comfortable peeling off all her clothes whilst traveling with two ex-boyfriends, Har, and the other male Bazeerka. Curiosity coupled with magical powers might prove too tempting, and Mara's stepmother had taught her girls that modesty was as important as good posture in young women.

Mara spotted Remy and Arnesto chatting amiably as the blankets, dinner utensils, and foodstuffs flew out of saddlebags, landing with precision at the edge of the sunflower meadow. The swelling in Remy's eye was nearly gone, and his front teeth were back in his mouth, courtesy of Zornamayne's remarkable healing skills. Mara shook her head. They behaved as if they'd not engaged in fisticuffs the previous evening. Meanwhile, her heart was battered over Arnesto, and she felt lonely, despite the throng of fays in her midst.

Zornamayne came alongside Mara and hissed softly, "I gave both boys a good ear boxing when they roused me from my sleep last night."

Mara glanced over at the hybrid. "They deserved it. I still can't believe they came to blows like that."

The feline-fay tilted her head, her green cat's eyes assessing Mara. "Why do you find it so surprising?"

"They used to be flat mates in Bellaryss and got along fine. They may not be the best of buddies, but why would they pommel each other?"

Zornamayne's whiskers twitched. "My dear lass, it is a common trait among males, whether human, fay, elven, or hybrid, to fight over a female, particularly when she has not yet chosen."

Mara approached the row of blankets and sat down, so everyone else would follow suit. Zornamayne sat next to her with a small purr of satisfaction when she saw the main course was broiled halibut in a light lemony sauce, with roasted vegetables and chunks of warm, yeasty bread on the side. Mara took a bite of her fish and waited until the rest of their company was eating before asking, "When she has not chosen...what?"

Zornamayne delicately wiped her mouth and whiskers

on a napkin before responding. "Her one true friend and life-mate, of course. Surely you understand that since you've broken your friendship pledge with Arnestarious, you are unattached and therefore, available once again for male suitors?"

Mara groaned. "I'd prefer not to think along those lines, and I certainly don't want anyone fighting because of me."

The feline-fay hybrid waved her paw. "Then consult your heart and in due time, make your choice public. I daresay you know whom it is you truly love."

Mara bit her bottom lip and didn't reply. Zornamayne gave her a shrewd look before returning to her fish dinner.

After the Bazeerka cleared away the remains of dinner and set up the pup tents, they took the horses farther afield, near the bank of a slow-moving stream. Six tasseled seat cushions, arranged in a circle, remained on the grass. Two thick pillar candles, unlit, occupied the center of the circle. Arnesto withdrew Rezebella's journal from the folds of his cape and placed the book between the candles.

Yelenarra said, "It is time we decide which of Rezebella's two paths we shall take in the morning. Please, take a seat." She nodded at Remy, who snapped his fingers, lighting both candles. Mara thought that was a nice touch —the elderly fay could have just as easily lit the candles with a snap of her fingers—but she seemed to want Remy to feel included. Mara wondered how Arnesto felt about that; she glanced over at him, but he was chatting with Katrine, his face in profile.

Mara sat on a cushion between Remy and Zornamayne. Arnesto sat opposite her, with Yelenarra to his right and Katrine to his left. Katrine pointed at Rezebella's journal. "I think we may need to refresh our memories on the two paths before we make our choice."

Zornamayne smoothed her whiskers. "Aye. The past is a wise teacher. Arnestarious, would you please read from the journal?"

"Very well." Arnesto picked up the book and carefully turned each brittle page. "I shall start at this same juncture, on the eve of the second day of Rezebella's travels." Arnesto read aloud in his rich baritone, pausing at times to decipher Rezebella's handwritten entries. He read through the first itinerary, and then the second, closing the journal when he was finished.

Yelenarra shook her head. "I am still unsure which is best. Much of the two itineraries appear very similar, with only slight differences in the number of times Rezebella encountered dead of winter."

Mara nodded at the journal. "Arnesto, would you mind reviewing the sections where Rezebella mentions dead of winter? Let's compare each of the last three days of both itineraries."

Arnesto gently turned the stiff parchment pages until he found what he was looking for. "On the third day in this itinerary, Rezebella encountered dead of winter six times out of thirty-two landings." He flipped farther back in the journal. "And in the other itinerary we are considering, she notates that of her thirty-four landings, seven were in dead of winter." Arnesto glanced at Mara. "Interesting. I had observed the same thing, and Rezebella's journal provides additional proof."

Remy asked, "Proof of what?"

"I noticed we were landing more frequently in dead of winter than we should be," said Mara. "And Rezebella's journal confirms it."

Arnesto added, "I would have expected to traverse through the seven seasons with approximately the same regularity. Statistically speaking, roughly fourteen percent of the time we should touch down in dead of winter." He paused to do some quick math. "However, in the first itinerary, Rezebella experienced dead of winter nineteen percent of the time on her third day, and in the second itinerary, twenty-one percent."

Yelenarra fluttered her hands at the book. "Most intriguing. Please, let us compare the last two days of the travelogue."

Arnesto complied, and they discovered that in both of Rezebella's accounts, she encountered dead of winter with greater frequency on each progressive day of travel. Arnesto held up the journal, "Here, wait a moment, she added a footnote to the second itinerary. Let me read it. 'Not only did I translocate through dead of winter with greater frequency, but I found the season grew increasingly harsher and less hospitable the closer I traveled to my destination.'"

Katrine had been scribbling calculations on a small pad of parchment she'd conjured. "Here, let's run through the numbers for the last two days of Rezebella's travels. In the first itinerary, she landed in dead of winter close to twenty-nine percent of the time; in the second, it was thirty-three percent!"

Remy yawned and glanced toward the tents longingly. "Our choice seems pretty obvious to me—let's take the first route, with fewer stopovers in dead of winter."

Zornamayne gave a soft yowl. "I concur with the lad. It seems logical."

"But why—in either case—would we encounter dead of winter with increasing frequency?" Mara canted her head. "Is it because we are traveling north?"

Arnesto shook his head. "That would be true in Valerra and elsewhere in the human realm, but not in Havynweal.

Here, the seasons are not fixed to a particular geography or physical location."

Mara frowned. This was one of those times when the fay lands made no sense whatsoever, leaving her feeling vaguely unmoored. "Then I'll pose the question differently: why would dead of winter crop up more frequently, if the seasons occur randomly?"

"Ah, but they are not random at all." Arnesto tapped the journal. "Nay, the seasons are shuffling themselves toward some purpose, which is why Rezebella made note of them in her journal."

Remy shrugged. "I'm finding it hard to believe the seasons shuffle themselves. What purpose does it serve for dead of winter to appear more often?"

Katrine ran a hand through her short blue curls. "To discourage travelers from heading to Alfweard."

Mara nodded. "My thoughts exactly. But who is doing the discouraging? Are the seasons shuffling around due to fay magic, or elven?"

Zornamayne picked up her black-tipped tail and stroked it thoughtfully. "An excellent query. Whilst we shall make the trip regardless, it would be wise to discern intentions."

Yelenarra folded her hands in her lap and stared at the journal. "Rezebella was traveling to Alfweard at the elven king's request. I think the elves would have made the route more hospitable for her and not less."

Katrine nodded. "Good point. Here's another theory: the magic may have been in place for so long that no one recalls who did it or why."

Remy clambered to his feet. "On that note, I think I'll turn in. I'm having trouble keeping my eyes open."

"Aye," said Zornamayne, who uncurled her tail and

stood up. "I believe we've settled on the first itinerary?" She paused and the others nodded. "Very well, then I must be off. It is high time for this feline-fay to get some rest. Particularly since two silly boys disturbed my slumber last night."

Remy dropped his head, mumbling his apologies. Arnesto cleared his throat. "I am terribly sorry—"

Zornamayne held up her paw. "No need for further apologies. My only request is that we have no repeat performances whilst we are traveling together." The healer marched toward her tent, her tail flicking in time with her steps. Remy followed a safe distance behind her.

Katrine scuttled around the candles and sat next to Mara, so the two of them were opposite Arnesto and Yelenarra. "I need to say something to the three of you, and this is as good a time as any. I feel partly responsible for the... tension...we're all sensing whenever Mara and Arnesto are in the same vicinity. I'm the one who encouraged Mara to break off the friendship pledge."

Yelenarra gasped. Arnesto's gray eyes flashed with anger. He thrust out his jaw and seemed to be struggling to formulate a sentence. He finally settled on a single word. "Why?"

Katrine waved her hand, causing both candles to flicker. "We're here to help Mara regain her magic because of all she's done for us and because we need her assistance in restoring balance in the lower realms. Your brother's spirit, and so many others, won't last much longer. Plus, there are fissures opening up inside Valerra, further threatening the human realm. We must focus."

Arnesto huffed, "I understand the urgency of the tasks at hand, which have nothing to do with the friendship pledge between Mara and me. Why did you interfere?"

Katrine cut her eyes to Yelenarra, who reached over and gently removed Rezebella's journal from Arnesto. He'd been gripping the book so hard the cover was bending. Yelenarra placed the journal between the candles and patted her nephew's knee. "As you well know, strong emotions—such as those between young couples with unresolved feelings—interfere with the flow of magic. Whilst I do not agree with Katrinareus's advice, I do understand her intent."

Mara's stomach roiled inside her. Valerrans would never have such a frank conversation about someone else's love life right under her nose. Fays could be so mystifying, all secretive one moment, and then entirely candid the next. "Katrine was trying to help, so there is no need to be angry with her, Arnesto." Mara's voice started to waver. She paused to gain control again. "It wasn't Katrine who hurt me with unkind words and long absences. It was you."

Mara stood up abruptly, whispered, "Goodnight," and hurried away. She sniffed and wiped a tear that escaped down her cheek. *I refuse to show any weakness—not in front of the rest of the group—and definitely not in front of Arnesto. I won't allow him to hurt me again.*

CHAPTER 17

MARA LED THE GROUP THROUGH THE REMAINDER OF REZEBELLA'S itinerary without incident, and without speaking to Arnesto unless absolutely necessary, and then only to reply "aye" or "nay."

On the thirty-fourth jump of their fifth travel day, Mara paused to allow the traveling mists to clear. They'd landed on a wind-blown, snow-capped hill in dead of winter. As her cape magically gained a fur lining, and thick woolen gloves appeared on her hands, she pulled up her hood and peered into the valley below. She turned in her saddle and shouted above the wind, "I see something glimmering faintly on the horizon. Could that be the Unseasonable Sea?"

Katrine squinted in the direction Mara was pointing. "I think you're right. We should make it in one final jump, precisely as Rezebella had indicated in her notes."

Mara nodded and gave the hand signal to move forward. They touched down on hard-packed snow, which Mara assumed would have been sandy beach if they'd landed in one of the warmer seasons. Instead, a frosty gray sea stretched out before them. Large chunks of ice bobbed and spun in the churning waves. An ugly boat, covered with painted images of gargoyles, goblins, and sea monsters, sat moored at the pier. Sharp spikes jutted out from its sides, prow, and stern, giving the boat a sinister appearance. Mara thought the ship might have been iced into the harbor but spotted men running about on the ship's deck, hoisting enormous red sails in the stiff breeze. Her heart sank at the prospect of crossing the water on such a strange-looking conveyance, but she'd learned to not judge anything involving magic by its outward form.

Mara held up her hand, and Har blew on his horn. Before dismounting, she leaned over and patted Seaworthy's neck. "Thank you for your patience throughout this trip. I've never led an expedition like this before, and I'm glad I could travel with such a lovely horse."

Seaworthy's ears flicked back and then stood straight up. He turned his head and gave her a wink. "You are quite a cheeky fellow, aren't you?" Seaworthy pulled back his lips in a toothy grin as Mara dismounted. She half-expected Seaworthy to say something, but the horse chose not to speak, unlike her vocal, opinionated griffin.

Gloria landed with a squawk next to Mara. "I had hoped we might be sailing on a proper vessel and not something so foreboding."

"It does have a scary exterior, but I suppose we must be grateful for what we have."

Gloria sniffed. "I suppose."

Mara watched as Har directed the Bazeerka to unload their bags and supplies, and transport them onto the ugly ship. In under a minute, everything that should have been loaded was onboard the ship, and Har approached Mara and the rest of their group. He removed his green top hat.

"The admiral awaits ye. May yer quest go as expected, and may the wind be always in yer faces."

Mara pursed her lips. She had no idea how the quest ought to go, but she expected complications. And if the wind was always in one's face, wouldn't that make for a more arduous journey? Perhaps it was the equivalent of a Bazeerka blessing. She realized Har was waiting for her reply. "Thank you for all of your assistance throughout the trip. Please travel safely, and, er, may the wind be always in your face."

Har sketched a low bow and returned to the horses. He patted Seaworthy's neck before mounting him, blew once on his horn, and disappeared, along with the remaining horses and their Bazeerka riders, into the mists. Katrine shook her head. "A most peculiar group of fays."

"But entirely trustworthy, despite their reputation," pointed out Yelenarra. "And now it is time for us to depart, as well. We must be off before sundown."

"What happens at sundown?" asked Remy.

"Rezebella never stayed long enough to find out," replied Arnesto.

"And neither shall we." Yelenarra's voice had a slight tremor. Mara had no doubts about the octogenarian's bravery. Perhaps Yelenarra was growing more concerned about Efram with each passing day, or perhaps the elderly fay was simply fatigued. Mara could sympathize; she was exhausted after five days of travel by fay mist, her quasi-leadership of the group, and her breakup with Arnesto.

Mara scanned the sky. "What about Xenestra?"

Katrine was already heading toward the ship, which was considerably larger than Mara had first realized. The fay chief called over her shoulder, "Xenestra planned to arrive before us. She should be onboard by now."

Mara said, "I still find it odd that a dragon wouldn't simply fly across the sea."

"Understandable." Yelenarra came alongside her and looped her arm through Mara's. "However, according to the dragon histories, none have ever crossed the Unseasonable Sea by air. And while there are no written records of any dragon visiting the Alfweard Archives, there are several oral traditions involving one of Xenestra's ancestors. Xenestra is determined to make the trip, study in the archives, and publish her research when she returns. The Dragon Mage no doubt encouraged her to travel by boat, although the ship's crew will have to remove half the cabins to accommodate her comfortably."

"I wonder whether the crew will be able to accommodate her appetite, as well."

Yelenarra laughed in her tinkling way. "They shall be fishing almost as much as sailing as we cross the sea."

They had no more time for conversation, as they arrived at the gangplank and were greeted by a wide man with a long platinum beard and hair to match. Both hair and beard were plaited in numerous small, white-blond braids and finished with colored beads that clicked when he walked. He wore a floppy yellow fedora, tied under his chin, and a long yellow mackintosh.

The admiral shouted to be heard above his noisy crew, preparing for departure. "Welcome to Nowhere, the finest ship on the Unseasonable Sea. Me name's Admiral Adley. Who's the leader of this here endeavor?"

Yelenarra gave Mara a gentle tap on the shoulder, so she stepped forward. "I am, sir."

The admiral drew his bushy eyebrows together and stared. "State yer purpose."

"I seek an audience with the elven king," said Mara,

deciding the admiral didn't need to know the details of her magical problems.

Adley threw back his head and laughed so loudly most of his crew paused to stare at Mara. She heard them muttering, "mixed blood," "half breed," or "part elf, part stupid."

Mara lifted her chin. "Will you transport us or must we wait for the next ship?" She was bluffing and had no idea whether there was a next ship. Plus, she knew Yelenarra didn't want to stay on shore past sundown.

The man stopped laughing as suddenly as he'd begun. "No need to get your knickers all twisted, lass. 'Course we'll transport ye. Yer dragon's already paid yer fares and is resting nicely below deck. Wouldn't want to disturb the draconic scholar, now would we?"

Mara was surprised to hear Xenestra referred to as a scholar by the admiral, and even more surprised the dragon had paid their fares. Mara had no idea what was involved and would have to thank her later for the kindness. "In that case, please tell us what we can expect on this voyage— how long it will take, where are our accommodations, and what are the mealtimes." She added that last part for Remy's sake.

Adley started to chortle again, but Mara put her hands on her hips and locked eyes with the man. "If you laugh one more time at my expense, I shall ask for our fares to be returned, and you can trust me on this: our dragon will ensure you comply."

The old seaman grunted, "There's no need to be high-handed."

"There's no need to be ill-mannered," Mara replied sharply. The crew had paused again, watching the exchange with interest.

The admiral waved his hand at the sailors, who turned back to their tasks, hoisting the red sails and unhooking cables from the pylons on the solitary pier. "The crossing will take most of a day, if the repairs hold and the sea monsters ain't too frisky."

"What sea monsters?" Remy's voice squeaked.

"What repairs?" frowned Katrine.

Adley gave a shrug, which Mara found far too casual for the admiral of a ship. "The monsters are actually giant sea creatures that snack on jest about anything, including boats—that's why we have all them pikes sticking outta the ship, to discourage 'em—and why we've painted the ship to look like we're ferrying creatures on board."

"You are elves; would not your spells keep you safe?" asked Arnesto.

"They do—however, the sea contains strong counter-spells that favor creatures of the deep."

"And the repairs?" Katrine folded her arms.

Adley pointed at the main sail. "The mast came down in our last crossing and needs to be replaced when we reach port. And afore ye ask, 'tis our magic that's keepin' the whole thang together, but those same counterspells that favor sea creatures also wreak havoc on wood and metal." The admiral scratched his beard, causing the beads to click together. "We sailors have another name fer the Unseason-able Sea."

"What's the other name?" asked Remy, who looked peaky. Like Mara, he suffered from seasickness.

"The Unreasonable Sea," said the admiral.

Mara stifled a sigh and vowed to eat as little as possible until she reached dry land. She reminded Adley about her other query regarding meal times and accommodations.

"Ye shall join us in the galley fer meals. Timing is catch-as-catch-can, gen'rally at sunup, midday, and sundown. Fish—smoked, stewed, steamed, or pickled—is on the menu. As fer yer quarters, follow Telly." Adley barked at a slender lad, also attired in a bright yellow fedora and mackintosh.

Telly saluted his admiral and then turned to Mara and the group. "Follow me an' please watch yer step." He guided them below deck to the cabins, each fitted with a bunk bed, washbasin, small shelf, one candle, and two hooks. Their saddlebags were piled into one of the rooms, and Telly quickly sorted them out. Arnesto and Remy had no choice but to room together, although Mara noticed they seemed to have reached an accord. She and Katrine took one cabin, Yelenarra and Zornamayne the other, and Farleigh went to stay with "his dragon friend."

Telly took them to the galley, where he served them pickled herring, dry crackers, and dark ale, the equivalent of "high tea on the Unseasonable Sea," as he called it. After Telly left, the group split up to their separate cabins.

Katrine noticed Mara covering her mouth to hide a yawn. "Why don't you lie down, and try to get some rest while you can? I have a feeling this is going to be a bumpy ride."

Mara nodded. "Good advice. What do you want, bottom or top?"

Katrine pointed to the bottom bunk and grinned. "Elders always take the bottom. 'Tis a shorter fall."

"Very funny." Mara hung her cape on one of the hooks, pulled off her boots, and climbed to the top, careful not to smack her head on the low ceiling. Gloria flapped her wings, flew up to join her, and curled up at her feet. Mara's eyes fluttered closed, and she drifted to sleep, only to be awakened by Gloria's squawking and a noisy foghorn blaring above deck.

Mara found herself airborne as the ship pitched from side to side. She landed on top of Katrine, who'd tumbled from her bunk. They untangled themselves but fell back to the floorboards as the ship rolled again. Mara crawled over the washbasin, her stomach already heaving as much as Nowhere, which she decided was an apt name for the boat. They were getting nowhere fast—and she'd rather be anywhere else—instead of bent over a basin on a rocking ship, sailing through an unreasonable sea.

CHAPTER 18

Mara rinsed out her mouth with Katrine's minty mouthwash and washed her face one more time. Patting her cheeks dry, she said, "I think I can walk now without losing my stomach."

"I don't think there's anything left in your poor stomach. When you said you got seasick, I thought you meant a bit queasy." Katrine pulled both their capes from the hooks and handed the blue cape to Mara. "Everyone else, except for Xenestra, is already above deck with our bags. I'll let Xenestra know you're ready to leave—she preferred to wait in her cabin until it was time to go. She's not a fan of extreme cold."

"Wise dragon." Mara smiled. She was starting to feel almost human again, or rather, elven-human—she'd have to get used to thinking of herself as part elf. Mara adjusted her cape and followed Katrine up the steps, her pulse quickening with excitement. *I'm finally here, in Alfweard, about to see the elven king!*

They exited the ship, which looked like an exploding catapult had hit its masts and rigging, the sails hanging torn and ragged, the main mast gone. Yelenarra surveyed the damage. "It appears Admiral Adley was not exaggerating about the peculiarities of the Unseasonable Sea."

"Or the amount of fish served with every meal," grumbled Remy.

Telly helped them load their bags onto Xenestra's spiky tail and wished them well. Xenestra peered down at Mara and bleated, "Maragold, please mount first and climb up behind my shoulder blades. I want an extra pair of eyes to help me locate the elven king's enclave. I am simply not accustomed to this much snow and ice. Everything looks frosty and white, and the afternoon sun is reflecting from every surface."

Mara gripped the sharp spinal plates on Xenestra's back, careful not to cut her hand, and hauled herself up. She settled into the small indentation between the dragon's shoulders. As Mara waited for everyone else to climb onto the dragon's shiny, dark green back, she said, "Thank you for paying our fares. It was totally unexpected and very kind. How can I ever repay you?"

"You are most welcome, Maragold, and there is no need for repayment. I am honored to be included in this novel expedition. Besides, I have been paring down my hoard. I started running out of room in my nest and brought some of my castoffs along, precisely for this purpose. I offered the admiral dinnerware for twenty-four—two dozen silver plates, bowls, mugs, and matching flatware—which he readily accepted as payment. Now, the admiral and his crew shall be eating their delicious fish recipes on silver plates, instead of battered tin."

"Oh, I'm glad to hear it...and thank you again for your generosity." Mara strongly suspected Adley would melt down the silver dinnerware, but she kept that to herself.

She confirmed everyone was seated, even Gloria, who had flown up and was tucked in front of Mara. Cupping her hands, Mara called out, "Prepare for departure, and hang tight!"

Xenestra spread her massive green, gold, and teal wings and ran across the snow-covered ground. The moment of liftoff, when Mara felt the air surge beneath the dragon's wings and they soared upward, filled her bruised heart with joy. Whatever happened next, with the elven king and with Arnesto, Mara had no regrets about making this trip. She hoped, however, she might find another means home, other than a return trip on the Unseasonable Sea.

As Xenestra mounted into the blue sky, Mara brought her free hand up to shield her eyes from the sun's glare. All she could see were white-capped mountains and valleys buried in huge drifts of snow. She scanned the horizon, searching for a speck of something different, an outpost, a building, or a stronghold.

Rezebella's various itineraries ended with her ship docking in port, so Mara had no indication how much farther they needed to travel. Yelenarra believed the king would have sent someone to accompany Rezebella to the palace, which the fay reaper didn't record in her journal out of respect for elven privacy customs.

"There! I think I see an outpost!" shouted Mara. "Bank starboard."

Xenestra turned right, gliding lower on an air current for a closer inspection. "Look," cried the dragon, "that must be the castle on top of that mountain."

"Aye," called Mara. "However, I believe we must first present ourselves to the guardhouse, about a third of the way up the mountain."

Xenestra agreed and continued her descent, soaring

over a snow-covered village, each miniature building so perfectly charming Mara thought they'd flown inside a snow globe. Mara spotted a bakery, a pub, two dress shops, a haberdashers, and a toyshop, all of which she'd enjoy exploring later.

The palace, made of pale gray stone and glass, with at least a dozen towers thrusting into the sky, teetered on the mountaintop overlooking the village. Mara couldn't imagine how the castle had been constructed, but then she reminded herself it was the home of the elven king, so plenty of magic must have been involved. Still, she thought it looked more like an illustration she'd seen in one of her old storybooks, than an actual place where people lived. She didn't even see any obvious roads leading from the village to the palace. Did the elves translocate everything up to that monstrous peak?

Xenestra landed in a spray of snow and ice, sliding to a stop in front of the guardhouse. The village was spread out below them, clinging to the base of the mountain. Gloria flew to the frosty ground, while Mara and the others descended down Xenestra's tail and jumped off, landing on the hard-packed snow. Mara inspected the guardhouse, knitting her brows. In contrast to the lovely mountain village, the elven king's guardhouse was uninviting, bordering on hostile. Square, squat, and constructed from dark gray stones, it sat like an ugly blemish on an otherwise pristine surface. Long icicles hung from its roof, which sloped over the windows and doors, obscuring the view inside the building.

A towering elf about Katrine's age, with a long platinum braid, trim beard, and dark violet eyes, emerged from the guardhouse accompanied by a younger, scowling elf. Both elves wore dappled capes in shades of white, silver, and gray that Mara figured was their version of camouflage. Their tunics and trousers were made of the same material, and hanging from their belts were a long sword, a short sword, and various-sized daggers, tucked into silver scabbards. Each man had slung two coils of silvery reaping rope across their shoulders, crisscrossing their chests. The tall elf introduced himself as the captain of the guard and asked them to state their business.

Mara took a deep breath, stepped forward, and said, "We have traveled from Havynweal for several purposes. In my case, I have come to request an audience with the elven king because—"

Both elves burst out laughing, and Mara compressed her lips, trying to keep her temper in check. The captain said, "Out of the question. No one sees the king. Now be gone, all of you. Alfweard does not recognize any of you, nor your right to set foot on our snow." He brought his hand to the hilt of his long sword and rested it there.

Xenestra stomped her feet, causing the icicles hanging over the front of the guardhouse to crash to the ground. The captain raised one white-blond eyebrow. "You broke my icicles."

Xenestra emitted two small puffs of smoke from her nostrils. Mara suspected she was making an effort to be civil and not blast the elf with a fireball. "I do apologize, sir. However, I am a credentialed draconic scholar who wishes to conduct historical research in your famed archives. This is a grave disappointment indeed."

The captain of the guard stared up at Xenestra as if assessing her sincerity. He rubbed his blond beard and took his time replying. "Perhaps the king might permit a draconic scholar access to his archives. Norris, what do you think?"

Norris, the other guard, appeared to be in his mid-twenties, with a pointy beard and permanent glower. He shrugged. "I can see no harm in a scholarly visit, Captain." He and the captain seemed to be the only guards on duty. Mara wondered whether they'd arrived on some elven holiday. The guardhouse had a distinctly empty feel to it, as if inhabited more by ghosts than elves.

Zornamayne yowled to draw the captain's attention. When he glanced her way, she gave him an elaborate bow, her long veils swishing around her legs. "Sir, I am a rare species, a feline-fay hybrid and master healer. I wish to learn more about elven healing techniques."

Katrine poked Arnesto in the shoulder. He picked up her cue. Clearing his throat, he gave a deep bow. "And I am a twelfth-level fay wizard with elemental magic capabilities. I wish to study how elven mages manipulate the elements."

One by one, the entire group shared their reasons for wanting to study in the king's archives: Remy to study baking techniques, Katrine to research elven parliamentary proceedings, and Yelenarra to learn more about elven architecture. Only Farleigh and Mara remained.

The wolf-man crossbreed gave a small yip, dropped to all fours, and spun around in a circle three times before sitting on his haunches. His antics brought a smile to the guards' faces. Clearly they had a soft spot for canine types.

The captain turned to Mara with a furrowed brow. "What brings you to request an audience with the king? You must know half-breeds are unwelcome here."

So he knows I'm part elven, and he's biased against anyone with mixed bloodlines. My week just keeps getting better. Mara pulled up her shoulders and took two more steps forward, to demonstrate she was not afraid of either the elven king or his towering captain. "As you correctly surmised, sir, I am half-elven. My mother was from Alfweard. I wish to trace my roots and uncover the reason my magic has stopped working."

The captain folded his arms across his chest, his silver ropes glittering in the sunshine, and glared down at her. "You used the past tense. Does your mother no longer walk among the living?"

Mara shook her head. "Nay, sir. My mother passed into the lower realms fourteen years ago."

The captain blinked slowly a few times and glanced skyward, as if thinking. His voice sounded like sandpaper on wood as he rasped, "And your human father? Was he not a mage? Could he not assist you now?"

"My father is an accomplished Serving Mage. However, he evacuated from Bellaryss with his second wife when our capital was attacked. I have not seen him since."

The captain glared at Mara, as if blaming her for her father's absence. "How old are you?"

"Eighteen."

Norris sniffed. "Old enough to solve your own problems and not bother the king."

"I daresay you are correct, Norris."

Mara hated it when people, especially men, spoke about her as if she wasn't standing before them. "But sir, I have traveled so far. I am seeking answers—"

"Silence!" boomed the captain. "The king permits no visitors to his palace, conducts no private audiences, and does not care how far one has traveled to Alfweard. He does, however, respect scholarly research." Ignoring Mara, the captain addressed the rest of the group over her head. "If you would kindly wait here, I will send Norris to the palace to explain the merits of your various research requests to the head librarian."

Norris's jaw dropped. Perhaps he hadn't expected the captain to be so accommodating to the odd assortment of scholarly visitors. However, Mara was not about to go quietly, not when so much was at stake. She refrained from stomping her feet like Xenestra. Instead, she put her hands on her hips and shouted in her loudest voice, "I will *not* be silenced, sir! Much is at stake in Bellaryss, where the streets are caving in due to activities below—and in the realms of the dead, where the Choirmaster has asked for my help. Good spirits are fading to nothing, and the dark fay king must be defeated once for all. I own one of the Swords of Five, and I must regain my magical connection to the sword!"

The captain of the guard reared back, his violet eyes narrowing at Mara. "*You* own one of the ensorcelled swords?"

"Aye."

Norris turned to his captain. "But how can this be? And only half elven at that?"

Zornamayne had suggested Mara wear the sword when they docked, if for no other reason than as a defensive weapon. Now Mara was glad she'd strapped the scabbard around her waist.

The older guard pointed to her sword. "Show me."

Mara gripped the hilt of her sword and slowly withdrew it, praying the blade would react to her touch—even a few flashes would do—anything to demonstrate to the overbearing captain she was the rightful owner of the sword. She held the sword above her head, pointing to the crystal-clear sky.

The blade's hieroglyphs pulsed blue, shining brightly for several moments before blinking on and off, and then finally going out. Mara blew a puff of air through her lips.

"It's been like this since I sealed Bazra into the lowest realm."

Norris shook his head. "Impossible. No half-breed could wield such power in the realms of the dead. Besides, that sword barely lights up for you, which means it's stolen. You are a liar and a thief."

Mara took several deep breaths, struggling to keep her temper in check, and re-sheathed her sword. "I did not travel so far to be insulted by an ignorant, prejudiced elf." She'd have to find another means of regaining control of her magic and her sword. Clearly, the elves were useless.

Remy put a hand on Mara's left shoulder. "I have known Mara all my life, and I can assure you, she never lies. I was there when the blue sword chose her, and I was one of many she rescued from the dark fay king's tower."

Arnesto stepped forward and stood on Mara's right. "Maragold is the rightful owner of the blue sword, and she is the one who sealed Bazra into the lowest realm. Whilst all of us have scholarly reasons for accessing the archives, our primary purpose for coming to Alfweard is to seek your king's help in restoring Maragold's magic. Without her and her blue sword, I fear the underworld will grow increasingly unstable."

The captain glanced at Xenestra. "Is this true, dragon?"

Xenestra bleated, "Aye. The lass owns the blue sword, and she imprisoned the dark fay king in the realms of the dead." The rest of their group nodded in agreement. Xenestra added in a draconic whisper, loud enough to wake the undead, "And I also wish to conduct research in your archives."

The older elf ignored the last part of the dragon's statement and pointed at Mara's scabbard. "May I?"

Mara's eyebrows peaked, surprised at the request. She

debated handing over the blade, but decided she had nothing more to lose at this point. "Aye, sir." Mara withdrew her sword and handed it, hilt first, to the captain.

The elf grasped the jeweled hilt firmly and waited. Nothing happened; the blade remained a dull gray. He handed the sword to Norris, who eagerly grabbed the hilt and raised the sword halfway to the sky. The younger elf cried out in pain, clasping his gloved hand as the sword clattered onto the snow-packed ground. Mara bit her bottom lip to prevent herself from smirking.

The captain nodded at the sword lying on the frozen ground. "We have validated your claim of ownership. Perhaps you ought to retrieve it."

As Mara picked up her sword, she noticed the blade flared up a bit brighter and sparkled a bit longer before fizzling out again. She re-sheathed it, puzzling over the subtle change.

"You mentioned the Choirmaster herself has requested your aid. When was this?" asked the captain.

Mara glanced at Arnesto. "It's been a week, hasn't it?"

Arnesto nodded and described their encounter with the Choirmaster.

"And have you visited the lower realms since then?" asked the captain.

Mara and Arnesto shook their heads. Yelenarra asked in a low voice, "Has anything transpired, sir? My late nephew is one of those spirits in danger of fading to nothing. Further, one of Bazra's creatures killed my sister some years ago—I have a vested interest in the outcome."

"As do we all," said Katrine. The captain's pale eyebrows arched in surprise when she introduced herself as Chief of the Fay Nation. "We must end the acrimony between fays and elves and work together to defend all the realms—fay, elven, and human. And to dispatch Bazra for good, we will need Mara's magic and blue sword to be functioning again."

Yelenarra stared at the captain. "Sir, you have not answered my question."

The elven captain waved at the guardhouse, which expanded to nearly four times its original size as they watched, the doorway growing wide enough and tall enough to accommodate everyone in their party, including Xenestra. "Let us repair inside, out of the wind, to continue this conversation." He turned to Norris. "Please make all necessary accommodations for our visitors to access the archives."

"But, Phineas—"

The captain gave the younger guard a withering glare. Norris's scowl deepened as he saluted his superior officer. "Aye, sir, as you wish."

Phineas watched as Norris stretched out both hands, his palms open to the sky. He disappeared on a puff of white mist that froze instantly, tiny icicles tinkling to the ground in his wake.

CHAPTER 19

THE CAPTAIN TURNED BACK TO HIS GUESTS AND USHERED EVERYONE inside a cavernous white room with a domed ceiling. Xenestra pulled back her lips in a toothy grin when she saw the elf had conjured a set of large, silver nesting cushions at one end of a long, shiny black table that was set for tea. "Thank you, sir. I was growing somewhat chilled on this windy hillside."

The captain nodded. "I understand dragons prefer the warmer climes."

"That is most certainly true. And this dragon is no exception." Xenestra pummeled the cushions with her hind legs and settled in with a happy sigh. Farleigh nestled next to next to her, his tail wagging.

Phineas stood at the head of the table and waited until everyone else was seated before lowering himself onto a cushion. He lifted his right hand, and steaming pots of tea and platters of scones, sandwiches, and small cakes floated into the room and whisked about the table. The captain magically served all the guests with a few wags of his finger and then settled the teapots and platters on the table for his guests to help themselves to seconds.

Mara noticed Remy, seated to her right, pulled one of the platters a bit closer to his plate. She refrained from an eye roll. Remy did have a troll ancestor, after all. She'd have to make allowances for his sizable appetite. Yelenarra sat between Mara and the elven captain, with Katrine, Arnesto, and Zornamayne seated across from them. Yelenarra sighed softly; Mara gave the elderly fay's hand a sympathetic squeeze. She was as impatient as Yelenarra for the captain's reply about circumstances in the underworld.

Phineas addressed Yelenarra, his voice far gentler than when he'd addressed Mara. "The lower realms grow more chaotic with each passing of the moon, but no spirits have faded from view as yet." He spoke to the group, but his eyes bored into Mara's. "However, even if this young woman's magic is fully repaired, she will not be powerful enough—despite assistance from the rest of you—to restore balance in the realms of the dead."

Mara set her cup down when the captain referred to her once again in the third person. At least he hadn't called her a half-breed, which she supposed was an improvement, but not much. On the other hand, she had more important things to worry about than rude elves. "Then what more do we need to defeat the dark fay king?"

"You will need all six ensorcelled swords and their owners, working in tandem, to take back the lower realms. And you will need as many elves as I am able to muster."

"*Six* swords? You are mistaken, Captain. There are only five," said Katrine, who had first told Mara the legend of the Swords of Five.

Phineas shook his head. "Your fay historians have gotten it all wrong. There were six swords in the beginning;

all of them forged by a giant, spelled by *elven* dust from the forest floor, and melded with young Sollara's fay magic. The elves and fays had agreed to divide the remarkable weapons evenly between them. However, the fays got greedy"—here he gave a short bow from his shoulders—"and decided to snatch up an extra two swords for themselves."

The captain stood up and withdrew his long sword from his scabbard. His blade flared into orange flames, from hilt to pointy tip. He re-sheathed the fiery weapon and took his seat once again. "As you can plainly see, I carry one of the Swords of *Six*."

Mara wasn't sure which version of the legend was the truth, and a millennium or more afterward, it probably no longer mattered. Then she recalled how elves had suddenly popped up in Yelenarra's triptych, and the lone figure wielding a sixth, orange sword in the painting's background. Perhaps the rude elven captain had his facts straight after all. No one knew how the other five swords wound up at the Valerran Museum, hidden in plain sight for centuries. Katrine believed a very wise fay seer had stashed away the weapons until they would be needed.

"Why do you wield one of the swords intended for your king?" asked Mara.

Phineas took a sip of tea before answering. "The captain of the elven guard is the king's representative and wields the blade in his place." Mara had a feeling he was holding something back, but she couldn't very well interrogate him, not when she needed his help.

Remy frowned, a half-eaten sandwich in his right hand. "Pardon my confusion, sir, but did you say we'll need *all* the ensorcelled swords—and their owners—in order to patch up things in the lower realms?"

"Aye, we need everyone who wields one of the Swords of Six."

"That is going to be difficult, since three of the swords and their owners are in Faynwood," said Remy.

"And Bazra has the last sword, the red one," added Arnesto.

"Aye, I know about the red sword. The lower realms have been a disaster ever since." Phineas leaned forward, pinning Arnesto with a hard stare. "How did that dark fay scoundrel come to possess such a valuable weapon?"

Arnesto stared down at his plate for a moment and then looked directly at the captain. "Bazra sent his creatures to the human realm to capture me and the red sword. If not for Maragold, I would still be imprisoned in the lower realms. She rescued me and expended her magic in the process."

Phineas rubbed his white-blond beard. His eyes roved around the table, finally coming to rest on Mara. "Allow me to summarize the situation as I understand it," he drawled. "You traveled from Havynweal to Alfweard, ostensibly to visit our remarkable archives, but truly to seek aid for a half-elven girl in the hopes both her magic and her sword would be restored to full strength. And from here, you were planning on descending into the lower realms to take on Bazra and his undead creatures, steal back the red sword, and help the Choirmaster direct the good spirits once more. Oh, let's not forget you were also hoping all this bravery would no doubt reverse the chasms appearing in the human realm. You are fools. Brave fools, no doubt, but fools nonetheless."

Mara clenched her jaw, her hands curling into fists on the tabletop. She waited until the sarcastic captain of the guard paused to take another bite of his sandwich. "Thank you for summarizing the situation so succinctly, Captain," she said, her tone clipped. "However, you failed to mention one vital fact."

The captain nodded. "Please enlighten me."

"If the elven reapers had been doing their jobs, Bazra wouldn't be controlling the realms of the dead. This 'situation' would be very different."

Phineas grimaced and tossed the remainder of his sandwich onto his plate. *Good,* thought Mara. *I've struck a nerve.*

Katrine cleared her throat. "Mara makes a good point, Captain. While some fays are reapers by choice and talent, we are not responsible for overseeing the lower realms—they are under Alfweard's jurisdiction. Elves are the guardians of the portals separating the living realms from the dead. But we saw no elven villagers as we flew overhead, and just you and Norris appear to be manning this station. What has happened here in Alfweard? Where is everyone?"

"You wish to know what is happening?" Roared the captain, jumping up from the table. He held his hands in front of him, cupping his palms. "See for yourselves!" The flickering image of a miniature battle scene appeared between his hands. Elven reapers fought against a pack of undead creatures in the lower realms. A sudden flash of light blinded the elves, who were overpowered by the bristly creatures. Many reapers lay sprawled on the ground.

"At the precise moment Bazra and the red sword landed in the lowest, last realm, elven magic wavered," cried Phineas. "I was in the midst of a reaping when my fiery sword momentarily sputtered out, and I barely escaped with my life. I lost many good reapers—good friends, that day."

Yelenarra said softly, "I am sorry for your losses,

Captain. I am no stranger to grief, myself. But where are the other elves to assist you? We have encountered no one else, other than you and Norris."

The captain waved his hand at the mountains beyond the walls of the guardhouse. "Elves, like fays, were once as numerous as the stars above. But infighting amongst rival lords, and the ever-present dangers of reaping in the lower realms, have taken their toll. Our numbers have dwindled to less than a thousand, a third of whom are children.

Zornamayne gasped. "Less than *a thousand elves*? Why have you not asked for assistance from the fays?"

"Or from Serving mages in Valerra and Faynwood?" added Mara. "Many would be willing to help."

"Elves never ask for help!" snapped Phineas, his violet eyes flashing.

"It's high time you did, sir." Katrine nodded curtly, her short blue curls bouncing. "I'm truly sorry for your losses, and I extend the condolences of the entire Fay Nation. However your elven pride, which has prevented you from seeking help, has created a crisis for all peoples and species."

"Do you not think I know this? The elves have failed for the first time in our glorious history." Phineas dropped his head to his chest, his anger deflating as suddenly as it had flared.

Mara found herself starting to feel sorry for the overly proud man, until she remembered his rude "half-breed" comments. "With your population dwindling and your problems guarding the underworld, why are you so quick to insult my mixed heritage? Surely there are others like me. Why not encourage inward migration from anyone with elven ancestry and train them to help safeguard the portals?"

"Mixed bloods are not welcome," sniffed Phineas.

"Why?" Mara narrowed her eyes. "Until I expended my magic during my last mission, I was as fully capable as any other mage."

Remy's plate still had uneaten teacakes, but he tossed his napkin onto the table and stood up. He reached his hand down toward Mara. "Let's go, Mara. The captain's not going to help, and I'll not sit here any longer while he hurts you." Mara gave him her hand and rose as gracefully as she could from the silver floor cushion, grateful for Remy's loyalty, which overrode even his appetite. Gloria clicked her beak and trotted behind Mara.

Arnesto jumped up and skirted around the glossy black table to join them. Mara assumed he didn't want to be outdone by Remy's gallantry. "Remy is quite right. There is no need for you to listen to any more insults. The elves are losing much more than they realize this day. We shall find a cure for your magic elsewhere, I promise."

At Arnesto's words, "*we* shall find a cure," Mara's heart lurched. He promised to help her, despite everything they'd said and not said over the past week. They still had a lot to resolve, but maybe, just maybe, if the elven king had agreed to an audience—and if Arnesto had asked her to renew their friendship pledge—she might have asked the king's permission to become formally betrothed. All of that was best left for another day to sort through. For now, she needed to retain whatever shred of dignity she had remaining and depart from Alfweard. Mara looped her arms through Remy's on her right and Arnesto's on her left, and marched past Phineas without a backward glance.

Everyone else silently rose from the table and followed them out of the guardhouse. Xenestra was the last to leave. "I shall not require access to your king's archives after all,

Captain. Thank you for tea." Mara wanted to hug the giant dragon, who trundled away from her love of research to demonstrate solidarity.

They had trudged about halfway down the main street of the quiet, deserted village, their boots crunching on the snow, when Phineas translocated in front of them, icicles from his frosty traveling mists clinging to his face, beard, and reaping ropes. He planted himself in front of Mara. "I know why your magic has faltered."

Mara drew herself up to her full height, but she still had to bend her neck to look up at the captain. "I don't need you to tell me why. I expended too much magic during my battle with Bazra and his necromancers in the lower realms. It is a common disorder among Serving mages."

"It may be common among human mages, but it never happens to elves."

Mara crossed her arms and glared at the towering elf. "Since I'm only half-elven, I suppose you're going to blame my weaker human nature for my malady."

Phineas crossed his arms and glowered at her. He growled, "Your magic is failing because of your elven nature, not human. You will not find a cure elsewhere."

Zornamayne yowled, "Sir, please explain. As Maragold's healer, I must understand the particulars in order to help my patient."

Phineas uncrossed his arms and waved both hands, palms open, in front of him. The snow-globe village disappeared, as well as the turreted castle on the mountaintop. Instead, the guardhouse reformed itself into a walled crystalline fortress, as shiny as a piece of cut glass. Mara blinked, murmuring in surprise.

"But what happened to the village? And the bakery and pub?" Remy sounded disappointed. "Where did they go?"

Yelenarra shook her head wearily. "They never existed —all an elven illusion. I can understand masking the palace, sir, but why bother to create an imitation village?"

"Four powerful fays, a dragon, a canine crossbreed, a griffin, a baker-mage, and a half-elven girl arrive uninvited in your port, which hasn't welcomed a single visitor from Havynweal since the illustrious Rezebella. You have no idea what mischief they might be bringing to your already troubled kingdom. Do you roll out the white carpet, or do you use subterfuge to discern their motives first?"

Katrine narrowed her eyes at the captain. "Point taken, Captain, although we did send a missive to your king when we docked, explaining the reason for our visit."

"Aye. And I followed the king's orders."

Arnesto had been silently observing the discussion, but Mara could sense his impatience. "It is all well and good to follow orders, sir. But we must make haste. Please tell us what we must do to cure Maragold's magic."

Zornamayne hissed her agreement. "Aye. Once you have provided us with the cure, we shall be on our way."

Xenestra emitted a small puff of smoke from each nostril. "Perhaps I might make a small detour through the archives whilst Maragold is undergoing her treatment?"

Phineas cocked his head to the side as if listening to a conversation elsewhere. He didn't appear to like whatever he was hearing and straightened up, the lines on his brow deepening. Mara wondered whether it had something to do with further negative developments in the underworld. Turning to Xenestra, he said, "An excellent suggestion, madam. I believe all of you, with the exception of Maragold, expressed a desire to conduct research in the archives."

With a clap of Phineas's hands, icy mists surrounded everyone, except for Mara. Gloria clicked her beak furiously, and Arnesto appeared to be struggling to break free. Mara heard him shouting, "Now just a minute, sir—" but he vanished on the elven mists along with the others, icicles tinkling onto the snow where they'd been standing.

The captain must have forgotten about Farleigh, who whined, "Mara, friend." He sat on his haunches and growled softly at Phineas, the fur along his back standing up in spiky tufts. Mara patted his shoulder, grateful she wasn't entirely alone with the mercurial captain of the guard.

Phineas peered down at the crossbreed and smiled. "I shall ask Norris to provide you with a meaty bone and a big bowl of water. How does that sound?"

"Sound nice," grunted Farleigh. *So much for my large, furry protector,* thought Mara. She couldn't really blame poor Farleigh. His wolfish instincts overrode his loftier human traits. The captain lifted his hand. Frosty tendrils of elven mist swirled around Farleigh, who yipped, "Mara!" before disappearing in an icy puff.

Mara still hadn't decided whether Phineas was a friend or foe, but she had very little leverage at the moment, and she desperately needed his help to cure her magic—that is, if he was telling the truth. If he was lying, then perhaps his real purpose was to separate her from her friends so he could...do what? Toss her in a dungeon designed for half-breeds? Whisk her away to some wintry work camp for wayward elves, where she'd be cold and miserable all the time?

Snap out of it, Mara; that's enough mental moaning. Time to find out what Phineas is really after. She flexed her fingers and toes, achy with cold. "What now?"

"I shall escort you to my master healer, of course. First, we must set your magic to rights as best we can, and then we must retrieve the ensorcelled swords—and their owners —from Faynwood."

Mara's mouth formed an O, but before she could reply, frigid coils of mist wrapped around her legs, snaked up her waist, and encircled her shoulders and head. She couldn't part her lips to cry out, and her eyelashes froze shut. Mara's heart raced in terror for several long moments, until a blast of warm air melted the icicles from her hair, face, and clothes, forming a small puddle at her feet. Rubbing the moisture from her eyes, she glanced around. She and Phineas stood inside a wing of the palace, its sheer walls of opaque crystal surrounding them.

Phineas thrust Mara toward a willowy female elf in a wispy, white gown. The woman's thick platinum braid was draped over a short white cape, which covered her right shoulder only; slung across her left was a coil of silver reaping rope. Her long sword hung from a silver belt at her waist. "This half-elven lass requires the treatment."

The woman gave the captain a low bow. "As you wish, Captain." Phineas disappeared in a frosty mist without bothering to say goodbye.

Mara turned to the woman with a huff. "Is he always so rude, or is he just like that with his guests?"

The beautiful healer pursed her full lips before answering. "Phineas is a leader with too many problems and not enough time to solve them. He is not rude, but efficient."

Mara rolled her eyes, and the elven woman pointed. "Why did you do that?"

"What, you mean this?" Mara rolled her eyes again, and the woman nodded. "I roll my eyes when I don't necessarily agree or when something is difficult to believe."

"Ah, I see. So you do not believe Phineas has many problems to solve?"

"Oh, I believe that's true enough. But I don't agree he is just being efficient, when I've experienced his rudeness firsthand. He referred to me as a half-breed more than once and made it clear I was not welcome here."

"That is because you had an elven parent who"—the woman hesitated and seemed to be choosing her words with care—"ignored her duties. She did not help you complete the rituals. Phineas is a stickler for tradition."

"But my mother died when I was very young."

"Then your human father should have seen to it. He knew the requirements."

"What requirements?" asked Mara, falling into step beside the healer, who led her down the passageway, their footsteps echoing on the polished, white stone floors. Mara didn't see or hear anyone else.

The beautiful elf fluttered her hand. "Those needed for your elven magic to blossom, rather than wither. You are here to re-make your magic, correct?"

"Aye, if that's required to cure my condition." Mara couldn't imagine how to re-make her magic. It sounded complicated. "How long will it take?"

"As long as necessary."

Mara refrained from another eye roll. "Could you please be more specific? A day? A week?"

"As if." The elven healer snorted.

"What's that supposed to mean?"

"None could survive the elemental rites for even a full day. You shall require half a day at the most."

Mara shrugged. "That doesn't sound too bad."

"I should warn you the ritual is quite painful when not completed by the time a child is twelve years of age."

Mara flattened her lips. "Fine. Show me the way before I change my mind."

"Very well." They'd reached the end of the corridor. Frosted crystalline walls enveloped them; Mara hadn't noticed any doors or archways as they walked and wondered about the location of the infirmary or sanatorium—or wherever the healing ritual would take place.

The elf pressed her hand against the smooth surface in front of them. The wall receded, revealing a dark cavern lit by one candle mounted on a pedestal near the entrance, its tiny flame sputtering in the draft created by the opening. A small pool of water bubbled off to the left, emitting a slightly acrid odor. Razor-sharp stalactites hung down from the ceiling, some of them nearly touching the stalagmite pillars rising from the floor.

The woman nodded to indicate Mara should enter the cave. Mara cautiously stepped inside, all her internal alarm bells going off, her stomach twisting with dread. Whatever was about to happen felt less like a cure and more like a test, one she'd struggle to pass, since she was half human. Why hadn't her father told her the truth about her elven mother—and helped prepare her for these rites?

The elven healer remained in the corridor. "Do not worry. You can make as much noise as you like—no one will hear your screams."

Mara spun around to face her. *"What?"*

"Do not turn your back on the flame!" called the elf. The wall slid closed, cutting off the light from the corridor and plunging Mara into near darkness, broken only by the flickering candle.

CHAPTER 20

SOMETHING COLD, WET, AND SLIMY SNAKED AROUND MARA'S
waist. She yelped, slapping at a thick rope of black-as-
midnight water twining around her torso. Two more damp
coils curled up her legs. Mara tried kicking free as the
water tightened its grip. She felt herself tumbling backward into the acrid pool. She opened her mouth to scream
but swallowed water as the coils pulled her under. *It's no
surprise Father never told me about this place. Elves are
horrible!*

Mara paddled upward using her arms—her legs and
body entangled beneath her—straining to raise her head
above the surface long enough for a gulp of air before the
watery coils ripped her away. She bobbed up again,
inhaled, and then slipped under, over and over, her arms
growing heavy as she struggled to the surface, her movements slowing with each repetition.

Mara fought against her rising panic, her heart pounding, her lungs burning as she tried to break clear of the
water long enough for another gasp of air, before the black
water ripped her away, dragging her down again. *Strain*

upward, break the surface, breathe. Repeat. How many times can I do this until my muscles cramp up completely?

She thought about her quest to heal her magic and wondered whether, in the end, any of it mattered. Even if she cured whatever ailed her, Phineas made it clear she couldn't fix the problems in the underworld alone. If Bazra and the red sword had overcome a group of elven reapers, what made her think she could do any better?

Then there was the stab of pain in her chest whenever she so much as glanced at Arnesto. Restoring her magic wouldn't fix her broken heart. Mara's arms grew wooden, her hands fluttering uselessly as the watery bindings tightened around her waist. *Should I keep fighting or just give up?*

Mara was desperate for oxygen, for just one more breath of air so she could think clearly. Her chest heaved as she fought to the surface, thrashing her arms. She raised her head above the black pool, coughing and inhaling...and then the watery ropes tugged her down under again. Exhausted, she debated letting the water take her and be done with it.

Phineas doesn't want to cure me—he wants to kill me so he can take my blue sword! Mara shook her head, furious she allowed herself to be tricked by the elven captain. She remembered the first time she'd picked up the sword in the Valerran Museum, and her excitement when the blade's hieroglyphs blazed bright blue for her. *Can my sword help me now?*

The fingers of her right hand felt for the scabbard pressed against her side. Mara grasped the hilt and struggled to pull it free, as the coils around her legs and torso tightened further. Her arm shook as she strained to withdraw her blade, the weight of water dragging her down toward the bottom of the pool. Rather than fight the coils,

Mara allowed her body to go slack, all the while tugging on her sword.

As her feet touched down on the rocky floor, the coils loosened slightly. Mara managed to free her blade, its runes pulsing with blue light, and she slashed at the snake of water twined around her middle. She heard a soggy keen as the largest coil dissolved. Her head pounding, her lungs desperate for air, she stabbed at the two remaining coils wrapped around her boots. They melted into the floor of the pool with a squelch.

Mara pushed off the rocks and swam for the surface, breaking free of the black water and gulping in the dank air of the cave. She pulled herself onto a flat rock and vomited, her sides heaving until she had nothing left inside. She glanced at her dripping sword, now dull and gray once more and whispered, "You belong to me, and I'll not give you up without a fight."

Mara propped herself against the wall of the cavern, and recalling the elven woman's final warning, she kept an eye on the single candle on its pedestal. The water had been bad enough; she didn't want to find out what the candle's flame could do to her.

Mara stared at the opposite wall, where the opening to the corridor ought to be, and saw no seams or lines, nothing to indicate a doorway existed. She clambered to her feet, still shaky, and sidestepped farther away from the spring, which bubbled quietly now, its pools no longer appearing dark and threatening. She heard a crunching, gravelly sound, as if someone was grinding stones overhead. Glancing up, Mara yelled, "Oh, come on!" The rocky ceiling was dropping toward her, its sharp stalactites threatening to pierce her.

Mara grabbed her sword and looked around, no longer

worried about the water or candle flame as a fresh threat emerged—if she didn't find a place to hide, she'd be buried alive or stabbed by a stalactite—or both. She ran, dodging around boulders and pillars, searching for a gap or crevice in the walls. Stones and gravel continued raining down on her, and a particularly sharp rock smashed into her forehead, cutting her above the left eye.

Mara swiped away the trickle of blood and ducked around a stalactite that crashed to the ground in front of her. The ceiling continued to descend, and Mara dropped to all fours, scrabbling on her knees and left hand, while dragging her sword along with her right. Finally, she could move no farther, trapped between two stalagmites.

Mara thought she might be safe, until the pillar on her left collapsed, followed by the one on her right. The ceiling ground its way down, and she whimpered. She had no moves left, no way to save herself from being crushed alive. Mara choked on the dust and thought of Arnesto, wishing they could have had just one happy day together before their lives splintered apart. She rubbed her sword, the blade lighting up faintly through the layers of dust and grime.

A crazy idea came to her, but she had nothing left to lose. Gripping the hilt, she jammed the sword into the ground, its tip catching inside a narrow crevice. The rocky ceiling ground downward, bending the sword's blade. Mara flattened herself and desperately tried thinking of some sort of counterspell, but nothing came to her—not that it mattered, since her magic was useless, and soon, her sword would be too.

The only thing to pop in her head was an old nursery rhyme her father sang to soothe her when she woke up screaming from a nightmare. The bad dreams had started after her mother's death and always left Mara feeling drained and exhausted, although she could never recall the details.

As the grinding noise grew louder Mara closed her eyes, waiting for the sharp rocks to break her skin, and whispered:

> *"All creatures lay thee down,*
> *To your own realms return.*
> *Calm wild seas and fiery woods,*
> *Be still the quaking stones.*
> *Mend spells and dreams and broken wings;*
> *Heal shattered hearts and ruined kings."*

She took a deep breath, and another, but she felt no painful jabs in her back. The sound of rocks smashing against each other continued, but it wasn't as jarring or as close. She pushed herself to her knees and glanced up; the stones, rocks, and stalactites were receding to their original position. Snatching up her sword, she rose on shaky legs. *Did Father's old nursery rhyme hold some hidden magic?*

Mara had no time to ponder or rejoice, because the cave started filling with black smoke. She remembered the elf's admonition never to turn her back on the flame and spun around. Sure enough, the candle was gone, replaced by a fiery maw spreading rapidly, its flames consuming the front wall of the cavern—even if Mara could locate the exit, the fire blocked her way. She hollered, "Can't you let me catch my breath?"

The wall of flames responded to Mara's voice, reaching two fiery arms toward her. Mara backed up, but the fire continued advancing until her legs touched the back wall of the cavern. Fire raged on three sides, the flames creeping toward her boots and licking the air around her. Mara choked on the thick smoke stinging her eyes. She dropped back down to her knees, seeking whatever air she could find.

One fiery finger leapt toward Mara's head, and she screeched in terror. She remembered a much younger Remy pulling a hair from her head and then snapping his fingers to show her how quickly hair could catch fire. She wished for Remy's magic or Arnesto's wizardry, anything to fight back against the flames hemming her in.

Wait a minute, thought Mara. *I've fought water and earth, and now fire. I'm battling the elements inside this cave—but I'm not an elemental mage! I'm a Serving mage, or I was, until I lost my magic.*

Mara glanced at the sword on the ground next to her. She'd channeled her blade's elemental magic in the realms of the dead once before, using it to defeat the dark fays. Although she'd depleted her magical reserves, she couldn't have used *all* her Serving magic, not really—because elemental magic overruled the other magical systems in the lower realms. But in Alfweard, Serving magic should function as well as elemental magic. At least she hoped so.

Mara ran through her Serving magic spells for commanding fire, but they were all for starting fires or shape-shifting fiery objects, not stopping fires. Mara's left leg felt hot and she shrieked—her leather boot was smoking. She scraped her boot across the ground to snuff out the fire and drew her legs under her chest. She lowered the left side of her face to the floor of the cave, gasping as the smoke choked out all the oxygen. Soon, she'd be out of air, the one element she truly needed at the moment. And water, of course. Water could put out flames.

Mara frowned. *If I can't stop this fire with a spell, maybe I can shape-shift it into something else.* She gripped her sword's hilt, hoping for whatever elemental magic her blade still possessed, and croaked out the words to a basic fire-shifting spell she'd learned as a mage apprentice. Since she didn't trust the creepy pond inside the cave, she had to shift the fire into something other than water. "Make tongues of fire petal soft, from fiery maw to garden shop!"

Her throat raw from smoke inhalation, Mara choked on the words to the spell, repeating them over and over, but the fire still roared in her ears. Tears and sweat streaked down her sooty face as Mara hissed at her blue sword, "It's now or never—your magic and mine—or we're both headed to the lower realms and this time, we're not coming back!" Squeezing her eyes shut, she gripped her sword tighter and wheezed out the words of the spell once more.

The roaring of the flames dimmed somewhat, the heat at her back lessening. Mara didn't dare raise her face from the ground, not yet, not with the all the dark smoke still inside the cave. She drew her sword closer and opened one eye. A layer of white daisies with yellow centers covered the blade, which shone bright blue beneath the petals. The hieroglyphs pulsed with raw power, and they remained blue, not diminishing as before. She arched her eyebrow. "Did you have to wait until we faced total annihilation to show up again?" She couldn't be sure, but she thought the blade might have winked on and off at her. *What a sassy sword.*

Slowly, she raised her head from the floor and took a breath, then another. The smoke was clearing, whether by magic or a well-concealed vent, Mara didn't know or care. All she knew was she'd used magic to shapeshift the fire into flowers—red poppies, yellow roses, blue hydrangeas, orange mums, and pink geraniums had sprung up from the ground or grew in glazed pots, while vines of coral honey-

suckle and purple clematis climbed the walls of the cave—
she'd turned the ugly cavern into a botanical garden! Even
the black water had cleared, becoming a clear, bubbling
spring. Mara eyed the formally evil candle, now a bleeding
heart plant in a bronze urn, its delicate pink buds draped
over the pedestal.

Mara stood, sheathed her sword, and stared at the vine-
covered front wall. She still had no clue how to activate the
exit, and she wasn't about to stand around, waiting for
someone to help her—clearly, that wasn't the elven way, at
least not during a ritual. Mara was furious she'd been shut
inside the horrible cavern and left there to fend for herself.

On the other hand, the "cure" seemed to have worked.
She could feel her old magic thrumming within her,
vibrating with fresh energy—but different, as if she'd fused
a new bond with her sword—and perhaps with the cavern
too. She could sense the cave's wards now, a complex web
of spells crisscrossing the room, a mishmash of elemental
magic, Serving magic, and something else too. Mara realized she was sensing *elven* magic, as much a part of her now
as her violet eyes and pale blonde hair.

Mara folded her arms. She wanted her next move to be
a smooth exit from the cavern, followed by a bath to
cleanse off all her grime and soot, and then a cup of tea.
Afterward, she might be able to have a civil word with
Phineas—or perhaps find another elf to answer her myriad
of questions about her elven heritage and her mother—
surely someone here knew of her. And then Mara planned
to find the rest of the group and head back to the ship.
They'd determine their next move later, once they were
together. Meanwhile, she had to find the doorway.

Mara examined the wall with a sigh. *I've been tested by
water, earth, and fire. The only element remaining is air. Do I*

need to manipulate air to create an escape route? The more Mara considered her options, the more the idea of somehow using air made sense. But she still had to find the actual exit.

She pushed through the plants on the ground, skirted around the colorful pots, and pushed aside the vines on the front wall. Pressing her palms against the rough-hewn surface, she felt along the wall, beginning in the middle and then fanning out, up, and down. She went to the left and the right, and felt along the floor and ceiling. The elf had sealed the room shut. Mara couldn't find so much as a tiny crack in the wall.

Mara returned to the center of the cavern and flexed her fingers, thinking. Finally, she nodded. Withdrawing her sword, she pointed at the opposite wall and called out, "Mighty windstorm, gale-force air; break through this rock with your power!"

A soft breeze stirred the flowers briefly and then settled again. She repeated the spell, putting more energy into each word. The breeze quickly became a gust that whipped around the room, causing the bleeding heart plant to wobble on its pedestal. She jabbed the tip of her sword into the wall, shouting the spell once more. This time, the gust turned into a tempest, tearing the vines from the wall.

The pedestal toppled over, sending the bronze urn crashing to the ground. As the bleeding heart plant fell, the wind shredded all its flowers, flinging the mass of dark pink petals at the wall. The squall spiraled into a mini-twister, flinging more planters and flowers at the middle of the wall. The cavern quaked and shuddered beneath Mara's boots. In a mighty swoosh of vines, leaves, and petals, the windstorm blew through the front wall, leaving a large archway in its wake.

CHAPTER 21

MARA HASTILY SHEATHED HER SWORD AND DASHED THROUGH THE opening before it closed up again. She ran headlong into the corridor where the elven healer greeted her with a cool, assessing glance. Mara waited for her to say something but the healer merely stared back, unblinking. Mara found herself annoyed by the woman's stony silence and blurted out, "Aren't you going to congratulate me?"

The beautiful elf reared back. "I do not understand."

"I survived your ritual." Mara put her hands on her hips and furrowed her brow. "Don't you congratulate people when they pass a challenge, especially one so dangerous?"

The elven woman tilted her head to the side. "You are cured, your magic even more powerful than before. It is not congratulations we should be discussing, but gratitude— yours for Phineas. He could have turned you away; many men in his boots would have. Instead, he asked me to arrange your healing ritual. I suggest you thank him when you see him."

"Thank Phineas for insulting me and sending me into a

deadly cave?" Mara sputtered, her scowl deepening. "That crazy ritual nearly killed me three times!"

"I warned you it would be more painful since you are older—and only half-elven. Still, I am surprised..." The woman's voice trailed off.

"Surprised at what?"

"You completed the ritual in a little more than half an hour. I expected you would need longer, that is, if you made it through at all." The elven healer lifted her shoulders slightly. Mara wondered how many young elves didn't make it through and shuddered. *It's no surprise Father never told me about Alfweard—he probably feared for my life.*

"I have arranged a private suite, where you may bathe and change. Is that agreeable?" asked the elf.

Mara glanced down at her grimy, torn tunic and leggings and nodded.

The woman's frosty traveling mists wrapped around Mara. They arrived in a spacious suite, sparsely furnished with a bed, dresser, and chair. The room was soothing in its simplicity but devoid of color—walls, floor, and furnishings all in muted shades of gray and white—so unlike the Amber Room in Yelenarra's mansion.

The elven healer opened a door at the far end of the room and showed Mara to the bathing suite, where a large soaking tub filled with clean, clear, normal-looking water beckoned Mara. Bottles lined the tub containing bathing soap, shampoo, and lotion.

"I have left something suitable for you to wear in the adjoining room. I shall return within the hour to escort you to the ceremony." Mara frowned, wondering whether she'd missed something important. Before Mara could ask any questions about the ceremony, the elven woman departed on icy mists.

Mara shook her head. *Elves have no manners. On the other hand, that bath looks divine.* She dropped her ruined clothes on the floor and winced as the water touched her cuts. After scrubbing and shampooing and scrubbing again, the bathwater was still warm and clear, another bit of elven magic. Mara leaned back against the tub and closed her eyes. She dozed lightly until she heard a squawk and felt droplets of water tickling her face.

Mara opened one eye and grunted, "I just survived the ordeal of a lifetime. Can't you give me a few more minutes of peace and privacy? I was having a particularly pleasant dream about Arnesto and our first mission together."

Gloria picked up a large, fluffy towel with her beak and dropped it next to the tub. "Sorry, milady, but you are needed immediately."

Mara grabbed the towel, draped herself in it, and stepped out of the tub. "What disaster has befallen us now?" she grumbled.

"Not a disaster so much as a development."

Mara tented her eyebrows. Gloria could be such a drama princess at times. "Please continue."

"Phineas has announced, on behalf of the king—who apparently never leaves his chambers—a celebration in your honor. You are to be recognized as an elf and accorded all the rights and privileges of an Alfweardian. He claims your performance during the healing ritual—which you must tell me about sometime—was superlative, better than most elves. Phineas said only he was faster."

Of course he would have been faster, thought Mara, *he is an elf. But why the change of heart toward me? Is it really because I completed a deadly ritual intended for full-blooded elves, or is something else at play here?*

Then she realized this must be the ceremony the elven

healer had mentioned. If Mara didn't want to learn more about her mother, and find out if any of her relatives still lived, she might have declined outright. After all, she'd nearly died trying to complete the ritual. On the other hand, Mara reasoned, she had survived, and her magic was back to its full potency. Although Phineas was tactless and overbearing, he'd been right about the cure.

Gloria clicked her beak. "Now hurry. Hortensia said she would be back for you shortly, and you are to wear the gown she has provided."

"Who is Hortensia?

"Tall, attractive—I think she may be Phineas's consort. She told me she arranged for your cure."

Mara snorted. "You must mean the healer-slash-ice-queen whose ritual nearly killed me."

Gloria leaned against Mara's legs. "If it is any consolation, I paced around the archives the entire time, frantic with worry."

Mara bent down and rubbed Gloria's mane until she started purring. "So tell me about this gown."

"Hortensia may be snooty, but the gown she left for you is gorgeous."

Mara padded after Gloria, who had better fashion taste than most women. If her griffin liked the dress, it must be truly stunning. Mara sighed. She hoped elves served tea at their celebrations; otherwise that cup she'd been craving would have to wait a bit longer.

When Mara opened the door, Hortensia's hand was raised, preparing to knock. The elven woman wore a forest green ball gown, with a short golden cape draped over one shoulder, and her sword strapped to her waist. Her long side braid, woven with gold and green ribbons, lay over her cape.

Mara thanked her for the dress and accessories. Hortensia nodded gravely and twirled her finger. Mara raised an eyebrow but rotated slowly to show off her pale yellow ball gown, carefully disguised to hide its split-skirt underneath. Around her waist Mara had buckled a new gold leather belt, outfitted with a jeweled scabbard for her blue sword, and on her feet were a pair of buttery-yellow tall boots, her daggers tucked inside. A short ivory cape, lined with creamy yellow satin, completed the outfit. Mara had brushed out her long, straight, pale blonde hair, leaving it free of her ponytail.

Hortensia pointed to Mara's cape, which she was wearing like any Valerran or fay, tossed around both shoulders. "May I?" asked the elf.

"Please do."

Hortensia layered the cape over Mara's right shoulder. "There. You must wear the formal cape elven style."

"Is there significance to the style?"

Hortensia pursed her full lips. "Naturally. Our capes are short and worn over one shoulder to permit freedom of movement." She pulled back the front panel of her gown to reveal her split-skirt beneath, the same as Mara's. "Elven women are always prepared for battle in the lower realms, same as the men."

"What about reaping ropes?"

"An excellent question." Hortensia almost smiled, and Mara felt as if she'd scored points with the frosty woman. "They are too ungainly to wear all the time. We conjure them as we're heading to battle."

"But not the swords?"

Hortensia shook her head solemnly. "Nay. We keep our weapons close at hand. The few seconds needed to conjure them may prove fatal." Hortensia pointed down the corridor. "Come along now. Everyone else is already gathered."

They turned down a series of passages, their boot heels clacking on the stone floors. Mara tried keeping track of the number of left and right turns but soon gave up. Every corridor looked the same, shiny, opaque crystal walls with an occasional polished white door breaking the monotony.

Hortensia finally stopped, small lines crinkling her forehead. Katrine was hovering in the corridor, blocking a set of double doors. Katrine wore a sparkly blue-and-silver cape over a beaded blue dress. She gave Hortensia a small bow, just low enough to be polite. "This will not take long, but I must speak with Mara privately. We will be right behind you."

Hortensia tossed her white-blonde braid. "Very well. I shall remain just inside the doors. Please understand this is a high honor we are bestowing on a half, well, on a young woman who is not a pureblood elf. Do not keep Phineas waiting long."

Katrine and Mara waited for Hortensia to enter the room. Mara caught a glimpse of glitz and glitter—on the walls, floors, and the ladies' gowns—before the double doors closed. *Phineas is holding a* ball *in my honor?* She had no time to ponder it further, because Katrine whispered something that made her frown. Mara asked her to repeat it.

Katrine hissed in her ear, "Alfweard has no king!"

"No king?" Mara shook her head, feeling confused—could there be a kingdom without a king?—and unexpectedly sad. She'd held onto a glimmer of hope she might yet meet the mysterious elven king. He'd probably been the monarch when her mother had lived in Alfweard. "But the stories and legends all revolve around the king. Sometimes there's an elven queen, but more often, a consort. The king plays the central role. How can this be?"

"Elves are masters of subterfuge, even better than we fays."

Mara folded her arms. "Have you been spying again?" She knew her old boss's talents for undercover work. Katrine had trained her, after all, in the art of spy craft.

Katrine gave her a sly grin. "After Phineas dropped us in the archives, and a sleepy old elf gave us a tour, I slipped away. I visited the kitchens, the stables, the servants quarters, and even snuck up to the 'king's chambers.'"

"You didn't!"

"Those chambers need a good cleaning. In fact, that whole wing needs a thorough airing out. The layer of dust is this thick." Katrine held up her thumb and forefinger to indicate half an inch. "By the looks of it, I don't think there's been an elven king for decades, perhaps longer."

"But why keep up the pretense? And who's running Alfweard?"

Katrine shrugged. "Officially? Everyone seems to think there's still a king, albeit a reclusive one. Unofficially, it's got to be Phineas. He seems to be the one everyone else listens to around here."

"Aye, he's bossy enough," huffed Mara. "How should we play this?"

"We have no choice but to pretend along with them. Despite the fact your magic is healed, according to every elf I've chatted up, the underworld is so chaotic they think we'll need a miracle to set the place to rights—along with all the ensorcelled swords, ropes, mages, and reapers at our disposal."

"You do realize what this means, don't you?"

Katrine compressed her lips. "Aye. It means a trip to

Faynwood to ask for help from Linden, Corbahn, and Jayna."

The tall double doors opened, and Hortensia glared at Katrine, who nodded. "Thank you for this short break. We appreciate the high honor the king is bestowing on Maragold." Katrine's smile showed plenty of teeth, and Mara bit her bottom lip to keep from snorting out loud.

MARA FOLLOWED the two women into a glittering gold, silver, and crystal ballroom, with frosted glass panels for walls and a gilded dome ceiling. Candelabras floated overhead, casting a soft glow over gowns and faces. Platters of food and drink flitted among the guests, who served themselves. A low crystalline dais occupied the wall opposite the entrance.

Mara's heart stuttered painfully as she spotted Arnesto, dashing in a long, silvery cape, navy blue tunic with bright silver buttons, and navy slacks. His tall, black boots were polished to a high sheen. He was chatting with Remy, sporting a dark red jacket and brown pants, and Yelenarra, in a silver-and-gold, sequined empire-waist gown. Zornamayne, covered head to toe in diaphanous veils inlaid with jewels, stood next to Yelenarra.

Xenestra lounged on an assortment of large nesting pillows in one corner of the room, as a constant supply of tea, cakes, sandwiches, and savory appetizers hovered on platters in front of her. Farleigh had joined the giant dragon on one of the pillows and appeared to be savoring the meatier foodstuffs.

Gloria's head swiveled toward the corner and the

floating food platters. "I think I shall keep an eye on those two," said the griffin, trotting over to join them.

Phineas had exchanged his camouflaged uniform for a formal white jacket trimmed with gold braid and buttons, and white slacks. He'd draped a short gold cape over one shoulder. The other male elves were dressed similarly, in white, blue, or black jackets with gold or silver trim, and short capes in a rainbow of colors.

Phineas clapped his hands once, and the candles dimmed. He clapped again, and the trays of food and drinks floated over to high-topped tables scattered around the perimeter. The third time he clapped, high-backed, cushioned chairs materialized in three neat rows in front of the dais. The ballroom grew quiet as everyone paused to turn toward the entrance and stare at Mara. She took a deep breath to steady her nerves. *Whatever is about to happen is something I want...isn't it?*

Hortensia escorted her to Phineas, who stood on the dais. Mara climbed the two steps onto the platform, an uneasy knot settling into her stomach. Everything about Alfweard had differed from her expectations and at this point, she had no idea what to expect.

Phineas extended a hand, and Mara reached over to take it. As he gripped her hand, a wave of nostalgia washed over her, as if she were traveling through her own past and glancing backward in time. Memories of her mother—laughing at her toddler antics, kissing her scraped knee, and clasping her hand as they traveled on chilly mists to the lower realms—flooded her head. Mara blinked back a tear threatening to slide down her cheek.

Phineas snapped the fingers of his free hand and a scroll hovered in the air in front of him. "Maragold Gracelyn Raeburn"—as he spoke, the words wrote themselves onto the scroll. Mara noticed Phineas didn't use her full name, probably because he didn't want to acknowledge her human father—"has completed the passage rites at age eighteen, without interference, assistance, or rescue, and in near-record time. She has demonstrated the skills and courage of a pureblood elf and henceforth shall be accorded the full rights and privileges of an Alfweardian."

The captain paused, and the elves broke into polite applause. Phineas flicked his wrist. The scroll rolled itself up and winked out of sight. Turning to Mara, he asked her to withdraw her blue sword. Two thin lines formed on Mara's brow. *What's up? Why does Phineas want to see my sword again?* Phineas noticed her confusion and smiled— the first sign of encouragement she'd received from the austere elf.

Mara decided to go along and gripped the sapphire-encrusted hilt at her side. She held her breath as she withdrew the weapon from its scabbard. *How will my sword react, now the immediate danger has passed?* Mara raised her sword above her head, pointing at the gilded ceiling. The blade's hieroglyphs blazed bright blue, pulsing with magical energy, and they remained lit. She exhaled slowly, relieved her sword was behaving. What she really wanted to do was hop off the platform and run a lap around the ballroom, holding her blue sword aloft.

Phineas raised both his arms, palms open, and cried, "Another Sword of Six for Alfweard!"

The elves, who had been lukewarm before, roared their approval. Mara's frown lines deepened, and she noticed Arnesto jump up from his seat. Squaring his jaw, he moved toward the dais. She hastily resheathed her sword, hoping to avoid a confrontation between Phineas and Arnesto inside a ballroom full of elves.

But Arnesto strode forward and leapt onto the dais, shouting, "The sword belongs to Mara, not to the fays or humans or elves!" The crowd booed him, reinforcing in Mara's mind the rudeness of elves.

Phineas hissed, "Not now, fay wizard. Your gallantry is overdue, and you do not comprehend the true significance of this occasion."

Mara's heart swelled at Arnesto's chivalry, however ill-timed. She looked up at Phineas. "Do I comprehend the significance?"

"Perhaps not yet, but I promise you shall, soon enough. But first, we must step aside." Phineas nodded at Norris, who'd charged the dais and Arnesto, tackling him to the crystalline flooring. "They need some space to roll about."

"Aren't you worried someone will get hurt?"

Phineas guided Mara down the steps on the opposite side of the platform. "Nay. I shall not allow this to continue for very long. My king would not wish to learn of such brawling inside the palace."

Phineas waved his hand, and the platters of food and drink began circulating among the guests again, most of whom lost interest in Arnesto and Norris, wrestling on the floor of the platform. Only a handful of younger male elves remained near the dais, shouting encouragements to Norris or, surprisingly, Arnesto—apparently, Norris wasn't uniformly well liked among his peers.

Mara decided this was the ideal moment to ask about the king. "Some from my party believe the elven king is merely a legend." She surprised herself by how interested she was in the captain's answer.

The captain scowled. "While the king grants no audiences, as I have explained, he is as true to Alfweard today as he ever was."

"But where does he reside?" Mara knew she was pressing her luck, but this was the most forthcoming Phineas had been since she'd first set foot in Alfweard.

"The king is here, within the walls of this palace." Phineas turned away, the conversation over. He waved his hand at the dais, which collapsed into the floor. "They have tussled long enough for each of them to make their point. Come, you must mingle, and I must have Hortensia see to their injuries."

Mara brought a hand to her throat. "Injuries?"

"Nothing serious, but both are bleeding. I do not wish to see blood when I am at a ball, and I daresay my guests agree."

Hortensia had already made her way over to Arnesto and Norris, who was holding his nose. Her chilly mists twined around the three of them, and they winked out of sight.

Phineas clapped his hands twice. The three rows of chairs vanished, and the first few chords of a spirited melody filled the room, sending a frisson down Mara's spine. Most of the elves lined up in two rows, men on one side, and women opposite. They began a series of complex dance moves involving bowing, toe pointing, and a lot of stepping forward, backward, and sideways. Mara decided it must be some sort of elven minuet.

She felt another quiver down her back and glanced about, looking for the source of the music. Finding no musicians in the ballroom, she remarked, "Even the music, which is both strange and exhilarating, appears magically conjured by you."

"'Tis true, my magic courses through this palace." Phineas bestowed another smile on her. *If this keeps up, I might revise my opinion of the overbearing captain. He's being practically civil.* He addressed someone behind her. "I am certain Maragold would be pleased to join you on the dance floor."

Mara turned around and came face-to-face with one of the elves who'd been encouraging Arnesto as he wrestled on the dais. Although he was tall and blond like the rest, his skin tone was closer to Arnesto's rich brown than Hortensia's pale ivory. He wore a maroon jacket and slacks, trimmed in gold, with a short gold cape over his left shoulder. The elf bowed and introduced himself as Dowell, his violet eyes twinkling. Mara had no desire to dance, but she wanted information, and the complicated minuet seemed the best means at the moment.

Mara returned the bow. As she straightened, Dowell took her hand and led her toward the line of couples in the middle of the dance floor. "I'm not familiar with elven dances. I'm afraid I'll be a clumsy dance partner."

Dowell smiled at Mara, his teeth bright white. "That is why I asked for this first dance. I figured as much and want to help. I shall transfer a bit of my dance magic to you for the evening."

"Oh, thank you." She could never leave well enough alone, as Katrine had pointed out more than once. Mara's curiosity often got her in trouble, but it was the main reason she'd succeeded as a Valerran spy. "Why do you want to help me?"

"Do you always inquire about someone's motives?"

When Mara nodded, the tall elf chuckled. "Excellent. Phineas is always telling me I am not nosy enough—or perhaps he said smart enough—ah well, no matter. Since I believe you possess enough curiosity and wit for both of us, I shall learn from you."

It was Mara's turn to laugh. Here was an elf who was

polite, charming, and clever. "Oh dear. This simply won't do. I may have to alter my opinion of elves after all. I thought you were all rude, arrogant, and rather dull."

Dowell threw his head back and laughed. "I can see why you managed to beat Hortensia's carefully crafted passage ritual." They both fell silent as the music's tempo increased; even with Dowell's magic, Mara had to concentrate to avoid tripping over her feet. When the music slowed again, Dowell said, "I have walked in your boots. I know how intimidating Alfweardians may seem at first."

"You mean you are not a pureblood elf?"

Dowell's eyebrows peaked. "I shall have to brace myself for your frankness."

"I'm terribly sorry if I've said anything I shouldn't have." Mara liked the elf and didn't want to offend him.

He grinned. "No apology needed. You are forthright, unlike elves and for that matter, fays. You remind me of Granny Annabel, who was human. I am three-quarters elven—I had to earn my Alfweardian citizenship just like you. However, I had two advantages: my father was a pureblood and prepared me well, and I underwent the passage rites when I turned twelve."

"I can't imagine going through that ordeal at such a young age," Mara shook her head.

"Oh, the rites become increasingly more difficult, based on one's age. They are far less rigorous for a seven-year-old than they were for me or for you. In fact, you are the oldest person to complete the elven passage rites. You have broken the record."

"Is that a good thing?" asked Mara. She recalled Phineas telling her she didn't understand the significance yet. The truth seemed just beyond her reach—like the elven king himself—hidden somewhere within the palace compound.

"Phineas seems pleased, and that is always a good thing." Their dance had ended and Dowell nodded to an elf behind Mara. "Maragold, may I present my good friend, Ignatius? He may prove nearly as light on his feet as I."

Ignatius bowed. "Please, call me Iggy, and I am a far better dancer than Dowell."

Dowell shook his head at his friend. "Do not believe a word he says, and you shall be as well informed as you are now." Both elves chuckled, and Dowell gave Mara another sweeping bow.

The tallest elf in the room, Iggy had an olive complexion, round face, and a long platinum braid down his back. He wore a black jacket trimmed with pewter buttons and a bright green cape flung over his shoulder.

Iggy led Mara through the intricate dance steps, keeping the conversation light and amusing. As the last few bars of music played out, he spoke so softly Mara had to lean in to hear him. "Thank you, milady, for joining our ranks."

"Joining your ranks? I don't understand."

"The cobalt sword was one of the original Swords of Six promised to the elven king. Now that you have completed your passage rites and earned your citizenship, you wield the sword on our king's behalf."

Mara pursed her lips—all of this fuss over a stolen sword—or two stolen swords, if Phineas's tale was accurate. Then she recalled the havoc Bazra was wreaking in the lower realms with the red sword. Perhaps the elves had every right to be upset...and perhaps the lower realms wouldn't be quite so messy if the elves had had possession of the ensorcelled swords from the very beginning.

Iggy bowed and stepped aside as one of the elves who'd been encouraging Norris came up to claim the next dance.

Although Mara expected him to be boorish, the elf surprised her. He was polite, soft-spoken, and good company.

By the time Remy made his way over to Mara, she had danced with all of the unattached elves present. Her feet ached, and she wanted nothing more than to lie down in a soft bed. "What took you so long?" she whispered. "You could have rescued me sooner." Instead of another elven minuet, which Mara never wanted to dance again, couples were dancing some sort of slow waltz she and Remy were able to follow.

Remy nodded at the platters of food hovering around the perimeter of the large room. "I was starving. Plus, I knew you wanted to talk to as many elves as possible, and what better way than at a ball in your honor?"

Remy knew her well, but Mara wasn't about to admit he was right. "Fine. I spoke with a lot of elves this evening. Most are witty, charming even, but there's something not quite right about this whole set up."

Remy sighed. "What could possibly be wrong? Your magic is healed, you've been formally welcomed into Alfweard, and even Phineas turned out to be a decent chap after all."

Mara told him about Katrine's discovery there was no elven king, Phineas's insistence otherwise, and what she'd learned about her blue sword. She wondered whether the red sword *could* be the last, lost sword of Alfweard and then drew her brows together, deep in thought. A dark idea flickered through Mara's head, making her wince. Remy noticed. "Aw come on, my dancing can't be that bad!"

"It's not your dancing that's giving me heartburn. I just thought of something: what if nasty, wicked Bazra is the rightful owner of the red sword?"

Remy snorted. "I think the passage rites have shaken something loose in your head. There's no way my old sword chose the dark fay king. I'd wager quite the opposite. I think we'll find the rightful owner for the red sword—whether elven, fay, or human—after we retrieve it from Bazra." He shrugged. "Who knows? Maybe I'll be the one to wield the sword again."

Every time Mara thought about returning to the realms of the dead and fighting Bazra, she shuddered. She still dreamt of the final bend in the river, the point of no return, where the dark, churning water arced over the lake of fire. She'd never forget the screaming and weeping of the spirits swept into the burning embers.

"Are you cold?" asked Remy. "You're shivering."

Mara smiled. "Just a little tired. It's been a long day."

Remy glanced around the still-crowded ballroom. "I suppose as the guest of honor, you can't exactly slip away unnoticed."

"Please do not slip away—at least, not until we have danced together." Arnesto stood next Remy, who nodded reluctantly at him and stepped aside.

"I see you are not much worse for the wear." Remy pointed at a small cut above Arnesto's eye.

"Hortensia forced us to rest whilst we healed, so both Norris and I are mostly back to normal. He is not such a bad chap after all—and I do regret breaking his nose—but he never should have tackled me. We have both apologized." Arnesto gave Mara a low bow. "I owe you an apology as well, for creating a scene. Whilst I am still uncertain of Phineas's meaning behind his blue sword comment, I should not have stormed the dais. According to Norris, that is tantamount to starting a revolt in Alfweard."

Remy grunted, "Serves 'em right. They weren't exactly

chummy when we first arrived, and they forced Mara to undergo some crazy ritual before they recognized her elven ancestry." He gave Mara a peck on the cheek, which caused Arnesto to scowl and step closer to her.

"Well, I think I'll go check out the corner where Xenestra is lounging." Remy nodded in the dragon's direction. "There may be some meat pies I haven't sampled yet."

Arnesto stared at the elven couples trotting up and down the center of the ballroom to music that reminded Mara of a parade march. He raised one eyebrow and lowered the other. "How about we simply observe this dance and attempt the next one?"

"I could use a break, but I'm afraid if I sit down now, I won't be getting back up until the morning."

Arnesto looped Mara's arm through his and guided her to the room's perimeter. "In that case, let us stroll as you tell me about your passage rites. I was quite anxious when Phineas whisked you away, but I can now see there was no cause for concern."

"Oh, there was plenty of cause for concern," muttered Mara.

Arnesto glanced at her sharply. "Tell me—please." Mara took a deep breath and plunged ahead. She told him how she'd battled each of the elements, how she was nearly drowned, crushed, and burned, and how terrified she'd been. Arnesto's face hardened as Mara spoke. When she described choking on the smoke inside the cave, he put his arm around her waist and drew her closer. "I shall kill him."

Mara's stomach flipflopped at Arnesto's nearness; she inhaled the heady scent of him—loamy earth and tangy citrus—which always left her feeling slightly breathless. *I'm such a bundle of nerves and contradictions. I don't want to react like this...but Arnesto is very hard to resist when he looks at me like that and pulls me close.*

She twisted out of Arnesto's grasp and locked eyes with him. "You will do no such thing," she insisted. "The ritual is over, I survived, and my magic is stronger than ever. We need to focus on what's most important, and that's fixing the mess in the lower realms. Katrine has been doing a lot of reconnaissance, and every elf she's spoken to says the same thing—we're going to need a lot of help."

"Fine," grumbled Arnesto. "I shall wait until we have defeated Bazra, saved my brother from fading away, and fixed the cracks in the streets of Bellaryss. And then I shall kill him."

Mara rolled her eyes. "Tell you what. Let's see how much help Phineas provides. If he is extremely helpful, perhaps you could merely frighten him."

"Do not roll your eyes at me, Maragold. I am serious." Mara's pulse sped up as Arnesto leaned toward her, their faces inches apart. She wavered; she wanted to kiss him, but not now. They still had too much unfinished business, and she wasn't ready to risk her heart again.

Mara turned her head away and the moment passed. "You're always so serious, ever since..."

"Ever since I bungled everything so badly." Arnesto sighed as they resumed their slow walk. "My brother's spirit might fade away forever because of me."

The music was winding down, and so were the couples on the floor. Mara hoped for a slow waltz, something intimate and soothing for her and Arnesto. Instead, Phineas stood near the entrance to the ballroom and boomed in his captain of the guard voice, "I hope you have enjoyed this evening. I know it is a mere interlude between battles for us, but no matter—Bazra shall not prevail! We shall restore balance in the lower realms, and we shall reclaim the last, lost sword of Alfweard!"

The elves burst into loud cheers and applause. Iggy and a few others whistled through their teeth. The elven captain waited until the clapping died down. "And now, for the king's orders." A murmur rippled through the room, and Mara glanced around. None of the elves present seemed to doubt the king's existence. *Perhaps there is an elven king after all, but only a few trusted subjects have access to him?*

Phineas waved his hand, and the room grew quiet. "I shall leave momentarily for Faynwood, to seek assistance from the owners of the green sword, the gold sword, and the purple sword. Lady Reaper Maragold and Fay Chief Katrinareus shall accompany me." Mara and Arnesto locked eyes. He mouthed, "*Lady Reaper?*" and she lifted her shoulders in a shrug. "In the meantime, see Lieutenant Dowell for your instructions. Please prepare for departure to the lower realms."

Arnesto turned to Mara. "Quick, before Phineas whisks you away, withdraw your sword and hold it flat across your palms." He rolled up the left sleeve of his tunic.

Mara's eyebrows quirked upward, but she complied. Arnesto used the edge of his dagger to cut his forearm—a mere flesh wound, but it bled—and he smeared a few drops of blood on Mara's hilt, on the large sapphire on the base of the handle. "What are you doing?" she whispered, sheathing her sword again, careful not to touch the fresh stain.

"Ensuring you shall have what you need to send any undead to their permanent destination." Arnesto used a handkerchief to mop up his forearm and nodded at Mara.

"Promise me you will use my blood magic when the time comes."

Mara wanted to tell Arnesto she wouldn't need his blood magic; that he could command the undead as well as she could; that he'd be beside her throughout the ordeal to come; but in the end, she said none of those things. Instead, Mara stood on her tiptoes, her heart beating in her throat, and kissed Arnesto quickly on the lips. "Promise me you won't do anything stupid."

Arnesto's eyes softened and his voice was low, husky. "Maragold—"

Phineas clapped his hands once, and Mara felt tiny icicles forming on her face, neck, and arms. She heard Arnesto call out her name again as the chilly mists carried her away.

CHAPTER 22

Mara's boots touched down on hard-packed soil. After the shimmering lights of the ballroom, her eyes took a while to adjust to the darkness. She had no idea of the time but figured they'd arrived past midnight. Glancing down, she realized she was still wearing her ball gown. *Is this how Phineas sends his elves into battle in the lower realms? Or do they magically alter their clothes as they depart?*

Katrine landed next to Mara and murmured, "I'm sorry about the lack of notice, but Phineas did discuss this with me and Yelenarra. We decided that sending a small delegation to Faynwood made the most sense. Lieutenant Dowell and Yelenarra will prepare our group for departure, and everyone will travel together to the lower realms. We will meet them by Arnesto's portal."

"So you know about Arnesto's portal?"

Katrine nodded. "Aye, the entire fay council knows about the portal, but I have not told them Arnesto created it. They would be livid if they learned. They assume Bazra made the portal, and—"

Phineas cleared his throat. "Ladies? I believe we have urgent business to attend to. Which of you wishes to rouse the Liege? It is always best to be awakened in the middle of the night by a friend than a stranger, particularly when requesting assistance."

Mara looked around, trying to get her bearings. They had arrived inside a walled compound, and even this late, Mara heard the sounds of people and animals still settling in for the night. A horse neighed in a nearby stable yard, a dog barked, and several men and women, guards most likely, spoke in low tones near the main gate. Torches burned in front of each of the buildings lining the road, lighting doorways in an orange glow and plunging everything else in shadow.

Mara took a step back, too many memories flooding into her head. They stood in front of the largest building in the stronghold—the Liege's longhouse in the Faynwood province of Tanglewood—where Mara had once lived with Linden and Jayna. Remy's quarters, in the barracks nearby, had been far less luxurious. They'd lived here before Linden had met Corbahn, Chief of Arrowood, who was now her husband, and before Mara had met Arnesto. Although they'd been at war at the time, Mara and her friends had enjoyed a brief period of rest in this beautiful place. She inhaled the clean, fresh air, perfumed with hyacinth and lilies from the gardens.

"There's no need to rouse me," said a familiar voice behind them.

Mara spun around. Despite the lateness of the hour, Linden wore a long burgundy silk gown, overlaid with a pale gold robe. Her glossy black hair, streaked through with the blue highlights of her Faymon ancestors, was woven in an intricate braid that reached halfway to her waist. She looked the same as ever, except for the dark circles under her eyes. Mara threw her arms around her old friend. "Oh Linden—it's so good to see you again!"

Linden gripped Mara in a fierce hug. "We have so much to catch up on, and Jayna will be thrilled to see you too." Linden spotted Katrine, standing behind Mara, and bowed from the waist.

"There's no need for bowing between us, lass." Katrine smiled.

Linden asked about Pryl, her fay grandfather—and Katrine's half-brother. Chief Pryl had led the Fay Nation for decades, taking his first-ever holiday after the war. He intended to search for his son, Linden's father, who had evacuated from one of the border towns early in the conflict. Like Mara's family, Linden's parents had set their sights on the colonies, a difficult place to reach under the best of conditions.

Katrine shook her head. "No word yet, but don't worry. I'd know if something were wrong. I believe my brother found what he was looking for." Katrine stepped aside to introduce Phineas, standing in the shadows. "Allow me to introduce Sir Reaper Phineas August Maximere, Captain of the Elven Guard and His Majesty's Representative. We traveled here on Alfweardian mists." Mara was glad Katrine made the formal introductions; she had no idea how to address Phineas, other than "Captain."

Phineas and Linden bowed formally to one another, and then Linden asked them to follow her into the long-house. She paused to speak in soft undertones with her oldest maidservant, Garlan, as a black and white cat weaved in and out of her legs, and Gloria's youngest offspring, Kal, squawked at being roused from his nap.

Garlan left to retrieve beverages and refreshments for the guests.

They heard voices down the passage, coming from the library, which Mara knew also served as the hub for official Faymon gatherings. Phineas said, "I apologize; it appears we have interrupted something." Mara stared at Phineas, surprised he would apologize to Linden for anything. He'd never offered any apologies to Mara for his boorish remarks when she'd arrived in Alfweard, nor later, when she'd nearly died during the passage rites.

Linden smiled. "There's no need to apologize. The tribal chiefs and elders are gathered here for the week, and our council meetings are running later than usual. I had excused myself to get some fresh air when you arrived."

Linden led them into the receiving room in the front of the longhouse, where they sat on tasseled floor cushions around a low, circular table. Linden turned to Katrine. "I'm glad the second pair of scouts I sent were able to find you. The first pair must still be on your trail."

Katrine said, "None of your scouts tracked me down, which is not surprising, since we have been traveling to Alfweard for the past five days. Why did you send scouts after me, and why the extra-long council meetings?"

Linden took a sip from her glass and set it down on the low table. "Three chasms opened up inside Tanglewood this past week—we lost a farmer, a traveling merchant caravan, and a herd of cows. I sent fay scouts to Bellaryss and Havynweal with the news. Vas has confirmed the same thing is happening in Valerra. Chasms are opening up there too—and none of you are surprised by the news. Is this why you're here?"

Mara looked at Katrine, who gave her a head nod. She wanted Mara to explain. "Aye, we're not surprised—the chasms started appearing in Bellaryss a week ago—and it *is* related to why we're here, but it's complicated."

Linden snorted. "Life, boys, and magic—none of it has ever been straightforward or easy for us. Why should I expect anything different now?" She tilted her head, a small line forming between her dark eyebrows. "Please fill me in, and while you're at it, tell me what happened to your hair and eyes. I didn't notice the change when we were standing outside, but the lighting is better in here. It's obvious— you're part elven, aren't you?"

When Mara nodded, Linden grinned. "Now that sounds like a story Jayna and I both need to hear. But first, tell me what you know about the cracks."

Mara filled in Linden about the first chasm to appear, in front of the children's hospital, and her visit to the lower realms—Linden gasped when she heard her former mentor, Mage Mother Pawllah, was the current Choir-master—and how Efram and other good spirits were beginning to fade. Mara had to backtrack a bit and tell Linden about her battle with Bazra, and how she'd used her blue sword to seal him into the lower realms.

Linden leaned forward, her brow furrowed in concentration. "What I don't understand is how Bazra is able to create such chaos. After all, he is stuck in the lowest realm of the dead—it's not as if he can leave, right?"

"That's true enough," agreed Katrine. "But he has Remy's red sword. He's able to channel the power of the ensorcelled sword to command the elements, and the spirits, in the lower realms."

Linden looked stricken. "Remy's sword? You don't mean—"

Mara hastily added, "Remy is fine. He's in Alfweard with the rest of our group." She explained about the unremembered spell that severed Remy's connection to the red sword, which unfortunately fell into Bazra's hands.

Linden's frown lines deepened. "But I still don't understand what all this has to do with the cracks."

Phineas placed his mug on the table with a firm clack. "As Maragold has said, the situation is complicated. When I first learned of the fissures appearing in the human realm, I consulted every seer in Alfweard." Mara pursed her lips. Given their shrinking population, Phineas probably spoke to two or three elves at most. "Whilst the seers do not agree on the precise cause of the fissures, they concur the source of the problem is in the underworld—and they are certain we must combine the power of all six ensorcelled swords to restore balance and prevent additional cracks."

"All *six* swords?" queried Linden. "I am aware of only five."

Phineas bowed from his shoulders and then launched into the elven legend of the Swords of Six, which did not cast the fays in a positive light.

When he finished, Linden said, "That is an interesting account of the legend, to be sure."

Katrine spread her hands. "I've seen the captain's fire sword, which appears to be the sixth sword. And Xenestra, a draconic scholar, has reviewed the elven scrolls. She believes the elven version of events is more accurate." Katrine glanced at Phineas and gave him a bow. "Xenestra is certain the elves would have been better able to manage the underworld—which would have been far less leaky— had they been in possession of the swords from the beginning."

Mara was shocked at Katrine's admission, which sounded awfully close to an apology from one head of state to another. Of course, no one knew for sure how the elves had come up two swords short.

"Thank you for so stating," said Phineas. "I concur with the dragon. All realms have suffered as a result, the human realm most of all. Consider the dark tales of ghosts, monstrous creatures, and walking undead told by humans through the centuries; if elves had been better equipped to protect the underworld's portals, most if not all of those hauntings would never have occurred."

Linden took a deep breath and glanced at Mara. "And you're here now because you need my green sword, Corbahn's gold sword, and Jayna's purple sword to set things right again in the lower realms."

"Aye," said Mara softly. "If there was any other way—"

Linden raised her hand. "I get it. You're here because there is no other way." She sighed. "I'll go tell the others. We'll help, of course. We can be ready to go shortly. Let Garlan know if you need anything else in the meantime."

A short while later Mara heard a murmur of accents down the hall, including a familiar, lilting female voice. She jogged toward the voice. Jayna turned to greet her, arms outstretched. The two women hugged, laughed, and hugged again. "Linden told me you looked different, but what a surprise!"

"And you look happy," said Mara. "Life in Faynwood must agree with you."

Jayna's curly hair framed her pretty, dark face. She broke into a shy smile as Reynier draped an arm around her waist. "Life is very agreeable here." Her eyes clouded. "Or rather, it was, until those horrid cracks opened up last week. Now, everyone is afraid of what's next."

Reynier cleared his throat. "I wish there were another way, anything other than Jayna needing to take up her sword again. I thought the days of battling Fallow necromancers and dark magic were behind us."

Jayna pulled away from Reynier, her expression stern. "You know we are never entirely free from the darker powers. If we don't take up our swords now, all the realms will suffer. Faynwood must do its part."

Reynier sighed. "Aye, my love. I merely wish for a peace that lasts longer than several months—for a decade, at least—so we could retire your purple sword."

"You wish to retire your purple sword?" asked Phineas. Mara heard the eagerness in his voice.

"I will do my part to restore order to the lower realms, and afterward, I"—Jayna and Reynier glanced at each other, a silent agreement passing between them—"that is, *we*, wish for a more stable life together."

Mara read between the lines, and apparently so did Phineas, who said, "Ah, I see. Your wish is for a child in the future, and for someone else to be called upon to wield the purple sword."

"Aye," said Jayna. "I'm not like Linden or Mara. They are gifted leaders—in battle, in council meetings, and everywhere in between. I am a healer; that is where my true path lies."

Mara could almost see the wheels turning inside Phineas's head. She wasn't surprised when he replied, "I may be able to help. You see, three ensorcelled swords were originally destined for Alfweard. My fire sword, Maragold's cobalt sword, and the rose sword—which could be either red *or* purple—our scholars never agreed on that point." He raised both hands, palms facing up. "But the fays did not fulfill their part of the contract, and the swords never found their way true north."

Reynier rubbed the long scar that bisected his eyebrow

but did not reply. As a Faymon, he was two percent fay. Mara didn't think Reynier was insulted, so much as intrigued.

Phineas gave Jayna a small bow. "When you are ready to 'retire' your purple sword, with your permission, I could cast a spell to sever your connection to the sword. I would take the sword back to Alfweard; an elf will be the next owner of the purple sword. You will be doing us a great service, milady." Phineas smiled brightly at Jayna. "Does my offer interest you?"

Mara saw the hopeful expression on Jayna's face and realized Phineas's solution was brilliant. By releasing Jayna from her sword-fighting obligations, he was helping her and also securing a third sword for the elves.

Jayna and Reynier answered simultaneously, "Aye!" They glanced at each other and chuckled softly.

Linden peered at Reynier, who frowned. "I believe you are going to ask me to remain behind in Faynwood, my Liege."

"Aye," agreed Linden. "As Faymon Elder, you are second-in-command. Should anything happen—"

"Let's ensure nothing untoward happens to any of us," interjected Corbahn, Chief of Arrowood and Linden's husband. "I forbid it." Corbahn was perhaps the fiercest-looking man Mara had ever encountered, except when he looked at Linden. Then his features softened and a small smile came to his lips. Mara felt suddenly lonely. *Does Arnesto ever look at me that way? Perhaps he did, early on, but lately he is too focused on Bazra and the problems in the under-world to look at me at all.*

Mara glanced down at her gown and then at the others. None of them were dressed for battle. She opened her mouth to say something, but Phineas's frosty mists encircled everyone, except for Reynier, who called out goodbye, blowing a kiss to his wife; Kal, who raised his head and protested; and the small black and white cat, sleeping on a cushion.

The elven captain was not one for long goodbyes. Mara heard Corbahn exclaim, "What the—", but the rest of his words were lost in the mists.

CHAPTER 23

MARA LANDED IN GLOOM AND SHADOW, THE GROUND SPONGY beneath her boots. When Katrine told her they'd meet their group at Arnesto's portal, she'd assumed they would gather in Havynweal and then access the lower realms through the bug-infested passage. Mara sniffed the warm, sulfurous air and suppressed a shudder. Phineas's icy mists had translocated them directly into the realms of the dead.

"I thought we were meeting by Arnesto's portal," she whispered.

Phineas answered, his voice low. "Aye. Look to your left —everyone else has already assembled."

Mara cast her eyes over her shoulder. He was right; just outside the portal's egress stood all the elves who'd attended the ball earlier that evening—including Dowell, Iggy, Norris, and Hortensia—their violet eyes trained on the captain of the guard. The elven men and women were dressed in their ballroom finery, with two additions: they wore mesh vests beneath their capes and coils of reaping rope on their shoulders. Mara spotted Yelenarra and Zornamayne standing next to Dowell. Xenestra, Farleigh, and Gloria waited behind them.

Mara frowned and scanned the crowd a second time, and then a third. She didn't see Arnesto or Remy. Two questions competed for dominance in Mara's head: *Where are Arnesto and Remy? And how can a hundred elves and a smattering of other species arrive in the underworld without Bazra's knowledge?* Mara had her answer to the second question almost immediately.

A screechy yowl shattered the heavy silence in the land of the dead. Mara's scalp prickled as a second shriek echoed the first. Suddenly squeals and moans filled the lower realm, setting Mara's teeth on edge. *What—or who—is making all that racket?* She moved her hand to her sword's hilt and glanced at Linden, who compressed her lips in a straight, unhappy line. Linden hated the lower realms as much as Mara did.

"I've never heard that before," hissed Linden. Corbahn put one hand on his sword hilt and the other on Linden's shoulder.

Phineas sighed. "You shall see and hear many things heretofore unknown in the lower realms."

Dowell agreed. "Sealing Bazra and the red sword into the underworld—a living, breathing necromancer with an ensorcelled object—has ripped apart the very fabric of this realm. Nothing is as it should be."

Mara's shoulders drooped. She was beginning to understand the burden of guilt Arnesto had been carrying around since Bazra captured him and the sword. "I'm to blame for this—I sealed Bazra and the red sword into this realm—but I had no idea this would happen!"

Katrine's blue curls bounced as she shook her head. "This is *not* your fault, Mara. You had zero options at the time. And don't forget you rescued thirty of us from Bazra's prison."

Phineas waved over Iggy, who passed out reaping rope to Mara and her friends. When Iggy handed Mara her coil, she sensed the web of magic—elven and elemental—woven into the fibers. Unlike the spelled golden coils preferred by fays, the elven version was silver and translucent, reminding Mara of an iced-over lake in winter. "Take heart," said Iggy, "my grandfather foresaw a catastrophic event in the lower realms involving one of the swords. *Someone* had to set the whole thing off."

"Did he predict the outcome?" grumbled Mara as she draped the coil across her chest and settled it on her left hip. She'd had far too much practice withdrawing her sword and rope simultaneously—blue sword in her right hand and reaping lasso in her left—an overrated skill everywhere, except in the realms of the dead.

Iggy shrugged. "Grandfather said there were many possible futures, but he could not say with any certainty."

Linden accepted her rope from Iggy. "That's not especially comforting, although prophecies rarely are."

Phineas spoke so softly Mara thought perhaps she'd imagined it, but then she realized he was telepathically casting his voice. He must have been communicating with everyone else as well, because the entire group grew quiet. "Prepare for battle. Lieutenant Dowell, you have charge of the Alfweardian unit."

Dowell saluted Phineas and waved one hand forward, a signal to the elves to fan out. They formed a circle around Phineas, Mara, and the rest of her friends. Hands resting on sword hilts and ropes, the elves waited, ready to spring into action at the next command. Mara rolled her shoulders, trying to loosen the tightness in her neck and back.

"Reaper Maragold, Liege Linden, Chief Corbahn, and Healer Jayna, on the count of five, withdraw your swords and strike mine. All other honored allies, please join the outer circle." Phineas waited until the elves had expanded the circle wide enough to accommodate everyone, including Xenestra, who seemed entirely absorbed in the proceedings. *She's probably making mental notes for her next scholarly monograph,* thought Mara. Yelenarra held aloft her staff, the elderly fay's weapon of choice, in her right hand. Gloria gently tapped Mara's leg with her wing before scurrying off to join Katrine in the outer circle.

Mara glanced around, hoping to see Arnesto and Remy bounding back to them. The fact they were still at large filled her with dread. Before she could form the question, Phineas spoke inside her head. "Your two companions are performing reconnaissance. Remington has an affinity for the red sword, and he volunteered for the assignment. Arnestarious insisted on accompanying him. We cannot wait for them to return. Bazra is nearly upon us."

Mara swallowed the lump in her throat and nodded as Phineas started the telepathic countdown. Everyone else holding one of the ensorcelled swords must have "heard" the captain as well—Linden, Jayna, and Corbahn gripped the jeweled hilts of their blades with a grim determination. Although Mara would never wish this on any of them, she was glad her friends stood with her in the lower realms. They had battled Fallow sorcerers and necromancers before, and they'd never let her down.

Mara's pulse quickened as she withdrew her sword, anxious in case the hieroglyphs failed to flare bright blue, but she needn't have worried. Her sword blazed as bright and clear as Linden's green sword, Corbahn's gold, and Jayna's purple. Phineas withdrew his sword last, flames lighting up his blade in a burst of fiery runes, and held it steady in the center of their small circle.

As he reached the end of the countdown, their four blades struck the elven captain's fire sword. A rainbow of sparks—blue, green, gold, purple, and amber—burst forth, dancing over their heads before drifting to the ground. As they fell, Mara felt a slight tremor beneath her boots. *Did we just do that, or did Bazra and his creepy minions cause the pulsation?*

"Again!" shouted Phineas inside their heads, and they raised their blades, striking the fire sword a second time. The spongy ground vibrated like a long-hibernating creature shaking itself awake. Mara's heart thundered in her chest as Phineas cried aloud, "And again!" As their swords struck Phineas's blade the third time, the entire realm shuddered and quaked. Mara nearly toppled over, but Phineas reached out a strong hand to steady her. She heard a loud tearing sound, followed by a rumble of thunder, and then another. A bolt of lightning struck somewhere in the distance, near the river.

She looked at Phineas. "The lower realms don't experience weather patterns."

"Disregard all of this...temporary disruption, which is caused by our swords' magic working in tandem to rebalance this realm," replied the captain, sweeping his arm to indicate the gloomy, gray dunes, twiggy trees, black boulders, and rushing river. The choir still moaned eerily on the river's far shore, attempting to harmonize again. "This is precisely as our seers predicted."

Mara refrained from an eye roll. She truly hoped Phineas's insistence on bringing together their five ensorcelled swords had not been driven by some ancient, erroneous elven prophesy. "But don't we need to relieve Bazra of the red sword before we can fully restore this realm?"

"True, but—"

Mara never heard the remainder of Phineas's response. The air crackled with screeches and shrieks as a herd, or a pack, or simply a mob—Mara couldn't get her head around what she was seeing—as Bazra's undead creatures slithered, slunk, and charged toward them.

She'd seen their grotesque likenesses before, the strange panther-lizards with razor-sharp claws and the snaky-spiders with eight long, hairy legs. Thick, sharp bristles covered their hides, jagged teeth filled their mouths, and their eyes glowed blood red. The worst part, by far, wasn't the fistful of terror slamming into Mara's belly, but the darkness pressing in on her from all sides. Her spirit withered inside her, shrinking smaller and smaller, until she felt like a tiny insect trapped inside a monstrous web.

The springy soil heaved again beneath Mara's boots, and she lost her balance, falling to her hands and knees. She became vaguely aware of her friends and elves, some wailing, some whimpering, all of them kneeling or writhing on the ground. Her head throbbed, the pain obliterating every happy memory, every moment of joy and lightness she'd ever experienced, until only bleakness remained.

I've lost everyone I've ever cared about—my mother and father, my stepmother and sisters, countless friends—and now, Remy and Arnesto have disappeared too. The Fallow necromancers and dark fays have won. Why bother to fight back? Although Mara realized, somewhere deep in her soul, that Bazra was the source of her crushing sadness, she found him impossible to withstand. His twisted magic overwhelmed her, filling her mind with images of lost battles, ruined cities, and everywhere—death. She wept, her tears salty and bitter.

Something tickled at the back of her mind. A fragment of a memory started to surface. Mara frowned; she struggled through the fogginess clouding her brain, weighing down her thoughts. *Wait. I've navigated this dark landscape before—and not so long ago. I managed to escape. But how?*

Then she remembered. Mara concentrated on dragging herself out of the pit of her despair. Beads of sweat formed on her brow and her upper lip. She groped for her sword, gingerly wrapping her fingers around the jeweled handle. The blade pulsed uncertainly, as if waiting for Mara to pull herself and her magic together. Gritting her teeth, she pushed herself off the roiling ground, gripped her hilt more firmly, and shouted in her mage's commanding voice, "No! You will *not* win this day, Bazra! Not today—not ever!"

Mara sensed Bazra's hold starting to fray. Corbahn rose slowly to his feet and reached down his hand to Linden, who stood up shakily. Linden held her sword in front of her, her eyes wide as she scanned the realm. "Those things—those snakes with legs and panthers with crocodile jaws—they're everywhere!"

"Aye," agreed Jayna. "We're surrounded—and unless the elves wake up and help us—we'll be meeting our own deaths here soon enough." She nodded at Phineas and the circle of elves, all of them still curled over on their sides, keening.

Corbahn shouted, "Snap out of it, Captain Phineas! We're losing this war, and we need you and your elves to help us."

Phineas groaned, but didn't shift his position. "I seem... unable...to resist. I am utterly powerless."

Mara bent over the elven captain and gave his shoulder

a hard shake. "You are *not* powerless. And you are *not* alone. But if you don't get up now, we're all going to die." One of the elves in the outer circle screamed as the jaws of a panther-lizard closed over the poor man's head.

Mara grimaced, wishing in her heart she could help the elf, but knowing in her head he was already gone. "That's one of *your* friends, slaughtered by Bazra's undead fiends. *Get up* and *get moving*, Captain! Now!"

Phineas's eyes blinked open. He levered himself onto one elbow, groped for his sword, and slowly stood up. Then he reared back, spotted the horde descending on them, and hollered at his elves, "On your feet, reapers! Swords and ropes at the ready! Bazra is upon us!" Phineas charged toward the outer circle and stabbed the panther-lizard snacking on the dead elf. The creature lifted its snout and roared angrily, which seemed to rouse the elves lying nearby. They shook their heads and scrambled to their feet, a pair of them tossing lassos around the bristly panther.

Mara saw a snaky-spider bearing down on Yelenarra, who was leaning on her staff. The older woman shook her head as if to clear the cobwebs, her wispy blue hair tumbling into her eyes. Mara charged the creature, the blue runes on her sword radiating with ancient magic and power. She pushed Yelenarra aside, facing the monster head-on. Yelenarra cried, "Lass, what are you doing?" but Mara focused on the red-eyed demon, his pointy teeth designed to shred and tear.

Mara felt his hot breath on her face as the monster worked his jaws. His wide, open mouth was poised above her, ready to clamp down on her head. Mara gripped her blade in both hands and jammed it through the roof of the snaky-spider's mouth. The creature screeched and backed away, dragging Mara and her sword with him.

Mara tried withdrawing her blade, but it was stuck fast —and so was she—she'd never allow Bazra to retain another ensorcelled sword. Yellow goop seeped from the open wound in the monster's mouth, spattering Mara's ruined gown and burning holes in the fabric. She grimaced and leaned right, still holding onto her sword and attempting to avoid the spray of acid from the creature's mouth. Mara unwound her silver coil but didn't have enough space to form a proper lasso. Instead, she flicked the rope like a whip at the beast's front legs, causing it to stumble. The creature pitched forward, and Yelenarra slammed her staff through its left eye. As the fiend screamed and reared up, Mara finally managed to withdraw her sword from its mouth. She jammed her blade into the creature's other eye. The monster crumbled onto the ground.

Mara slipped behind the beast, twirling her lasso above her head. She tossed the loop over the snaky-spider's snout and pulled tight. Meanwhile, Katrine dashed over and tossed a second lasso around the creature's hind legs. Mara and Katrine tugged the creature toward the river. Although he appeared defeated, the only way to ensure the evil spirit didn't rise again to possess another form was to send him downriver, into the lake of fire.

As Mara and Katrine prodded and dragged the monster, Yelenarra used her staff to clear the path to the river. She batted away three large, crowing roosters running toward them, each bird covered in metallic fish scales, the crests on top of their heads as sharp as ice picks. On all sides elves and undead beasts battled. Out of the corner of her eye, Mara noticed Zornamayne starting to load the injured onto Xenestra's broad back. Jayna ran over to lend a hand with the injured. Norris fought with a sword in each hand, fending off any undead creatures as they approached the dragon, Jayna, and Zornamayne.

Mara and Katrine shoved the snaky-spider into the churning water, loosened their lassos, and watched as the current swept the beast away. Mara heard the creature squeal as it struggled before sinking beneath the surf. She used the back of her hand to wipe her brow, which came away bloody.

Yelenarra pointed. "I think that will need stitches, my dear."

Mara shook her head. "Later. Right now, we need to help Linden and Corbahn." Katrine sprinted over to her great-niece, who was trying to stop a flock of scaly roosters from pecking at an injured elf. Meanwhile, Corbahn had squared off against another snaky-spider, and although he was getting the better of the creature, he didn't see the panther-lizard prowling toward him.

"Corbahn! Behind you!" hollered Mara. She reached into her left boot, withdrew one of her daggers, and flung it at the panther. The knife sank into the beast's flank, garnering both its attention and its fury. The creature charged Mara and leapt in the air, a strange, fascinating sight—panther body, lizard snout and tail, hanging for a moment in the still air of the underworld—before falling on top of Hortensia.

CHAPTER 24

OH NO! PHINEAS WILL NEVER FORGIVE ME! MARA STILL WASN'T quite clear on the relationship between Phineas and Hortensia, but she knew there was one. Mara threw her other dagger at the panther-lizard, who shook itself, barely registering it had a screaming elf pinned beneath it. The creature leapt again, aiming for Mara's throat—this time, its aim was true—and Mara was ready. She brought her sword up against her chest, cross-wise, and as the beast tumbled on top of her, she slit its throat.

Hortensia had recovered sufficiently to toss a lasso around the monster, and Iggy ran over to assist her. The panther-lizard screeched and extended its claws, slicing Mara's left leg. She hissed in pain, rolled onto her right side, and shouted, "Retrieve my daggers before you haul him into the water! No point in losing my blades!"

Hortensia rolled her eyes—which made Mara grin, since Hortensia had learned about eye rolls from her—but then the elf withdrew the knives from the struggling creature and dropped them near Mara's boots. "Thank you, Maragold," she called over her shoulder, as she and Iggy dragged the fiend toward the water. "You have earned my gratitude."

Scores of Bazra's panther-lizards, snaky-spiders, and scaly-roosters attacked them, joined by an entire infantry of undead troopers, wearing the tattered rags of a bygone regime. Mara had no time to process where the troopers had materialized from—and wondered at the metaphysical impossibility—since any necromancer raising an undead army would use them to haunt the living realm, not the dead.

Bazra had relied on living, breathing dark fays, the Bazeerka, when he'd lived in his creepy tower in the second-lowest realm, and the creatures he'd sent to defeat her in the past had been the same bristly, toothy variety she was battling now. Well, except for the scaly-roosters, whom she'd not encountered previously.

Mara had no idea which were worse, Bazra's hideous creatures or the new arrivals, the undead soldiers with flesh hanging in strips from their skeletal frames, their eye sockets empty, and their lower jaws missing from their skulls. She focused on the spiky beasts, because they seemed particularly interested in attacking anyone with an ensorcelled sword.

Every time Mara managed to lasso a creature and drag it to the river—assisted by either Katrine or Linden or one of the elves—it seemed two more popped up in its place. Mara had no way of keeping track who was winning or losing, but she had a sinking feeling in the pit of her stomach things weren't going according to Phineas's plan. Too many elves had fallen, and the undead monsters and soldiers were too numerous and resilient. Many of the injured beasts scurried off, before anyone could lasso them and haul them into the river—which meant they'd be back after they'd healed.

The ground quaked and rumbled beneath Mara's boots, and she stumbled to maintain her balance on the squashy soil. A series of screeches filled the realm, a cross between a scream, a yowl, and a roar that hurt Mara's ears.

"What's making that horrid noise?" yelled Linden. "It sounds *big*, whatever it is!"

"I don't know, but it's giving me a headache!" shouted Mara, who gripped her sword more firmly, the runes blazing brightest blue.

Corbahn pointed. "I think it's coming from that...monstrous spiky thing...which is heading right toward us!" Corbahn pulled Linden and Mara back into a stand of black, scraggly trees, their leaves gray and sparse in the constant gloom of the lowest realm.

"Is that Bazra, riding a giant *boulder*?" hissed Katrine, who'd run up next to them.

Mara squinted at the figure, wearing a long, black, hooded cape and thick goggles over his eyes, wielding a dull red blade. Remy's old sword was now in the hands of the darkest, nastiest fay in any realm. Although the sword didn't sparkle and glimmer brightly like it used to, Bazra had obviously discovered a way to channel some of the sword's elemental magic.

The dark fay king stood on top of a massive, bristly, mound-like creature, one of many sprinkled throughout the realm, which Mara had thought was a boulder but was actually a mostly ossified spirit. The dark fay urged the mound forward, and the boulder-thing rumbled toward the trees where they were gathered.

"Fan out!" shouted Mara. "I don't think we can lasso that thing—any ideas?"

Corbahn sheathed his sword and reached for his bow and a handful of arrows. As they ran from Bazra and his strange mount, Corbahn fired off a series of arrows. The spiky creature screeched and reversed course, retreating in double time as Bazra raise his sword in the fetid air of the realm and hissed an incantation in the fay tongue. Bolts of black lightning struck the trees, the river, and the far shore, frightening the living, the dead, and the undead.

Spirits—both the good and the unsavory—started fleeing, floating upward through the chasms toward the human realm. The undead soldiers, screaming and wailing, winked out suddenly, yanked into another realm by an invisible necromancer. Meanwhile, Bazra's panther-lizards, snaky-spiders, and scaly-roosters kept coming at them, compelled by the dark fay's magic.

"What's wrong—why isn't this working?" hollered Mara, as she helped Phineas drag a massive panther-lizard into the river. "If anything, we've made things even worse! Spirits are departing through every conceivable exit, and I can't say I blame them. And all of the undead soldiers have vanished—back to wherever they came from." Mara hastily stepped out of range of the monster's snapping jaws, which could easily sever a hand or foot.

Even the far shore was quiet, deserted now. The Choirmaster and her chorus had retreated well beyond the far shoreline. Mara only hoped the Choirmaster knew the way back when—or if—she could figure out how to repair the lowest realm. Without the choir, Mara knew she could never rebalance the underworld. Efram's spirit would disperse into the ether, and it would be all her fault.

Phineas yelled above the creature's caterwauling. "I am equally flummoxed! The power of our combined swords should have overcome Bazra and his legion."

Linden joined them, tossing her lasso around the creature as they alternately dragged and pushed the thrashing, wailing monster into the water. "Did we neglect something essential, something so obvious we simply missed it?"

Perspiration trickled into Mara's eyes, making them blur and sting. She blinked rapidly, considering Linden's question. *What, if anything, did we forget?* A thought rattled around inside Mara's weary, sleep-deprived brain. *Could the answer be that simple?* "Not something—someone! A powerful, Fallow necromancer has to be helping Bazra. Nothing else makes sense."

Linden's eyes widened. "Of course—crazy King Roi! He's been slipping in and out of Vas's grasp ever since the end of the war with Glenbarra."

"I have heard of this Glenbarran king, but I find it hard to believe a human could wield such power," sputtered Phineas, as he used his shoulder to shove the monster farther into the churning current. "And let's not forget Fallow sorcery is useless in this realm."

"Release your lassos," shouted Mara, as her rope slackened. The creature sank beneath the surface, screeching curses at them until it disappeared into the surf. She used her torn sleeve to wipe her brow. "Roi doesn't operate alone. He has a strong following among disaffected Fallow mages and anyone else looking to make trouble."

Linden reeled in her rope. "Fallow necromancers could be raising the dead in the human realm and sending them here for Bazra to command. Those soldiers, for instance. They were wearing really old uniforms...I seem to remember seeing them in one of my father's military history books." Linden adjusted her coil on her shoulder.

Suddenly Linden's head snapped up, and she locked eyes with Mara. "Those were royal guards—*Glenbarran* royal guards, from old King Barre's reign—I think that's evidence enough Roi is helping Bazra." King Roi was the lunatic son of the late King Barre, who had eschewed Fallow magic during his lifetime, or at least, until he became so enfeebled his son took over the day-to-day running of the kingdom.

Phineas groaned. "That is a most unhelpful scenario, but one we must consider." He glanced at the fighting all around them, his elves engaged in battling the bristly, toothy beasts, aided by Yelenarra and her staff. Meanwhile Corbahn and Katrine deposited another spidery creature into the river farther downstream. Nodding at Mara and Linden, he said, "Would you mind handling those roosters heading our way? I need to provide Dowell with fresh instructions."

Mara frowned. *Can't the elven captain handle the creatures and then issue new orders?* Perhaps telepathic communication required all of Phineas's magical focus. She glanced at Linden, who shrugged. "Fine. Then let's regroup and figure out our next move."

Three squalling, scaly-roosters charged toward them. They ran with their heads down, their pointy crests facing forward, ready to impale anyone unfortunate enough to cross their path. Mara hissed, "How about I go left and you go right? Let's try both ropes at the same time."

Linden pushed a chunk of blue-and-black hair out of her eyes. "And to think I could be safely tucked into bed, dreaming of Faymon politics and endless debates, instead of hauling ugly roosters toward their ultimate demise."

Mara grinned as she tossed Linden one end of her coil, and Linden did the same, handing off the end of her coil. "On three. One, two, three!" She and Linden sprinted to either side of the squawking flock, dragging their two ropes on the ground. Once the roosters were less than a foot away, the two girls pulled their lines taut, and circling behind the birds, entrapped them in the two lengths of coil. They dragged the wriggling, screeching roosters to the river and flung them into the fast-moving current.

"Whew!" said Linden. "They're nothing like my aunties' chickens back in Valerra." Mara started to chuckle, but the laugh died on her lips.

"Scary ghosts," huffed Farleigh, bounding toward Mara and Linden on all fours, with Gloria riding on his back. "Bad men."

Mara knew Gloria would not have condescended to a ride from Farleigh unless she'd been injured. She raced over to her griffin, bleeding from a cut on top of her head. "Let's get you to Zornamayne right away!" Mara gently lifted Gloria from Farleigh's back, cradling the griffin against her chest. "What happened?"

Gloria clicked her beak weakly. "We decided to track Remington and Arnestarious, in case they needed assistance. Farleigh's nose is quite sensitive."

Farleigh woofed. "Bazra escaped through crack. Boys followed. So did soldiers and ghosts."

Mara glanced around, a chill settling in her spine. "Can you track them again?"

Farleigh nodded his shaggy head. "Bellaryss."

Mara's heart sank—it was the worst possible outcome—Roi and Bazra meeting up in the Valerran capital, along with undead soldiers, free-floating spirits, and anything else the necromancers decided to raise. She carried Gloria to Zornamayne, who was settling another injured elf on Xenestra's back. Jayna stood by the dragon's tail, deciding which patients needed to be seen immediately by Zorna-mayne. Mara glanced up; the dragon's broad back was nearly full. Zornamayne and Jayna would have to set up a triage unit where their healing spells would be effective, since they couldn't use Serving magic in the lower realms.

Mara carefully placed her griffin in Jayna's outstretched arms. "We're leaving soon for Havynweal. Don't worry, we'll take good care of her," said Jayna. "Kal would never forgive me if something happened to his mother." Mara mouthed a silent "thank you" to her old friend.

Gloria squawked. "Find those boys...and then come home."

"Aye," whispered Mara, running a hand over her griffin's mane. "I'll bring them home." *But where is home? Where do I belong?*

Corbahn jogged toward them, an injured blue-haired fay in his arms. Mara's heart seized up. The fay was too small to be Arnesto, but that left only Katrine and—"Oh Yelenarra!" cried Mara. She glanced at Zornamayne, who'd hopped down from Xenestra's back and dashed over to examine the elderly fay. Yelenarra clutched her middle, a dark stain spreading beneath her fingers.

Zornamayne's eyes met Mara's, her whiskers rigid. "The wound is deep." *But can you heal her? Will she live, and love, and laugh again?* Mara wanted to shout at the impassive hybrid, demanding answers, but she forced herself to remain calm.

Yelenarra opened her mouth to speak, and Mara leaned closer, blinking back tears. The fay woman sputtered, pausing a few times to catch her breath. "Take my blood... for your sword...you know what to do." Mara shook her head. She wanted neither Yelenarra's blood, nor what she could do with it. Yelenarra choked on the words. "Take... use...only way."

Tears streaking down her face, Mara used two fingers to

swipe at the dark blot on Yelenarra's abdomen. Mara rubbed her fingers across the center of her blade, making sure she didn't touch Efram's reddish-brown stain lower down. With Arnesto's smear covering the large sapphire on the bottom of the hilt, her sword now carried the blood magic of all three fays.

Katrine stood behind Mara. She placed a hand on her shoulder but said nothing; Mara knew she loved Yelenarra too. They stepped back as Corbahn and Jayna carefully laid Yelenarra near the base of the giant dragon's tail. Corbahn hopped down and hollered, "All clear!"

"Wait! We have one more." Iggy and another elf carried an unconscious Dowell between them. They helped Jayna find a spot for the injured lieutenant on the dragon's crowded back.

Jayna called down, "That's all we can take. Stand back."

The giant dragon glanced behind her and bellowed, "Hold tight to my spinal plates!" Extending her wings, Xenestra ran forward on her powerful hind legs. At the last possible moment, when it looked as if she might crash into a low dune covered in limp, gray grass, she flapped her wings and lifted off. The dragon flew upward in looping, graceful spirals, gaining distance with each beat of her gold-flecked green, teal, and blue wings.

Corbahn draped his arm around Linden's shoulders, and she leaned back against him. He kissed the top of her head. Mara tried not to compare herself and Arnesto to the Liege of Faynwood and Chief of Arrowood—whose relationship ran the gamut from contentious to lovestruck on any given day—and yet, they were as grounded and secure as Yelenarra's mountain. Corbahn and Linden had managed to overcome a lot of old prejudices and hurts.

Maybe there's a lesson here for Arnesto and me—if I can find the impossible fay!

Phineas rejoined them, watching as Xenestra flew out of sight. The elven captain's eyes softened when he addressed Mara. "I am truly sorry about Lady Yelenarra's injuries."

Mara sniffed and blinked. Her heart ached for Yelenarra, and for Arnesto, who would be beside himself with grief. However, she didn't need sympathy at the moment; she needed a plan. "Thank you. I know you've suffered many casualties today, as well."

"Aye," the captain agreed, his voice gravelly. "The toll has been heavy, and far too many good spirits—elven, fay, and human—remain in limbo, with no means of moving on."

Mara pointed to Farleigh, panting by her side. "We need to go after Remy and Arnesto—and the red sword and Bazra—who managed to escape through one of the rifts above. Farleigh will help us find them; they're somewhere in Bellaryss. Will you join us?"

Phineas drew his white-blond eyebrows together. "With Lieutenant Dowell injured, I must remain here to lead the mop up operation. We still have many undead creatures, temporarily incapacitated, to send downriver, as well as a number of elves with more minor injuries that I'll need to translocate back to Alfweard. I am afraid I will be detained for quite some time."

"Then I suppose this is goodbye." Mara sheathed her sword. Placing her left hand beneath her right forearm, she extended her right hand to the captain.

Phineas shook her hand gravely and turning toward Hortensia and Iggy, took several steps in their direction. Suddenly, he spun back around. "Do take care, Maragold.

You just completed your passage rites, which are taxing, and your elven powers are new. You have much to learn."

Did I hear correctly? Phineas just admitted Hortensia's healing rituals are hard. And did the elven captain just tell me to be careful? Mara knew she'd never be able to learn elven ways without a mentor. Who better than the captain himself? She had nothing left to lose. "Will you teach me?"

Phineas quirked an eyebrow and seemed to be considering Mara's question. Finally, he gave her a curt nod. "I will find you when my work—and yours—is done."

Mara watched as he jogged toward Iggy and Hortensia, and then she turned back to Katrine, Linden, and Corbahn. "Are you ready?"

Linden glanced around and shivered. "More than ready."

Mara placed a hand on Farleigh's furry shoulder. "This next part is up to you, old friend. Help us find Remy and Arnesto."

"Aye," grunted Farleigh. "Help friends!"

CHAPTER 25

Farleigh dropped down to all fours and jogged away from the river, running past stands of spindly trees and clumps of tall, gray grass. He paused beneath the same crack Mara had tumbled through with Arnesto, which had opened next to the children's hospital. Mara glanced up; how in Queen's Crown had Remy, Arnesto, and Bazra ascended to street level?

Farleigh woofed at Mara, who scratched her head. "I'm sorry, Farleigh, but I have no idea how to track them through that crack. Did you see how they managed it?"

Farleigh shook his head, his tail drooping. Corbahn rubbed his beard thoughtfully. "Spirits can rise to the surface that way, but not flesh-and-blood mages. There must be a hidden portal nearby."

They spread out and searched the area, careful not to disturb any slumbering, ossified spirits—Mara really didn't want to lasso any more of them. They waded through tall grasses, examined rock formations, and tapped on tree trunks. "This isn't getting us anywhere," grumbled Linden.

"They did not *climb* out." Corbahn stood beneath the chasm, craning his neck.

Katrine scowled at the opening. "We know fay traveling mists don't work down here. Only elves have the ability to teleport within the realms of the dead." Katrine sounded a tad bitter, and Mara couldn't really blame her. Fays were the dominant magical species everywhere—except in Alfweard, of course—and in the underworld.

"I suppose we could ask Phineas for a lift to the surface," reasoned Mara.

Katrine shook her head. "Elven magic is unknown in Valerra. The last thing we need is to alarm Vas and the other Serving mages in the city. We'll need to properly introduce Vas and Phineas first."

"Bazra, Remy, and Arnesto deployed magic of some sort to get out of here." Linden shrugged. "We just need to figure out what."

"Or, one of them used magic and the others tagged along," said Mara, an idea slowly forming. Katrine asked her to explain. "Bazra figured out how to use the red sword's magic to turn this realm upside down. Perhaps he's found a way to use it to escape too."

Katrine slowly nodded. "If he's figured out a way, then we can too."

Linden turned to Mara. "You've done this before; you've awakened the elemental magic in your sword. Please show Corbahn and me how to do it."

Mara blew out a puff of air. It was strange—disconcerting even—for Linden, the Liege of Faynwood and a master mage, to be asking for *her* advice. "I mashed together a spell and focused on channeling the elemental energy in my sword...I was guessing the entire time. I'm no expert."

"But what you did worked," pointed out Corbahn.

Linden gave Mara an encouraging smile. "You can do this. I have faith in you."

Mara pursed her lips. "Thanks for the vote of confidence. Now let me think." She withdrew her sword, the blue hieroglyphs lighting up the blade, and stared up at the fissure. Last time, she'd used the elemental magic in her sword to call down Xenestra, and later to seal Bazra and his creatures into the lowest realm. The incantations she'd used before wouldn't work without some serious editing. Then again, the actual words would have been powerless without the magical energy she'd directed through her sword.

She remembered a version of the old mage's mantra Yelenarra had quoted the last time they'd done this, and she repeated it out loud. "We have to Focus, Funnel, Find, Flow...focus our sword's magic, funnel our mental energy, and find us a conveyance in the flow of the elements."

"Huh?" said Linden and Corbahn.

Katrine pointed at Mara's sword. "Mara, I think this is up to you. Last time, you were able to channel *both* types of magic through your sword—elemental and elven— although we didn't realize you were half-elven at the time. You'll need to do it again, but this time without calling down Xenestra, who is otherwise occupied."

Mara narrowed her eyes at the crack overhead. From this distance it looked like a thin black line in the firmament of the underworld. She glanced around, trying to figure out what she could use to lift them up and out of the lower realms. She scanned the gray dunes and black grasses, the creepy, spindly trees, and the dark rocks and boulders, her eyes coming to rest on a low rise in the ground not far from where they stood. Nodding, she indicated the rest of the group should follow her. She raised a finger to her lips and said under her breath, "We're climbing onto that low rise over there—but we need to be very quiet and not shift our feet once we're on it."

Katrine smacked her forehead. "You've got to be kidding me!"

"Do you have a better idea?" whispered Mara. Linden and Corbahn glanced at each other and shrugged.

"Let's just get this over with," hissed Katrine. Everyone clambered onto the mound, which shuddered slightly. Farleigh whined and Katrine patted his shoulder.

Mara raised her sword and shouted, "Spirit of the dead ascend, take us to the living realm. Deposit us safely therein —then to your present state return."

The undead beast-mound grunted and groaned and rose in the air. Linden's eyes widened, and she reached out for Corbahn's hand. The creature soared upward, screeching and trembling the entire way. Mara held her sword aloft and repeated the incantation continuously as they ascended, barely pausing for a breath in case the monster got any other ideas. As their heads emerged from the crack, the beast shook itself violently, tossing them off its back and onto the road. Mara feared for a moment it would disobey her instructions, but the beast-mound juddered, belched, and with a final groan plunged back down through the chasm.

Farleigh yipped and took off down the street. Mara and the others jogged behind the crossbreed, who paused periodically to sniff the cobblestones. He stopped, lifted his head, and let out a mighty, mournful howl before taking off on all fours and disappearing out of view. Mara didn't slow down. "He's heading toward the cemetery," she called out to the others. "And I don't think he's howling like that because he's found Bazra."

"Then who's he chasing after?" grumbled Katrine. "And who are *we* chasing?"

"The man who legalized crossbreeding in Glenbarra and funded Mordahn's grihm program," shouted Mara. "The one man Farleigh truly hates—King Roi."

"Just great," grunted Corbahn. "Now all we need is for Bazra and Roi to meet at the cemetery."

"Aye," panted Linden as she jogged. "Two Fallow sorcerer kings—one fay and the other human—with the power to raise the dead."

They turned onto High Street and stopped in their tracks. Mara caught her breath. Her beloved city was a warzone once again—but this time, instead of battling their Glenbarran oppressors, the citizens of Bellaryss were fighting an *undead* occupation.

Valerrans, wielding clubs, knives, pots, and pans, battled an undead mob swaying in front of the cemetery. The metropolitan constables pitched in to aid them, but the Valerrans were losing. The undead men and women, in various stages of decomposition, ignored their severed limbs and stab wounds—after all, they were already dead—and kept shambling out of the cemetery gates and down the street.

Mara scanned the cemetery grounds, searching for any patterns as the undead continued rising from their graves. She narrowed her eyes at a grisly duo, probably guards when they'd lived, their uniforms now moldy rags hanging from skeletal frames. They tilted their skulls, screeched something unintelligible and skirted around the battle, heading up High Street.

A gruesome-looking couple followed them out of the

cemetery, the woman wearing a tattered gown, the man in shredded black coattails. They shuffled away in the opposite direction. Mara watched as the men and women, from soldiers and shopkeepers to horse breeders and blacksmiths, little bits of rotten cloth and decayed skin sticking to their bones, lumbered away. They didn't engage in the battle but seemed to be guided by some purpose, in a shuffling, lurching, undead sort of a way.

Mara spotted Chef Desna, wielding a pair of kitchen knives in his large hands, circling one of Bazra's pantherlizards that had managed to escape from the lower realms. "Chef!" she shouted. "Aim for its eyes!"

Desna must have heard her above the groans and cries of battle. He rotated both knives so their handles pointed toward the monster and raised the weapons to shoulder height. In one fluid motion, he flung his knives at the beast, their sharp tips sinking into the creature's eyes. The monster reared back, roaring, and then collapsed, yellow goop from his eyes sizzling as it spattered the pavement.

Two of Desna's apprentices attempted to stop a lurching soldier from leaving the cemetery. One apprentice lopped off the undead man's arm. The skeletal soldier leaned over, picked up his limb, which was mostly bone with a few patches of flesh and cloth, and continued on his way. The apprentice looked ready to give pursuit, but Desna called out, "Leave it be, lad. All we're doing right now is slowing 'em down, but we're not stopping 'em. It's time to scrap the dough and start over."

Desna carefully removed his blades from the pantherlizard, wiped them on his apron—which smoked from the acid burning the starched white fabric—and glanced up at Mara. "We need a strategy, and I hope, Miss Pensk, you have something in mind?"

"Not quite yet, Chef," admitted Mara. "But I'm working on it." Mara thought Chef Desna was giving her too much credit. Though she'd rescued a lot of folks from Bazra once before—including both her ex-boyfriends, Katrine, Vas, and Desna—Mara was hoping Katrine or maybe Linden might have some ideas for capturing the dark fay king now they were in Valerran territory.

"Might I suggest focusing on the best counter-measures for reversing all of this nonsense?" The chef pointed at the lurching clusters of undead wandering away from the cemetery. Most of the citizens had stopped fighting them by then, realizing the futility. No additional panther or snake monsters made an appearance, so Mara hoped the last one had snuck through with Bazra himself. The more Mara pondered various means of escape from the lower realms, the more she became convinced Bazra had escaped the same way she had—on an ossified spirit that still moved when prodded—and Arnesto and Remy had somehow hitched a ride.

A cloud of fay mists formed in front of them, depositing Vas and Talias on the sidewalk. For as long as Mara knew her, Chief Inspector Talias had taken great pains to hide her fay heritage while on the job, but not any longer. Rather than disguising herself as a bespectacled, staid Valerran inspector, her black hair pulled back into a tight bun, Talias's long, wavy blue locks flowed down her back, and she'd lost her spectacles. Perhaps in the current crisis, Talias had decided to telegraph her fayness as a means of calming Valerrans, especially among the non-magical population, who were more apt to panic at the first sign of anything supernatural.

Whatever Talias's reason for dropping the glamour spells, Mara applauded the decision—she thought everyone should be able to embrace their ancestry and be fully themselves—even girls who were part elven, like herself, or part fay, like Linden.

Vas's eyes blazed as he hollered at Katrine and Mara. "What took you so long? I thought you'd never come! What are you doing about this undead mess?" He spotted Linden and Corbahn behind them and bowed. "Oh, ah, Liege Linden, Chief Corbahn. It's good to see you again, despite these circumstances."

Vas looked ready to resume his shouting, but Katrine put her hands on her hips. "Stop hollering, Vas, and tell us how long this has been going on."

Vas ran a hand through his short-cropped, blue-streaked hair. "Bodies started disappearing two nights ago—just a few at first. We assumed they'd been taken by body snatchers."

Talias nodded. "And then last night, we found a whole section of the cemetery with coffins unearthed, and we knew the problem was far bigger than body snatchers digging up the dead for profit."

Desna spoke up. "When a couple of my bakers told me a skeleton army was invading High Street, I closed the shop and dashed over. This chaos here"—he waved his arm—"started about an hour ago." He nodded, his ice-blue eyes narrowed at the cemetery. "I'll be in my shop should you need me. Times like these, my customers want their breads and sweets more than ever."

Mara's stomach rumbled; she thought of the chef's famous puff pastry and sighed. "Have you figured out where they're heading?"

Vas shook his head. "They're fanning out all across the city, and we're not able to contain them. I'm hoping they can lead us to the necromancers who are raising them."

Mara whistled and Farleigh bounded over to her. He sat on his haunches, his tongue hanging out of his mouth and his sides heaving. He'd been howling non-stop. "Has King Roi been here?"

Farleigh yipped, "Aye. His smell here."

"Where's he now?" shouted Vas, sounding like the marine colonel he'd been during the war. "Tell me!"

Farleigh whimpered and started shaking. Mara glared at the provisional president, who lowered his voice. "Sorry, Farleigh. I'm so frustrated—I can't seem to catch Roi—he's slippery as an eel."

Mara placed a hand on Farleigh's shoulder. "Can you tell us which direction Roi was headed?"

Farleigh yowled, "Under cemetery. Bad men."

Vas's forehead furrowed. He turned to Talias as if she could translate grihm-speak for him. The chief inspector crouched down in front of the giant crossbreed. "Roi went *under* the cemetery?" When Farleigh nodded, she asked, "Is he hiding in one of the mausoleums?"

Farleigh shook his shaggy head. "Tunnels!"

"How?" Vas scrubbed his face with his palm. "We patrol the tunnels regularly. There's been no sign of Roi anywhere near here and only isolated sightings elsewhere."

"But there've been enough sightings of Roi in the outskirts of Bellaryss to confirm he's in the area," Talias pointed out. "He's managed to stay two steps ahead of us."

"Let's face it, those tunnels are impossible to patrol entirely. We've spent enough time in them to know that much," said Katrine. The Valerran resistance had employed the tunnels running beneath Bellaryss throughout the war and occupation. The tunnel system was vast, confusing, and never completed. There were twists, turns, and dead ends enough to hide a crazy necromancer and his followers.

"Aye," agreed Linden, "and only the main tunnel system has been properly mapped."

"Since no one has mapped the tunnels entirely, how are we going to track down Roi and Bazra without getting lost ourselves?" asked Corbahn. "I'd rather not rely solely on Farleigh's superior nose."

Farleigh grunted, "I track them. But tunnels scary."

A sickening roar reverberated through the streets, followed by fresh screaming from Valerrans—the living variety. The sounds of boots, hooves, and paws striking the pavement grew louder.

Vas groaned, "What now?"

Talias glanced at Vas, her brow furrowing. "Could someone have let animals out of the city zoo?" The city zoo, otherwise known as the Bellaryss Zoological Society, was considered the finest—and largest—collection of exotic animals anywhere in the continent.

"Sounds like a stampede to me!" grunted Corbahn. "Something more than a few animals set loose."

Linden massaged her forehead. "I have a bad feeling about this. I sense dark magic at play here." As both a mage and a seer, Linden often had visions, accompanied by nasty headaches. While Mara was no seer, she sympathized with Linden and her headaches. Every time Mara used a powerful new combination of spells, her head hurt afterward.

Mara had a feeling Corbahn and Linden were both right, and this was much worse than a typical stampede. "We need to get Valerrans off these streets, now!"

Talias was already barking orders at her constables, who immediately began shepherding adults and children into the government offices across from the cemetery.

Katrine helped a mother corral her three children, carrying the youngest into the building.

The fastest animals—the cheetahs, antelopes, and gazelles—rounded the corner six blocks away, followed by much smaller hares and foxes, darting about wildly, and then the wildebeests, kangaroos, and a throng of other species. Mara heard elephants trumpeting behind them and shuddered to think of the damage the frightened, rampaging animals were causing. She felt certain something had spooked them; they all appeared driven by the same impulse to run, but Mara couldn't fathom where were they headed or who was in control.

As the entire city zoo bore down on them, Mara realized, with sickening dread, what had set them off. "Oh no! They're possessed!"

CHAPTER 26

"Any ideas?" yelled Linden, as a pack of wild dogs howled nearby. The cheetahs, antelopes, and gazelles sprinted past them; at least their goal wasn't to trample Mara and her friends. Were they merely a distraction, then?

A faintly glowing apparition flickered on the pavement in front of them. Mara stared as the ghost attempted to solidify. She bit down on her bottom lip and winced. *This can't be...Efram?* Arnesto's brother nodded in greeting, but his head detached from his neck and floated in the air. Vas, the tough marine colonel and famed leader of the Valerran resistance, fainted. Corbahn caught the provisional president and lowered him onto the cobbled street.

"Time's almost up." Efram's head bobbed in front of Mara. She strained to hear his voice, more of a sigh than a whisper. "A few hours, at most, and I'll fade to nothing. Find Arnesto and use our blood magic—auntie's, mine, and his—to defeat the ghost army." He reached out, his arms mere wisps, and tried grasping his head, which wobbled and rolled. Mara shut her eyes for a few seconds, unable to watch. When she opened them again, Efram's head was more or less where it belonged. He wavered and slowly winked out

"Was that...Efram's ghost?" asked Linden, her face ashen.

Mara nodded. "We have just hours left to reset the lower realms."

"He said something about blood," Corbahn frowned, "but I couldn't hear the rest."

Mara hastily explained about the blood magic running through Arnesto's family line, and how she'd combined it once before with her sword's magic to command Bazra's undead beasts. "But it's more complicated now. We're no longer in the lower realms—and we have spirits, both good and bad, roaming the streets of Bellaryss—plus possessed animals, risen bodies, and both Bazra and Roi on the loose. This is a nightmare!"

Katrine had rejoined them, and she gave Vas a hand up from the cobblestones. Talias and four of her constables were down the street, attempting to calm the elephants and prevent them from crashing through a row of shop windows. Katrine glanced at Mara. "I think you need to start with those poor animals. You know what you need to do."

Mara withdrew her sword from its scabbard and stared down at the old smear from Efram and the newer, brighter smear from his aunt. "I need to separate the spirits from the animals—and do it safely. These are living creatures, and I don't want to destroy them." Which meant she'd need to improvise again, stitch together yet another spell, and hope it did the trick.

Mara touched the reddish-brown spatter of Efram's

blood above the hilt and then raised her blade to the over-cast sky. Her sword's hieroglyphs lit up, a bright blue beacon in her right hand. Mara shouted:

> *"Roaming spirits, your rest delayed,*
> *Stop and listen to my command:*
> *Leave these living beasts alone—*
> *Lowly, frightened creatures all.*
> *Return at once to the lowest realm,*
> *Return to where you now belong."*

Nothing happened. The animals kept running, roaring, yowling, and bleating. Mara hung her head; she had no moves left, nothing she could think of to fix this necro-mantic disaster. She could really use Arnesto's fay wizardry at the moment—actually, she'd feel a whole lot better if she could just *see* Arnesto—and Remy too, and know they were safe.

Linden whispered, "I think it's working. Take a look!"

The wild dogs stopped howling and lay down on the road, panting. Instead of running madly, the gazelles and antelopes wandered into the cemetery and started grazing on the grass. Even the elephants became more cooperative. They ceased their trumpeting and trampling, and one of them playfully grabbed a constable's hat with its trunk.

Mara's legs wobbled from the expenditure of so much energy. She dropped down onto the curb, leaned her elbows on her knees, and propped her chin in her hands. "Alright then. At least *that* problem's solved, although the consta-bles and zookeepers will be busy for the rest of the day."

"Well done, lass." Katrine smiled down at her.

"But we still have Bazra and Roi to catch, and this undead mob to deal with," sighed Mara. *Plus I haven't slept in two days; I almost died yesterday during my elven passage rites; I'm rattled about my two ex-boyfriends' whereabouts; and I'm heartsick over Yelenarra.*

"Could you do the same thing with the undead mob—separate the ghosts from the bodies they're inhabiting—and send the spirits back to the lower realms?" asked Linden.

Mara shook her head. "When I started my spell, I sensed the intentions of the ghosts possessing the animals, and they were positive, perhaps even a bit protective. I think they were good spirits, attempting to flee from Bazra and Roi, who would have forced them to rise again and submit to the necromancers' control. Instead, the spirits chose to join themselves to the animals.

"But I'm afraid it's not the same with the undead roaming the streets. The unsavory ghosts that escaped from the underworld inhabit bodies again—however gruesome and decayed—and they have no intention of leaving. Many are quite nasty and will fight me all the way. As for the rest," Mara shook her head, "the spirits must obey the necromancer that raised them."

Farleigh lifted his head and whined, "Scary."

"Very scary indeed." Mara rose from the curb and stretched, pushing against her aching muscles and all-over fatigue.

"We need to find Roi and Bazra and put an end to this for good!" grumbled Vas.

Mara thought about the many hiding places where Roi and Bazra could be holed up—whether in the tunnels themselves, the caves along the coast, or even a private residence—the possibilities were endless. "Even if Roi and Bazra met up in the tunnels and used them to escape, they could be anywhere by now. Maybe we can flush them out into the open."

"Sounds preferable to searching the tunnels, which could take days, and Efram said we only have hours." Corbahn rubbed his beard. "But how?"

"What sort of leverage can we use to induce them to come to us?" Vas grunted.

Mara withdrew her sword and pointed at the reddish smear from Yelenarra's wound. She glanced at Katrine, whose eyes widened. "That's a dangerous gamble, Mara. Are you sure about this?"

"No." Mara frowned. "I'm not sure...but Yelenarra and Efram believe it's the only way." She didn't want to think about Yelenarra or her injury. Had the elderly fay already passed into the lower realms? Mara didn't think even Zornamayne could reverse the damage.

Linden squeezed Mara's arm. "If you think this is the best option—or our only option—then let's do it."

Mara murmured her thanks. "I'd feel better if we could tip off Arnesto and Remy somehow." Mara knelt down in front of Farleigh. "Have you picked up their scents?"

"Not sure," grunted Farleigh. "Think nearby."

Mara glanced at Katrine and Linden. "Are you sensing their magical signatures in the area?" Master mages could sense the presence of other mages and even determine who had recently cast a spell, conjured a protection charm—or raised the dead. They shook their heads. Mara tucked a loose lock of hair behind her ear and tried not to lose heart. *Where are you, Arnesto? Are you and Remy safe...or lying injured somewhere, hidden under a veil of drabness?*

Mara wondered whether she really could go through with it, and more importantly, whether she should. What gave her the right to invoke forbidden magic, one that

Mordahn, Roi, and Bazra had used so freely and to such disastrous effects? What if she became corrupted by the dark magic and couldn't find her way back afterward? Who would rescue *her*?

No one had come to her aid during her passage rites, when she was nearly drowned, crushed, and burned to death. And she'd been on her own the last time she'd commanded Bazra and his creatures inside the lower realms, although Arnesto and Katrine had done what they could.

Mara squared her shoulders. She had no choice, not really. If she didn't at least try this, then Efram and the others would fade entirely, becoming fleeting wisps of light in the stillness and gloom of the lowest realm. She gingerly touched the stain from Yelenarra's wound and raised her sword, its blue runes blazing. And then she chanted the strangest spell she'd ever mashed together. "Commendable spirits, help us please—rise up against Fallow sorcery. Spirits into bodies newly raised; help the living defeat the undead."

Mara felt nothing at first, no ripple or rumble beneath her feet, no stirring in the warm summer air, no sense she'd actually *done anything*. And then she heard it—the sound of something, or many somethings, being unearthed—a thousand clods of soil hitting the ground, and hundreds of rusty hinges creaking as coffin lids swung open.

Men and women slowly clawed and climbed their way out of the earth. Mara's spell had called forth every Valerran willing to help, regardless of when they'd died, and their clothing—or what was left of it—ranged from the past two decades to the past two centuries. Fragments of black bombazine, navy wool, or gray silk clung to their skeletal frames. Mara clamped her jaw shut to keep the bile down;

she hoped to never become immune to the sight and smell of decomposing human flesh.

One woman reached up to pat her hair but instead pulled away a chunk of her scalp. Her jaw fell open and she wailed. The marine standing next to her, his uniform hanging in raggedy strips from his bones, rotated his skull. Mara noticed half of his head was missing, probably lopped off in some long-ago border war.

The marine raised his voice in concert with the screeching woman, their long, mournful cries sending shivers down Mara's spine. That seemed to set off everyone else, because the saddest, most awful keening emerged from the spirits Mara had raised. She brought a hand to her mouth, horrified—the ghosts sounded as if they were in pain. Farleigh howled along with them.

"What's *wrong* with them?" asked Linden, covering her ears.

"Hurry up and do something," hissed Vas. "That noise can't be normal."

"Sounds like a lamentation to me," said Corbahn. "Perhaps not so surprising, given where they find themselves."

Katrine agreed. "Corbahn makes a good point. I believe this is entirely normal. The spirits are lamenting their current state of being, trapped as they are between two realms, the living and the dead."

Mara winced. This was *her* doing, and she had to get this right. Now came the hard part, much harder than raising the dead. She had to tell them what she wanted them to do; she had to *control* them. Before she could utter the next incantation, the shrieking and yowling grew louder, more shrill, and if possible, more sinister. She glanced at the cemetery. Mara's undead army—for she supposed that's what they were—shifted and swayed in place. Though they were still moaning, they weren't the ones making her skin crawl with dread. The screams and howls grew louder, accompanied by a rhythmic thumping noise, like bootheels slapping against pavement.

The other undead mob, the ones raising the goose bumps along Mara's arms and legs, shuffled back onto High Street at an alarmingly fast pace, as if they were being driven by something, or more precisely, someone. They streamed in from all directions, clogging the road and sidewalks. Their screeches overpowered the quieter moans from the newly undead waiting in the cemetery—waiting for Mara to tell them what to do.

"Well, lass, I think you did it. You're drawing out Bazra and Roi's screaming minions. I'm not sure we're prepared to handle all of them at once though," shouted Vas, unsheathing his sword. Katrine held her lasso and sword aloft, one in each hand, ready for battle with the undead. She gave Mara an encouraging nod.

"No time like the present to engage, Mara. Do your crazy magic before we're overrun," yelled Corbahn, his sword shimmering with gold hieroglyphs.

Linden's sword flared bright green next to him. "Ready when you are, my friend. Just say the word, or better yet, the spell!"

Mara had hoped for more time, even a few minutes would have helped, to think through the next part of her incantation. As usual, her enemies gave her zero leeway. Turning toward her own undead throng, she touched Efram's smear, waved her blue sword in a wide arc over the cemetery, and shouted: "All good spirits, hear me now. All not friends are our foes. By my command, hold them at bay; from the living keep them away."

Nothing happened. The cemetery undead continue to

wail, moan, and sway. Everyone looked at Mara as if she had all the answers. Mara gritted her teeth and thought hard. *It worked last time. Why isn't this working now?* She didn't think the incantation itself was wrong; maybe the undead she'd raised simply couldn't hear her above all the racket they were making. Mara touched the smear again and repeated the incantation, using her mage's commanding voice to scream at the friendly undead.

Slowly at first, and then with more speed than accuracy, Mara's undead army responded. They hobbled, staggered, and limped out of the cemetery, colliding with the roaring mob in the street. The two armies slapped, kicked, punched, and wrestled, rolling around on the road and grass, crashing into shop windows and churning flowerbeds to mud. Mara winced as hands, feet, limbs, and even a few heads went flying in all directions, with enough yowling, screaming, and shrieking to fill the entire under-world with sound. Mara hoped the citizens of Bellaryss would recover from the latest battle unfolding in their streets—and not have too many nightmares as a result.

Katrine cried, "Maybe we should concentrate on finding Roi and Bazra, and let the undead bury the undead, so to speak."

"Good idea! I'll clean this up with another spell later," yelled Mara. *But first, I'll have to figure out the incantation. I have a pretty good idea what to do—I think.* She squinted at the undead mob raised by Bazra and Roi, wondering whether she'd finally identified a pattern. Even if she had, she wasn't sure how helpful it would be. She noticed the mob paused every so often and tilted their heads, as if waiting for their next command. Whenever they paused, about half the undead crowd stared up High Street, while the rest focused their vacant orbs in the opposite direction.

"Any thoughts on where we can find Roi and Bazra?" bellowed Vas.

"I know where they are."

Mara spun around at the familiar voice. "Remy," she cried. She bit back the rest of her words—*Who did this to you? And what's happened to Arnesto?*—as she ran toward her oldest friend.

CHAPTER 27

REMY STAGGERED INTO MARA'S ARMS, HIS SWORD CLATTERING TO the ground. She laid him down gently, her heart constricting so tightly it hurt. Linden, Corbahn, Katrine, and Vas formed a cordon around them, their swords out and ready to strike anyone who approached.

"Oh Remy," Mara said softly, her voice shaking, "you're hurt." She could hardly process Remy's injuries—his clothes shredded and covered with burn holes—his face, hands, and chest bleeding from gashes.

Remy coughed, took several gulps of air, and then coughed harder, staining his lips red. Mara gripped his hand, blinking back tears. "Listen...not much time," he rasped, "Roi is under...museum."

"In the tunnels or the museum's basement?" whispered Mara, wondering how to get Remy to the infirmary.

"Basement," he rasped. Not so very long ago, Mara and her friends had battled Mordahn in the Valerran Museum. It wasn't surprising Roi decided to hole up there, given the many magical artifacts within its thick, well-fortified walls.

Remy's eyes rolled back in his head, but Mara shook

him awake. "Don't you leave me like this, Remington Richard Zel!"

Remy tried laughing, as if amused by the thought of dying, but he gasped for breath, his chest heaving. His eyelids fluttered as he struggled to open his eyes. "You look...so pretty."

Mara choked back a sob. "My gown is ruined, silly."

"I meant you, silly. *You're* pretty." Remy winced and then groaned. "Palace... Bazra's there...Arnesto needs you." He let out a long, sorrowful wheeze as his head rolled to the side.

Mara sobbed out loud, "No, Remy! No!" She ran her fingers through his tangled hair, hoping he'd waken and tell her this was all some elaborate prank. Then he'd crack one of his eye-rolling jokes, or explain why she needed more cookies and fewer carrots for true happiness. Farleigh lifted his shaggy head and howled his wolfish version of a funeral dirge, so mournful and sad it broke Mara's heart a little bit more.

Linden knelt down and closed Remy's eyes, and then she reached her arm around Mara's shoulders. The two girls hugged and cried—Remy had been Linden's friend and schoolmate too. Together they'd learned their magic spells, discovered their ensorcelled swords, escaped from Mordahn multiple times, and ultimately defeated him. They'd wept together when they lost Remy's best friend, and Linden's old flame, Toz Valti. Mara's only comfort was knowing Remy and Toz would be reunited again—that is, if she could help the Choirmaster rebalance the lower realms in time.

Mara whispered the words to a benediction recited at mages' funerals. "May you find peace in the realms of the dead, having followed Serving magic until the end of your days. This is the true path."

Katrine asked Vas to give up his jacket, which he removed without complaint. Katrine tenderly draped it over Remy and remained kneeling beside Mara and Linden. "Look," whispered Katrine. "His sparks of magic are releasing."

Mara squeezed her eyes shut and concentrated on sensing Remy's magical energy. She caught and indwelled several of his sparks, honoring him as both a mage and a friend. When the sparks had passed by, Mara wiped her streaming face with the back of her hand and stood up wearily. Every joint and muscle ached, but none could compare to the pain radiating inside her chest, where Remy's loss sat like an open wound, raw and weeping.

"Remy's gone," Mara said shakily. "But we have two necromancers to catch, and Arnesto to find."

Linden grabbed Mara's arm. "Wait. Remy's sword."

"What about"—Mara paused and stared down at the sword, its hilt inlaid with rubies, garnets, and red spinel— "the red sword! Remy stole it back!"

Corbahn leaned over to retrieve the sword, the hiero- glyphs along its blade dormant and nearly invisible. The jeweled handle gave the only clue to its provenance. This was *the* red sword of legend.

Vas reached out a hand toward the weapon. "May I?" Corbahn offered him the sword, hilt first, which Vas gripped firmly. "Ouch!" he cried, as smoke rose from his right hand. He quickly dropped the sword. "What a devilish instrument."

Katrine shook her head at Vas, her short, blue curls still bouncy despite the battle and the heat, and bent down. She picked up the sword and her eyebrows peaked, as if recognizing an old friend, one whose path had crossed hers after many years.

"Oh," Katrine murmured, as the blade's hieroglyphs glimmered a deep claret-red. "Oh!" she repeated, as the truth sank in. The red sword had picked its new owner: Katrinareus Maybella Orion the Fifteenth, Chief of the Fay Nation, former resistance leader, and one-time purveyor of clockwork toys.

Katrine rotated the sword, watching as the runes shimmered along the blade. "It's an honor to be chosen." She glanced at Mara, Linden, and Corbahn. "And a burden, too, isn't it?"

"Aye," agreed Corbahn. "Carrying one of these swords is a burden. But their magic helped us rout Mordahn and his Fallow mages, and they'll help us again, no doubt."

"But I also understand why Jayna is ready to give up her purple sword," said Linden. "She is a healer, heart and soul. The weight of bearing such a sword is too much for her."

Vas waved his unremarkable sword in the air. "Enough about magical swords. I'm going after Roi—who's coming with me?"

Mara and Linden locked eyes, a look passing between them. *Linden knows how heartsick I am over Remy, and how weary and ready for this fight to be over—she lost Toz in the midst of battle—and she still picked up her sword and faced Mordahn again. Linden and Corbahn need to defeat King Roi, and I need to dispatch Bazra to the realms of the dead.*

"Time to split up," Mara said firmly. "I have to go after Bazra and Arnesto, and I could use some backup." She waited, hoping the new owner of the red sword would volunteer. Katrine's loyalties were naturally split between Linden, her great-niece, and Arnesto, her cousin. Since

Mara and Katrine shared no kinship ties, Mara didn't feel she had any claim, except perhaps friendship.

"Aye, lass," Katrine nodded at Mara. "I'm in this with you to the end." Mara blew out a puff of air, relieved she wouldn't be entirely alone. Perhaps friendship *was* a legitimate claim after all.

Farleigh yipped, "Me too. Find Arnesto!"

Linden recited the old mages' blessing, "May your magic serve in peace and lead through service; this is the true path," which everyone else, even Farleigh, repeated. Linden gave Mara one more quick hug before joining Corbahn and Vas. Mara watched as the three of them jogged in the direction of the Valerran Museum, dodging clusters of undead still brawling up and down High Street.

"Are you ready?" asked Katrine.

Mara adjusted the reaping coil over her shoulder and bent down to withdraw a dagger from inside her left boot. When she had some distance to cover through occupied territory—and the streets of Bellaryss were certainly occupied at the moment, although not by the living—Mara preferred running with a weapon in each hand. "Aye, let's go."

Mara started to jog, Farleigh and Katrine running alongside her. She glanced back for one final look at Remy. He looked so small and insignificant, lying there beneath Vas's jacket, but she knew better. Remy had been the best of them all, and Mara would not let his death go unremarked —or unpunished.

~

"Are you sure about this, Farleigh?" Mara craned her neck, staring up at the Fortress Tower, the oldest and highest part of the city's western wall. The palace, which was built centuries later, connected to the ancient tower.

"Aye," he yipped. "Arnesto here."

"What about Bazra?" asked Katrine.

Farleigh cocked his head to one side. "Not sure his smell."

"Let's find Arnesto and maybe he can lead us to Bazra," said Mara.

Katrine nodded. "After what happened to Remy..." Her voice trailed off, but Mara didn't need to hear the rest. Both of them were worried about Arnesto.

"Are you sensing any undead, Farleigh?" Mara didn't like going in blind; she couldn't help Arnesto if she and Katrine were attacked as soon as they entered. However, the tower was so massive, there was no way she could do any reconnaissance in advance.

The grihm growled, "Smell 'em everywhere."

Mara and Katrine glanced at each other. "I'm going to outlaw necromancy when I convene the next fay council meeting," grumbled Katrine.

"But it's already outlawed," pointed out Mara.

"I know." Katrine waved her sword, its hieroglyphs glinting brightly despite the overcast sky. "So I'll outlaw it again."

Mara understood Katrine's extreme frustration, since she shared it. Necromancy had been outlawed centuries earlier. Any Serving mage who practiced it was banished, their magic considered polluted. "But I committed the forbidden act, too—although for very good reasons."

"True, but you didn't use a Fallow spell. You used Yele-narra's blood magic and snippets of Serving magic that you stitched together—a very creative interpretation, by the way."

Mara didn't feel she deserved any compliments. "So then, do you approve of using necromantic magic, under the right circumstances?"

Katrine furrowed her brow. "Why, do you plan to start raising the dead on a regular basis?"

Mara shuddered. "No way. I just want to know what it means, that I can do it." She lightly tapped the reddish-brown smears on her blade. "Maybe I should give up my blue sword when this is all over."

"Perish the thought! You did nothing wrong, lass, and I encouraged you, let's not forget." Katrine pointed down the winding road behind them. "It's more like fighting fire with fire. What choice do we have?"

Farleigh whined. Mara patted his shoulder and said, "Alright, let's go." She turned to Katrine. "Can you translocate us into the lowest part of the tower? We can begin our search for Arnesto at the bottom level and work our way up."

"Aye," said Katrine, gripping the red sword. "Ready?"

"Ready." Mara sucked in her breath and prayed she'd find Arnesto at the other end of Katrine's traveling mists.

But even before the vapors had cleared, Mara heard the grunts and groans of the undead. Farleigh's nose proved infallible again—Bazra's gruesome minions were everywhere.

CHAPTER 28

Mara was furious at herself; she'd forgotten to cast a veil of drabness when they entered the tower, but now it was too late. Farleigh barked, ran toward the stairwell, and dashed up the steps. *Ugh...how inconvenient. Farleigh has picked up Arnesto's scent, but we have to fight an undead mob before we can follow him.*

Mara's hands were full, literally, with her dagger and her sword, and the undead gave her no time to cast any spells to control them. They charged, wailing and screaming.

Mara and Katrine formed a tight fighting circle, their backs to one another, as the skeletal remains of a dozen palace guards—their tattered red and gold uniforms clinging to their pale bones—turned toward them. This crew looked as bad as the mob in the streets, most of them missing a hand, arm, or foot.

Mara stabbed and jabbed at the screeching undead. A skeletal guard, missing his entire lower jaw, screamed at her and reached out bony hands. He grabbed her sword and the two of them struggled, Mara and the skeleton each tugging back and forth. The guard was strong, too strong for Mara, and she felt her sword slipping away. She dropped her dagger and held onto her sword's hilt with both hands, praying for strength as the skeleton grasped her blade and pulled hard.

But instead of wresting the weapon out of her hands, the creature shuddered, all his bones creaking and rattling. He turned his blank orbs on Mara, hastily released her sword, and stepped back. Then he shifted from side to side, waiting, but Mara had no idea what he was waiting for, or what to do next. One of his undead comrades attempted to charge her, but the one missing his jaw stepped in front of Mara, shielding her.

Mara stared down at her blade, confused. *What just happened? Why did the skeleton suddenly drop my sword? And why did he* protect *me?* If she hadn't been so exhausted from her passage rites and the battle in the lower realms, followed by Remy's loss, the charging zoo animals, and the undead mob on High Street, perhaps she'd have realized it sooner. *Better late than never, as Father used to say.*

Mara tapped Efram's blood smear, and modifying her last spell somewhat, shouted, "All good spirits, hear me now. All not friends are our foes. Guard us please, front and back; protect the living from attack."

All of the undead guards stopped shrieking—the silence alone was a blessed relief—and turned toward Mara. One of them had threaded his bony digits through Katrine's hair, and the fay batted him away. The skeletons retreated several steps and then swayed in place, waiting for Mara to command them. She cried out, "Protect us—and the grihm who arrived with us—and lead us to the top of the tower."

The skeletal guard unit surrounded Mara and Katrine, their bones rattling as they shuffled into place. The one missing his lower jaw seemed to be in charge and led them to the narrow, spiral staircase Farleigh had taken.

Katrine whispered, "This is extremely unnerving."

Mara didn't want to say anything aloud, in case she broke the command spell controlling the undead, so she nodded in agreement. Katrine must have realized why Mara remained silent, because she added, "Good thinking."

The skeletons shuffled along at a good pace, but their bones made such a racket Mara feared they would lose any element of surprise. They climbed past the main level of the palace and kept ascending the twisting stairs.

Mara saw no one, not a single living guard or servant, and she hoped they were hiding somewhere safe. Though the queen had evacuated during the war, a small staff still maintained the palace and its grounds. *Then again, we're in the Fortress Tower, the least-used part of the palace—so it makes sense no one else is here—except for a dark fay king with an affinity for old towers.*

Mara heard faint howling nearby—Farleigh perhaps?—and wondered whether they were walking into one of Bazra's traps. "Halt!" she shouted.

"What are you doing?" hissed Katrine.

The skeletons stopped so suddenly the two of them directly in front of Mara became entangled, and they collapsed on the steps in a heap of bones and faded red rags. The lead guard grunted as he pulled them apart, and Mara had the feeling she was watching a replay of something that had occurred fairly regularly during their lifetime—two clumsy, perhaps even tipsy, guards stumbling through their rounds—and their overworked captain reestablishing order.

"Captain," she said softly, and the skeletal guard missing his lower jaw turned toward her. *Good,* she thought, *perhaps I don't need to shout at the top of my lungs and give Bazra any more of a warning than he already has.*

"Can you tell me whether there are any others like your-selves in this tower?" The skeleton shook his head.

"And how many of the living will we find above us?" He raised one pale finger.

One? Is it Bazra or Arnesto? If Arnesto needed her, Mara wasn't going to wait any longer—trap or not. "I'll take the lead. Unless I command otherwise, please keep ten paces behind my friend and me." The guard brought his bony hand up to his skull and gave her a surprisingly jaunty salute for a skeleton, before stepping aside to allow her and Katrine to jog past.

"Only one?" whispered Katrine. "I don't get it."

"Me neither." Mara barreled up the steps until she reached the landing and paused. She brought her finger to her lips, and the skeletons stopped moving and rattling. Glancing at Katrine, she mouthed, "On the count of three. One. Two. Three!" Mara flung open the door to the upper floor of the tower, where the Bellaryss Bell hung from the nave.

A sparkly silver cape, with a pair of black boots dangling beneath, swung from a rope attached to the bell's support beam. The edge of the cape flapped in the breeze as the body slowly swayed overhead. Mara screamed "Arnesto!" Her heart pounded, radiating bursts of pain from the center of her chest to the tips of her fingers.

Every harsh word they'd exchanged, and every hurtful misunderstanding, came flooding into her head, blocking every happy memory. *Regret—so much regret!* She felt utterly, completely consumed by it. "Arnesto!" she wailed more softly, tears trickling down her cheeks.

Katrine gripped Mara's shoulder. "That's not Arnesto. Look again!"

Mara ran beneath the bell and craned her neck. "Who is it?" The dead man in Arnesto's clothes had a long black braid and beard to match.

The undead captain shuffled alongside her and screeched. Mara stared up at the dead man. Perhaps the skeleton was attempting to give her an answer. "Maybe he was one of the guards here, whom Bazra killed when he entered the palace. But why is he wearing Arnesto's cape?"

"Tricked! Tricked!" yipped Farleigh as he loped from the walkway that connected the Fortress Tower to the palace's six smaller towers.

Mara gripped her sword more firmly and scanned the adjacent towers. She saw no one else, neither living nor undead. Farleigh sat on his haunches in front of her, his tongue hanging out as he panted. "What trick?" she asked.

"Tricked me. Arnesto not here," grunted Farleigh.

Mara sighed. Farleigh had tracked Arnesto's scent up the tower steps, right to the dead man dressed in Arnesto's clothes. The only living creature in the tower when they stormed it had been Farleigh. Technically, the skeletal guard had been correct, but that meant she was no closer to finding Arnesto than she'd been in the streets below.

Mara sheathed her sword and rubbed her temples. She'd sobbed so much in the past hour and had expended so much magical energy that her head throbbed. The undead captain creaked toward her and bowing, handed her the dagger she'd dropped during their initial struggle. She thanked him and slipped it inside her boot.

Mara walked to the tower's edge to clear her head and think. The lush green valley, dotted with neat squares of wheat and maize planted by Valerran farmers, had an ugly new chasm bisecting it. She shook her head, disgusted at the destruction wrought by Bazra. She had to end this; she had to send him downriver, over the falls, and into the lake of fire.

But first, she had to find Arnesto—Remy had sent her to the palace to help him. Arnesto had been there long enough to exchange his cape for a dead guard's uniform. Whether Arnesto had hung up the dead man to lure Bazra, or the dark fay had done it to mock Arnesto, she didn't know, and it didn't matter. All that mattered was that she find Arnesto before it was too late.

Katrine pointed at the fresh rift in the valley below. "Something's very strange about that fissure."

The sun peeked out from behind the clouds just then, illuminating the valley in beam of yellow light. Mara used her hand to shield her eyes. "What do you mean?"

"It's advancing. "

"Advancing?" Mara studied the crack running from the outer wall of the palace, through fields and meadows, and stopping about halfway across the valley. But then she noticed the crack *extending itself* a bit farther into the valley. As she watched, it advanced again. "I don't know much about these chasms, except all the others just suddenly opened up. None of them kept enlarging themselves."

Katrine squinted into the valley. "I've been thinking about them. We know Bazra used the red sword to amplify his elemental magic and create chaos in the underworld. I'm convinced he also used the sword to make these fissures. I think he was looking for a way out and kept experimenting until he escaped."

Mara leaned against the rough stone wall of the tower and watched as the crack traveled another few feet across the valley floor. "So who's opening up a new crack inside our realm now?"

"There are only two mages in the human realm today who can wield that kind of raw elemental power."

Mara straightened up. "Bazra...and Arnesto! Do you think they started battling in the tunnel that runs beneath the palace, and just kept going—and making their own tunnel as they continued fighting?"

Katrine rubbed her chin. "Aye, I think that's a good hypothesis."

"Then let's go! We need to help Arnesto dispatch Bazra back to the underworld."

The undead captain screeched and shuffled over to the opposite side of the tower. Mara crossed the floor and looked where the skeletal guard was pointing. Mara stared down at the battle in the streets below, which had spread through most of the downtown, the undead crushing bushes and trampling gardens, tearing shutters from windows and limbs from trees as they pommeled each other. She spotted squads of Valerrans, brawling with the undead as they attempted to protect their neighborhood from the incursion. "Oh my stars! Katrine—come take a look!"

Katrine glanced over the wall and groaned. "You need to do something about this undead mess right now, lass. They're going to destroy what's left of the city if this keeps up."

"But what about Arnesto?"

"He's holding his own against Bazra—the fresh opening in the valley floor is evidence of that. Arnesto can hang on another few minutes, but Vas, Talias, and the rest of Bellaryss can't wait much longer."

Mara needed to construct a spell to stop the bedlam. She had zero room for error—no learning on the job for her —and no time for do-overs. She stared at the bloodstains on her blade, recalling an old fay prophecy about needing the red sword to defeat the dark fays and maintain order in the underworld.

Mara always thought the prophecy had gotten it wrong —since she'd rescued Arnesto, defeated Bazra, and subdued his undead creatures once before—using her magic, her blue sword, and Efram's reddish-brown smear to control the undead. On the other hand, Bazra had created even more problems in the realms of the dead, Arnesto was in trouble again, and Bellaryss had an enormous undead population roaming its streets. Maybe she and her blue sword could use a little help.

Mara quickly explained her theory to Katrine, who shrugged. "Sounds plausible. Tell me what you need me to do."

"Let me say goodbye, and then I'll be ready." Mara addressed the skeletal captain of the guard. "When I send back the undead raised by necromancy, you and your unit will return as well. Thank you for your loyalty to our exiled queen and for your help today." The undead guard saluted Mara and then shuffled back to his unit. He grunted a few unintelligible syllables, and the skeletons trained their empty orbs on Mara, swaying slightly as they waited.

"Alright, let's do this," said Mara, her hand hovering over her blade. "When I tap Arnesto's smear on my hilt, wave your sword in a wide arc over the city and palace, repeating each line of the incantation after me."

Nodding, Katrine withdrew her red sword and raised it to shoulder level. "Ready."

Mara took a deep breath, tapped the large sapphire on her sword's hilt, and shouted in her loudest commanding voice, "All undead, in bodies raised, now return to your final place. Good spirits to the distant shore, evil ones to the lake of fire." Katrine repeated the incantation, waving her red sword over the city and swiveling around in a complete circle to include the skeletal guards behind them.

Mara and Katrine repeated the incantation and sword waving until the undead armies and skeletal tower guards dropped to the ground. Their bodies vanished in one blink, reappearing in the graveyard. The city was silent for a moment, as if holding its collective breath; then Mara heard weirdly welcome sounds—the thumping of corpses dropping into their coffins, the squeaking of hinges as the lids closed, the thudding of soil clods hitting the wooden boxes. Mara also heard a distant, eerie moan, as the bad spirits found themselves heading toward their just desserts—the lake of fire in the lowest realm.

Mara shuddered and surveyed the city cemetery again, where fresh soil covered every plot, although a number of headstones had fallen over. She exhaled a long sigh of relief. At least she'd been able to return the good spirits to the far shore, which they'd inhabited before she'd called them forth. She wished she could do the same for Efram, but Arnesto's blood magic only worked on spirits that had been raised through necromancy.

Katrine glanced around the empty Fortress Tower and grinned. "I never thought I'd say this, but I think I'm going to miss our skeletons. Well, the captain, anyway."

Mara gave her old boss the ghost of a smile, relieved they'd reversed the bedlam in the city's streets. But nothing could make Mara feel better on the inside, where Remy's loss gnawed at her. She would not lose anyone else to the dark fay king. "Can you translocate us into that fresh crack below, as far down as your mists will take us? It's time to help Arnesto—and make sure Bazra can't hurt anyone else."

CHAPTER 29

KATRINE'S TRAVELING MISTS DROPPED THEM INTO THE FISSURE. The smell of freshly tunneled earth reminded Mara of the new clods of soil covering the graves in the cemetery. The mists held them aloft most of the way down, the air becoming warm and humid as they descended. Katrine's mists gradually waned, winking out before they reached the lowest, last realm of the dead. They tumbled onto the spongy ground and quickly scrambled to their feet.

Mara saw no ghosts in the area, probably due to the presence of two powerful fays crossing swords and blasting each other with enough elemental magic to shift the earth around them. She heard the clang of their blades and the buzz of their spell casting before she saw them. Mara reached into her boot to withdraw a dagger. She crept along, taking point, short blade in her left hand and blue sword in her right.

Mara spotted Bazra first. The dark fay king's black robe hung in tatters, and his thick goggles were missing one of their lenses. He limped, favoring his right leg. *Good,* thought Mara, *Arnesto has slowed Bazra down. Now we're here, we can finish the job.*

But then she saw Arnesto, and her relief was short-lived. Though Arnesto was still upright and fighting, he seemed nearly spent. Scorch marks covered his borrowed red uniform, where one of Bazra's fire spells had burned through the fabric to the skin underneath, and the tips of his wavy blue hair were blackened and singed. Arnesto clutched his side, lurching toward Bazra, his movements jerky as he countered Bazra's blade.

Bazra saw Mara and Katrine before Arnesto was aware of their arrival. The dark fay must have deduced the odds now tipped in their favor, because he screeched, "Never! Never again will I be imprisoned in this half-life!"

Arnesto stumbled, providing Bazra with the opportunity to inflict more damage. The dark fay withdrew something from his robe—a wicked-looking disc covered with jagged points—and threw the weapon at Arnesto, piercing him in the side. Arnesto cried out, crumbling to the ground. Bazra ran toward Arnesto, swinging his sword wildly with both hands like a crazed executioner.

Mara hurled her dagger, spearing Bazra in the shoulder. "*Hands off my boyfriend!*" she hollered, charging into the fray, her blue sword pulsing with magical energy.

Bazra screeched and retreated, dashing behind a huge pile of dirt. Katrine positioned herself in front of Arnesto, ready to defend him if the dark fay emerged for another attack.

Mara dropped to her knees beside Arnesto, her heart in her throat, frantic to save him. She pressed her hand over his wounded side, trying to stem the bleeding. "Oh, Arnesto! Why didn't you wait for me?" she cried.

Arnesto gasped, "Mara. You said..." Coughing up blood, he winced and tried speaking again, but Mara gently touched his lips with her finger.

"Hush now. We're going to get you to Zornamayne. She'll fix you up in no time."

"Not leaving you..." Arnesto sputtered and wheezed, trying to catch his breath. His eyelids flickered closed... open...closed. And then he fell silent.

"No!" Mara wailed. "Don't you dare leave me, Arnesto!" Mara grabbed his wrist, desperate to find a pulse. She groped around, sobbing, her fingers slipping and shaking, until she found it—faint and erratic—but his heart was still beating.

"Katrine," Mara called out, "you have to take Arnesto home to Havynweal, right now! He can't wait!"

Methodically scanning the dirt pile, Katrine paused to glance over her shoulder. Worry lines creased her brow. "How? My mists don't work in this realm, and there's no portal nearby."

Mara picked up her sword. She'd gotten them out of this realm once before, and she could do it again—she'd just have to find another mostly ossified spirit and order it to lift them to the surface. Mara glanced around, but there were no convenient spirits in this part of the underworld, only fresh piles of dirt and somewhere, off in the distance, the sound of running water.

Mara thought of Xenestra. Had the dragon safely delivered all her patients by now? Mara took a chance and raised her sword, adding more urgency to her commanding spell. "Please come to us, Xenestra," she shouted, "take us to the home of the fays. Our need is great, our mission worthy— Arnesto requires healing without delay!"

Mara held her breath, hoping Xenestra might respond. But she heard no bleating from the scholarly dragon, no scraping of her talons as she landed on the ground. Mara didn't know whether to alter the spell, or whether Xenestra was still unloading patients, but she couldn't wait any longer. Arnesto's breathing was growing shallow and raspy, and far too uneven.

Mara thought of Phineas and his elven mists; he could traverse through the realms of the dead as well as the living. Arnesto groaned, and Mara made up her mind. She had nothing left to lose. She hadn't the first clue how to conjure elven traveling mists—but she'd had no clue how to raise the dead or how to send them back to their graves, or how to call down a dragon or command the elements—and that had never stopped her before.

Mara raised her sword, its blue runes lighting up like a beacon in the gray gloom of the lowest realm, and shouted, "Chilly mists of truest north, send frosty vapors to transport. Icy tendrils to carry us forth, lift us from this underworld." She knew fays and elves didn't have to shout spells when they traveled, but she had no idea how else to conjure the mists.

Mara repeated the spell until her voice grew hoarse, desperate for some change to come over her, but she didn't feel any different. Her heart sank. She nearly gave up as another wave of exhaustion washed over her, until she realized her teeth were chattering, and icicles were forming on Arnesto's face and hair. "It's working," Mara paused her incantation long enough to holler at Katrine, still on the lookout for another appearance by Bazra. "Get ready to take over as soon as your mists become active."

Katrine's eyes grew round. "Aye, lass," she whispered. Mara was grateful Katrine didn't try giving her any tips on how to translocate. Her old fay boss clamped her mouth shut, probably to keep herself from shrieking.

The icicles on Arnesto's face started melting when Mara had briefly paused her spell casting, and so she focused all her dwindling strength on channeling her elven magic through her sword. Shaking with cold, Mara resumed the incantation. Slowly, oh so slowly, frosty tendrils encircled the three of them, and they started to rise.

Mara shivered, her fingers growing numb as she gripped her sword, but she held on, casting and praying she could raise them far enough above the lowest realms for Katrine's fay mists to take over. They wobbled a few times, sliding sideways once, which caused Katrine to yelp. Then she hissed, "Sorry!" as Mara's elven mists strengthened, drawing them upward once more.

Mara felt dampness on her upper lip and assumed the ice was melting again. She pushed herself and her magic harder, until she felt the mists shuddering around her. "What's happening!" she cried, knowing she'd given it her all, and ready to weep over her failure to save Arnesto.

"'Tis me, lass!" yelled Katrine, as her fay mists increased around them. "I've got you and Arnesto firmly in my vapors now, so you can let go."

Trembling from energy loss and her chilly elven mists, Mara shook her head. "I'm going after Bazra. We may not get another chance."

Katrine's mists swirled about them, maintaining their altitude, but she didn't translocate them out of the realm. "You've done enough, lass, more than enough. You're worn out, and your nose is bleeding from the strain of all your spell casting."

Mara glanced below them and spotted a lone figure in a black robe scurrying toward Arnesto's unguarded portal.

Mara leapt out of Katrine's vapors, hoping she had enough stamina left to maintain her icy tendrils as she tumbled toward the portal and Bazra.

"Lass! What are you—" cried Katrine, the rest of her words lost as she and Arnesto vanished on her cloud of mist.

Mara narrowed her eyes at Bazra, willing her icy ethers, which were diminishing as rapidly as her strength, to drop her near the dark fay king. She didn't think she had the stamina to run after him for very long.

Mara didn't expect to land *on top* of him, but her mists gave out directly above Arnesto's portal, just as Bazra was about to enter. "Bazra!" she shouted as she fell toward him. "Stand down, and I'll show you mercy."

Bazra looked up, spotted Mara's boot heels plunging toward his face, and screamed. Mara crashed onto his back, but Bazra reared up on his knees and tossed her off. She tumbled in front of the portal, effectively blocking the exit, but her sword slipped out of her chilled, numb fingers and clattered to the ground. Bazra snatched up her weapon and skirted the nearest dune, heading toward the river.

Her legs trembling from exhaustion, Mara scrambled to her feet and followed Bazra, who was waving *her* blue sword over one of the ossified spirits. Mara gritted her teeth. She wouldn't let the dark fay king misuse her weapon, but without it she was powerless in the lower realms.

Or was she? Mara thought about her mother, a full-bloodied Alfweardian elf and reaper. *Could I access my elven magic—and cast spells—without channeling them through my sword?*

The spirit-mound started to rise from the ground, with Bazra perched on top; Mara was out of options. One of

Linden's favorite Serving magic spells popped into her head. Wrinkling her brow, Mara reached for her elven magic—which felt different somehow than her Serving magic—cooler, contained, coiled, as if ready to spring into action. She cried out, "Freeze all magic swirling about; stop our spells 'til the hour runs out!"

The mound shuddered, tilted, and crashed down onto the black soil of the lowest realm. Bazra threw back his head and shrieked curses at Mara, which she ignored as she dashed toward him, wondering how to distract him long enough to seize her blue sword.

Bazra hopped down and limped toward the river, dragging his right leg behind him. He clasped Mara's sword against his chest. *Fine,* she thought grimly. *He's not surrendering my sword without a fight—and so I'll give him one.* She hobbled after the dark fay, every muscle aching, her nose bleeding, and her head hurting so much she wondered whether she'd popped a blood vessel. She'd take the sorcerer downriver with her, if that's what it took to wrest her blade from his pale, bony fingers.

"Turn around and face me like a man, Bazra!" she hollered.

Bazra neither stopped nor turned but kept shambling toward the river. Mara had no choice but to drag herself along, wondering how she'd be able to defeat the dark fay without access to her magic or her sword. She glanced down at the filthy, tattered ball gown she'd donned after completing her passage rites—had that been only yesterday?—and grimaced at her lack of weapons. She was down to one dagger in her right boot, and a coil of reaping rope that had lost its translucent sparkle when she'd frozen all magic for the next hour. Mara fingered the rope and tied one end securely around her waist; if she caught the dark fay king, she wouldn't let him escape again.

She stared at Bazra's skinny, black-robed form. He was almost to the river, still clutching her sword to his chest. Where did he think he was going? There were no boats left, and he couldn't possibly swim across to the far shore. Then it dawned on her—the crazy necromancer didn't want to *keep* her sword—he wanted to *toss* it in the dark, churning water! Mara winced as picked up her pace, straining to catch up with him. She had to stop him before he reached the shoreline.

Unfortunately, Bazra started to shuffle faster, and Mara fell farther behind. She had to find a way to slow him down. Reaching into her right boot, she withdrew her knife. "Bazra," she shouted, "surrender now, or suffer the consequences."

Bazra half-turned and cackled over his shoulder. "No sword, no magic, no way!" He pulled her blue sword away from his chest and raised it over his head, ready to fling it into the river.

Mara took a deep breath. She had once chance to get this right. She positioned her knife, its tip pointing behind her shoulder, its hilt aimed at Bazra's sword hand. She whipped the dagger at Bazra and held her breath as it sailed through the fusty air of the lowest realm. Her blade hit its mark, spearing the fleshy part of Bazra's hand. He screamed, the blue sword clattering to the ground. Raining down curses on Mara and her future progeny, Bazra barreled toward her.

Good, she thought. *Come just a little bit closer.* Mara unwound the long coil that was still tied around her waist and started twirling the loose end of rope. Bazra didn't seem to notice she held a lasso, or he didn't care. Perhaps the dark fay believed he had enough physical strength to overcome Mara, and perhaps he was right. She was running on fumes and barely able to stand.

Bazra came within range of her lasso, and she tossed the loop over his shoulders, pulling the rope taut. He could still move his forearms, but rather than struggling to free himself, Bazra gave her a mirthless grin. He turned, stumbled toward the river, and pulled Mara into the rushing current with him.

Mara gasped at the bone-chilling water, so different from the warm, moist air around them. She didn't have time to register anything else, because Bazra used the rope to tug Mara closer and stretched out his hand—the good one, without the dagger wound. Grabbing her by the hair, he plunged her head beneath the surface. Mara resisted, trying to break free, kicking at Bazra underwater, but her kicks had no impact. She punched and slapped at Bazra, but his grip didn't loosen as he continued pressing down on her head.

Mara kept fighting but she had little strength left, her hands fluttering uselessly in the surf, the weight of water impeding every movement. Her ball gown became entangled around her legs, and she felt heavy, sodden, and shattered. Her lungs burned as she realized she might not win this fight—the crafty dark fay had outfoxed her.

Mara saw stars in front of her eyes and knew soon, very soon, she'd open her mouth and instead of gulping air, she'd swallow the river water and be done with it. At least she'd managed to save Arnesto from Bazra, and she'd sent the spirits back to their graves. But she'd lost Remy.

The current picked up speed, and Mara flailed her arms, punching through the water at Bazra, but his grip on her head didn't loosen. She sensed they'd passed the last bend in the river, the no-turning-back point. Straight ahead would be the white, frothing waterfall that would deposit both Mara and the dark fay king into the lake of fire. There'd be no escape now—the flames knew no mercy and would engulf them both.

Mara closed her eyes and opened her mouth, ready to inhale the water and drown before she hit the scorching blaze, the final destination for the unsavory and downright wicked. But before she could gulp down any water, *something* plucked her out of the river.

When Mara's head broke the surface, she gasped, coughing and panting as she inhaled sizzling hot air. Blinking several times to clear her streaming eyes, Mara found herself hovering over smoke and flames as far as she could see. The blazing sea was filled with bubbling eddies of brimstone where burning spirits groaned and wailed, reaching out their wraith-like arms to grab at her and Bazra, still attached to her reaping rope.

Mara screamed and looked away, trying to figure out who or what had saved her—and hoping they were strong enough to keep her suspended and not drop her into the fiery gulf below. She glanced up at something very large, scaly, and green—Xenestra's underbelly! The giant dragon clutched Mara carefully between her damp talons; Bazra dangled from the other end of the rope, shrieking as a scorching geyser flared up, singeing his robe. He kicked his legs to escape the flames, and the lasso slipped from his shoulders. Bazra tumbled, screeching curses, as he fell into the inferno.

Mara averted her eyes. She didn't need to see anything more to know Bazra would not be rising again. She called up to the giant dragon, "You are a welcome sight!"

Xenestra bleated, "I am pleased that I could rescue you

and retrieve your weapon." The dragon raised her other claw, which clutched Mara's blue sword. "And now, I believe it is time for you to see Zornamayne without any further delay."

Mara nodded gratefully, her eyes already closing as Xenestra flapped her massive wings and carried her home.

CHAPTER 30

THE HEALER WITH THE GENTLE TOUCH PLACED A LAVENDER-scented cloth on Mara's forehead. Mara had sensed different healers hovering over her—for how many days?—she had no concept of time. There was the furry one with many veils who hissed a lot, the gentle one with the kind, soothing voice, and the icy, efficient one who spoke in crisp tones. Mara winced as she tried moving her arms and legs, weak and achy beneath the bed sheets. Her temples throbbed painfully as if gripped by a giant vise. "Where am I?" she croaked.

"Zornamayne's infirmary," replied Jayna.

Mara forced her eyelids open and groaned—it even hurt to blink. She recognized Zornamayne's decorating touches; hot pink, neon yellow, and lime green floral patterns adorned the window curtains, the bedding, and even the walls of her infirmary room. Although Mara was surprised to see Jayna in Havynweal, she was even more surprised to find herself recovering in a fay infirmary instead of the Amber Room inside Yelenarra's mansion. "Why...where...

how is Arnesto? And Yelenarra? And Gloria? And everyone else?"

Gloria popped her head up from the foot of the bed and clicked her beak. "I am recovering, milady. Much more quickly than you, I might add. Your magic was drained down to its last few sparks, and well, the rest of you is not much better."

Mara reached for her magic and panicked—*not again!*—then she took a shaky breath and waited. She felt a few strains of magical energy pulsing weakly, but still there and very much a part of herself. "Tell me about the others—please." *But don't tell me if anyone else I care about has passed on to the lower realms. I can't take any more losses.*

Jayna pulled up a chair next to Mara's bed. "Both Arnesto and Yelenarra are healing, although Yelenarra more slowly, given her age and injuries."

Mara exhaled, a tear slipping down her cheek. The pain in her temples eased a smidge. "I was so worried," she whispered, "I'd lost them both."

"Arnesto asks about you nearly every hour. Zornamayne has told him she will only provide updates at sunrise and sundown," Jayna said, her eyes twinkling, "so I've been popping in during my rounds to tell him how you're doing. All the updates have been pretty much the same: 'Mara moved her head a little. Mara lifted her right arm. Mara called out your name in her sleep.'"

Mara smiled, which appeared to be the only movement that didn't cause her any pain. "I called out his name? Really?" When Jayna nodded, Mara said, "and you *told* him?"

Jayna grinned. "Nah, I didn't tell him that part, but it's obvious he's a man in love, and I strongly suspect he's captured your heart, too."

Mara flattened her lips, which hurt, so she stopped. She

couldn't deny her feelings for Arnesto any longer, but she also wasn't ready to talk about them just yet. "What about Linden and the others?"

"Linden and Corbahn captured King Roi, who is shackled in twisted steel and sitting in the palace dungeon in Bellaryss, awaiting trial. They've gone to a meeting hosted by Katrine—in dead of winter, of all seasons—to confer about the absent Choirmaster and the cracks. All the Faymon clan chiefs, including Reynier, went with them. Phineas and Vas are there, too, representing Alfweard and Valerra."

Mara's heart sank. Now that Bazra was gone and Katrine possessed the red sword, Mara had hoped the other problems would be resolved. "So I take it the choir hasn't returned, and the chasms haven't healed?"

Jayna shook her head, her dark curls springing around her face. "The good news is the cracks have stopped spreading, and the spirits have stopped fading away, so Efram and the others are safe for the moment."

"But we haven't found the key to rebalancing the lower realms—and until we do—nothing will be back to normal."

"Aye. However, this is not a problem for you to solve, and certainly not in your current condition. You need to get some rest." Jayna stood to leave.

An old memory tickled at the back of Mara's aching head, something to do with King Roi and the palace dungeon. "The palace guards know to wear ear plugs when they feed Roi, don't they?" When Mara and her friends had been falsely imprisoned, they'd escaped from the palace dungeon and their twisted steel manacles by singing an old fay lullaby that magically put their guards to sleep.

"Aye, Linden made sure of that. Now get some rest."

Mara was certain she'd just dozed off when Hortensia

—the chilly, businesslike healer—shook her awake. Mara yawned and kept her eyes firmly closed. "I just fell asleep. Can you come back later?" Mara would have forced herself awake for Jayna or Zornamayne, but she wasn't ready to make the extra effort for Hortensia.

Hortensia snorted and ripped the covers off the bed. "Nay. I am here and shall not leave until you get out of that bed."

"What?" Mara squinted at the bright light streaming through the window. When she'd spoken with Jayna she remembered the sky had been dark. How long had she slept? "I can barely move my legs. How can I possibly get out of bed?"

"Simple," huffed Hortensia. "I shall pull you up to a seated position, then you shall swivel your legs around to the side of the bed, then you shall—"

Mara raised her hand to stem the tide of step-by-step instructions from Hortensia. "I understand the concept of rising from bed. I don't believe I have the strength to do it. Besides, everything hurts. And my head feels like it's going to explode."

Hortensia tossed her lustrous white-blonde hair. "Your headaches shall lessen with each day; you expended nearly all your magic, and it takes time for your reserves to replenish. As for your aches and pains, you shall improve faster if you begin to move. It is the elven way."

Mara grumbled, "Fine. I want to visit Arnesto anyway, so I guess I'm getting out of bed."

Hortensia nodded and then pulled and prodded Mara until she was sitting on the edge of her bed. Mara gritted her teeth to keep from crying out loud from the pain in her joints and muscles and head. She ran a hand through her hair and stopped. "Do you have a looking glass handy?"

Hortensia silently incanted a spell, turned her palm over, and handed Mara a portable looking glass, set in gold plate, with a long handle. Mara gripped the handle and brought the mirror up to her face. "I look like I belong in the underworld!" Mara grimaced. "I can't go visit Arnesto like this. Help me, Hortensia. Please."

"Very well; on one condition. You shall make an effort to get up and walk at least twice daily until you are recovered. You are an elf. Elves expedite their healing with movement."

Mara mumbled her assent. She noticed Hortensia had not called her a "half breed" or "part elven" but recognized her Alfweardian citizenship, which Mara had earned the hardest way possible. Hortensia helped her into a fresh pale blue nightgown and matching robe. The elf brushed out Mara's hair, her hands gently detangling the knots, an almost motherly gesture. *I might warm up to the ice queen after all,* thought Mara, who felt marginally better as Hortensia helped her take her first few steps out of bed. Hortensia conjured an ivory walking stick, covered in runes, and instructed Mara to use the walking stick until she felt strong enough to move about without assistance.

Mara hobbled through Arnesto's open door; he was sitting up in bed, his pillows propped behind him. A pretty hybrid healer giggled at something he said. Mara raised her eyebrows, which hurt, so she smiled instead. "You are a sight for sore eyes, and arms, and legs, for that matter."

"Maragold! You are up!" Arnesto's bow-shaped mouth bent downward. "But you are in pain." He started to swing his legs over the side of his bed but both the healer and Mara said, "No, stay put." The young hybrid bowed as she left the room.

Arnesto reached out his hand and Mara limped over,

trying not to wince too much as she sat on the neon green chair beside the bed. Mara threaded her fingers through his. "I peeked in on Yelenarra. She is resting comfortably, but Zornamayne says she'll need to stay here, where the healers can keep an eye on her, for quite some time. The good news is Zornamayne thinks you'll be able to leave in two moonrises."

Arnesto nodded. "Aye. I will need to look after Auntie Yelenarra once she is well enough to go home. Zornamayne has ordered her to slow down and allow me to take on more magical duties around the manor. Auntie has been wearing herself out." He narrowed his eyes. "But you will need some looking after as well."

Mara shook her head and frowned. "Not according to Hortensia, who is about as brusque as Jayna is gentle. Hortensia says I need to be up and about, and my constant migraines will lessen as my magic strengthens."

"Your migraines are a consequence of being drained down to your last few sparks." Arnesto looked away and seemed to be struggling to say what was on his mind. He took a deep breath. "And, I believe, losing Remy. I know I feel his loss in here." Arnesto used his other hand to tap his chest. "And you must feel his loss even more keenly."

Mara's eyes welled up and she sniffed. "Aye," she said softly, "it hurts so much I can't speak of it, except to say my pain would have been multiplied had it been you instead of him. And that's the truth."

"Oh, Mara!" Arnesto brought her hand to his lips and kissed it. "I am so sorry we lost Remy—he stepped in front of me when Bazra attacked us—and I am sorry for all the misunderstandings that came before. I have been a fool, but I promise to do better...that is, if you will have me."

Mara suppressed a moan as she stood up from her chair

and moved over to sit on the bed beside Arnesto. She inhaled his rich scent, of loamy earth and tangy citrus, so unlike anyone she'd ever known—or loved. Mara cupped his ridiculously handsome face in both her hands and kissed him gently on the lips. "Aye, I'll have you. But first we need to have that chat we never seem able to have."

Arnesto brushed a lock of Mara's pale blonde hair out of her eyes. "Whatever." He pulled her down and kissed her squarely on the mouth, and then he kissed her again, and once more for good measure. Mara's pulse raced, butterflies roiling her stomach.

She reached her arms around Arnesto's neck and smiled. "*Whatever?* You've never been so agreeable, especially about our long-delayed chat."

Arnesto leaned in for another long, sweetly satisfying kiss. "I have never nearly lost everything I have ever loved before. It changes a man."

Mara nuzzled against Arnesto's chest before straightening up with a sigh. "Zornamayne will have my hide if I'm not back in bed before she makes her rounds. Apparently, she and Hortensia disagree on how much bed rest I need. Although I do feel slightly better—my headache's even eased a bit—so I think the frosty elven healer might have a point."

Mara rose, her legs weak and wobbly as a newborn kitten's, and leaned against the bed so Arnesto wouldn't notice. She didn't want to admit to herself or her fay boyfriend that his breathtaking kisses were mostly to blame for her trembles.

Arnesto shook his head, his wavy blue hair wilder than usual, and smiled up at her. "It has nothing to do with either healer, and you know it." He raised one eyebrow and lowered the other. "Your magic will be healing much faster now."

"Why is that?"

"Because I love you and you will have me, which means you love me too—although I sense you are not ready to admit it yet. In any case, love is the ultimate magical balm."

"Whatever," said Mara, chuckling softly.

CHAPTER 31

Z ORNAMAYNE DECIDED H ORTENSIA WAS CORRECT AND DEMANDED Mara begin walking about the infirmary and even taking a spin around the small woods outside her cottage. Mara squinted the first time she stepped into the bright light; after the overcast skies in Valerra, and the gloom in the lower realms, her eyes were unaccustomed to so much glorious daylight. Mara wandered through the feline-fay's woodsy grounds until she came to the opening where she'd taken tea with Xenestra and Zornamayne, before their trip to Alfweard to heal her magic.

"Oh, I'm sorry," she said with a start. "I don't mean to intrude upon your privacy."

A tall man in a hooded cape sat on the bench where Mara had been heading. As she approached, she saw his cape was actually a snowy-white ceremonial robe covered in shimmering golden runes that pulsed with their own magical energy. The man's back was to her, and he had pulled up his hood. Mara frowned. Something about the man seemed familiar, but she'd never met anyone whose raiments glowed. Even so, she felt drawn to the golden runes on the robe and wanted to reach out her hand to touch them.

The man said, "You are not disturbing me, Maragold. Please come sit beside me."

"Phineas?" Mara exclaimed. "Why are you here, instead of in dead of winter with the other leaders?"

Phineas dropped his hood, his platinum braid gleaming as brilliantly as his robe. "I learned from Hortensia you had awakened...and decided it is past time for me to tell you the rest."

"The rest of what?" Mara asked, a small line forming on her brow. Her head still ached, but the pain was lessening with each passing day. Still, she found it hard to concentrate for very long without her temples beginning to throb. She hoped whatever Phineas was about to tell her wouldn't bring on another pounding migraine.

"The rest of your origin story." Phineas made room on the bench for Mara to be seated.

"My *origin* story?" In the ballroom celebrating her Alfweardian citizenship—which seemed half a lifetime ago—Mara recalled Phineas telling her she didn't quite grasp the significance of the occasion, but she would soon enough. Had he traveled to Havynweal to explain the significance now?

"Aye. More precisely, it is your mother's story, which is where your story begins, in a manner of speaking."

"Huh?" Mara wanted to learn more about her mother, but Phineas was speaking in riddles. She felt a spike of pain in her temples and reached up to massage them.

Phineas rose from the bench and began to pace, little twigs and leaves snagging beneath his boots. "Are you always this obtuse?"

"Not when someone is forthright and prepared to tell me the truth," huffed Mara, crossing her arms.

Phineas stopped pacing and turned toward her. Instead of scowling or glaring, which Mara fully expected from the towering, arrogant elf, he bowed his head. Then he did an even more remarkable thing—he looked straight at her as tears slowly trickled down his face. He didn't attempt to wipe them away, either.

Mara tilted her head, all her earlier annoyance evaporated. "Please tell me," she whispered.

Phineas sniffed. "Your mother—Gracelyn Saturna Maximere Pensk—was my daughter. Which means you are..."

"Your *granddaughter*?" Mara's eyebrows formed a downward *V*. "Then why were you so mean to me?" She waved her hand, fuming as she remembered Phineas's offensive comments. "You called me a half-breed, and you didn't even want to help me! *Why*?"

Phineas heaved a sigh. "I told you the truth when I said I had to confirm the veracity of your claim—and that of your friends. Visitors to Alfweard are rare; rarer still are the unusual assortment of companions who traveled to true north with you. I sensed immediately you had elven blood, and you look remarkably like your mother, but I suspected a glamour at first. I thought perhaps your great-aunt had sent an imposter to try and trick me."

Mara's head was spinning; she felt a migraine forming behind her eyes. *I have a grandfather and a great-aunt who obviously don't get along. Do I have any other elven relatives?* Then she recalled how dismissive the other palace guard had been of her and her claim to the blue sword. She sighed. "Is Norris my cousin?"

"Aye. Norris and my sister are quite at odds—not that I

blame the lad, who lives with me—no one can tolerate my sister's chicanery for long. She betrayed my father, deceived my mother, and tried to kill me. We do not see eye to eye."

Mara shook her head at Phineas's understatement. She might have been better off not knowing about her elven relatives. She could have carried on quite nicely, blissfully ignorant of her heritage, except for her faltering magic and unresponsive sword, of course. Mara realized she was stuck with them now, or at least with a rude elven grandfather and cousin. She wasn't going to even think about a tricksome great-aunt. Then she thought of the icy elven healer. "Please don't tell me Hortensia is my grandmother!" Although she was growing accustomed to Hortensia's brusqueness, Mara couldn't imagine a less-grandmotherly sort of a woman.

"Then I shall not."

"Well, is she or is she not my grandmother?"

Phineas stared off at a spot above Mara's head, as if peering through a scope, peeling back layer by layer the years and the memories. "Hortensia is my second wife. Your dear grandmother passed away many years ago, when Gracelyn was sixteen. I believe Gracelyn's grief and sadness over the loss of her mother was behind her request."

"What request was that?"

"When Gracelyn turned seventeen and came of age, she asked for a transfer. She wanted to fulfill her duties in the human realm. I have never really understood her fascination for humanity, but Gracelyn was adamant. She told me 'her destiny lay beyond the frosty bounds of true north.'"

"What do you mean, her duties?"

"Her duties as a reaper."

"And all elves are reapers, no exceptions?"

"Naturally. I granted Gracelyn's wish, of course, but I

had two stipulations: that she return home to Alfweard once a year, and that when the time came for her to marry, she would choose an elf."

Mara rolled her eyes. *Why do adults—whether elven, fay, or human—think they know what's best for everyone else?* "We all know how well that second part turned out, don't we?"

Phineas pursed his lips, ignoring her remark. "When Gracelyn brought your father home for her annual visit, I was furious at first. However, after she explained the circumstances, where they met and how they fell in love, I relented."

"Where did my parents meet?"

"On a lonely battlefield, during one of the border wars humans are so fond of—your father had been severely wounded and in terrible pain. When Gracelyn bent over him, she asked whether he was ready to move on. He said he would not leave his post until every one of his comrades had crossed over first. Gracelyn was so moved by his bravery and compassion, she took care of all the others first, guiding each of their spirits to the lower realms and ensuring they boarded boats for the far shore. When she returned to your father, his life force was nearly spent, but Gracelyn's heart was so moved she knelt down and kissed him. And well, something quite unexpected happened."

Mara swallowed a lump in her throat. She knew her father had been injured; he always walked with a limp, but she had no idea he'd nearly died. After he'd been stripped of his command and demoted to corporal, her father saw a lot of heavy action that he never discussed. She leaned forward and asked, "What happened?"

"Gracelyn's elven magic and your father's Serving magic became intertwined. She did not want him to depart for the lower realms, and he agreed. She used her elven mists to transfer him to a master healer who asked no questions, but got to work saving his life."

"Did my mother stay with him?"

"Aye. They had become inseparable by then and had fallen in love. I felt I had no choice but to give them my blessing."

"To be married?"

Phineas frowned at the memory. "Not exactly. They were already married, so I blessed their union instead. And I demanded something in return."

Mara closed her eyes and tried to recall her mother's last words, about a promise to keep, and her father's remark, something about hoping whoever they'd promised would forget. If her father had been referring to Phineas, there was no chance of that ever happening. "You made them promise to train any children in the elven ways—to train them to be reapers?"

Phineas nodded. "I asked for the firstborn only, as the reaping skills are always strongest in firstborns. But after Gracelyn died, your father refused to send you to me."

"Whoa." Mara held up her palm. "You expected my father to send me to Alfweard to train as a reaper at age four?"

"You make me sound like a barbarian." Phineas jutted out his jaw. "I merely requested regular training sessions —monthly visits to the lower realms to train with me—so I could prepare you for both your passage rites and your reaping duties. But I suspect your father paid a master mage a great deal of money to cast a powerful protection spell around you, which effectively cut me out of your life."

Mara could understand her father's motivations, and she could also empathize with Phineas, who'd lost both his daughter and his granddaughter. No wonder he didn't like humans very much, and she said as much to Phineas.

Phineas shook his head. "Elves are no better—we have nearly destroyed our own race with our fighting and factions—and the worst of it has been directed against the royal blood lines. We have assassinated or poisoned or imprisoned far too many kings and queens, princes, and princesses. This is why the elven king has taken the extraordinary step of isolating himself from the public. He hopes that by remaining sequestered, he might stop the bloodshed once and for all." The elven captain stopped speaking and knitted his brow.

Mara realized she was missing something vitally important, something to do with her mother's story, with her story—and with Phineas. She tucked a lock of hair behind her ear and stared at Phineas's glimmering robe. She'd noticed when he was speaking, the runes sparkled brighter, twinkling with energy. Now the runes, still beautiful and golden, pulsed occasionally, but they seemed passive, as if waiting for something to happen to inspire their magic again.

Mara frowned, a crazy idea forming in the back of her mind. *It can't be that simple...can it?* She looked at Phineas. He'd stopped pacing but was glancing down at her, his hands clasped in front of him. "You are...or you were...the elven king. But you did something to make people forget who you were, didn't you?"

Phineas nodded slowly. "Well done, Maragold. You are as perceptive as your mother, who never wanted to be the next elven queen. Nor, I believe, do you."

"Absolutely not! I'd never want to be queen of the elves —or queen of anything else!" Mara thought of Linden, who had inherited the title, duties, and headaches of the

Faymon Liege. Things had worked out for Linden in the end, but Mara was still not interested. She hated politics and negotiation, and she didn't even like Alfweard all that much. It was just too cold in true north. Plus, she'd have to avoid assassination plots all the time, and elves were perhaps the most tricksome of all the species.

Mara angled her head and said, "Your robe, and your sword, and even the castle itself...all of them are endowed with your magic, aren't they? That's what you meant when you said you were magically connected to everything in the palace."

"Aye." Phineas smoothed the folds of his robe. "After Gracelyn left Alfweard, I knew I had to do something. Otherwise, there would be another battle for the throne and more elves would lose their lives. I decided the elven king would become a mythical leader, wise and strong, someone to *emulate*—but difficult to find and *eliminate*. I worked on the spell for years, poring over manuscripts in the archives and consulting with seers, until I was finally ready. On the eve of my forty-fifth birthday, I gave myself a gift; I gave up my birthright. I took on a new identity, as the king's captain of the guard and his personal representative."

"And no one misses the king of the elves?"

"Why should they? He still exists, after a fashion."

Mara recalled her initial meeting with Phineas, as the unyielding, insulting captain of the guard. Why did he work in the guard station at all? Didn't he worry about an assault on the guards from some rebellious elves? Even in disguise, Phineas was still vulnerable—and still the closest thing to a king in Alfweard.

When she asked Phineas about it, he shrugged. "Generally, I do not work at the guard station, but I made an exception on the day of your arrival. I decided to check out the peculiar group of travelers myself. Given the dwindling elven population and general lack of visitors, the risk of physical assault is quite low. The true threat comes from deceit and subterfuge, my sister's domain; I am best equipped to identify her trickery and repel it." Phineas glanced at Mara and nodded. "Go ahead and ask me the next part of your question."

Mara frowned, trying to work out the best way to phrase it. She soon gave up and blurted, "What happens if —er, when—you travel to the lower realms for the last time? Who will speak for the king then?"

"An excellent question. Since no one has attempted such a spell before, I can only share my hypothesis: the *magic* will choose the next captain. And in a twinkling, the new elven captain will comprehend all that is needed to carry on." Phineas smiled. "Let us hope that eventuality is in the far, distant future."

Mara had a lot more questions for Phineas, but she decided only one was truly important at the moment. "Even though you're technically the elven king, are you still willing to tutor me?"

"Technically, I am *not* the elven king, and aye, I wish to tutor you in elven ways."

Mara said, "I'm glad to hear it—and I want to learn from you. But for the record, I really don't like the cold. Perhaps I could spend just part of each year in Alfweard?"

Phineas chuckled. "I believe we could come up with a suitable arrangement."

Mara liked the idea of honing her reaping and translocation skills with Phineas, which brought to mind the missing Choirmaster in the lower realms, and the chasms in the human realm. She asked whether any progress had been made to come up with a solution, but Phineas shook his head. He explained the leaders had decided to gather as many mages and reapers as possible, and then go together to the lower realms. They would plead, as one united voice, with the Choirmaster to return.

"When are you leaving for the lower realms?"

"The day after tomorrow. Why?"

"Because I want to come along."

Phineas's brow puckered. "You are not sufficiently recovered. It could be dangerous for you to cast even a simple spell in your condition."

Mara raised her shoulders. "I promise I won't cast any spells, but I want to come help you call back the Choirmaster. I have a feeling you're going to need as many mages and reapers as you can gather."

CHAPTER 32

THE LARGEST ASSEMBLY OF MAGES AND REAPERS MARA HAD EVER seen stood on the riverbank in the lowest, last realm of the dead. The elves who had survived the battle with Bazra's creatures were there—including Iggy, Norris, and Dowell, still recovering from his injuries—as well as Hortensia, standing at Phineas's side. She and Mara seemed to have reached an unspoken truce. At least the icy step-grand-mother no longer huffed or snorted whenever Mara asked her a question.

Linden, Corbahn, Jayna, and Reynier stood near Mara. The chiefs and commanders from the other Faymon clans gathered nearby. Vas and Talias represented Valerra in the lower realms, accompanied by Chef Desna, of the Best Bellaryss Bakery, and Gemala, owner of the Cracked Caul-dron and Mara's overly lenient boss.

Katrine and half the fay council were present, plus Zornamayne and her hybrid healers, and Farleigh and Jerdahn, his grihm friend. Gloria sat at attention next to her son, Kal, both miniature griffins clicking their beaks. Even Xenestra had swooped down to join them, despite the dragon's intense dislike of the oppressive gloom in the lower realms.

The spirits of the deceased hovered behind them. Most were silent, although some murmured a greeting or called out some advice, none of it helpful. With such an enormous backlog of ghosts waiting to cross the river to the far shore, Mara found it impossible to locate either Efram's or Remy's vaporous forms. Arnesto reached for Mara's hand, interlacing their fingers. He whispered in her ear, his breath tickling her cheek, "Nothing is happening."

Mara's voice wavered. "Aye. This isn't working." They had been standing along the river for two hours, calling out to the Choirmaster, at times in unison, at other times in their various tongues, the fays in their strange buzzing language, the hybrids in hisses and susurrations, and the elves in austere, clipped syllables.

Linden leaned over. "I feel like we're neglecting an important clue. Any thoughts?"

Mara tried to ferret out the missing ingredient. Linden was right—something hovered in the back of Mara's mind, something to do with being trapped in a dreary place, unable to move on. "I think the Choirmaster might be stuck —unable to return without our assistance. We need to find a way to help her and the choir break free."

"Break free? But how? We don't even know where she is!"

Mara bit her bottom lip, deep in thought. She'd managed to break out of the horrible cave after surviving her passage rites—using elemental magic and her sword— but she was pretty sure that wasn't what the Choirmaster needed.

Mara recalled another time she'd had to break free— from the Valerran palace dungeon, where King Roi was now imprisoned. She and Linden and their friends had sung an old fay lullaby that put the prison guards to sleep. "Wait a minute! What's missing from the lower realms?"

Arnesto ran his free hand through his wavy blue hair. "Other than the Choirmaster and her choir, you mean?"

Mara nodded. "Aye. What else?"

Linden snapped her fingers, which made a loud popping sound that caused a number of heads—living and ghostly—to turn her way. "Sorry," she said, adding, "Music! That's what's missing."

"What's this about music?" asked Katrine.

Mara waved an arm at the empty, silent far shore. "I think we need to *sing* to the Choirmaster to help her break free from wherever she is. 'Tis music that keeps this realm running smoothly...and I think the silence has worn her down."

Katrine nodded excitedly. "I think you're on to something, lass!" Katrine bellowed to Phineas and Vas, who jogged over to join them, and she explained Mara's theory.

Phineas's eyebrows shot up. "An excellent suggestion, Maragold. Music might hold the key to unlocking this realm and freeing the Choirmaster. At the very worst, raising our voices in song shall cheer us up a bit whilst we consider other alternatives."

"Makes sense to me," grunted Vas. "Now we just need to come up with the right song." The Faymon clan chiefs joined in the discussion, and the fay council too, until so many competing opinions were bandied about that Mara's head started to throb again.

During a lull in the debate, Mara asked, "What is the opposite of a lullaby, do you think?"

Jayna canted her head. "I suppose something rousing and uplifting."

Phineas agreed, and the fays and elves launched into another round of debate. Mara stopped listening as a lovely memory of her father, holding her hand like Arnesto was doing at the moment, came to her. He had accompanied Mara to her first day of school, and they sang a cheerful little song as they walked. When she was older and walked to school alone, Mara used to hum the tune under her breath.

Mara didn't offer any more suggestions, or ask anyone's opinion, or wait for consensus that might never come. Instead, she started to sing in her rich contralto, the words and tune feeling just right:

> *"Travel safely my precious one—*
> *Love is all around.*
> *Forget your fears; leave worries behind—*
> *Love is all around.*
> *Cling to the joy that freely abounds—*
> *Love is all around.*
> *'Tis love, only love, that truly lives on."*

Linden and Jayna joined her, and so did Arnesto and Katrine. Soon the rest of their contingent—the fays, elves, Valerrans, Faymons, hybrids, crossbreeds, griffins and a singular dragon—joined in, humming, clicking, bleating, and singing along.

Jayna heard it first—the tiniest echo—a small, thin, reedy sound coming from across the churning water. Encouraged, Mara focused on the distant shore, singing with gusto and a joy that surprised her. Despite her injuries and pain and fresh loss, Mara felt hopeful about the future —*her* future, with her fay boyfriend and elven grandfather, and her friends, so many of them, in so many places and realms.

"Look!" shouted Arnesto, pointing across the river at a bluish light spreading across the opposite shore. In the center of the light stood a small, dark-skinned woman dressed in a long, billowing robe. "The Choirmaster has returned!"

Whoops and cheers reverberated across the gloomy realm, and the bluish light glowed even more brightly. Mara hummed beneath her breath, not quite ready to stop, at least not until she was sure the choir was there to stay. But then the Choirmaster lowered her hood, threw back her head, and began to chant the haunting melody of the spirit realm. The rest of the choir joined their leader, raising their voices in song, the tune so heart-rending and otherworldly it sent shivers up and down Mara's spine.

The boats for ferrying spirits appeared along the river-bank, and the waiting ghosts lined up in an orderly fashion, without any pushing or shoving from the unsavory specters at the back of the line, who were forced to wait until every good spirit had left the shore. Mara knew the nasty ghosts would attempt to cross, and she also knew they would never make it to the other side, but they'd try anyway.

Mara, Arnesto, Phineas, and Katrine stayed behind long after the rest of the mages and reapers had left for their homes. Arnesto and Mara waved at Efram as he boarded the boat and crossed to the far shore. And much later, they waved again at Remy, who didn't see them, which Mara thought was just as well. She brushed away a tear, suddenly so exhausted she wanted to sleep all the way through to the next moonrise—which is exactly what she did, after Phineas and Arnesto dropped her off at Zorna-mayne's cheerful infirmary, where the feline-fay alternately scolded Mara for staying too long in the lower realms, and praised her for singing the Choirmaster home.

MARA GAVE the mahogany bar one final swipe before draping the damp towel over the lip of the sink. She picked up her reticule from the tiny office in the back of the Cracked Cauldron and called out, "I'm leaving now—see you in a few hours."

Gemala poked her head out of the kitchen, where she'd been conferring with her cook on the menu. "What are you still doing here? I thought you'd left half an hour ago to start getting ready."

"The bar needed a good scrubbing."

"You're nervous, aren't you?"

Mara shook her head, her ponytail swishing. "Not nervous...just worried our families will start squabbling again. I get a headache whenever fays and elves argue—all that buzzing, hissing, and yelling hurts my ears. Plus, every time Arnesto and Norris are together more than five minutes, they wind up on the ground, wrestling."

"I think both their egos are a bit bruised, don't you?"

"You mean over the Swords of Six?"

Gemala nodded. "Katrine carries the red sword, which Arnesto believed was destined for him, and—"

"And Dowell wields the purple sword, which Norris wanted for himself." Mara sighed. "I think Arnesto is relieved Katrine owns the red sword; as a twelfth-level fay wizard, he carries the weight of too many expectations already. And I'm glad Phineas's spell worked, so Jayna no longer has to be called into action. But it's going to take a while before Norris stops pouting."

"Aye, true enough," agreed Gemala, guiding Mara to the front door of the pub. "And now it's time for you to get dressed. Otherwise, Gloria will be showing up here any minute to scold you for being late. Don't fret; the food and beverages are well in hand, and Chef Desna has been baking for the past two days."

Three hours later, the rented horse-drawn carriage pulled up in front of the boardwalk, its wooden planks forming a sand-free path from the cobbled road down to the beach. Gloria clicked her beak furiously at the footman, who wasn't fast enough opening the door and assisting Mara down the carriage steps.

Vas had offered to provide a steam-powered locomobile for Mara, but she declined. She wasn't the romantic type, but she'd wanted to arrive in a carriage—not in elven frosty mists or fay wispy vapors or any other magical means, either. In fact, other than the traveling mists her guests would need for arrival and departure, she'd insisted on no magic.

Mara could have chosen Yelenarra's lovely hillside in Havynweal, or Phineas's crystalline palace in Alfweard, or Linden's woodsy longhouse in Faynwood, but Mara had wanted a Valerran ceremony. Arnesto agreed, reminding her they had met in Valerra, and so pledging themselves by the Pale Sea was the perfect setting.

Mara stood on the wooden planks and smoothed her gown, handmade by Madame Zostra. After much debate with the fashionable Zostra, Mara had opted for a simple, V-neck sleeveless gown in champagne-colored satin, hemmed to fall just above her ankles. Mara had wanted to wear her new brown leather boots, so she could slip her twin daggers inside, but Gloria had squawked and flapped her wings, so Mara relented, choosing a pair of golden sandals instead.

Mara ran her fingers through her straight, pale-blonde hair, which she left loose on her shoulders instead of pulled back in a ponytail. She'd decided to skip the traditional bonnet-and-veil worn by Valerran brides, since elves and fays had quite different notions about appropriate "headgear" as Hortensia called it. Mara refused to wear any of the other suggestions—a pert trilby, a peaked cap, or a cone-shaped hat with a flag on top.

Mara shifted her bouquet of two-dozen yellow roses to one hand and shielded her eyes with the other, scanning the beach. The late afternoon sun sparkled on the turquoise water as small white caps rolled into shore, and a summer breeze stirred the green dune grasses on either side of the boardwalk. Gemala and Chef Desna had constructed a wooden dais with a bright yellow awning over it, so the guests seated on folding chairs or cotton blankets could watch the ceremony from the beach. A large white-and-yellow, striped tent sat next to the dais, where Gemala, Chef Desna, and their staffs had set out food, drinks, and desserts for the party afterward.

Mara and Arnesto had decided to hold their ceremony —known as binding rites in Faynwood, betrothal pledges in Havynweal and Alfweard, and simply a wedding in Valerra—at the end of summer, on the cusp of fall. They wanted to give Yelenarra and everyone else plenty of time to recover from their injuries and traumas, both physical and emotional. Mara still teared up when she thought about Remy, and she'd cried when Chef Desna told her he'd funded a baker's scholarship in Remy's name at his shop.

Mara and Arnesto had another reason for waiting until

late summer for the ceremony. They wanted to be absolutely certain they'd restored balance in the lower realms, beginning with Bazra's demise and ending with the Choirmaster's return. Mara and Arnesto had expected to see the fissures inside Valerra and Faynwood close up almost immediately, which didn't happen. Although the rifts gradually began closing, what they had assumed would be a fast process took months, and the chasm created by Bazra and Arnesto during their final battle could still be seen in the valley outside the palace walls. The crack had narrowed to a long, raggedy ditch that continued to close, several inches each day.

When Mara had asked Phineas why the chasms were taking so long to disappear, his answer surprised her. "'Tis a healing process, lass, much like recovering from a wound or recharging your magic, except it takes much longer for the human realm to repair itself after such catastrophic meddling. Be patient and you shall see the fissures closing; each time the Choirmaster sings the good spirits home to the far shore, a bit more of the ground and soil shall be healed."

Har spotted Mara standing on the boardwalk with Gloria, who'd been grooming herself all day, the griffin insisting on wearing a large yellow bow on her tail. Har gave a hand signal, and one of the formerly dark fays blew two short notes on his ram's horn. The guests took their seats or nestled on their blankets, and the jumble of voices fell silent as all eyes—elven, fay, human, hybrid, crossbreed, griffin, and dragon—turned toward Mara.

She took a deep, calming breath and smiled at her ridiculously handsome fiancé, standing on the dais next to Phineas, Katrine, and Vas, who were jointly officiating at the first-ever elf-fay-human wedding. Xenestra, who'd been scouring through ancient scrolls for weeks, claimed this was a historic event, and she planned to write a monograph marking the occasion. Arnesto, wearing a sparkly gold cape over ivory-colored tunic and slacks, gave Mara one of his bedazzling smiles that made her feel slightly weak in the knees.

Gloria led the way up the wooden aisle, taking her time, her tail flicking proudly from side to side. Mara decided to go with the flow and try not to anticipate all the things that could go wrong, all the fights that could break out or feelings that could get hurt. Phineas, Katrine, and Vas would handle the ceremony, and Gemala and Chef Desna could manage the rest. She and Arnesto deserved a day to celebrate, without worrying about inter-species politics or crazy necromancers or giant chasms or rebalancing the underworld.

When Mara stepped onto the dais, even that last thought disappeared from her head, as if by magic. She knew, of course, it wasn't magic at all that drove every rational thought out of her head, but it was Arnesto—the way he laughed, which he did much more these days, the way he entwined his fingers in hers, and the way he leaned close for a kiss. Her heart, scarred by loss and misunderstandings and loneliness, was slowly healing—thanks to her impossible fay boyfriend, who was providing the cure.

Arnesto stood by her side as they faced the three heads of state; it had been Arnesto's idea to ensure their marriage would be recognized in the elven, fay, and human realms, and Mara had readily agreed, hoping it would pave the way for smoother family relations in the future.

Phineas, Katrine, and Vas each led a part of the service, which Mara tried but failed to follow, since the ceremony bounced between elven, fay, and human matrimonial customs, with few natural transitions. She did, however, respond "Aye" or "I do" or "I shall" at the appropriate moments, along with Arnesto.

Vas asked them to exchange their vows, and Arnesto and Mara turned to face each other. Arnesto grasped both her hands and smiled. "Maragold Gracelyn Raeburn Pensk," he said softly, so as not to cause any tremors or rumbles on their special day. Mara felt the platform vibrate slightly and then settle back down. "On this day I take you to be my wedded wife, in every stage of life and in every realm, on joyful days and sad days and all those in between, with magic or without, with health or without, I promise to stand by your side, to love you and to cherish you always, until I pass, at last, into that final realm from which no mortal man returns."

Butterflies fluttered in Mara's stomach, and she took a moment to center herself. She looked into Arnesto's twinkling gray eyes and murmured, "Arnestarious Aziel Windstorm Lucato the Fourteenth," and the platform shook a second time. She recited her vows, which were identical to Arnesto's, her throat catching on the last part. "I promise to stand by your side, to love you and to cherish you always, until I pass, at last, into that final realm from which no mortal woman returns." Then Katrine asked them for their rings. Arnesto looked momentarily panicked until Gloria stepped forward with a knotted handkerchief in her beak.

Arnesto and Mara grinned, each withdrawing a ring from inside the linen wrapping. At Mara's request, they'd chosen matching slender gold bands, without any jewels or other adornments; she feared anything larger would catch on her reaping ropes or interfere when she withdrew her daggers from her boots.

Mara went first, and as she placed the gold band on

Arnesto's finger, she said, "With this ring I plight you my troth."

Arnesto held her ring aloft and repeated, in a loud, clear voice, "With this ring I plight you my troth." As he slipped the gold band on the middle finger of Mara's right hand, Arnesto whispered, "You have made me the happiest of men."

Mara felt herself growing warm at Arnesto's steady, smoldering gaze, and a burst of pure joy bloomed in her chest, spreading to her fingers and toes and the roots of her hair.

Phineas said, "By the authority vested in me, as the elven king's representative—" and Vas interjected, "and vested in me, as the provisional president of Valerra—" and Katrine added, "and vested in me, as fay chief, we three pronounce you husband and wife. You may now seal your troth with a kiss."

Arnesto pulled Mara closer, brushed his lips against hers, and straightened. Mara placed her hands on either side of her fay husband's chiseled, gorgeous face and drew him down for a longer, deeper kiss. When she was finished, Arnesto gave her one of his heart-stopping smiles. "I believe we have properly sealed our troth."

Mara smiled. "Shall we?" He nodded, and they turned around to wave at the assembled guests. Their family and friends burst into applause. Yelenarra, wearing a yellow-and-green plaid shawl over her neon orange gown, beamed at them and waved back. Next to her sat Zornamayne, elegant in her jeweled veils, and Penray Talias, who'd dispensed entirely with her chief inspector attire, opting for a blue-and-white linen dress and a floppy fedora. Linden and Jayna, with Corbahn and Reynier, sat behind them in the second row, clapping and chuckling.

And across the aisle, Hortensia, stunning in a flowing pale pink gown, nodded austerely. Norris raised his hand in a half-wave, while Iggy and Dowell laughed and applauded. Well-wishers from the Valerran resistance and Gemala's pub and Chef Desna's bakery were there too, cheering for the newlyweds and trying not to stare at the giant green dragon sunning herself on a large yellow blanket, nor the oversized grihms, Farleigh and Jerdahn, dashing in and out of the surf.

Just beyond Xenestra's blanket, the air shimmered and brightened. Mara stared at the glowing figure, her mouth forming an O. Her mother, wearing a long, sparkling, silver gown, her platinum hair flowing around her face and shoulders, smiled and blew her a kiss. Mara blinked and her mother was gone.

"Are you crying?" whispered Arnesto.

Mara blinked again and sniffed. "A happy tear is all." She sent up a silent prayer of thanks to Pawllah, the Choirmaster, who for obvious reasons was unable to attend the wedding but still sent a gift—Mara's mother, from beyond the far shore, to give her blessing.

Arnesto reached for Mara's hand, entwining their fingers firmly together. They descended from the platform to the sandy beach, where their loved ones crowded around to offer congratulations before heading to the striped tent for refreshments and dinner. Mara leaned against Arnesto's shoulder, kicked off her sandals, and wriggled her toes in the warm sand. "This is as good as it gets," she sighed happily.

Arnesto raised one eyebrow and lowered the other. "You are quite wrong, my dear."

A small line formed on Mara's brow as she prepared to argue her point. "How am I wrong?"

He brought her hand to his lips and kissed her palm, sending tingles down Mara's spine. "Tomorrow shall be equally good, and the day after that, and every day to come —so long as you are my friend—in the deepest, truest, fay sense of the word."

A ghost of a smile crossed Mara's lips, and she didn't argue. She saw no reason to disagree with her talented, dashing, and dearly beloved fay husband.

BOOKS BY TONI CABELL

A fast-paced adventure full of magic, romance, humor, sword fighting, dangerous creatures, and the power of light versus darkness, **Serving Magic** is a YA Epic Fantasy series with Steampunk and Regency vibes. Winner of The Wishing Shelf Book Awards and recognized by Indies Today as a Top 5 YA Fantasy series by an indie author:

- *Lady Apprentice, Book 1*
- *Lady Mage, Book 2*
- *Lady Liege, Book 3*
- *Lady Spy, Book 4*
- *Lady Reaper, Book 5*

In the arid hills of Toresz, there's one thing more dangerous than divining for water... falling in love with the enemy. **Water Witch** is YA Romantasy duology packed with action, danger, intrigue, royal politics, and romance. Winner of The Wishing Shelf Book Awards:

- *The Lightness of Water, Book 1*
- *The Way of Water, Book 2*

If you're looking for sweet, slow-burn romance with swoony kisses, second chances, and funny, heartwarming characters, don't miss the complete **Faeries of Door County** series. Winner of Best Paranormal Romance, each novel is a standalone story set in the same cozy small town:

- *Rhyme, Riddle, and Romance*
- *Half a Faerie*
- *Return to Mooncrest Inn*

Find all Toni's available books and upcoming new releases on tonicabell.com and Amazon. All her novels are also available in audiobook format on Audible and Apple Books.

About the Author

When Toni told her fifth-grade teacher that she wanted to be a writer, neither of them expected Toni's journey to include stints as a nurse's aid, personal banker, instructional designer, real estate broker, systems analyst, and youth director. Toni is thrilled to be an indie author and does at least half her writing in the middle of the night, which may explain her wild plot twists and unforgettable characters.

Today, Toni writes award-winning fantasy stories filled with spunky gals, protective guys, imaginative magic, and romance that sizzles without the spice. Whether you're a fan of fast-paced, YA fantasy adventures with a dash of swoon or cozy paranormal romance packed with heart-stealing kisses and small town charm, you're sure to find something to love.

Toni's novels have earned Silver and Bronze Medals in The Wishing Shelf Book Awards, two Gold Medals in the Global Book Awards, and Best Paranormal Romance from Indies Today.

She makes her home in a small village along the shores of Lake Michigan with her handsome husband, where she enjoys generous supplies of strong coffee, too many pastries, and more books than she can ever read.

Want a free novella and to stay current on Toni's upcoming releases, sales, and giveaways? Then visit tonicabell.com and sign up for her newsletter.

Toni posts regularly about her indie author journey, life lessons, what inspires her, and her books on Instagram and Facebook. Also consider joining her Reader Group on Facebook, @onceuponaswoon, where she hangs out with some of her closed-door author friends and readers like you.

Soli Deo Gloria. ✝